TALES
OF
EDGAR
ALLAN
POE

PARENTS' MAGAZINE'S CULTURAL INSTITUTE
A Division of Parents' Magazine Enterprises, Inc.
New York

PREFACE

These strange, chilling, brilliant tales have captivated young people, and of course their elders, for more than a hundred years. In the shadows behind them is the solitary figure of a young writer, with dark, haunted eyes. Edgar Allan Poe and his work are unique in our country's literary history. He left a few poems of rare beauty and some short stories that are classics of the English language. These had brought him small success when he died in lonely poverty at the age of forty.

Many biographers have searched for facts and motives in the life of this unhappy genius. They theorize about Poe's two selves, which they claim to see in his photographs: one side of his face appearing mild and tender, the other side harsh and cold. His inner weaknesses finally ruined him; but weakness in this man contrasts oddly with the power and originality of his writing.

Edgar Poe was born in Boston in 1809, of gifted parents who were actors. They died when he was three, and he went to live with the wealthy Allan family of Richmond. The Allans did not legally adopt the attractive little boy, but he kept their name with his own. They prepared him for living as a gentleman of means. During his youth when they spent several years in England, Poe attended English schools. At the same time he was storing away impressions of crumbling castles and their great ghostly halls. For much of his life he was to dwell in a realm of phantoms.

Back in this country and ready for college, the young man was soon breaking rules at the University of Virginia, then at West Point. Poe and his foster family severed relations, ending the only security he would ever know. From then on Poe shared the home of his devoted but impoverished aunt, Maria Clemm. In time she encouraged him to marry his young cousin Virginia. He worked hard at several newspaper jobs, but none lasted because Poe was unreliable. The three lived together in Philadelphia and elsewhere. Finally they moved to Fordham, then outside New York, now in the Bronx. Their poor unheated cottage was without decent food or bedding as Virginia lay ill with consumption. When she died, only twenty-five years old, Poe wrote the melancholy "Annabel Lee" in her memory (see *A Treasure Chest of Poetry*).

For the sensitive, moody, unstable Poe there was no escape from the morbid experiences of his life. He described utter despair in "The Raven," the first of his poems to receive wide notice. The usual themes of his verses are sorrow, lost loveliness, and untimely death. All are set apart by his unerring sense of melody.

Poe longed to be known as a poet, but story-writing earned better pay, which he desperately needed. Between the years of 1838 and 1843, when Poe could least combat his problems, he wrote his most notable stories. "The Fall of the House of Usher," and others of his best, serve as models to teach technique in writing. "The Murders in the Rue Morgue," published in Graham's Magazine in 1841, set a pattern for detective tales, being the first of its kind. Poe's keen mind delighted in mysteries and their solutions. The pseudo-scientific knowledge of his time influenced all his work. It, in turn, almost certainly influenced Stevenson, Doyle, and Verne.

Poe spent his last years giving lectures from Boston to Richmond, revising his best poems, getting his stories published. His death in 1849 was blamed on alcoholism. All his characters are different reflections of the self only he could fully know.

IRENE SMITH
Former Superintendent of Work with Children
Brooklyn Public Library
Brooklyn, New York

CONTENTS

THE TELLTALE HEART

TRUE! Nervous—very nervous, dreadfully nervous I had been and am. But why will you say that I am mad? The disease had sharpened my senses—not destroyed, not dulled them. Above all was the sense of hearing acute. I heard all things in the heaven and in the earth. I heard many things in hell. How then am I mad? Hearken, and observe how healthily, how calmly I can tell you the whole story.

It is impossible to say how the idea first entered my brain. But once conceived, it haunted me day and night. Object there was none. Passion there was none. I loved the old man. He had never wronged me. He had never given me insult. For his gold I had no desire. I think it was his eye! Yes! it was this! He had the eye of a vulture, a pale blue eye, with a film over it. Whenever it fell upon me my blood ran cold; and so by degrees, very gradually, I made up my mind to take the life of the old man, and thus rid myself of the eye forever.

Now this is the point. You fancy me mad. Madmen know nothing. But you should have seen *me*. You should have seen how wisely I proceeded. With what caution, with what foresight, with what dissimulation I went to work! I was never kinder to the old man than during the whole week before I killed him.

And every night, about midnight, I turned the latch of his door and opened it—oh, so gently! And then, when I had made an opening sufficient for my head, I put in a dark lantern, all closed, closed so that no light shone out, and then I thrust in my head. Oh, you would have laughed to see how cunningly I thrust it in! I moved it slowly— very, very slowly, so that I might not disturb the old man's sleep. It took me an hour to place my whole head within the opening so far that I could see him as he lay upon his bed. Ha! Would a madman have been so wise as this? And then, when my head was well in the room, I undid the lantern cautiously—oh, so cautiously—cautiously (for the hinges creaked)—I undid it just so much that a single thin ray fell upon the vulture eye. And this I did for seven long nights, every night just at midnight, but I found the eye always closed; and so it was impossible to do the work. For it was not the old man who vexed me, but his Evil Eye.

And every morning when the day broke, I went boldly into the chamber and spoke courageously to him, calling him by name in a hearty tone, and inquiring how he had passed the night. So you see he woud have been a very profound old man indeed to suspect that every night, just at twelve, I looked in upon him while he slept.

Upon the eighth night I was more than usually cautious in opening the door. A watch's minute hand moves more quickly than did mine. Never before that night had I *felt* the extent of my own powers—of my sagacity. I could scarcely contain my feelings of triumph. To think that there I was, opening the door, little by little, and he not even dreaming of my secret deeds or thoughts! I fairly chuckled at the idea. And perhaps he heard me, for he moved on the bed suddenly, as if startled. Now you may think that I drew back—but no. His room was as black as pitch with the thick darkness (for the shutters were close fastened, through fear of robbers), and so I knew that he could not see the opening of the door, and I kept pushing it on steadily, steadily.

I had my head in, and was about to open the lantern, when my thumb slipped upon the tin fastening, and the old man sprang up in bed, crying out, "Who's there?"

I kept quite still and said nothing. For a whole hour I did not move a muscle, and in the meantime I did not hear him lie down. He was still sitting up in the bed listening—just as I have done, night after night, hearkening to the death watches in the wall.

Presently I heard a slight groan, and I knew it was the groan of mortal terror. It was not a groan of pain or of grief. Oh, no! It was the low stifled sound that arises from the bottom of the soul when overcharged with awe. I

3

knew the sound well. Many a night, just at midnight, when all the world slept, it has welled up from my own bosom, deepening, with its dreadful echo, the terrors that distracted me. I say I knew it well. I knew what the old man felt, and pitied him, although I chuckled at heart. I knew that he had been lying awake ever since the first slight noise, when he had turned in the bed. His fears had been growing upon him ever since. He had been trying to fancy them causeless, but could not. He had been saying to himself, "It is nothing but the wind in the chimney. It is only a mouse crossing the floor." Or, "it is merely a cricket which has made a single chirp." Yes, he had been trying to comfort himself with these suppositions, but he had found them all in vain. *All in vain,* because death, in approaching him had stalked with his black shadow before him, and enveloped the victim. And it was the mournful influence of the unperceived shadow that caused him to feel, although he neither saw nor heard— to *feel* the presence of my head within the room.

When I had waited a long time, very patiently, without hearing him lie down, I resolved to open a little, a very, very little crevice in the lantern. So I opened it—you cannot imagine how stealthily, stealthily—until at length a single dim ray, like the thread of the spider, shot from out the crevice and fell full upon the vulture eye.

It was open, wide, wide open, and I grew furious as I gazed upon it. I saw it with perfect distinctness—all a dull blue, with a hideous veil over it that chilled the very marrow in my bones. But I could see nothing else of the old man's face or person, for I had directed the ray, as if by instinct, precisely upon the damned spot.

And have I not told you that what you mistake for madness is but overacuteness of the senses? Now, I say, there came to my ears a low, dull, quick sound, such as a watch makes when enveloped in cotton. I knew *that* sound well, too. It was the beating of the old man's heart. It increased my fury, as the beating of a drum stimulates the soldier into courage.

But even yet I refrained and kept still. I scarcely breathed. I held the lantern motionless. I tried to see how steadily I could maintain the ray upon the eye. Meantime the hellish tattoo of the heart increased. It grew quicker and quicker, and louder and louder every instant. The old man's terror *must* have been extreme! It grew louder, I say, louder every moment! Do you mark me well? I have told you that I am nervous; so I am. And now at the dead hour of the night, amid the dreadful silence of that old house, so strange a noise as this excited me to uncontrollable terror. Yet for some minutes longer I refrained and stood still. But the beating grew louder, louder! I thought the heart must burst. And now a new anxiety seized me. The sound would be heard by a neighbor! The old man's hour had come! With a loud yell, I threw open the lantern and leaped into the room. He shrieked once—once only. In an instant I dragged him to the floor, and pulled the heavy bed over him. I then smiled gaily, to find the deed so far done. But, for many minutes, the heart beat on with a muffled sound. This, however, did not vex me; it would not be heard through the wall. At length it ceased. The old man was dead. I removed the bed and examined the corpse. Yes, he was stone, stone dead. I placed my hand upon the heart and held it there many minutes. There was no pulsation. He was stone dead. His eye would trouble me no more.

If you still think me mad, you will think so no longer when I describe the wise precautions I took for the concealment of the body. The night waned, and I worked hastily but in silence. First of all I dismembered the corpse. I cut off the head and the arms and the legs.

I then took up three planks from the flooring of the chamber, and deposited all between the scantlings. I then replaced the boards so cleverly, so cunningly, that no human eye—not even *his*—could have detected anything wrong. There was nothing to wash out, no stain of any kind, no bloodspot whatever. I had been too wary for that. A tub had caught all—ha! ha!

When I had made an end of these labors, it was four o'clock—still dark as midnight. As the bell sounded the hour, there came a knocking at the street door. I went down to open it with a light heart, for what had I *now* to fear? There entered three men, who introduced themselves, with perfect suavity, as officers of the police. A shriek had been heard by a neighbor during the night, suspicion of foul play had been aroused, information had been lodged at the police office, and they (the officers) had been deputed to search the premises.

I smiled, for *what* had I to fear? I bade the gentlemen welcome. The shriek, I said, was my own in a dream. The old man, I mentioned, was absent in the country. I took my visitors all over the house. I bade them search— search *well*. I led them at length to *his* chamber. I showed them his treasures, secure, undisturbed. In the enthusiasm of my confidence I brought chairs into the room, and desired them *here* to rest from their fatigues, while I myself, in the wild audacity of my perfect triumph, placed my own seat upon the very spot beneath which reposed the corpse of the victim.

The officers were satisfied. My *manner* had convinced them. I was singularly at ease. They sat, and while I answered cheerily, they chatted of familiar things. But ere long I felt myself getting pale and wished them gone. My head ached and I fancied a ringing in my ears. But still they sat and still chatted. The ringing became more distinct. It continued and became more distinct. I talked more freely to get rid of the feeling, but it continued and gained definiteness, until at length I found that the noise was *not* within my ears.

No doubt I now grew *very* pale, but now I talked more fluently and with heightened voice. Yet the sound increased. And what could I do? It was a low, dull, quick sound, much such a sound as a watch makes when enveloped in cotton. I gasped for breath—and yet the officers heard it not. I talked more quickly, more vehemently—but the noise steadily increased. I arose and argued about trifles, in a high key and with violent gesticulations—but the noise steadily increased. Why *would* they not be gone? I paced the floor to and fro with heavy strides, as if excited to fury by the observations of the men—but the noise steadily increased.

Oh God! would *could* I do? I foamed—I raved—I swore! I swung the chair upon which I had been sitting, and grated it upon the boards, but the noise arose over all and continually increased. It grew louder—louder—*louder!* And still the men chatted pleasantly and smiled. Was it possible they heard not? Almighty God! No, no! They heard! They suspected! They *knew!* They were making a mockery of my horror! This I thought and this I think. But anything was better than this agony! Anything was more tolerable than this derision! I could bear those hypocritical smiles no longer! I felt that I must scream or die! And now, again—hark! Louder! Louder! Louder! *Louder!*

"Villains!" I shrieked. "Dissemble no more! I admit the deed! Tear up the planks! Here, here! It is the beating of his hideous heart!"

THE MURDERS IN THE RUE MORGUE

INTRODUCTION

THE mental features discoursed of as the analytical are, in themselves, but little susceptible of analysis. We appreciate them only in their effects. We know of them, among other things, that they are always to their possessor, when inordinately possessed, a source of the liveliest enjoyment. As the strong man exults in his physical ability, delighting in such exercises as call his muscles into action, so glories the analyst in that moral activity which *disentangles*.

He derives pleasure from even the most trivial occupations that bring his talents into play. He is fond of enigmas, of conundrums, of hieroglyphics, exhibiting in his solutions of each a degree of *acumen* which appears to the ordinary apprehension preternatural. His results, brought about by the very soul and essence of method have, in truth, the whole air of intuition. The faculty of resolution is possibly much invigorated by mathematical study, and especially by that highest branch of it which, unjustly, and merely on account of its retrograde operations, has been called, as if *par excellence,* analysis. Yet to calculate is not in itself to analyze. A chess player, for example, does the one without effort at the other. It follows that the game of chess in its effects upon mental character is greatly misunderstood.

I am not now writing a treatise, but simply prefacing a somewhat peculiar narrative by observations very much at random. I will therefore take occasion to assert that the higher powers of the reflective intellect are more decidedly and more usefully tasked by the unostentatious game of checkers than by all the elaborate frivolity of chess. In this latter, where the pieces have different and *bizarre* motions, with various and variable values, what is only complex is mistaken (a not unusual error) for what is profound. The *attention* is here called powerfully into play. If it flags for an instant, an oversight is committed, resulting in injury or defeat. The possible moves being not only manifold but involute, the chances of such oversights are multiplied; and in nine cases out of ten it is the more concentrative rather than the more acute player who conquers.

In checkers, on the contrary, where the moves are *unique* and have but little variation, the probabilities of inadvertence are diminished, and the mere attention being left comparatively unemployed, the advantages by either party are obtained by superior *acumen.* To be less abstract—let us suppose a game of checkers where the pieces are reduced to four kings and where, of course, no oversight is to be expected. It is obvious that here the victory can be decided (the players being at all equal) only by some *recherché* movement, the result of some exertion of the intellect. Deprived of ordinary resources, the analyst throws himself into the spirit of his opponent, identifies himself therewith, and not infrequently sees thus, at a glance, the sole methods (sometimes indeed absurdly simple ones) by which he may seduce into error or hurry into miscalculation, his opponent.

Whist had long been noted for its influence upon what is termed the calculating power; and men of the highest order of intelect have been known to take an apparently unaccountable delight in it, while eschewing chess as frivolous. Beyond doubt there is nothing of a similar nature so greatly tasking the faculty of analysis. The best chess player in Christendom *may* be little more than the best player of chess; but proficiency in whist implies capacity for success in all these more important undertakings where mind struggles with mind. When I say proficiency I mean that perfection in the game which includes a comprehension of *all* the sources whence legitimate advantage may be derived. These are not only manifold but multiform, and lie frequently among recesses of thought altogether inaccessible to the ordinary understanding. To observe attentively is to remember distinctly; and, so far, the concentrative chess player will do very well at whist; while the rules of Hoyle (themselves based upon the mere mechanism of the game) are sufficiently and generally comprehensible. Thus to have a retentive memory, and to proceed by "the book," are points commonly regarded as the sum total of good playing.

But it is in matters beyond the limits of mere rule that the skill of the analyst is evinced. He makes, in silence, a host of observations and inferences. So perhaps do his companions. And the difference in the extent of the information obtained lies not so much in the validity of the inference as in the quality of the observation. The necessary knowledge is that of *what* to observe. Our player confines himself not at all; nor, because the game is the object, does he reject deductions from things external to the game. He examines the countenance of his partner, comparing it carefully with that of each of his opponents. He considers the mode of assorting the cards in each hand, often counting trump by trump, and honor by honor, through the glances bestowed by their holders upon each. He notes every variation of face as the play progresses, gathering a fund of thought from the differences in the expression of certainty, of surprise, of triumph, or chagrin. From the manner of gathering up a trick he judges whether the person taking it can make another in the suit. He recognizes what is played through feint, by the air with which it is thrown upon the table. A casual or inadvertent word, the accidental dropping or turning of a card with the accompanying anxiety or carelessness in regard to its concealment, the counting of the tricks with the order of their arrangement, embarrassment, hesitation, eagerness or trepidation—all afford, to his apparently intuitive perception, indications of the true state of affairs. The first two or three rounds having been played, he is in full possession of the contents of each hand, and thenceforward puts down his cards with as absolute a precision of purpose as if the rest of the party had turned outward the faces of their own.

The analytical power should not be confounded with simple ingenuity, for while the analyst is necessarily ingenious, the ingenious man is often remarkably incapable of analysis. The consecutive or combining power, by which ingenuity is usually manifested, and to which the phrenologists, I believe erroneously, have assigned a separate organ, supposing it a primitive faculty, has been so frequently seen in those whose intellect bordered otherwise upon idiocy as to have attracted general observation among writers on morals. Between ingenuity and the analytic ability there exists a difference far greater indeed than that between the fancy and the imagination, but of a character very strictly analogous. It will be found, in fact, that the ingenious are always fanciful, and the truly imaginative never otherwise than analytic.

The narrative which follows will appear to the reader somewhat in the light of a commentary upon the propositions just advanced.

THE MURDERS IN THE RUE MORGUE

RESIDING in Paris during the spring and part of the summer of 18—,I there became acquainted with a Monsieur C. Auguste Dupin. This young gentleman was of an excellent—indeed of an illustrious family, but by a variety of untoward events had been reduced to such poverty that the energy of his character succumbed beneath it, and he ceased to bestir himself in the world, or to care for the retrieval of his fortunes. Books, indeed, were his sole luxuries; in Paris these are easily obtained.

Our first meeting was at an obscure library in the Rue Montmartre, where the accident of our both being in search of the same very rare and remarkable volume, soon brought us into closer communion. We saw each other again and again. I was deeply interested in the little family history which he detailed to me with all that candor in which a Frenchman indulges whenever mere self is the theme. I was astonished, too, at the vast extent of his reading; and above all I felt my soul enkindled within me by the wild fervor, and the vivid freshness of his imagination. Seeking in Paris the objects I then sought, I felt that the society of such a man would be to me a treasure beyond price; and this feeling I frankly confided to him. It was at length arranged that we should live together during my stay in the city; and as my worldly circumstances were somewhat less embarrassed than his own, I was permitted to be at the expense of renting, and furnishing, in a style which suited the rather fantastic gloom of our common temper, a time-eaten and grotesque mansion, long deserted through superstitions into which we did not inquire, and tottering to its fall in a retired and desolate portion of the Faubourg St. Germain.

Had the routine of our life at this place been known to the world, we should have been regarded as madmen, although as madmen of a harmless nature. Our seclusion was perfect. We admitted no visitors. Indeed the locality of our retirement had been carefully kept a secret from my own former associates, and it had been many years since Dupin had ceased to know or be known in Paris. We existed within ourselves alone.

It was a freak of fancy in my friend (for what else shall I call it?) to be enamored of Night for her own sake; and into this *bizarrerie*, as into all his others, I quietly fell, giving myself up to his wild whims with a perfect abandon. The sable divinity would not herself dwell with us always, but we could counterfeit her presence. At the first dawn of the morning we closed all the massive shutters of our old building, lighted a couple of tapers which, strongly perfumed, threw out only the ghastliest and feeblest of rays. By the aid of these we then busied our souls in dreams—reading, writing, or conversing, until warned by the clock of the advent of the true darkness. Then we sallied forth into the streets, arm in arm, continuing the topics of the day, or roaming far and wide until a late hour, seeking amid the wild lights and shadows of the populous city that infinity of mental excitement which quiet observation can afford.

At such times I could not help remarking and admiring (although from his rich ideality I had been prepared to expect it) a peculiar analytic ability in Dupin. He seemed, too, to take an eager delight in its exercise—if not exactly in its display—and did not hesitate to confess the pleasure thus derived. He boasted to me, with a low chuckling laugh that most men, in respect to himself, wore windows in their bosoms. And he was wont to follow up such assertions by direct and very startling proofs of his intimate knowledge of my own. His manner at these moments was frigid and abstract; his eyes were vacant in expression; while his voice, usually a rich tenor, rose into a treble which would have sounded petulant but for the deliberateness and entire distinctness of the enunciation. Observing him in these moods, I often dwelt meditatively upon the old philosophy of the bi-part soul, and amused myself with the fancy of a double Dupin—the creative and the resolvent.

Let it not be supposed, from what I have just said, that I am detailing any mystery or penning any romance. What I have described in the Frenchman was merely the result of an excited, or perhaps of a diseased intelligence. But of the character of his remarks at the periods in question an example will best convey the idea.

We were strolling one night down a long dirty street in the vicinity of the Palais Royal. Being both, apparently, occupied with thought, neither of us had spoken a syllable for fifteen minutes at least. All at once Dupin broke forth with these words:

"He is a very little fellow, that's true, and would do better for the Théâtre des Variétés."

"There can be no doubt of that," I replied unwittingly, and not at first observing (so much had I been absorbed in reflection) the extraordinary manner in which the speaker had chimed in with my meditations. In an instant afterwards I recollected myself, and my astonishment was profound.

"Dupin," said I gravely, "this is beyond my comprehension. I do not hesitate to say that I am amazed, and can scarcely credit my senses. How was it possible you should know I was thinking of—?" Here I paused, to ascertain beyond a doubt whether he really knew of whom I thought.

"— of Chantilly," said he. "Why do you pause? You were remarking to yourself that his diminutive figure unfitted him for tragedy."

This was precisely what had formed the subject of my reflections. Chantilly was a quondam cobbler of the Rue St. Denis, who, becoming stage-mad, had attempted the role of Xerxes in Crébillon's tragedy, and been notoriously pasquinaded for his pains.

"Tell me, for heaven's sake," I exclaimed, "the method

—if method there is—by which you have been enabled to fathom my soul in this matter." In fact I was even more startled than I would have been willing to express.

"It was the fruiterer," replied my friend, "who brought you to the conclusion that the mender of soles was not of sufficient height for Xerxes *et id genus omne.*"

"The fruiterer! You astonish me—I know no fruiterer whomsoever."

"The man who ran up against you as we entered the street—it may have been fifteen minutes ago."

I now remembered that in fact a fruiterer, carrying upon his head a large basket of apples, had nearly thrown me down, by accident, as we passed from the Rue C— into the thoroughfare where we stood; but what this had to do with Chantilly I could not possibly understand.

There was not a particle of *charlatanerie* about Dupin. "I will explain," he said, "and that you may comprehend all clearly, we will first retrace the course of your meditations from the moment in which I spoke to you until that of the encounter with the fruiterer in question. The larger links of the chain run thus—Chantilly, Orion, Dr. Nichols, Epicurus, stereotomy, the street stones, the fruiterer."

There are few persons who have not, at some period of their lives, amused themselves in retracing the steps by which particular conclusions of their own minds have been attained. The occupation is often full of interest, and he who attempts it for the first time is astonished by the apparently illimitable distance and incoherence between the starting point and the goal. What, then, must have been my amazement when I heard the Frenchman speak what he had just spoken, and when I could not help acknowledging that he had spoken the truth. He continued:

"We had been talking of horses, if I remember aright, just before leaving the Rue C—. This was the last subject we discussed. As we crossed into this street, a fruiterer with a large basket upon his head, brushing quickly past us, thrust you upon a pile of paving stones collected at a spot where the causeway is undergoing repair. You stepped upon one of the loose fragments, slipped, slightly strained your ankle, appeared vexed or sulky, muttered a few words, turned to look at the pile, and then proceeded in silence. I was not particularly attentive to what you did; but observation has become with me of late a species of necessity.

"You kept your eyes upon the ground—glancing with a petulant expression at the holes and ruts in the pavement (so that I saw you were still thinking of the stones), until we reached the little alley called Lamartine, which has been paved, by way of experiment, with the overlapping and riveted blocks. Here your countenance brightened up, and perceiving your lips move, I could not doubt that you murmured the word 'stereotomy,' a term very affectedly applied to this species of pavement. I knew that you could not say stereotomy to yourself without being brought to think of atomies, and thus of the theories of

Epicurus. And since, when we discussed this subject not very long ago, I mentioned to you how singularly, yet with how little notice, the vague guesses of that noble Greek had met with confirmation in the late nebular cosmogony, I felt that you could not avoid casting your eyes upwards to the great nebula in Orion, and I certainly expected that you would do so. You did look up, and I was now assured that I had correctly followed your steps. But in that bitter tirade upon Chantilly, which appeared in yesterday's *Musée*, the satirist, making some disgraceful allusions to the cobbler's change of name upon assuming the buskin, quoted a Latin line about which we have often conversed. I mean the line: *Perdidit antiquum litera prima sonum*.

"I had told you that this was in reference to Orion, formerly written Urion. And from certain pungencies connected with this explanation, I was aware that you could not have forgotten it. It was clear, therefore, that you would not fail to combine the two ideas of Orion and Chantilly. That·you did combine them I saw by the character of the smile which passed over your lips. You thought of the poor cobbler's immolation. So far, you had been stooping in your gait; but now I saw you draw yourself up to your full height. I was then sure that you reflected upon the diminutive figure of Chantilly. At this point I interrupted your meditations to remark that as, in fact he *was* a very little fellow, that Chantilly. He would do better at the Théâtre de Variétés."

Not long after this, we were looking over an evening edition of the *Gazette des Tribunaux*, when the following paragraphs arrested our attention.

EXTRAORDINARY MURDERS.—This morning, about three o'clock, the inhabitants of the Quartier St. Roch were aroused from sleep by a succession of terrific shrieks, issuing apparently from the fourth story of a house in the Rue Morgue, known to be in the sole occupancy of one Madame L'Espanaye, and her daughter, Mademoiselle Camille L'Espanaye. After some delay, occasioned by a fruitless attempt to procure admission in the usual manner, the gateway was broken in with a crowbar, and eight or ten of the neighbors entered, accompanied by two *gendarmes*. By this time the cries had ceased; but, as the party rushed up the first flight of stairs, two or more rough voices, in angry contention, were distinguished, and seemed to proceed from the upper part of the house. As the second landing was reached, these sounds also had ceased, and everything remained perfectly quiet. The party spread themselves, and hurried from room to room. Upon arriving at a large back chamber in the fourth story (the door of which, being found locked with the key inside, was forced open), a spectacle presented itself which struck everyone present not less with horror than with astonishment.

The apartment was in the wildest disorder—the furniture broken and thrown about in all directions. There was only one bedstead, and from this the mattress had

21

been removed and thrown into the middle of the floor. On a chair lay a razor besmeared with blood. On the hearth were two or three long and thick tresses of gray human hair, also dabbled in blood, and seeming to have been pulled out by the roots. Upon the floor were found four napoleons, an earring of topaz, three large silver spoons, three smaller of *métal d'Alger,* and two bags, containing nearly four thousand francs in gold. The drawers of a bureau which stood in one corner were open, and had been apparently rifled, although many articles still remained in them. A small iron safe was discovered under the mattress (not under the bedstead). It was open, with the key still in the door. Its apparent contents, a few old letters and other papers of little consequence, were spread beside it.

Of Madame L'Espanaye no traces were here seen. But an unusual quantity of soot being observed in the fireplace, a search was made in the chimney, and (horrible to relate!) the corpse of the daughter, head downwards, was dragged therefrom, it having been thus forced up the narrow aperture for a considerable distance. The body was still quite warm. Upon examining it, many excoriations were perceived, no doubt occasioned by the violence with which it had been thrust up and disengaged. Upon the face were many severe scratches, and upon the throat, dark bruises and deep indentations of fingernails, as if the deceased had been throttled to death.

After a thorough investigation of every portion of the

house without further discovery, the party made its way into a small paved yard in the rear of the building, where lay the corpse of the old lady, with her throat so entirely cut that, upon an attempt to raise her, the head fell off. The body as well as the head was fearfully mutilated—the former so much so as scarcely to retain any semblance of humanity.

To this horrible mystery there is not as yet, we believe, the slightest clue.

The next day's paper had these additional particulars. THE TRAGEDY IN THE RUE MORGUE—Many individuals have been examined in relation to this most extraordinary and frightful affair, but nothing whatever has transpired to throw light upon it. We give below all the material testimony elicited:

PAULINE DUBOURG, laundress, deposes that she has known both the deceased for three years, having washed for them during that period. The old lady and her daughter seemed on good terms, very affectionate towards each other. They were excellent pay. Could not speak in regard to their mode or means of living. Believed that Madame L. told fortunes for a living. Was reputed to have money put by. Never met any persons in the house when she called for the clothes or took them home. Was sure that they had no servant in employ. There appeared to be no furniture in any part of the building except in the fourth story.

PIERRE MOREAU, tobacconist, deposes that he has been

in the habit of selling small quantities of tobacco and snuff to Madame L'Espanaye for nearly four years. Was born in the neighborhood, and has always resided there. The deceased and her daughter had occupied the house in which the corpses were found for more than six years. It was formerly occupied by a jeweler, who sublet the upper rooms to various persons. The house was the property of Madame L. She became dissatisfied with the abuse of the premises by her tenant and moved into them herself, refusing to let any portion. The old lady was childish. Witness had seen the daughter some five or six times during the six years. The two lived an exceedingly retired life, but were reputed to have money. Had heard it said among the neighbors that Madame L. told fortunes. Did not believe it. Had never seen any person enter the door except the old lady and her daughter, a porter once or twice, and a physician some eight or ten times.

Many other persons, neighbors, gave evidence to the same effect. No one was spoken of as frequenting the house. It was not known whether there were any living connections of Madame L. and her daughter. The shutters of the front windows were seldom opened. Those in the rear were always closed, with the exception of the large back room, fourth story. The house was a good house, not very old.

ISIDORE MUSSET, *gendarme*, deposes that he was called to the house about three o'clock in the morning, and found some twenty or thirty persons at the gateway endeavoring to gain admittance. Forced it open, at length, with a bayonet, not with a crowbar. Had but little difficulty in getting it open, on account of its being a double or folding gate and bolted neither at bottom nor top. The shrieks continued until the gate was forced, and then suddenly ceased. They seemed to be screams of some person (or persons) in great agony—were loud and drawn out, not short and quick. Witness led the way upstairs. Upon reaching the first landing, heard two voices in loud and angry contention, the one a gruff voice, the other much shriller—a very strange voice. Could distinguish some words of the former, which was that of a Frenchman. Was positive that it was not a woman's voice. Could distinguish the words *sacré* and *diable*. The shrill voice was that of a foreigner. Could not be sure whether it was the voice of a man or of a woman. Could not make out what was said, but believed the language to be Spanish. The state of the room and of the bodies was described by this witness as we described them yesterday.

HENRI DUVAL, a neighbor, and by trade a silversmith, deposes that he was one of the party who first entered the house. Corroborates the testimony of Musset in general. As soon as they forced an entrance they reclosed the door, to keep out the crowd, which collected very fast, notwithstanding the lateness of the hour. The shrill voice, the witness thinks, was that of an Italian. Was certain it was not French. Could not be sure that it was a man's voice. It might have been a woman's. Was not acquainted with the Italian language. Could not distinguish the words, but was convinced by the intonation that the speaker was an Italian. Knew Madame L. and her daughter. Had conversed with both frequently. Was sure that the shrill voice was not that of either of the deceased.

—— ODENHEIMER, restaurant owner. This witness volunteered his testimony. Not speaking French, was examined through an interpreter. Is a native of Amsterdam. Was passing the house at the time of the shrieks. They lasted for several minutes, probably ten. They were long and loud, very awful and distressing. Was one of those who entered the building. Corroborated the previous evidence in every respect but one. Was sure that the shrill voice was that of a man, of a Frenchman. Could not distinguish the words uttered. They were loud and quick, unequal, spoken apparently in fear as well as in anger. The voice was harsh—not so much shrill as harsh. Could not call it a shrill voice. The gruff voice said repeatedly *sacré*, *diable*, and once, *mon Dieu*.

JULES MIGNAUD, banker, of the firm of Mignaud et Fils, Rue Deloraine. Is the elder Mignaud. Madame L'Espanaye had some property. Had opened an account with his banking house in the spring of the year—(eight years previously). Made frequent deposits in small sums. Had checked for nothing until the third day before her death, when she took out in person the sum of 4000 francs. This sum was paid in gold, and a clerk sent home with the money.

ADOLPHE LE BON, clerk to Mignaud et Fils, deposes that on the day in question, about noon, he accompanied Madame L'Espanaye to her residence with the 4000 francs, put up in two bags. Upon the door being opened, Mademoiselle L. appeared and took from his hands one of the bags, while the old lady relieved him of the other. He then bowed and departed. Did not see any person in the street at the time. It is a side street, very lonely.

WILLIAM BIRD, tailor, deposes that he was one of the party who entered the house. Is an Englishman. Has lived in Paris two years. Was one of the first to ascend the stairs. Heard the voices in contention. The gruff voice was that of a Frenchman. Could make out several words, but cannot now remember all. Heard distinctly *sacré* and *mon Dieu*. There was a sound at the moment as of several persons struggling, a scraping and scuffling sound. The shrill voice was very loud, louder than the gruff one. Is sure that it was not the voice of an Englishman. Appeared to be that of a German. Might have been a woman's voice. Does not understand German.

Four of the above-named witnesses, being recalled, deposed that the door of the chamber in which was found the body of Mademoiselle L. was locked on the inside when the party reached it. Everything was perfectly silent, no groans or noises of any kind. Upon forcing the door no person was seen. The windows, both of the back and front room, were down and firmly fastened from within. A door between the two rooms was closed, but not locked. The door leading from the front room into the passage was locked, with the key on the inside. A small room in the front of the house, on the fourth story at the head of the passage, was open, the door being ajar. This room was crowded with old beds, boxes and so forth. These were carefully removed and searched. There was not an inch of any portion of the house which was not carefully searched. Sweeps were sent up and down the chimneys. The house was a four-story one, with garrets (*mansardes*). A trap door on the roof was nailed down very securely—did not appear to have been opened for years. The time elapsing between the hearing of the voices in contention and the breaking open of the room door, was variously stated by the witnesses. Some made it as short as three minutes, some as long as five. The door was opened with difficulty.

ALFONZO CARCIO, undertaker, deposes that he resides in the Rue Morgue. Is a native of Spain. Was one of the party who entered the house. Did not proceed upstairs. Is nervous, and was apprehensive of the consequences of agitation. Heard the voices in contention. The gruff voice was that of a Frenchman. Could not distinguish what was said. The shrill voice was that of an Englishman—is sure of this. Does not understand the English language, but judges by the intonation.

ALBERTO MONTANI, confectioner, deposes that he was among the first to ascend the stairs. Heard the voices in question. The gruff voice was that of a Frenchman. Distinguished several words. The speaker appeared to be expostulating. Could not make out the words of the shrill voice. Spoke quick and unevenly. Thinks it the voice of a Russian. Corroborates the general testimony. Is an Italian. Never conversed with a native of Russia.

Several witnesses, recalled, here testified that the chimneys of all the rooms on the fourth story were too narrow to admit the passage of a human being. Sweeps, or cylindrical sweeping-brushes such as are employed by those who clean chimneys were passed up and down every flue in the house. There is no back passage by which anyone could have descended while the party proceeded upstairs. The body of Mademoiselle L'Espanaye was so firmly wedged in the chimney that it could not be got down until four or five of the party united their strength.

PAUL DUMAS, physician, deposes that he was called to view the bodies about daybreak. They were both then lying on the sacking of the bedstead in the chamber where Mademoiselle L. was found. The corpse of the young lady was much bruised and excoriated. The fact that it had been thrust up the chimney would sufficiently account for these appearances. The throat was greatly chafed. There were several deep scratches just below the chin, together with a series of livid spots which were evidently the impression of fingers. The face was fearfully discolored, and the eyeballs protruded. The tongue had been partially bitten through. A large bruise was discovered upon the pit of the stomach produced, apparently, by the pressure of a knee. In the opinion of M. Dumas, Mademoiselle L'Espanaye had been throttled to death by some person or persons unknown. The corpse of the mother was horribly mutilated. All the bones of the right leg and arm were more or less shattered. The left tibia much splintered, as well as all the ribs of the left side. Whole body dreadfully bruised and discolored. It was not possible to say how the injuries had been inflicted. A heavy club of wood, or a broad bar of iron, a chair, any large, heavy and obtuse weapon would have produced such results if wielded by the hands of a very powerful man. No woman could have inflicted the blows with any weapon. The head of the deceased, when seen by witness, was entirely separated from the body, and was also greatly shattered. The throat had evidently been cut with some very sharp instrument, probably with a razor.

ALEXANDRE ETIENNE, surgeon, was called with M. Dumas to view the bodies. Corroborated the testimony and the opinions of M. Dumas.

Nothing further of importance was elicited, although several other persons were examined. A murder so mysterious, and so perplexing in all its particulars, was never before committed in Paris, if indeed a murder has been committed at all. The police are entirely at fault—an unusual occurrence in affairs of this nature. There is not, however, the shadow of a clue apparent.

The evening edition of the paper stated that the greatest excitement still continued in the Quartier St. Roch, that the premises in question had been carefully re-searched, and fresh examinations of witnesses instituted, but all to no purpose. A postscript, however, mentioned that Adolphe Le Bon had been arrested and imprisoned, although nothing appeared to criminate him beyond the facts already detailed.

Dupin seemed singularly interested in the progress of this affair, at least so I judged from his manner, for he made no comments. It was only after the announcement that Le Bon had been imprisoned that he asked me my opinion respecting the murders.

I could merely agree with all Paris in considering them an insoluble mystery. I saw no means by which it would be possible to trace the murderer.

"We must not judge of the means," said Dupin, "by this shell of an examination. The Parisian police, so much extolled for acumen, are cunning, but no more. There is no method in their proceedings beyond the method of the moment. They make a vast parade of measures; but not unfrequently these are so ill-adapted to the objects pro-posed as to put us in mind of Monsieur Jourdain's calling for his *robe de chambre—pour mieux entendre la musique*. The results attained by them are not unfrequently surprising, but for the most part are brought about by simple diligence and activity. When these qualities are unavailing, their schemes fail. Vidocq, for example, was a good guesser and a persevering man. But without edu-cated thought, he erred continually by the very intensity of his investigations. He impaired his vision by holding the object too close. He mght see, perhaps, one or two points with unusual clearness, but in so doing he necessarily lost sight of the matter as a whole.

"Thus there is such a thing as being too profound. Truth is not always in a well. In fact, as regards the more important knowledge, I do believe that she is invariably superficial. The depth lies in the valleys where we seek her, and not upon the mountaintops where she is found. The modes and sources of this kind of error are well typified in the contemplation of the heavenly bodies. To look at a star by glances, to view it in a sidelong way, by turning towards it the exterior portions of the retina (more susceptible of feeble impressions of light than the interior), is to behold the star distinctly, is to have the best appreciation of its luster—a luster which grows dim just in proportion as we turn our vision fully upon it. A greater number of rays actually fall upon the eye in the latter case, but in the former there is the more refined capacity for comprehension. By undue profundity we perplex and enfeeble thought, and it is possible to make even Venus herself vanish from the firmament by a scrutiny too sustained, too concentrated, or too direct.

"As for these murders, let us enter into some examinations for ourselves, before we make up an opinion respecting them. An inquiry will afford us amusement." (I thought this an odd term, so applied, but said nothing.) "And besides, Le Bon once rendered me a service for which I am not ungrateful. We will go and see the premises with our own eyes. I know G——, the Prefect of Police, and shall have no difficulty in obtaining the necessary permission."

The permission was obtained, and we proceeded at once to the Rue Morgue. This is one of those miserable thoroughfares which intervene between the Rue Richelieu and the Rue St. Roch. It was late in the afternoon when we reached it, as this quarter is at a great distance from that in which we resided. The house was readily found, for there were still many persons gazing up at the closed shutters, with an objectless curiosity, from the opposite side of the way. It was an ordinary Parisian house, with a gateway, on one side of which was a glazed watch box, with a sliding panel in the window, indicating a *loge de concierge*. Before going in we walked up the street, turned down an alley, and then again turning, passed in the rear of the building. Dupin meanwhile examined the whole neighborhood as well as the house with a minuteness of attention for which I could see no possible object.

Retracing our steps we came again to the front of the dwelling, rang, and having shown our credentials, were admitted by the agents in charge. We went upstairs, into the chamber where the body of Mademoiselle L'Espanaye had been found, and where both the deceased still lay. The disorders of the room had, as is usual, been suffered to exist. I saw nothing beyond what had been stated in the *Gazette des Tribunaux*. Dupin scrutinized everything, not excepting the bodies of the victims. We then went into the other rooms, and into the yard, a *gendarme* accompanying us throughout. The examination occupied us until dark, when we took our departure. On our way home my companion stopped in for a moment at the office of one of the daily papers.

I have said that the whims of my friend were manifold, and that *Je les ménageais.* (For this phrase there is no exact English equivalent.) It was Dupin's humor now to decline all conversation on the subject of the murder until about noon the next day. He then asked me suddenly if I had observed anything peculiar at the scene of the atrocity.

There was something in his maner of emphasizing the word peculiar which caused me to shudder without knowing why.

"No, nothing *peculiar*," I said. "Nothing more, at least, than we both saw stated in the paper."

"The *Gazette*," he replied, "has not entered, I fear, into the unusual horror of the thing. But dismiss the idle opinions of this print. It appears to me that this mystery is considered insoluble, for the very reason which should cause it to be regarded as easy of solution—I mean for the *outré* character of its features. The police are confounded by the seeming absence of motive—not for the murder itself, but for the atrocity of the murder. They are puzzled, too, by the seeming impossibility of reconciling the voices heard in contention with the facts that no one was discovered upstairs but the assassinated Mademoiselle L'Espanaye, and that there were no means of egress without the notice of the party ascending. The wild disorder of the room, the corpse thrust with the head downwards up the chimney, the frightful mutilation of the old lady's body—these considerations with those just mentioned, and others which I need not mention, have sufficed to paralyze the powers by putting completely at fault the boasted acumen of the government agents. They have fallen into the gross but common error of confounding the unusual with the abstruse. But it is by these deviations from the plane of the ordinary that reason feels its way, if at all, in its search for the true. In investigations such as we are now pursuing, it should not be so much asked 'what has occurred,' as 'what has occurred that has never occurred before.' In fact, the facility with which I shall arrive, or have arrived, at the solution of this mystery, is in the direct ratio of its apparent insolubility in the eyes of the police."

I stared at the speaker in mute astonishment.

"I am now awaiting," continued he, looking toward the door of our apartment, "a person who, although perhaps not the perpetrator of these butcheries, must have been in some measure implicated in their perpetration. Of the worst portion of the crimes committed, it is probable that he is innocent. I hope that I am right in this supposition, for upon it I build my expectation of reading the entire riddle. I look for the man here, in this room, at any moment. It is true that he may not arrive, but the probability is that he will. Should he come, it will be necessary to detain him. Here are pistols, and we both know how to use them when occasion demands their use."

I took the pistols, scarcely knowing what I did or believing what I heard, while Dupin went on very much as if in a soliloquy. I have already spoken of his abstract manner at such times. His discourse was addressed to me, but his voice, although by no means loud, had that intonation which is commonly employed in speaking to someone at a great distance. His eyes, vacant in expression, regarded only the wall.

"That the voices heard in contention," he said, "by the party upon the stairs, were not the voices of the women themselves, was fully proved by the evidence. This relieves us of all doubt upon the question of whether the old lady could have first destroyed the daughter and afterward have committed suicide. I speak of this point chiefly for the sake of method, for the strength of Madame L'Espanaye would have been utterly unequal to the task of thrusting her daughter's corpse up the chimney as it was found; and the nature of the wounds upon her own person entirely preclude the idea of self-destruction. Murder then has been committed by some third party, and the voices of this third party were those heard in contention. Let me now advert, not to the whole testimony respecting these voices, but to what was peculiar in that testimony. Did you observe anything peculiar in it?"

I remarked that while all the witnesses agreed in supposing the gruff voice to be that of a Frenchman, there was much disagreement in regard to the shrill, or as one individual termed it, the harsh voice.

"That was the evidence itself," said Dupin, "but it was not the peculiarity of the evidence. You have observed nothing distinctive. Yet there *was* something to be observed. The witnesses, as you remark, agreed about the gruff voice; here they were unanimous. But in regard to the shrill voice, the peculiarity is not that they disagreed, but that while an Italian, an Englishman, a Spaniard, a Hollander and a Frenchman all attempted to describe it, each one spoke of it as that of a foreigner. Each is sure that it was not the voice of his own countryman. Each likens it, not to the voice of an individual of any nation with whose language he is conversant, but the converse.

The Frenchman supposes it the voice of a Spaniard, and might have distinguished some words had he been acquainted with the Spanish. The Dutchman maintains it to have been that of a Frenchman; but we find it stated that 'not understanding French this witness was examined through an interpreter.' The Englishman thinks it the voice of a German, and 'does not understand German.' The Spaniard 'is sure' that it was that of an Englishman, but 'judges by the intonation' altogether, 'as he has no knowledge of the English.' The Italian believes it the voice of a Russian, but 'has never conversed with a native of Russia.' A second Frenchman differs moreover with the first, and is positive that the voice was that of an Italian, but, not being cognizant of that tongue, is, like the Spaniard, convinced by the 'intonation.' Now, how strangely unusual must that voice have really been, about which such testimony, as this could have been elicited! In whose *tones*, even, denizens of the five great divisions of Europe could recognize nothing familiar! You will say that it might have been the voice of an Asiatic, of an African. Neither Asiatics nor Africans abound in Paris; but, without denying the inference, I will now merely call your attention to three points. The voice is termed by one witness 'harsh rather than shrill.' It is represented by two others to have been 'quick and *unequal.*' No words, no sounds resembling words, even, were mentioned as distinguishable by any witness.

"I know not," continued Dupin, "what impression I may have made, so far, upon your own understanding. But I do not hesitate to say that legitimate deductions even from this portion of the testimony—the portion respecting the gruff and shrill voices—are in themselves sufficient to engender a suspicion which should give direction to all further progress in the investigation of the mystery. I said 'legitimate deductions,' but my meaning is not thus fully expressed. I designed to imply that the deductions are the sole proper ones, and that the suspicion arises inevitably from them as the single result. What the suspicion is, however, I will not say just yet. I merely wish you to bear in mind that, with myself, it was sufficiently forcible to give a definite form, a certain tendency, to my inquiries in the chamber.

"Let us now transport ourselves, in fancy, to this chamber. What shall we first seek here? The means of egress employed by the murderers. It is not too much to say that neither of us believe in preternatural events. Madame and Mademoiselle L'Espanaye were not destroyed by spirits. The doers of the deed were material, and escaped materially. Then how? Fortunately, there is but one mode of reasoning upon the point, and that mode *must* lead us to a definite decision.

"Let us examine, each by each, the possible means of egress. It is clear that the assassins were in the room where Mademoiselle L'Espanaye was found, or at least in the room adjoining, when the party ascended the stairs. It is then only from these two apartments that we have to seek issues. The police have laid bare the floors, the ceilings and the masonry of the walls in every direction. No secret issues could have escaped their vigilance. But not trusting to their eyes, I examined with my own. There were, then, no secret issues. Both doors leading from the rooms into the passage were securely locked, with the keys inside.

"Let us turn to the chimneys. These, although of ordinary width for some eight or ten feet above the hearths, will not admit, throughout their extent, the body of a large cat. The impossibility of egress by means already stated being thus absolute, we are reduced to the windows. Through those of the front room no one could have escaped without notice from the crowd in the street. The murderers must have passed, then, through those of the back room. Now, brought to this conclusion in so un-equivocal a manner as we are, it is not our part, as reason-ers, to reject it on account of apparent impossibilities. It is only for us to prove that these apparent impossibilities are in reality not such.

"There are two windows in the chamber. One of them is unobstructed by furniture, and is wholly visible. The lower portion of the other is hidden from view by the head of the unwieldy bedstead which is thrust close up against it. The former was found securely fastened from within. It resisted the utmost force of those who endeav-ored to raise it. A large gimlet hole had been pierced in its frame to the left, and a very stout nail was found fitted therein, nearly to the head. Upon examining the other window, a similar nail was seen similarly fitted in it, and a vigorous attempt to raise this sash failed also. The police were now entirely satisfied that egress had not been in these directions. And, therefore, it was thought super-fluous to withdraw the nails and open the windows.

"My own examination was somewhat more particular, and was so for the reason I have just given, because here it was, I knew, that all apparent impossibilities must prove to be quite possible in reality.

"I proceeded to think thus—*à posteriori*. The murderers *did* escape from one of these windows. This being so, they could not have refastened the sashes from the inside, as they were found fastened—the consideration which put a stop, through its obviousness, to the scrutiny of the police in this quarter. Yet the sashes *were* fastened. They must then have the power of fastening themselves. There was no escape from this conclusion. I stepped to the unobstructed casement, withdrew the nail with some difficulty, and attempted to raise the sash. It resisted all my efforts, as I had anticipated. A concealed spring must, I now knew, exist; and this corroboration of my idea convinced me that my premises, at least, were correct, however mysterious still appeared the circumstances attending the nails. A careful search soon brought to light the hidden spring. I pressed it, and satisfied with the discovery, forbore to upraise the sash.

"I now replaced the nail and regarded it attentively. A person passing out through this window might have reclosed it, and the spring would have caught, but the nail could not have been replaced. The conclusion was plain, and again narrowed the field of my investigations. The assassins must have escaped through the other window. Supposing the springs upon each sash to be the same, there must be a difference between the nails, or at least between the modes of their fixture. Getting upon the sacking of the bedstead, I looked over the headboard minutely at the second casement. Passing my hand down behind the board, I readily discovered and pressed the spring, which was, as I had supposed, identical in character with its neighbor. I now looked at the nail. It was as stout as the other, and apparently fitted in the same manner, driven in nearly up to the head.

"You will say that I was puzzled; but if you think so, you must have misunderstood the nature of the inductions. To use a sporting phrase, I had not been once at fault. The scent had never for an instant been lost. There was no flaw in any link of the chain. I had traced the secret to its ultimate result, and that result was the *nail*. It had, I say, in every respect the appearance of its fellow in the other window, but this 'fact' was an absolute nullity when one considered that here, at this point, terminated the clue.

" 'There must be something wrong,' I said, 'about the nail.' I touched it, and the head, with about a quarter of an inch of the shank, came off in my fingers. The rest of the shank was in the gimlet hole, where it had been broken off. The fracture was an old one (for its edges were incrusted with rust), and had apparently been accomplished by the blow of a hammer, which had partially imbedded, in the top of the bottom sash, the head portion of the nail. I now carefully replaced this head portion in the indentation whence I had taken it, and the resemblance to a perfect nail was complete; the fissure was invisible. Pressing the spring, I gently raised the sash for a few inches. The head went up with it, remaining firm in its bed. I closed the window, and the semblance of the whole nail was again perfect.

"The riddle, so far, was now unriddled. The assassin had escaped through the window which looked upon the bed. Dropping of its own accord upon his exit (or perhaps purposely closed), it had become fastened by the spring; and it was the retention of this spring which had been mistaken by the police for that of the nail, further inquiry being thus considered unnecessary.

"The next question was that of the mode of descent. Upon this point I had been satisfied in my walk with you around the building. About five and a half feet from the casement in question there runs a lightning rod. From this rod it would have been impossible for anyone to reach the window itself, to say nothing of entering it. I observed, however, that the shutters of the fourth story were of the peculiar kind called by Parisian carpenters *ferrades*—a kind rarely employed at the present day, but frequently seen upon very old mansions at Lyons and Bordeaux. They are in the form of an ordinary door, a single not a folding door, except that the upper half is latticed or worked in open trellis, thus affording an excellent hold for the hands. In the present instance these shutters are fully three and a half feet broad.

"When we saw them from the rear of the house they were both about half open, that is to say, they stood off at right angles from the wall. It is probable that the police as well as myself examined the back of the tenement; but if so, in looking at these *ferrades* in the line of their breadth as they must have done, they did not perceive this great breadth itself, or at all events failed to take it into due consideration. In fact, having once satisfied themselves that no egress could have been made in this quarter they would naturally bestow here a very cursory examination. It was clear to me, however, that the shutter belonging to the window at the head of the bed would, if swung fully back to the wall, reach to within two feet of the lightning rod. It was also evident that, by exertion of a very unusual degree of activity and courage, an entrance into the window from the rod might have been thus effected. By reaching to the distance of two and a half feet—we now suppose the shutter open to its whole extent —a robber might have taken a firm grasp upon the trellis-work. Letting go, then, his hold upon the rod, placing his feet securely against the wall, and springing boldly from it, he might have swung the shutter so as to close it, and if we imagine the window open at the time, might even have swung himself into the room.

"I wish you to bear especially in mind that I have spoken of a *very* unusual degree of activity as requisite to success in so hazardous and so difficult a feat. It is my design to show you, first, that the thing might possibly have been accomplished. But second and chiefly, I wish to impress upon your understanding the very extraordinary, the almost preternatural character, of the agility which could have accomplished it.

"You will say, no doubt, using the language of the law, that 'to make out my case' I should rather undervalue, than insist upon a full estimation of the activity required in this matter. This may be the practice in law, but it is not the usage of reason. My ultimate object is only the truth. My immediate purpose is to lead you to place in juxtaposition that very unusual activity of which I have just spoken, with that very peculiar shrill, or harsh, and unequal voice, about whose nationality no two persons could be found to agree, and in whose utterance no syllabification could be detected."

At these words a vague and half-formed conception of the meaning of Dupin flitted over my mind. I seemed to be upon the verge of comprehension, without power to comprehend—as men at times find themselves upon the brink of remembrance without being able, in the end, to remember. My friend went on with his discourse.

"You will see," he said, "that I have shifted the question from the mode of egress to that of ingress. It was my design to suggest that both were effected in the same manner at the same point. Let us now revert to the interior of the room. Let us survey the appearances here. The drawers of the bureau, it is said, had been rifled, although many articles of apparel still remained within them. The conclusion here is absurd. It is a mere guess, a very silly one, and no more. How are we to know that the articles found in the drawers were not all these drawers had originally contained? Madame L'Espanaye and her daughter lived an exceedingly retired life, saw no company, seldom went out, had little use for numerous changes of habiliment. Those found were at least of as good quality as any likely to be possessed by these ladies. If a thief had taken any, why did he not take the best— why did he not take all?

"In a word, why did he abandon four thousand francs in gold to encumber himself with a bundle of linen? The gold *was* abandoned. Nearly the whole sum mentioned by Monsieur Mignaud, the banker, was discovered in bags upon the floor. I wish you, therefore, to discard from your thoughts the blundering idea of motive, engendered in the brains of the police by that portion of the evidence which speaks of money delivered at the door of the house. Coincidences ten times as remarkable as this—the delivery of the money and murder committed within three days upon the party receiving it—happen to all of us every hour of our lives without attracting even momentary notice. Coincidences, in general, are great stumbling blocks in the way of that class of thinkers who have been educated to know nothing of the theory of probabilities— that theory to which the most glorious objects of human research are indebted for the most glorious of illustration. In the present instance, had the gold been gone, the fact of its delivery three days before would have formed something more than a coincidence. It would have been corroborative of this idea of motive. But under the real circumstances of the case, if we are to suppose gold the motive of this outrage, we must also imagine the perpe- trator so vacillating an idiot as to have abandoned his gold and his motive together.

"Keeping now steadily in mind the points to which I have drawn your attention—that peculiar voice, that unusual agility, and that startling absence of motive in a murder so singularly atrocious as this—let us glance at the butchery itself. Here is a woman strangled to death by manual strength, and thrust up a chimney, head downwards. Ordinary assassins employ no such modes of murder as this. Least of all do they dispose of the murdered. In the manner of thrusting the corpse up the chimney, you will admit that there was something excessively *outré*—something altogether irreconcilable with our common notions of human action, even when we suppose the actors the most depraved of men. Think too how great must have been that strength which could have thrust the body *up* such an aperture so forcibly that the united vigor of several persons was found barely sufficient to drag it *down!*

"Turn now to other indications of the employment of a vigor most marvelous. On the hearth were thick tresses, very thick tresses, of gray human hair. These had been torn out by the roots. You are aware of the great force in tearing thus from the head even twenty or thirty hairs together. You saw the locks in question as well as myself. Their roots, (a hideous sight!) were clotted with fragments of the flesh of the scalp—sure token of the prodigious power which had been exerted in uprooting perhaps half a million of hairs at a time. The throat of the old lady

47

was not merely cut, but the head absolutely severed from the body, yet the instrument was a mere razor.

"I wish you also to look at the brutal ferocity of these deeds. Of the bruises upon the body of Madame L'Espanaye I do not speak. Monsieur Dumas and his worthy coadjutor, Monsieur Etienne, have pronounced that they were inflicted by some obtuse instrument; and so far these gentlemen are very correct. The obtuse instrument was clearly the stone pavement in the yard upon which the victim had fallen from the window which looked in upon the bed. This idea, however simple it may now seem, escaped the police for the same reason that the breadth of the shutters escaped them, because by the affair of the nails their perceptions had been hermetically sealed against the possibility of the windows having even been opened at all.

"If now, in addition to all these things, you have properly reflected upon the odd disorder of the chamber, we have gone so far as to combine the ideas of an agility astounding, a strength superhuman, a ferocity brutal, a butchery without motive, a *grotesquerie* in horror absolutely alien from humanity, and a voice foreign in tone to the ears of men of many nations, and devoid of all distinct or intelligible syllabification. What result, then, has ensued? What impression have I made upon your fancy?"

I felt a creeping of the flesh as Dupin asked me the question. "A madman," I said, "has done this deed, some raving maniac, who has escaped from a neighboring *maison de santé.*"

"In some respects," he replied, "your idea is not irrelevant. But the voices of madmen, even in their wildest paroxysms, are never found to tally with that peculiar voice heard upon the stairs. Madmen are of some nation, and their language, however incoherent in its words, has always the coherence of syllabification. Besides, the hair of a madman is not such as I now hold in my hand. I disentangled this little tuft from the rigidly clutched fingers of Madame L'Espanaye. Tell me what you can make of it."

"Dupin!" I said, completely unnerved, "this hair is most unusual. This is no human hair."

"I have not asserted that it is," said he. "But before we decide this point I wish you to glance at the little sketch I have here traced upon this paper. It is a facsimile drawing of what has been described in one portion of the testimony as 'dark bruises and deep indentations of fingernails,' upon the throat of Mademoiselle L'Espanaye, and in another, by Messrs. Dumas and Etienne, as a 'series of livid spots, evidently the impression of fingers.'

"You will perceive," continued my friend, spreading out the paper upon the table before us, "that this drawing gives the idea of a firm and fixed hold. There is no slipping apparent. Each finger has retained, possibly until the death of the victim, the fearful grasp by which it originally imbedded itself. Attempt, now, to place all your fingers at the same time in the respective impressions as you see them."

I made the attempt in vain.

"We are possibly not giving this matter a fair trial," he said. "The paper is spread out upon a plane surface, but the human throat is cylindrical. Here is a billet of wood, the circumference of which is about that of the throat. Wrap the drawing around it and try the experiment again."

I did so, but the difficulty was even more obvious than before.

"This," I said, "is the mark of no human hand."

"Read now," replied Dupin, "this passage from Cuvier."

It was a minute anatomical and general descriptive account of the large fulvous orangutan of the East Indian Islands. The gigantic stature, the prodigious strength and activity, the wild ferocity, and the imitative propensities of these mammalia are sufficiently well known to all. I understood the full horrors of the murder at once.

"The description of the digits," said I, as I made an end of reading, "is in exact accordance with this drawing. I see that no animal but an orangutan, of the species here mentioned, could have impressed the indentations as you have traced them. This tuft of tawny hair, too, is identical with that of the beast of Cuvier. But I cannot possibly comprehend the particulars of this frightful mystery. Besides, there were *two* voices heard in contention, and one of them was unquestionably the voice of a Frenchman."

"True. And you will remember an expression attributed almost unanimously, by the evidence, to this voice —the expression, *mon Dieu!* This, under the circumstances, has been justly characterized by one of the witnesses (Montani, the confectioner), as an expression of remonstrance or expostulation. Upon these two words, therefore, I have mainly built my hopes of a full solution of the riddle. A Frenchman was cognizant of the murder. It is possible, indeed it is far more than probable, that he was innocent of all participation in the bloody transactions which took place. The orangutan may have escaped from him. He may have traced it to the chamber, but under the agitating circumstances which ensued, he could never have recaptured it. It is still at large. I will not pursue these guesses, for I have no right to call them more, since the shades of reflection upon which they are based are scarcely of sufficient depth to be appreciable by my own intellect, and since I could not pretend to make them intelligible to the understanding of another. We will call them guesses then, and speak of them as such. If the Frenchman in question is indeed, as I suppose, innocent of this atrocity, this advertisement which I left last night upon our return home, at the office of *Le Monde* (a paper devoted to the shipping interest and much sought by sailors), will bring him to our residence."

He handed me a paper, and I read thus:

CAUGHT—In the Bois de Boulogne, early in the morning of the —— inst. [the morning of the murder] a very large, tawny orangutan of the Bornese species. The owner (who is ascertained to be a sailor belonging to a Maltese vessel) may have the animal again upon identifying it satisfactorily and paying a few charges arising from its capture and keeping. Call at No. ——, Rue ——, Faubourg St. Germain ——au troisième.

"How was it possible," I asked, "that you should know the man to be a sailor, and belonging to a Maltese vessel?"

"I do not know it," said Dupin. "I am not sure of it. Here, however, is a small piece of ribbon, which from its form and from its greasy appearance has evidently been used in tying the hair in one of those long queues of which sailors are so fond. Moreover, this knot is one which few besides sailors can tie, and is peculiar to the Maltese. I picked the ribbon up at the foot of the lightning rod. It could not have belonged to either of the deceased. Now if, after all, I am wrong in my induction from this ribbon, that the Frenchman was a sailor belonging to a Maltese vessel, still I can have done no harm in saying what I did in the advertisement. If I am in error, he will merely suppose that I have been misled by some circumstance into which he will not take the trouble to inquire. But if I am right, a great point is gained. Cognizant, although innocent of the murder, the Frenchman will naturally hesitate about replying to the advertisement, about demanding the orangutan. He will reason thus: 'I am innocent; I am poor. My orangutan is of great value—to one in my circumstances a fortune of itself. Why should I lose it through idle apprehensions of danger? Here it is, within my grasp. It was found in the Bois de Boulogne, at a vast distance from the scene of that butchery. How can it ever be suspected that a brute beast should have done the deed? The police are at fault. They have failed to procure the slightest clue. Should they even trace the animal, it would be impossible to prove me cognizant of the murder, or to implicate me in guilt on account of that cognizance. Above all, I am known. The advertiser designates me as the possessor of the beast. I am not sure to what limit his knowledge may extend. Should I avoid claiming a property of so great value, which it is known that I possess, I will render the animal, at least, liable to suspicion. It is not my policy to attract attention either to myself or to the beast. I will answer the advertisement, get the orangutan, and keep it close until this matter has blown over.'"

At this moment we heard a step upon the stairs.

"Be ready," said Dupin, "with your pistols, but neither use them nor show them until at a signal from myself."

The front door of the house had been left open and the visitor had entered without ringing, and advanced several steps upon the staircase. Now, however, he seemed to hesitate. Presently we heard him descending. Dupin was moving quickly to the door when we again heard him coming up. He did not turn back a second time, but stepped up with decision and rapped at the door of our chamber.

"Come in," said Dupin, in a cheerful and hearty tone.

A man entered. He was a sailor, evidently, a tall, stout and muscular-looking person, with a certain daredevil expression of countenance, not altogether unprepossessing. His face, greatly sunburnt, was more than half-hidden by whiskers and *mustachio*. He had with him a huge oaken cudgel, but appeared to be otherwise unarmed. He bowed awkwardly and bade us good evening in French accents which, although somewhat Neufchatel-ish, were still sufficiently indicative of a Parisian origin.

"Sit down, my friend," said Dupin. "I suppose you have called about the orangutan. Upon my word, I almost envy you the possession of him, a remarkably fine and no doubt a very valuable animal. How old do you suppose him to be?"

The sailor drew a long breath, with the air of a man relieved of some intolerable burden, and then replied in an assured tone, "I have no way of telling, but he can't be more than four or five years old. Have you got him here?"

"Oh, no. We had no conveniences for keeping him here. He is at a livery stable in the Rue Dubourg, just by. You can get him in the morning. Of course you are prepared to identify the property?"

"To be sure I am, sir."

"I shall be sorry to part with him," said Dupin.

"I don't mean that you should be at all this trouble for nothing, sir," said the man. "Couldn't expect it. Am very willing to pay a reward for the finding of the animal—that is to say, anything in reason."

"Well," replied my friend, "that is all very fair, to be sure. Let me think! What should I have? Oh! I will tell you. My reward shall be this. You shall give me all the information in your power about these murders in the Rue Morgue."

Dupin said the last words in a very low tone, and very quietly. Just as quietly, too, he walked toward the door, locked it, and put the key in his pocket. He then drew a pistol from his bosom and placed it, without the least flurry, upon the table.

The sailor's face flushed up as if he were struggling with suffocation. He started to his feet and grasped his cudgel; but the next moment he fell back into his seat, trembling violently, and with the countenance of death itself. He spoke not a word. I pitied him from the bottom of my heart.

"My friend," said Dupin, in a kind tone, "you are alarming yourself unnecessarily. You are, indeed. We mean you no harm whatever. I pledge you the honor of a gentleman and of a Frenchman that we intend you no injury. I perfectly well know that you are innocent of the atrocities in the Rue Morgue. It will not do, however, to deny that you are in some measure implicated in them. From what I have already said, you must know that I have had means of information about this matter, means of which you could never have dreamed. Now the thing stands thus. You have done nothing which you could have avoided—nothing, certainly, which renders you culpable. You were not even guilty of robbery, when you might have robbed with impunity. You have nothing to conceal. You have no reason for concealment. On the other hand, you are bound by every principle of honor to confess all you know. An innocent man is now imprisoned, charged with that crime of which you can point out the perpetrator."

The sailor had recovered his presence of mind in a great measure while Dupin uttered these words, but his original boldness of bearing was all gone.

"So help me God," said he, after a brief pause, "I will tell you all I know about this affair; but I do not expect you to believe one half I say—I would be a fool indeed if I did. Still, I am innocent, and I will make a clean breast if I die for it."

What he stated was, in substance, this. He had lately made a voyage to the Indian Archipelago. A party of which he formed one landed at Borneo, and passed into the interior on an excursion of pleasure. He and a companion had captured the orangutan. This companion dying, the animal fell into his own exclusive possession. After great trouble, occasioned by the intractable ferocity of his captive during the home voyage, he at length succeeded in lodging it safely at his own residence in Paris, where, not to attract the unpleasant curiosity of his neighbors, he kept it carefully secluded, until such time as it should recover from a wound in the foot, received from a splinter on board ship. His ultimate design was to sell it.

Returning home from some sailors' frolic on the night, or rather in the morning of the murder, he found the beast occupying his own bedroom, into which it had broken from a closet adjoining, where it had been, as was thought, securely confined. Razor in hand and fully lathered, it was sitting before a looking glass, attempting the operation of shaving, in which it had no doubt previously watched its master through the keyhole of the closet. Terrified at the sight of so dangerous a weapon in the possession of an animal so ferocious, and so well able to use it, the man was for some moments at a loss to know what to do. He had been accustomed, however, to quiet the creature, even in its fiercest moods, by the use of a whip, and to this he now resorted. Upon sight of it, the orang-utan sprang at once through the door of the chamber, down the stairs, and thence through a window, unfortunately open, into the street.

The Frenchman followed in despair. The ape, razor still in hand, occasionally stopped to look back and gesticulate at its pursuer, until the latter had nearly come up with it. It then again made off. In this manner the chase continued for a long time. The streets were profoundly quiet, as it was nearly three o'clock in the morning. In passing down an alley in the rear of the Rue Morgue, the fugitive's attention was arrested by a light gleaming from the open window of Madame L'Espanaye's chamber, in the fourth story of her house. Rushing to the building, it perceived the lightning rod, clambered up with inconceivable agility, grasped the shutter, which was thrown fully back against the wall, and by its means, swung itself directly upon the headboard of the bed. The whole feat did not occupy a minute. The shutter was kicked open again by the orangutan as it entered the room.

The sailor, in the meantime, was both rejoiced and perplexed. He had strong hopes of now recapturing the brute, as it could scarcely escape from the trap into which it had ventured, except by the rod, where it might be intercepted as it came down. On the other hand, there was much cause for anxiety as to what it might do in the house. This latter reflection urged the man still to follow the fugitive. A lightning rod is ascended without difficulty, especially by a sailor; but, when he had arrived as high as the window, which lay far to his left, his career was stopped; the most that he could accomplish was to reach over so as to obtain a glimpse of the interior of the room. At this glimpse he nearly fell from his hold through excess of horror. Now it was that those hideous shrieks arose upon the night which had startled from slumber the inmates of the Rue Morgue. Madame L'Espanaye and her daughter, clad in their nightclothes, had apparently been arranging some papers in the iron chest already mentioned, which had been wheeled into the middle of the room. It was open, and its contents lay beside it on the floor. The victims must have been sitting with their backs toward the window; and from the time elapsing between the ingress of the beast and the screams, it seems probable that the ape was not immediately perceived. The flapping-to of the shutter would naturally have been attributed to the wind.

As the sailor looked in, the gigantic animal had seized Madame L'Espanaye by the hair (which was loose, as she had been combing it) and was flourishing the razor about her face, in imitation of the motions of a barber. The daughter lay prostrate and motionless; she had swooned. The screams and struggles of the old lady (during which the hair was torn from her head) had the effect of changing the probably pacific purposes of the orangutan into those of wrath. With one determined sweep of its muscular arm it nearly severed her head from her body. The sight of blood inflamed its anger into frenzy. Gnashing its teeth, and flashing fire from its eyes, it flew upon the body of the girl, and imbedded its fearful talons in her throat, retaining its grasp until she expired. Its wandering and wild glances fell at this moment upon the head of the bed, over which the face of its master, rigid with horror, was just discernible. The fury of the beast, who no doubt bore still in mind the dreaded whip, was instantly converted into fear. Conscious of having deserved punishment, it seemed desirous of concealing its bloody deeds, and skipped about the chamber in an agony of nervous agitation; throwing down and breaking the furniture as it moved, and dragging the bed from the bedstead. In conclusion, it seized first the corpse of the daughter and thrust it up the chimney, as it was found, then that of the old lady, which it immediately hurled through the window, headlong.

As the ape approached the casement with its mutilated burden the sailor shrank aghast to the rod, and rather gliding than clambering down it, hurried at once home, dreading the consequences of the butchery and gladly abandoning, in his terror, all solicitude about the fate of the orangutan. The words heard by the party upon the staircase were the Frenchman's exclamations of horror and affright, commingled with the fiendish jabberings of the brute.

I have scarcely anything to add. The orangutan must have escaped from the chamber by the rod, just before the breaking of the door. It must have closed the window as it passed through it. It was subsequently caught by the owner himself, who obtained for it a very large sum at the Jardin des Plantes. Le Bon was instantly released, upon our narration of the circumstances (with some comments from Dupin) at the *bureau* of the Prefect of Police. This functionary, however well disposed to my friend, could not altogether conceal his chagrin at the turn which affairs had taken, and was fain to indulge in a sarcasm or two about the propriety of every person minding his own business.

"Let him talk," said Dupin, who had not thought it necessary to reply. "Let him discourse. It will ease his conscience. I am satisfied with having defeated him in his own castle. Nevertheless, that he failed in the solution of this mystery is by no means that matter for wonder which he supposes it, for in truth our friend the Prefect is somewhat too cunning to be profound. In his wisdom is no stamina. It is all head and no body, like the pictures of the Goddess Laverna, or at best, all head and shoulders, like a codfish. But he is a good creature after all. I like him especially for one master stroke of cant, by which he has attained his reputation for ingenuity. I mean the way he has *de nier ce qui est et d'expliquer ce qui n'est pas.*" [1]

[1] Rousseau, *Nouvelle Héloïse.*

THE PURLOINED LETTER

AT Paris, just after dark one gusty evening in the autumn of 18—, I was enjoying the twofold luxury of meditation and a meerschaum in company with my friend C. Auguste Dupin, in his little back library or book closet, *au trois-ème,* No. 33, Rue Dunôt, Faubourg St. Germain. For one hour at least we had maintained a profound silence, while each, to any casual observer, might have seemed intently and exclusively occupied with the curling eddies of smoke that oppressed the atmosphere of the chamber. For myself, however, I was mentally discussing certain topics which had formed matter for conversation between us at an earlier period of the evening. I mean the affair of the Rue Morgue and the mystery attending the murder of Marie Rogêt. I looked upon it, therefore, as something of a coincidence when the door of our apartment was thrown open and admitted our old acquaintance, Monsieur G——, the Prefect of the Parisian police.

We gave him a hearty welcome; for there was nearly half as much of the entertaining as of the contemptible about the man, and we had not seen him for several years. We had been sitting in the dark. Dupin now arose for the purpose of lighting a lamp, but sat down again without doing so upon G——'s saying that he had called to consult us, or rather to ask the opinion of my friend about some official business which had occasioned a great deal of trouble.

"If it is any point requiring reflection," observed Dupin, as he forbore to enkindle the wick, "we shall examine it to better purpose in the dark."

"That is another of your odd notions," said the Prefect, who had a fashion of calling everything odd that was beyond his comprehension, and thus lived amid an absolute legion of oddities.

"Very true," said Dupin, as he supplied his visitor with a pipe and rolled towards him a comfortable chair.

"And what is the difficulty now?" I asked. "Nothing more in the assassination way, I hope?"

"Oh no, nothing of that nature. The fact is, the business is very simple indeed, and I make no doubt that we can manage it sufficiently well ourselves; but then I thought Dupin would like to hear the details of it, because it is so excessively *odd*."

"Simple and odd," said Dupin.

"Why yes, and not exactly that, either. The fact is, we have all been a good deal puzzled because the affair *is* so simple, and yet baffles us altogether."

"Perhaps it is the very simplicity of the thing which puts you at fault," said my friend.

"What nonsense you do talk!" replied the Prefect, laughing heartily.

"Perhaps the mystery is a little *too* plain," said Dupin.

"Oh, good heavens! Who ever heard of such an idea?"

"A little *too* self-evident."

"Ha! ha! ha! ha! ha! ha! ho! ho! ho!" roared our visitor, profoundly amused. "Oh Dupin, you will be the death of me yet!"

"And what after all *is* the matter on hand?" I asked.

"Why I will tell you," replied the Prefect, as he gave a long, steady and contemplative puff and settled himself in his chair. "I will tell you in a few words; but before I begin, let me caution you that this is an affair demanding the greatest secrecy, and that I should most probably lose the position I now hold were it known that I confided it to anyone."

"Proceed," said I.

"Or not," said Dupin.

"Well, then. I have received personal information from a very high quarter that a certain document of the first importance has been purloined from the royal apartments. The individual who purloined it is known—this beyond a doubt; he was seen to take it. It is known also that it still remains in his possession."

"How is this known?" asked Dupin.

"It is clearly inferred," replied the Prefect, "from the nature of the document, and from the non-appearance of certain results which would at once arise from its passing out of the robber's possession—that is to say, from his employing it as he must design in the end to employ it."

"Be a little more explicit," I said.

"Well, I may venture so far as to say that the paper gives its holder a certain power in a certain quarter where such power is immensely valuable." The Prefect was fond of the cant of diplomacy.

"Still I do not quite understand," said Dupin.

"No? Well, the disclosure of the document to a third person, who shall be nameless, would bring in question the honor of a personage of most exalted station; and this fact gives the holder of the document an ascendancy over the illustrious personage whose honor and peace are so jeopardized."

"But this ascendancy," I interposed, "would depend upon the robber's knowledge of the loser's knowledge of the robber. Who would dare—"

"The thief," said G——, "is the Minister D——, who dares all things, those unbecoming as well as those becoming a man. The method of the theft was not less ingenious than bold. The document in question—a letter, to be frank—had been received by the personage robbed while alone in the royal boudoir. During its perusal she was suddenly interrupted by the entrance of the other exalted personage from whom especially it was her wish to conceal it. After

65

a hurried and vain endeavor to thrust it in a drawer, she was forced to place it, open as it was, upon a table. The address, however, was uppermost, and the contents thus unexposed, the letter escaped notice.

"At this juncture enters the Minister D——. His lynx eye immediately perceives the paper, recognizes the handwriting of the address, observes the confusion of the personage addressed, and fathoms her secret. After some business transactions, hurried through in his ordinary manner, he produces a letter somewhat similar to the one in question, opens it, pretends to read it, and then places it in close juxtaposition to the other. Again he converses for some fifteen minutes upon public affairs. At length, in taking leave he takes also from the table the letter to which he had no claim. Its rightful owner saw, but of course dared not call attention to the act in the presence of the third personage who stood at her elbow. The minister decamped, leaving his own letter, one of no importance, upon the table."

"Here, then," said Dupin to me, "you have precisely what you demand to make the ascendancy complete—the robber's knowledge of the loser's knowledge of the robber."

"Yes," replied the Prefect. "And the power thus attained has for some months past been wielded, for political purposes, to a very dangerous extent. The personage robbed is more thoroughly convinced every day of the necessity of reclaiming her letter. But this of course cannot be done openly. In fine, driven to despair she has committed the matter to me."

"Than whom," said Dupin, amid a perfect whirlwind of smoke, "no more sagacious agent could, I suppose, be desired or even imagined."

"You flatter me," replied the Prefect. "But it is possible that some such opinion may have been entertained."

"It is clear," said I, "as you observe, that the letter is still in possession of the minister, since it is this possession and not any employment of the letter which bestows the power. With the employment the power departs."

"True," said G——, "and upon this conviction I proceeded. My first care was to make thorough search of the minister's hotel; and here my chief embarrassment lay in the necessity of searching without his knowledge. Beyond all things, I have been warned of the danger which would result from giving him reason to suspect our design."

"But," said I, "you are quite *au fait* in these investigations. The Parisian police have done this sort of thing often before."

"Oh yes; and for this reason I did not despair. The habits of the minister gave me a great advantage. He is frequently absent from home all night. His servants are by no means numerous. They sleep at a distance from their master's apartment, and are readily made drunk. I have keys as you know with which I can open any chamber or cabinet in Paris. For three months a night has not passed during the greater part of which I have not been engaged personally in ransacking the D—— hotel. My honor is interested, and to mention a great secret, the reward is enormous. So I did not abandon the search until I had become fully satisfied that the thief is a more astute man than myself. I fancy that I have investigated every nook and corner of the premises in which it is possible that the paper can be concealed."

"But is it not possible," I suggested, "that although the letter may be in possession of the minister, as it unquestionably is, he may have concealed it elsewhere than upon his own premises?"

"This is barely possible," said Dupin. "The present peculiar condition of affairs at court, and especially of those intrigues in which D—— is known to be involved, would render the instant availability of the document, its susceptibility of being produced at a moment's notice, a point of nearly equal importance with its possession."

"Its susceptibility of being produced?" said I.

"That is to say, of being *destroyed*," said Dupin.

"True," I observed. "The paper is clearly then upon the premises. As for its being upon the person of the minister, we may consider that as out of the question."

"Entirely," said the Prefect. "He has been twice waylaid, as if by footpads, and his person rigorously searched under my own inspection."

"You might have spared yourself this trouble," said Dupin. "D——, I presume, is not altogether a fool, and if not, must have anticipated these waylayings as a matter of course."

"Not *altogether* a fool," said G——. "But then he's a poet, which I take to be only one remove from a fool."

"True," said Dupin, after a long and thoughtful whiff from his meerschaum, "although I have been guilty of certain doggerel myself."

"Suppose you detail," said I, "the particulars of your search."

"Why, the fact is we took our time and we searched everywhere. I have had long experience in these affairs. I took the entire building room by room, devoting the nights of a whole week to each. We examined first the furniture of each apartment. We opened every possible drawer, and I presume you know that, to a properly trained police agent, such a thing as a secret drawer is impossible. Any man is a dolt who permits a secret drawer to escape him in a search of this kind. The thing is so plain. There is a certain amount of bulk, of space, to be accounted for in every cabinet. Then we have accurate rules. The fiftieth part of a line could not escape us. After the cabinets we took the chairs. The cushions we probed with the fine long needles you have seen me employ. From the tables we removed the tops."

"Why so?"

"Sometimes the top of a table or other similarly arranged piece of furniture is removed by the person wishing to conceal an article; then the leg is excavated, the article deposited within the cavity, and the top replaced. The bottoms and tops of bedposts are employed in the same way."

"But could not the cavity be detected by sounding?" I asked.

"By no means if, when the article is deposited, a sufficient wadding of cotton were placed around it. Besides, in our case we were obliged to proceed without noise."

"But you could not have removed, you could not have taken to pieces *all* articles of furniture in which it would have been possible to make a deposit in the manner you mention. A letter may be compressed into a thin spiral roll, not differing much in shape or bulk from a large knitting needle, and in this form it might be inserted into the rung of a chair, for example. You did not take to pieces all the chairs?"

"Certainly not, but we did better; we examined the rungs of every chair in the hotel and indeed the jointings of every description of furniture by the aid of a most powerful microscope. Had there been any traces of recent disturbance we should not have failed to detect it instantly. A single grain of gimlet dust, for example, would have been as obvious as an apple. Any disorder in the gluing, any unusual gaping in the joints, would have sufficed to insure detection."

"I presume you looked to the mirrors, between the boards and the plates, and you probed the beds and the bedclothes, as well as the curtains and carpets."

"That of course, and when we had absolutely completed every particle of the furniture in this way, then we examined the house itself. We divided its entire surface into compartments, which we numbered so that none might be missed; then we scrutinized each individual square inch throughout the premises, including the two houses immediately adjoining, with the microscope, as before."

"The two houses adjoining!" I exclaimed. "You must have had a great deal of trouble."

"We had, but the reward offered is prodigious."

"You include the grounds about the houses?"

"All the grounds are paved with brick. They gave us comparatively little trouble. We examined the moss between the bricks and found it undisturbed."

"You looked among D——'s papers of course, and into the books of the library?"

"Certainly. We opened every package and parcel; we not only opened every book but we turned over every leaf in each volume, not contenting ourselves with a mere shake, according to the fashion of some of our police officers. We also measured the thickness of every book cover with the most accurate admeasurement, and applied to each the most jealous scrutiny of the microscope. Had any of the bindings been recently meddled with, it would have been utterly impossible that the fact should have escaped observation. Some five or six volumes, just from the hands of the binder, we carefully probed longitudinally with the needles."

"You explored the floors beneath the carpets?"

"Beyond doubt. We removed every carpet and examined the boards with the microscope."

"And the paper on the walls?"

"Yes."

"You looked into the cellars?"

"We did."

"Then," I said, "you have been making a miscalculation, and the letter is not upon the premises, as you suppose."

"I fear you are right there," said the Prefect. "And now, Dupin, what would you advise me to do?"

"To make a thorough re-search of the premises."

"That is absolutely needless," replied G——. "I am not more sure that I breathe than I am that the letter is not at the hotel."

"I have no better advice to give you," said Dupin. "You have of course an accurate description of the letter?"

"Oh yes!" And here the Prefect, producing a memorandum book, proceeded to read aloud a minute account of the internal and especially of the external appearance of the missing document. Soon after reading this description to us, he took his departure, more entirely depressed in spirits than I had ever known the good gentleman before.

In about a month afterwards he paid us another visit,

and found us occupied very nearly as before. He took a pipe and a chair and entered into some ordinary conversation. At length I said:

"Well, G——, what of the purloined letter? I presume you have at last made up your mind that there is no such thing as overreaching the minister?"

"Confound him, say I—yes; I made the re-examination, however, as Dupin suggested, but it was all labor lost, as I knew it would be."

"How much was the reward offered, did you say?" asked Dupin.

"Why, a very great deal, a very liberal reward. I don't like to say how much, precisely, but one thing I *will* say. I wouldn't mind giving my individual check for fifty thousand francs to anyone who could obtain me that letter. The fact is, it becomes of more and more importance every day, and the reward has been lately doubled. If it were trebled, however, I could do no more than I have done."

"Why, yes," said Dupin, drawling between the whiffs of his meerschaum. "I really—think, G——, you have not exerted yourself to the utmost in this matter. You might—do a little more, I think, eh?"

"How? In what way?"

"Why"—puff, puff—"you might"—puff, puff—"employ counsel in the matter, eh?"—puff, puff, puff. "Do you remember the story they tell of Abernethy?"

"No. Hang Abernethy!"

"To be sure! Hang him and welcome. But, once upon a time, a certain rich miser conceived the design of sponging upon this Abernethy for a medical opinion. Getting up, for this purpose, an ordinary conversation in private company, he insinuated his case to the physician as that of an imaginary individual.

" 'We will suppose,' said the miser, 'that his symptoms are such and such. Now, doctor, what would you have directed him to take?'

" 'Take!' said Abernethy, 'why, take *advice*, to be sure.' "

"But," said the Prefect, a little discomposed, "I am perfectly willing to take advice, and to pay for it. I would really give fifty thousand francs to anyone who would aid me in the matter."

"In that case," replied Dupin, opening a drawer and producing a checkbook, "you may as well fill me up a check for the amount mentioned. When you have signed it, I will hand you the letter."

I was astounded. The Prefect appeared absolutely thunderstricken. For some minutes he remained speechless and motionless, looking incredulously at my friend with open mouth and with eyes that seemed starting from their sockets. Then apparently recovering himself in some measure, he seized a pen. After several pauses and vacant stares, he finally filled up and signed a check for fifty thousand francs and handed it across the table to Dupin. The latter examined it carefully and deposited it in his pocketbook. Then, unlocking an *escritoire,* he took thence a letter and gave it to the Prefect. This functionary grasped it in a perfect agony of joy, opened it with a trembling hand, cast a rapid glance at its contents, and then, scrambling and struggling to the door, rushed at length unceremoniously from the room and from the house, without having uttered a syllable since Dupin had requested him to fill up the check.

When he had gone, my friend entered into some explanations.

"The Parisian police," he said, "are exceedingly able in their way. They are persevering, ingenious, cunning, and thoroughly versed in the knowledge which their duties seem chiefly to demand. Thus, when G—— detailed to us his mode of searching the premises at the Hôtel D——, I felt entire confidence in his having made a satisfactory investigation—so far as his labors extended."

"So far as his labors extended?" said I.

"Yes," said Dupin. "The measures adopted were not only the best of their kind, but carried out to absolute perfection. Had the letter been deposited within the range of their search, these fellows would, beyond a question, have found it."

I merely laughed, but he seemed quite serious in all that he said.

"The measures, then," he continued, "were good in their kind, and well executed; their defeat lay in their being inapplicable to the case and to the man. A certain set of highly ingenious resources are, with the Prefect, a sort of Procrustean bed, to which he forcibly adapts his designs. But he perpetually errs by being too deep or too shallow for the matter in hand, and many a schoolboy is a better reasoner than he.

"I knew one about eight years of age whose success at guessing in the game of 'even and odd' attracted universal admiration. This game is simple and is played with marbles. One player holds in his hand a number of these toys, and demands of another whether that number is even or odd. If the guess is right the guesser wins one, if wrong he loses one. The boy to whom I allude won all the marbles of the school.

"Of course he had some principle of guessing; and this lay in mere observation and admeasurement of the astuteness of his opponents. For example, an arrant simpleton is his opponent, and, holding up his closed hand, asks, 'Are they even or odd?' Our schoolboy replies, 'odd,' and loses; but upon the second trial he wins, for he then says to himself, 'the simpleton had them even upon the first trial, and his amount of cunning is just sufficient for him to make them odd upon the second; I will therefore guess odd. He guesses odd and wins.

"Now, with a simpleton a degree above the first, he would have reasoned thus: 'This fellow finds that in the first instance I guessed odd. In the second, he will propose to himself upon the first impulse, a simple variation from even to odd, as did the first simpleton; but then a second thought will suggest that this is too simple a variation, and finally he will decide upon putting it even as before. I will therefore guess even'; he guesses even and wins. Now this mode of reasoning in the schoolboy, whom his fellows termed 'lucky,'—what, in its last analysis, is it?"

"It is merely," I said, "an identification of the reasoner's intellect with that of his opponent."

"It is," said Dupin, "and upon inquiring of the boy by what means he effected the thorough identification in which his success consisted, I received answer as follows: 'When I want to find out how wise, or how stupid, or how good, or how wicked anyone is, or what his thoughts are at the moment, I fashion the expression of my face as accurately as possible in accordance with his, and then wait to see what thoughts or sentiments arise in my mind or heart to correspond with the expression.' This response of the schoolboy lies at the bottom of all the spurious profundity which has been attributed to Rochefoucauld, to La Bougive, to Machiavelli, and to Campanella."

"And the identification," I said, "of the reasoner's intellect with that of his opponent, depends, if I understand you aright, upon the accuracy with which the opponent's intellect is admeasured."

"For its practical value it depends upon this," replied Dupin; "and the Prefect and his cohort fail so, frequently —first by default of this identification, and secondly by ill-admeasurement, or rather through non-admeasurement, of the intellect with which they are engaged. They consider only their own ideas of ingenuity; and, in searching for anything hidden, consider only the modes in which they would have hidden it. They are right to this extent—that their ingenuity is a faithful representative of that of the mass; but when the cunning of the individual felon is diverse in character from their own, the felon foils them, of course.

"This always happens when it is above their own, and very usually when it is below. They have no variation of principle in their investigations; at best, when urged by some unusual emergency—by some extraordinary reward—they extend or exaggerate their old modes of practice, without touching their principles. What, for example, in this case of D——, has been done to vary the principle of action? What is all this boring, and probing, and sounding, and scrutinizing with the microscope, and dviding the surface of the building into registered square inches—what is it all but an exaggeration of the application of one principle or set of principles of search, which are based upon the one set of notions regarding human ingenuity, to which the Prefect, in the long routine of his duty, has been accustomed?

"Do you not see he has taken it for granted that *all* men proceed to conceal a letter—not exactly in a gimlet hole bored in a chair leg—but, at least in *some* out-of-the-way hole or corner suggested by the same tenor of thought which would urge a man to secret a letter in a gimlet hole bored in a chair leg? And do you not see also, that such *recherchés* nooks for concealment are adapted only for ordinary occasions, and would be adopted only by ordinary intellects. For in all cases of concealment, a disposal of the article concealed—a disposal of it in this *recherché manner*—is, in the very first instance, presumable and presumed. Thus its discovery depends, not at all upon the acumen, but altogether upon the mere care, patience, and determination of the seekers; and where the case is of importance or—it amounts to the same thing in policial eyes—when the reward is of magnitude, the qualities in question have *never* been known to fail.

"You will now understand what I mean in suggesting that, had the purloined letter been hidden anywhere within the limits of the Prefect's examination—in other words, had the principle of its concealment been comprehended within the principles of the Prefect—its discovery would have been a matter altogether beyond question. This functionary, however, has been thoroughly mystified, and the remote source of his defeat lies in the supposition that the minister is a fool because he has acquired renown as a poet. All fools are poets; this the Prefect feels; and he is merely guilty of a *non distributio medii* in thence inferring that all poets are fools."

"But is this really the poet?" I asked. "There are two brothers, I know, and both have attained reputation in letters. The minister I believe has written learnedly on the differential calculus. He is a mathematician, and no poet."

"You are mistaken. I know him well; he is both. As poet and mathematician, he would reason well; as mere mathematician he could not have reasoned at all, and thus would have been at the mercy of the Prefect."

"You surprise me," I said, "by these opinions, which have been contradicted by the voice of the world. You do not mean to set at naught the well-digested idea of centuries. The mathematical reason has long been regarded as the reason *par excellence*."

" '*Il y a à parier*,' " replied Dupin, quoting from Chamfort, " '*que toute idée publique, toute convention reçue, est une sottise, car elle a convenu au plus grand nombre*.' The mathematicians, I grant you, have done their best to promulgate the popular error to which you allude, and which is none the less an error for all its promulgation as truth. With an art worthy a better cause, for example, they have insinuated the term, analysis, into application to algebra. The French are the originators of this particular deception; but if a term is of any importance, if words derive any value from applicability, then analysis conveys algebra about as much as, in Latin, *ambitus* implies ambition, *religio*, religion, or *homines honesti*, a set of honorable men."

"You have a quarrel on hand, I see," said I, "with some of the algebraists of Paris, but proceed."

"I dispute the availability, and thus the value of that

reason which is cultivated in any special form other than the abstractly logical. I dispute in particular the reason educed by mathematical study. The mathematics are the science of form and quantity; mathematical reasoning is merely logic applied to observation upon form and quantity. The great error lies in supposing that even the truths of what is called pure algebra are abstract or general truths. And this error is so egregious that I am confounded at the universality with which it has been received. Mathematical axioms are *not* axioms of general truth. What is true of *relation*—of form and quantity—is often grossly false in regard to morals, for example. In this latter science it is very usually *un*true that the aggregated parts are equal to the whole. In chemistry also the axiom fails. In the consideration of motive it fails; for two motives, each of a given value, have not, necessarily, a value when united equal to the sum of their values apart.

"There are numerous other mathematical truths which are only truths within the limits of *relation*. But the mathematician argues, from his finite truths, through habit, as if they were of an absolutely general applicability—as the world indeed imagines them to be. Bryant, in his very learned *Mythology*, mentions an analogous source of error when he says that 'although the pagan fables are not believed, yet we forget ourselves continually, and make inferences from them as existing realities.' With the algebraists, however, who are pagans themselves, their 'pagan fables' *are* believed, and the inferences are made, not so much through lapse of memory, as through an unaccountable addling of the brains. In short, I never yet encountered the mere mathematician who could be trusted out of equal roots, or one who did not clandestinely hold it as a point of his faith that $x^2 + px$ was absolutely and unconditionally equal to q. Say to one of these gentlemen, by way of experiment, if you please, that you believe occasions may occur where $x^2 + px$ is *not* altogether equal to q, and, having made him understand what you mean, get out of his reach as speedily as is convenient, for, beyond doubt, he will endeavor to knock you down.

"I mean to say," continued Dupin, while I merely laughed at his last observations, "that if the minister had been no more than a mathematician, the Prefect would have been under no necessity of giving me this check. I knew him, however, as both mathematician and poet, and my measures were adapted to his capacity, with reference to the circumstances by which he was surrounded. I knew him as a courtier, too, and as a bold *intrigant*. Such a man, I considered, could not fail to be aware of the ordinary policial modes of action. He could not have failed to anticipate—and events have proved that he did not fail to anticipate—the waylayings to which he was subjected. He must have foreseen, I reflected, the secret investigations of his premises. His frequent absences from home at night, which were hailed by the Prefect as certain aids to his success, I regarded only as ruses, to afford opportunity for thorough search to the police, and thus the sooner to impress them with the conviction to which G——, in fact, did finally arrive—the conviction that the letter was not upon the premises. I felt, also, that the whole train of thought (which I was at some pains in detailing to you just now, concerning the invariable principle of policial action in searches for articles concealed) would necessarily pass through the mind of the minister. It would imperatively lead him to despise all the ordinary nooks of concealment. He could not, I reflected, be so weak as not to see that the most intricate and remote recess of his hotel would be as open as his commonest closets to the eyes, to the probes, to the gimlets, and to the microscopes of the Prefect. I saw, in fine, that he would be driven, as a matter of course, to simplicity, if not deliberately induced to it as a matter of choice. You will remember, perhaps, how desperately the Prefect laughed when I suggested, upon our first interview, that it was just possible this mystery troubled him so much on account of its being so very self-evident."

"Yes," said I, "I remember his merriment well. I really thought he would fall into convulsions."

"The material world," continued Dupin, "abounds with very strict analogies to the immaterial; and thus some color of truth has been given to the rhetorical dogma that metaphor, or simile, may be made to strengthen an argument as well as to embellish a description. The principle of the *vis inertiae,* for example, seems to be identical in physics and metaphysics. It is not more true in the former, that a large body is with more difficulty set in motion than a smaller one, and that its subsequent momentum is commensurate with this difficulty, than it is, in the latter, that intellects of the vaster capacity, while more forcible, more constant, and more eventful in their movements than those of inferior grade, and yet the less readily moved, and more embarrassed and full of hesitation in the first few steps of their progress. Again: have you ever noticed which of the street signs over the shop doors are the most attractive of attention?"

"I have never given the matter a thought," I said.

"There is a game of puzzles," Dupin resumed, "which is played upon a map. One party playing requires another to find a given word—the name of town, river, state or empire—any word, in short, upon the motley and perplexed surface of the chart. A novice in the game generally seeks to embarrass his opponents by giving them the most minutely lettered names; but the adept selects such words as stretch, in large characters, from one end of the chart to the other. These, like the over-largely lettered signs and placards of the street, escape observation by dint of being excessively obvious. And here the physical oversight is precisely analogous with the moral inapprehension by which the intellect suffers to pass unnoticed those considerations which are too obtrusively and too palpably self-evident. But this is a point, it appears, somewhat above or beneath the understanding of the Prefect.

He never once thought it probable, or possible, that the minister had deposited the letter immediately beneath the nose of the whole world, by way of best preventing any portion of that world from perceiving it.

"But the more I reflected upon the daring, dashing and discriminating ingenuity of D——, upon the fact that the document must always be at hand if he intended to use it to good purpose—and upon the decisive evidence obtained by the Prefect that it was not hidden within the limits of that dignitary's ordinary search—the more satisfied I became that, to conceal this letter, the minister had resorted to the comprehensive and sagacious expedient of not attempting to conceal it at all.

"Full of these ideas, I prepared myself with a pair of green spectacles, and called one fine morning quite by accident, at the ministerial hotel. I found D—— at home, yawning, lounging and dawdling as usual, and pretending to be in the last extremity of *ennui*. He is, perhaps, the most really energetic human being now alive—but that is only when nobody sees him.

"To be even with him, I complained of my weak eyes, and lamented the necessity of the spectacles, under cover of which I cautiously and thoroughly surveyed the apartment, while seemingly intent only upon the conversation of my host.

"I paid special attention to a large writing table near which he sat, and upon which lay confusedly some miscellaneous letters and other papers, with one or two musical instruments and a few books. Here, however, after a long and very deliberate scrutiny, I saw nothing to excite particular suspicion.

"At length my eyes, in going the circuit of the room, fell upon a trumpery filigree card rack of pasteboard that hung dangling by a dirty blue ribbon from a little brass knob just beneath the middle of the mantelpiece. In this rack, which had three or four compartments, were five or six visiting cards and a solitary letter. This last was much soiled and crumpled. It was torn nearly in two across the middle, as if a design, in the first instance, to tear it entirely up as worthless had been altered or stayed, in the second. It had a large black seal, bearing the D—— cipher *very* conspicuously, and was addressed, in a diminutive female hand, to D——, the minister himself. It was thrust carelessly and even as it seemed, contemptuously, into one of the upper divisions of the rack.

"No sooner had I glanced at this letter than I concluded it to be that of which I was in search. To be sure it was, to all appearance, radically different from the one of which the Prefect had read us so minute a description. Here the seal was large and black, with the D—— cipher; there it was small and red, with the ducal arms of the S—— family. Here the address, to the minister, was diminutive and feminine; there the superscription, to a certain royal personage, was markedly bold and decided; the size alone formed a point of correspondence. But then the radicalness of these differences was excessive. The dirt, the soiled and torn condition of the paper were inconsistent with the true methodical habits of D——, and suggestive of a design to delude the beholder into an idea of the worthlessness of the document. These things, together with the hyperobtrusive situation of this document, full in the view of every visitor, were thus exactly in accordance with the conclusions to which I had previously arrived. These things, I say, were strongly corroborative of suspicion in one who came with the intention to suspect.

"I protracted my visit as long as possible, and while I maintained a most animated discussion with the minister on a topic which I knew well had never failed to interest and excite him, I kept my attention really riveted upon the letter. In this examination I committed to memory its external appearance and arrangement in the rack, and also fell at length upon a discovery which set at rest whatever trivial doubt I might have entertained. In scrutinizing the edges of the paper, I observed them to be more chafed than seemed necessary. They presented the broken appearance which is manifested when a stiff paper, having been once folded and pressed with a folder, is refolded in a reversed direction, in the same creases or edges which had formed the original fold. This discovery was sufficient. It was clear to me that the letter had been turned, as a glove, inside out, redirected, and resealed. I bade the minister good morning, and took my departure at once, leaving a gold snuff box upon the table.

"The next morning, when I called for the snuff box, we resumed, quite eagerly, the conversation of the preceding day. While thus engaged, however, a loud report, as if of a pistol, was heard immediately beneath the windows of the hotel, and was succeeded by a series of fearful screams, and the shoutings of a mob. D—— rushed to a casement, threw it open, and looked out. In the meantime, I stepped to the card rack, took the letter, put it in my pocket, and replaced it by a facsimile (so far as regards externals), which I had carefully prepared at my lodgings; I imitated the D—— cipher very readily by means of a seal formed of bread.

"The disturbance in the street had been occasioned by the frantic behavior of a man with a musket. He had fired it among a crowd of women and children. It proved, however, to have been without ball, and the fellow was suffered to go his way as a lunatic or a drunkard. When he had gone, D—— came from the window, whither I had followed him immediately upon securing the object in view. Soon afterwards I bade him farewell. The pretended lunatic was a man in my own pay."

"But what purpose had you," I asked, "in replacing the letter by a facsimile? Would it not have been better, at the first visit, to have seized it openly and departed?"

"D——," replied Dupin, "is a desperate man, and a man of nerve. His hotel, too, is not without attendants devoted to his interests. Had I made the wild attempt you suggest, I might never have left the ministerial presence alive. The good people of Paris might have heard of me no more. But I had an object apart from these considerations. You know my political prepossessions. In this matter, I act as a partisan of the lady concerned. For eighteen months the minister has had her in his power. She now has him in hers; since, being unaware that the letter is not in his possession, he will proceed with his exactions as if it were. Thus will he inevitably commit himself, at once, to his political destruction. His downfall, too, will not be more precipitate than awkward. It is all very well to talk about the *facilis descensus Averni*, but in all kinds of climbing, as Catalani said of singing, it is far more easy to get up than to come down. In the present instance I have no sympathy—at least no pity—for him who descends. He is that *monstrum horrendum*, an unprincipled man of genius. I confess, however, that I should like very well to know the precise character of his thoughts, when, being defied by her whom the Prefect terms 'a certain personage,' he is reduced to opening the letter which I left for him in the card rack."

"How? did you put anything particular in it?"

"Why, it did not seem altogether right to leave the interior blank. That would have been insulting. D——, at Vienna once, did me an evil turn, at which time I told him, quite good-humoredly, that I should remember. So, as I knew he would feel some curiosity in regard to the identity of the person who had outwitted him, I thought it a pity not to give him a clue. He is well acquainted with

my ms., and I just copied into the middle of the blank
sheet the words:

> —*Un dessein si funeste,*
> *S'il n'est digne d'Atrée, est digne de Thyeste.*

They are to be found in Crébillon's *Atrée*."

MS. FOUND IN A BOTTLE

INTRODUCTION

OF my country and of my family I have little to say. Ill-usage and length of years have driven me from the one, and estranged me from the other. Hereditary wealth afforded me an education of no common order, and a contemplative turn of mind enabled me to methodize the stores which early study diligently garnered up. Beyond all things the works of the German moralists gave me great delight, not from my ill-advised admiration of their eloquent madness, but from the ease with which my habits of rigid thoughts enabled me to detect their falsities. I have often been reproached with the aridity of my genius; a deficiency of imagination has been imputed to me as a crime; and the Pyrrhonism of my opinions has at all times rendered me notorious. Indeed, a strong relish for physical philosophy has, I fear, tinctured my mind with a very common error of this age—I mean the habit of referring occurrences, even the least susceptible of such reference, to the principles of that science. Upon the whole, no person could be less liable than myself to be led away from the severe precincts of truth by the *ignes fatui* of superstition. I have thought proper to premise this much, lest the incredible tale I have to tell should be considered rather the raving of a crude imagination, than the positive experience of a mind to which the reveries of fancy have long been dead.

MS. FOUND IN A BOTTLE

AFTER many years spent in foreign travel, I sailed in the year 18—, from the port of Batavia, in the rich and populous island of Java, on a voyage to the Archipelago Islands. I went as passenger, having no other inducement than a kind of nervous restlessness which haunted me as a fiend.

Our vessel was a beautiful ship of about four hundred tons, copper-fastened, and built at Bombay of Malabar teak. She was freighted with cotton wool and oil from the Lucchadive Islands. We had also on board coir, jaggeree, ghee, coconuts, and a few cases of opium. The stowage was clumsily done, and the vessel consequently lurched and rolled.

We got under way with a mere breath of wind, and for many days stood along the eastern coast of Java, without any other incident to beguile the monotony of our course than the occasional meeting with some of the small grabs (boats) of the Archipelago to which we were bound.

One evening, leaning over the taffrail, I observed a very singular isolated cloud, to the northwest. It was remarkable, both for its color and for being the first cloud we had seen since our departure from Batavia. I watched it attentively until sunset, when it spread all at once to the eastward and westward, girding the horizon with a narrow strip of vapor, and looking like a long line of low beach. My notice was soon afterward attracted by the dusky-red appearance of the moon, and the peculiar character of the sea. The latter was undergoing a rapid change, and the water seemed more than usually transparent. Although I could distinctly see the bottom, yet, heaving the lead, I found the ship in fifteen fathoms. The air now became intolerably hot, and was loaded with spiral exhalations similar to those arising from heated iron. As night came on every breath of wind died away, and a more entire calm it is impossible to conceive. The flame of a candle burned upon the poop without the least perceptible motion, and a long hair, held between the finger and thumb, hung without the possibility of detecting a vibration. However, as the captain said he could perceive no indication of danger, and as we were drifting in to shore, he ordered the sails to be furled, and the anchor let go. No watch was set, and the crew, consisting principally of Malays, stretched themselves deliberately upon deck. I went below—not without a full presentiment of evil.

Indeed, every appearance warranted me in apprehending a simoom. I told the captain of my fears, but he paid no attention to what I said, and left me without deigning to give a reply. My uneasiness, however, prevented me from sleeping, and about midnight I went upon deck. As I placed my foot upon the upper step of the companion ladder, I was startled by a loud, humming noise, like that occasioned by the rapid revolution of a mill wheel, and before I could ascertain its meaning I found the ship quivering to its center. In the next instant a wilderness of foam hurled us upon our beam-ends, and, rushing over us fore and aft, swept the entire decks from stem to stern.

The extreme fury of the blast proved, in a great measure, the salvation of the ship. Although completely water-logged she rose, after a minute, heavily from the sea, and staggering awhile beneath the immense pressure of the tempest, finally righted. Her masts had gone by the board.

By what miracle I escaped destruction, it is impossible to say. Stunned by the shock of the water, I found myself, upon recovery, jammed in between the sternpost and rudder. With great difficulty I regained my feet, and looking dizzily around, was at first struck with the idea of our being among *breakers* in mid-ocean. Terrific beyond the wildest imagination was the whirlpool of mountainous and foaming ocean within which we were engulfed.

After a while I heard the voice of an old Swede, who had shipped with us at the moment of leaving port. I hallooed to him with all my strength, and presently he came reeling aft. We soon discovered that we were the sole survivors of the accident. All on deck, with the exception of ourselves, had been swept overboard; the captain and mates must have perished while they slept, for the cabins were deluged with water. Without assistance we could expect to do little for the security of the ship, and our exertions were at first paralyzed by the momentary expectation of going down. Our cable had of course parted like packthread at the first breath of the hurricane, or we should have been instantaneously overwhelmed.

We scudded with frightful velocity before the sea, and the water made clear breaches over us. The framework of our stern was shattered excessively, and in almost every respect we had received considerable injury; but to our extreme joy we found the pumps were unchoked, and we had made no great shifting of our ballast. The main fury of the blast had already blown over, and we apprehended little danger from the violence of the wind. But we looked forward to its total cessation with dismay, well believing that in our shattered condition, we should inevitably perish in the tremendous swell which would ensue.

But this very just apprehension seemed by no means likely to be soon verified. For five entire days and nights —during which our only substance was a small quantity of jaggeree[1], procured with great difficulty from the forecastle—the hulk flew at a rate defying computation before rapidly succeeding flaws of wind which, without equaling the first violence of the simoom, were still more terrific than any tempest I had before encountered. Our course for the first four days was, with trifling variations, southeast and by east, and we must have run down the coast of Australia.

On the fifth day the cold became extreme, although the

---

[1] Sugar from the jaggery palm.

wind had hauled round a point more to the northward. The sun arose with a sickly yellow luster, and clambered a very few degrees above the horizon, emitting no decisive light. There were no clouds apparent, yet the wind was upon the increase and blew with a fitful and unsteady fury. About noon, as nearly as we could guess, our attention was again arrested by the appearance of the sun. It gave out no real light, but a dull and sullen glow without reflection, as if all its rays were polarized. Just before sinking within the turgid sea, its central fires suddenly went out, as if hurriedly extinguished by some unaccountable power. It was a dim, silverlike rim alone, as it rushed down the unfathomable ocean.

We waited in vain for the arrival of the sixth day. That day to me has not yet arrived; to the Swede it never did arrive. Thenceforward we were enshrouded in pitch darkness, so that we could not have seen an object at twenty paces from the ship. Eternal night continued to envelop us, all unrelieved by the phosphoric sea-brilliancy to which we had been accustomed in the tropics. We observed, too, that although the tempest continued to rage with unabated violence, there was no longer to be discovered the usual appearance of surf, or foam, which had hitherto attended us. All around were horror and thick gloom, and a black sweltering desert of ebony. Superstitious terror crept by degrees into the spirit of the old Swede, and my own soul was wrapped in silent wonder. We neglected all care of the ship as worse than useless, and securing ourselves as well as possible to the stump of the mizzenmast, looked out bitterly into the world of ocean. We had no means of calculating time, nor could we form any guess of our situation. We were, however, well aware of having made further to the southward than any previous navigators, and felt great amazement at not meeting with the usual impediments of ice. In the meantime every moment threatened to be our last —every mountainous billow hurried to overwhelm us. The swell surpassed anything I had imagined possible, and that we were not instantly buried is a miracle. My companion spoke of the lightness of our cargo, and reminded me of the excellent qualities of our ship. But I could not help feeling the utter hopelessness of hope itself and prepared myself gloomily for that death which I thought nothing could defer beyond an hour, as, with every knot of way the ship made, the swelling of the black stupendous seas became more dismally appalling. At times we gasped for breath at an elevation beyond the albatross—at times became dizzy with the velocity of our descent into some watery hell, where the air grew stagnant, and no sound disturbed the slumbers of the kraken.[1]

We were at the bottom of one of these abysses, when a scream from my companion broke fearfully upon the night. "See! See!" cried he, shrieking in my ears. "Almighty God! See! See!"

As he spoke I became aware of a dull sullen glare of

[1] Scandinavian sea monster.

red light which streamed down the sides of the vast chasm where we lay, and threw a fitful brilliancy upon our deck. Casting my eyes upwards, I beheld a spectacle which froze the current of my blood. At a terrific height directly above us, and upon the very verge of the precipitous descent, hovered a gigantic ship, of perhaps four thousand tons. Although upreared upon the summit of a wave more than a hundred times her own altitude, her apparent size still exceeded that of any ship in existence. Her huge hull was of a deep dingy black, unrelieved by any of the customary carvings of a ship. A single row of brass cannon protruded from her open ports, and dashed from the polished surfaces the fires of innumerable battle lanterns which swung to and fro about her rigging. But what mainly inspired us with horror and astonishment, was that she bore up under a press of sail in the very teeth of that supernatural sea, and of that ungovernable hurricane. When we first discovered her, her bows alone were to be seen, as she rose slowly from the dim and horrible gulf beyond her. For a moment of intense terror she paused upon the giddy pinnacle as if in contemplation of her own sublimity, then trembled and tottered, and—came down.

At this instant, I know not what sudden self-possession came over my spirit. Staggering as far aft as I could, I awaited fearlessly the ruin that was to overwhelm. Our own vessel was at length ceasing from her struggles, and sinking with her head to the sea. The shock of the descending mass struck her, consequently, in that portion of her frame which was nearly underwater, and the inevitable result was to hurl me, with irresistible violence, upon the rigging of the stranger.

As I fell, the ship hove in stays and went about; and to the confusion ensuing I attributed my escape from the notice of the crew. With little difficulty I made my way, unperceived, to the main hatchway, which was partially open, and soon found an opportunity of secreting myself in the hold. Why I did so I can hardly tell. An indefinite sense of awe, which at first sight of the navigators of the ship had taken hold of my mind, was perhaps the principle of my concealment. I was unwilling to trust myself with a race of people who had offered, to the cursory glance I had taken, so many points of vague novelty, doubt, and apprehension. I therefore thought proper to contrive a hiding place in the hold. This I did by removing a small portion of the shifting boards, to afford me a convenient retreat between the huge timbers of the ship.

I had scarcely completed my work, when a footstep in the hold forced me to make use of it. A man passed by my place of concealment with a feeble and unsteady gait. I could not see his face, but had an opportunity of observing his general appearance. There was about it an evidence of great age and infirmity. His knees tottered beneath a load of years, and his entire frame quivered under the burden. He muttered to himself in a low broken tone some words of a language which I could not understand,

and groped in a corner among a pile of singular-looking instruments and decayed charts of navigation. His manner was a wild mixture of the peevishness of second childhood, and the solemn dignity of a god. He at length went on deck, and I saw him no more.

*

A feeling, for which I have no name, has taken possession of my soul—a sensation which will admit of no analysis, to which the lessons of bygone time are inadequate, and for which I fear futurity itself will offer me no key. To a mind constituted like my own, the latter consideration is an evil. I shall never—I know that I shall never—be satisfied with regard to the nature of my conceptions. Yet it is not wonderful that these conceptions are indefinite, since they have their origin in sources so utterly novel. A new sense, a new *entity* has now been added to my soul.

It is long since I first trod the deck of this terrible ship, and the rays of my destiny are, I think, gathering to a focus. Incomprehensible men! Wrapped up in meditations of a kind which I cannot divine, they pass me by unnoticed. Concealment is utter folly on my part, for the people *will not see.* Just a moment ago I passed directly before the eyes of the mate; it was no long while ago that I ventured into the captain's own private cabin and took thence the materials with which I write, and have written. I shall from time to time continue this journal. It is true that I may not find an opportunity of transmitting it to the world, but I will not fail to make the endeavor. At the last moment I will enclose the ms. in a bottle, and cast it within the sea.

＊

An incident has occurred which has given me new room for meditation. Are such things the operation of ungoverned chance? I had ventured upon deck and thrown myself down, without attracting any notice, among a pile of ratlin stuff and old sails, in the bottom of the yawl. While musing upon the singularity of my fate, I unwittingly daubed with a tarbrush the edges of a neatly folded studded-sail which lay near me on a barrel. The studding-sail is now bent upon the ship, and the thoughtless touches of the brush are spread out into the word *Discovery*.

I have made my observations lately upon the structure of the vessel. Although well armed, she is not, I think, a ship of war. Her rigging, build, and general equipment all negate a supposition of this kind. What she is *not*, I can easily perceive; what she *is*, I fear it is impossible to say. I know not how it is, but in scrutinizing her strange model and singular cast of spars, her huge size and overgrown suits of canvas, her severely simple bow and antiquated stern, there will occasionally flash across my mind a sensation of familiar things, and there is always mixed up with such indistinct shadows of recollection, an unaccountable memory of old foreign chronicles and ages long ago.

I have been looking at the timbers of the ship. She is built of a material to which I am a stranger. There is a peculiar character about the wood which strikes me as rendering it unfit for the purpose to which it has been applied. I mean its extreme *porousness,* considered independently of the worm-eaten condition which is a consequence of navigation in these seas, and apart from the rottenness attendant upon age. It will appear perhaps an observation somewhat overcurious, but this would have every characteristic of Spanish oak, if Spanish oak were distended by any unnatural means.

In reading the above sentence, a curious apothegm of an old weather-beaten Dutch navigator comes full upon my recollection. "It is as sure," he was wont to say, when any doubt was entertained of his veracity, "as sure as there is a sea where the ship itself will grow in bulk like the living body of the seaman."

❈

About an hour ago, I made bold to trust myself among a group of the crew. They paid me no attention, and although I stood in the very midst of them all, seemed utterly unconscious of my presence. Like the one I had at first seen in the hold, they all bore about them the marks of a hoary old age. Their knees trembled with infirmity; their shoulders were bent double with decrepitude; their shriveled skins rattled in the wind, their voices were low, tremulous, and broken; their eyes glistened with the rheum of years; and their gray hairs streamed terribly in the tempest. Around them, on every part of the deck, lay scattered mathematical instruments of the most quaint and obsolete construction.

*

I mentioned some time ago the bending of a studding-sail. From that period the ship, being thrown dead off the wind, has continued her terrific course due south, with every rag of canvas packed upon her, from her truck to her lower studding-sail booms, and rolling every moment her topgallant yardarms into the most appalling hell of water which it can enter into the mind of man to imagine. I have just left the deck, where I found it impossible to maintain a footing, although the crew seem to experience little inconvenience. It appears to me a miracle of miracles that our enormous bulk is not swallowed up at once and forever. We are surely doomed to hover continually upon the brink of eternity, without taking a final plunge into the abyss. From billows a thousand times more stupendous than any I have ever seen, we glide away with the facility of the arrowy seagull; and the colossal waters rear their heads above us like demons of the deep, but like demons confined to simple threats, and forbidden to destroy. I am led to attribute these frequent escapes to the only natural cause which can account for such effect. I must suppose the ship to be within the influence of some strong current, or impetuous undertow.

*

I have seen the captain face to face, and in his own cabin—but, as I expected, he paid me no attention. Although in his appearance there is, to a casual observer, nothing which might bespeak him more or less than man, still, there was a feeling of irrepressible reverence and awe mingled with the sensation of wonder with which I regarded him. In stature he is nearly my own height, that is, about five feet eight inches. He is of a well-knit and compact frame of body, neither robust nor remarkable otherwise. But it is the singularity of the expression which reigns upon the face—it is the intense, the wonderful, the thrilling evidence of old age so utter, so extreme, which excites within my sprit a sentiment ineffable. His forehead, although little wrinkled, seems to bear upon it the stamp of a myriad of years. His gray hairs are records of the past, and his grayer eyes are sibyls of the future. The cabin floor was thickly strewn with strange, iron-clasped folios, mouldering instruments of science, and obsolete long-forgotten charts. His head was bowed down upon his hands, and he pored with a fiery, unquiet eye over a paper which I took to be a commission, and which, at all events, bore the signature of a monarch. He murmured to himself—as did the first seaman whom I saw in the hold—some low peevish syllables of a foreign tongue; and although the speaker was close at my elbow, his voice seemed to reach my ears from the distance of a mile.

❊

The ship and all in it are imbued with the spirit of eld. The crew glide to and fro like the ghosts of buried centuries; their eyes have an eager and uneasy meaning; and when their fingers fall athwart my path in the wild glare of the battle lanterns, I feel as I have never felt before, although I have been all my life a dealer in antiquities, and have imbibed the shadows of fallen columns at Balbec, and Tadmor, and Persepolis, until my very soul has become a ruin.

*

When I look around me, I feel ashamed of my former apprehension. If I trembled at the blast which hitherto attended us, shall I not stand aghast at a warring of wind and ocean compared to which the words tornado and simoom are trivial and ineffective? All in the immediate vicinity of the ship is the blackness of eternal night and a chaos of foamless water. But about a league on either side of us may be seen, indistinctly and at intervals, stupendous ramparts of ice, towering away into the desolate sky, and looking like the walls of the universe.

*

As I imagined, the ship proves to be in a current—if that appellation can properly be given to a tide which, howling and shrieking by the white ice, thunders on to the southward with a velocity like the headlong dashing of a cataract.

To conceive the horror of my sensations is, I presume, utterly impossible; yet a curiosity to penetrate the mysteries of these awful regions predominates even over my despair, and will reconcile me to the most hideous aspect of death. It is evident that we are hurrying onward to some exciting knowledge—some never-to-be-imparted secret, whose attainment is destruction. Perhaps this current leads us to the South Pole itself. It must be confessed that a supposition apparently so wild has every probability in its favor.

The crew pace the deck with unquiet and tremulous step, but there is upon their countenance an expression more of the eagerness of hope than the apathy of despair.

In the meantime the wind is still in our poop, and as we carry a crowd of canvas, the ship is at times lifted bodily from out the sea.

Oh, horror upon horror! The ice opens suddenly to the right, and to the left, and we are whirling dizzily, in immense concentric circles, round and round the borders of a gigantic amphitheater, the summit of whose walls is lost in the darkness and distance. But little time will be left me to ponder upon my destiny! The circles rapidly grow smaller—we are plunging madly within the grasp of the whirlpool—and amid a roaring, and bellowing, and thundering of ocean and tempest, the ship is quivering—oh God! and—going down!

AUTHOR'S NOTE.—The *Ms. Found in a Bottle,* was originally published in 1831, and it was not until many years afterward that I became acquainted with the maps of Mercator, in which the ocean is represented as rushing, by four mouths, into the (northern) Polar Gulf, to be absorbed into the bowels of the earth; the Pole itself being represented by a black rock, towering to a prodigious height.

THE OVAL PORTRAIT

THE chateau into which my valet had ventured to make forcible entrance, rather than permit me in my desperately wounded condition to pass a night in the open air, was one of those piles of commingled gloom and grandeur which have so long frowned among the Apennines, not less in fact that in the fancy of Mrs. Radcliffe. To all appearance it had been temporarily and very lately abandoned. We established ourselves in one of the smallest and least sumptuously furnished apartments. It lay in a remote turret of the building. Its decorations were rich, yet tattered and antique. Its walls were hung with tapestry and bedecked with manifold and multiform armorial trophies, together with an unusually great number of very spirited modern paintings in frames of rich golden arabesque.

My incipient delirium, perhaps, had caused me to take a deep interest in these paintings which were displayed on the walls, and hung in the many nooks which the bizarre architecture of the château rendered necessary. Since it was already night, I bade Pedro, my valet, close the heavy shutters of the room, light the candles of a tall candelabrum which stood by the head of my bed, and open wide the fringed curtains of black velvet which enveloped the bed itself. I wished all this done that I might resign myself, if not to sleep, at least alternately to the contemplation of these pictures and the perusal of a small volume which lay on the pillow and which purported to criticize and describe the paintings.

Long, long I read and devoutly I gazed. Rapidly and gloriously the hours flew by and the deep midnight came. The position of the candelabrum displeased me, and rather than disturb my slumbering valet, I reached out and placed the light so that its rays fell more directly upon my book.

But the action produced an effect altogether unanticipated. The rays of the numerous candles, for there were many, now fell within a niche of the room which had hitherto been thrown into deep shade. I thus saw in vivid light a picture all unnoticed before. It was the portrait of a young girl just ripening into womanhood. I glanced at the painting hurriedly and then closed my eyes. Why I did this was not at first apparent to me. But while my lids remained shut, I ran over in my mind my reason for shutting them. It was an impulsive movement to gain time for thought, to make sure that my vision had not deceived me, to calm and subdue my fancy for a more sober and more certain gaze. In a few moments I again looked fixedly at the picture.

That I now saw aright I could not and would not doubt. For the first flashing of the candles upon that canvas had seemed to dissipate the dreamy stupor which was stealing over my senses and to startle me at once into waking life.

The portrait, I have already said, was that of a young girl. It was a mere head and shoulders, done as a vignette, much in the style of the favorite heads of Sully. The arms, the bosom, and even the ends of the radiant hair melted imperceptibly into the vague yet deep shadow which formed the background of the whole. The frame was oval, richly gilded and filigreed in a Moresque style. As a thing of art nothing could be more admirable than the painting itself. But it could have been neither the execution of the work nor the immortal beauty of the countenance which had so suddenly and so vehemently moved me. Could it have been that my fancy, shaken from its half-slumber, had mistaken the head for that of a living person? I saw at once that the peculiarities of the design, of the vignetting, and of the frame must have instantly dispelled such an idea, should have prevented even its momentary entertainment. I remained, for an hour perhaps, half-sitting, half-reclining, with my eyes riveted upon the portrait. At length, satisfied with the true secret of its effect, I fell back within the bed. I had found the spell of the picture in an absolute lifelikeness of expression, which first startled then confounded, subdued and finally appalled me. With deep and reverent awe I replaced the candelabrum in its former position. The cause of my deep agitation being thus shut from view, I sought eagerly the volume which discussed the paintings and their histories. Turning to the number which designated the oval portrait, I there read the vague and quaint words which follow:

"She was a maiden of rare beauty, and not more lovely than full of glee. And evil was the hour when she saw, and loved and wedded the painter. He was passionate, studious, austere, and already possessed a bride in his art; she was a maiden of rarest beauty and not more lovely than full of glee, all light and smiles, frolicsome as the young fawn, loving and cherishing all things but the art which was her rival, and hating only the palette, brushes and other instruments of that art which deprived her of the countenance of her lover. It was thus a terrible thing for this lady to hear the painter speak of his desire to portray even his young bride. But she was humble and obedient, and sat meekly for many weeks in the dark high turret chamber where the light dripped upon the pale canvas only from overhead. But he, the painter, took glory in his work, which went on from hour to hour and from day to day. He was a passionate and wild and moody man. Lost in reveries, he *would* not see that the light which fell so ghastly in that lone turret withered the health and the spirits of his bride, who pined visibly to all but him.

"Yet she smiled on and on uncomplainingly, because she saw that the painter—an artist of high renown—took a fervid and burning pleasure in his task, and wrought day and night to depict her, who loved him so much that *she* grew daily more dispirited and weak. And in truth some who beheld the portrait spoke in low words of its resemblance, as of a mighty marvel, and a proof not less of the power of the painter than of his deep love for her whom he depicted so surpassingly well. But at length, as the labor drew nearer to its conclusion, none were admitted into the turret. For the painter had grown wild with the ardor of his work, and turned his eyes from the canvas rarely, even to regard the countenance of his wife.

"And he would not see that the tints which he spread upon the canvas were the lifeblood drawn from the cheeks of her who sat beside him. And when many weeks had passed, and little remained to be done save one brush upon the mouth and one tint upon the eye, the spirit of the lady again flickered up as the flame within the socket of the lamp. And then the brush was given, and then the tint was placed. For one moment the painter stood entranced before the work which he had wrought; in the next, while he yet gazed, he grew tremulous and pallid and aghast, and crying with a loud voice, 'This is indeed Life itself,' turned suddenly to regard his beloved. *She was dead!*"

BERENICE

INTRODUCTION

MISERY is manifold. The wretchedness of earth is multiform. Like the rainbow, it overreaches the wide horizon, and its hues are as various as the hues of that arch, as distinct, too, yet as intimately blended. Overreaching the wide horizon as the rainbow! How is it that from beauty I have derived a type of unloveliness? From the covenant of peace a simile of sorrow? But as in ethics evil is a consequence of good, so in fact out of joy is sorrow born. Either the memory of past bliss is the anguish of today, or the agonies which *are* have their origin in the ecstasies which *might have been*.

My baptismal name is Egeus; that of my family I will not mention. Yet there are no towers in the land more time-honored than my gloomy, gray, hereditary halls. Our line has been called a race of visionaries. And in many striking particulars—in the character of the family mansion, in the frescoes of the chief saloon, in the tapestries of the dormitories, in the chiseling of some buttresses in the armory, and more especially in the gallery of antique paintings, in the fashion of the library chamber, and, above all, in the very peculiar nature of the library's contents, there is more than sufficient evidence to warrant the belief.

The recollections of my earliest years are connected with that chamber—and with the volumes of its library. Here died my mother. Herein was I born. But it is mere idleness to say that I had not lived before, that the soul has no previous existence. You deny it? Let us not argue the matter. Convinced, myself, I seek not to convince. There is however a remembrance of aërial forms, of spiritual and meaning eyes, of sounds, musical yet sad—a remembrance which will not be excluded. It is a memory like a shadow, vague, variable, indefinite, unsteady. And like a shadow, too, impossible to be rid of while the sunlight of my reason exists.

In that chamber was I born. Thus awaking from the long night of what seemed, but was not, nonentity, into the very regions of fairyland into a palace of imagination, into the wild dominions of monastic thought and erudition, it is not singular that I gazed around me with a startled and ardent eye. I loitered away my boyhood in books, and dissipated my youth in reverie. But it is singular that the years rolled away and the noon of manhood found me still in the mansion of my fathers. It is wonderful what stagnation there fell upon the springs of my life, then, wonderful how total an inversion took place in the character of my commonest thought. The realities of the world affected me as visions, and as visions only, while the wild ideas of the land of dreams became, in turn, not merely the material of my everyday existence, but my existence itself.

BERENICE

BERENICE and I were cousins, and we grew up together in my paternal halls. Yet how differently we grew! I was ill of health and buried in gloom, while she was agile, graceful and overflowing with energy. Hers the ramble on the hillside; mine the studies of the cloister. I lived within my own heart, addicted body and soul to the most intense and painful meditation. She roamed carelessly through life with no thought of the shadows in her path or the silent flight of the raven-winged hours. Berenice! I call upon her name, and from the gray ruins of memory a thousand tumultuous recollections are startled at the sound! Ah, vividly is her image before me now, as in the early days of her lightheartedness and joy! Oh gorgeous yet fantastic beauty! Sylph amid the shrubberies of Arnheim! Naiad among its fountains! And then, then all is mystery and terror, and a tale which should not be told. Disease, a fatal disease, fell like the simoom upon her frame, and even while I gazed upon her the spirit of change swept over her, pervading her mind, her habits and her character, and in a manner most subtle and terrible, disturbing even the identity of her person! Alas! the destroyer came and went, and the victim—where was she? I knew her not, knew her no longer as Berenice.

Among the lingering maladies brought on by the fatal and primary one, which effected a revolution of so horrible a kind in the moral and physical being of my cousin, I mention, as the most distressing and obstinate in its nature, a species of epilepsy not unfrequently terminating in trance itself. This trance very nearly resembled positive dissolution, and her manner of recovery from it was, in most instances, startlingly abrupt.

In the meantime, my own disease—for I have been told that I should call it by no other appellation—grew rapidly upon me. It assumed, finally, a monomaniac character of a novel and extraordinary form, hourly and momently gaining vigor, and at length obtaining over me the most incomprehensible ascendency. This monomania, if I must so term it, consisted in a morbid irritability of those properties of the mind in metaphysical science termed the *attentive*. It is more than probable that I am not understood. But I fear that it is not possible to convey to the mind of the general reader an adequate idea of that nervous *intensity of interest* with which, in my case, the powers of meditation busied themselves in the contemplation of even the most ordinary objects.

I mused for long unwearied hours with my attention riveted to some frivolous device on the margin or in the typography of a book. I became absorbed, for the better part of a summer's day, in a quaint shadow falling upon the tapestry or the door. I lost myself for an entire night in watching the steady flame of a lamp or the embers of a fire. I dreamed away whole days over the perfume of a flower. I repeated monotonously some common word until the sound, by dint of frequent repetition, ceased to convey any idea whatever to my mind. I lost all sense of motion or physical existence, by means of absolute bodily quiescence long and obstinately persevered in. These were a few of the most common and least pernicious vagaries induced by a condition of the mental faculties, not altogether unparalleled, but certainly bidding defiance to analysis or explanation.

Yet let me not be misapprehended. The undue, earnest and morbid attention thus excited by objects, in their own nature frivolous, must not be confounded in character with that ruminating propensity common to all mankind, and more especially indulged in by persons of ardent imagination. It was not even, as might be at first supposed, an extreme condition or exaggeration of such propensity, but essentially distinct and different. In the one instance, the dreamer or enthusiast, being interested by an object usually *not* frivolous, imperceptibly loses sight of this object in a wilderness of deductions and suggestions issuing therefrom until, at the conclusion of a daydream often replete with luxury, he finds the *incitamentum* or first cause of his musings entirely vanished and forgotten. In my case the primary object was invariably frivolous, although assuming, through the medium of my distempered vision, a refracted and unreal importance. Few deductions, if any, were made; and those few pertinaciously returned to the original object. The meditations were never pleasurable. At the termination of the reverie the first cause, so far from being out of sight, had attained that supernaturally exaggerated interest which was the prevailing feature of the disease. In a word, the powers of mind more particularly exercised were, with me, as I have said before, the *attentive,* and are, with the daydreamer, the *speculative.*

If my books at this period did not actually serve to irritate the disorder, they partook it will be perceived, by their imaginative and inconsequential nature, of the characteristic qualities of the disorder itself. I well remember among others the treatise of the noble Italian Coelius Secundus Curio, *De Amplitudine Beati Regni Dei,* St. Augustine's great work, *The City of God,* and Tertullian's *De Carne Christi,* in which the paradoxical sentence, "*Mortuus est Dei filius; credibile est quia ineptum est: et sepultus resurrexit; certum est quia impossibile est,*" occupied my undivided time, for many weeks of laborious and fruitless investigation.

Thus it will appear that, shaken from its balance only by trivial things, my reason bore resemblance to that ocean crag spoken of by Ptolemy Hephestion, which, steadily resisting the attacks of human violence and the fiercer fury of the waters and the winds, trembled only to the touch of the flower called asphodel. A careless thinker might assume that the alteration, produced by her unhappy malady in the *moral* condition of Berenice, would afford me many objects for the exercise of my intense and abnormal meditation. Yet such was not the case. In the lucid intervals of my infirmity, her calamity indeed gave me pain. And taking deeply to heart that total wreck of her fair and gentle life, I did not fail to ponder frequently and bitterly upon the wonder-working means by which so strange a revolution had been so suddenly brought to pass. But these reflections partook not of the idiosyncrasy of my disease, and were such as would have occurred, under similar circumstances, to the ordinary mass of mankind. True to its own character, my disorder reveled in the less important but more startling changes wrought in the *physical* frame of Berenice—in the singular and most appalling distortion of her personal identity.

During the brightest days of her unparalleled beauty, most surely I had never loved her. In the strange anomaly of my existence, feelings with me had never been of the heart, and my passions always were of the mind. Through the gray of the early morning, among the trellised shadows of the forest at noonday, and in the silence of my library at night, she had flitted by my eyes. And I had seen her, not as the living and breathing Berenice but as the Berenice of a dream, not as a being of the earth earthy, but as the abstraction of such a being. I saw her then not as a thing to admire but to analyze, and not as an object of love but as the theme of the most abstruse although desultory speculation. *Now*—now I shuddered in her presence, and grew pale at her approach. Yet bitterly lamenting her fallen and desolate condition, I called to mind that she had loved me long, and in an evil moment I spoke to her of marriage.

The period of our nuptials was approaching, when upon an afternoon in the winter of the year—one of those unseasonably warm, calm, and misty days which are the nurse of the beautiful Halcyon[1]—I sat, as I thought, alone in the inner apartment of the library. But lifting my eyes I saw that Berenice stood before me.

Was it my own excited imagination, the misty influence of the atmosphere, the uncertain twilight of the chamber, or the gray draperies which fell around her figure that gave it so vacillating and indistinct an outline? I could not tell. She spoke no word, and I—not for worlds could I have uttered a syllable. An icy chill ran through my frame. A sense of insufferable anxiety oppressed me. A consuming curiosity pervaded my soul, and sinking back upon the chair, I remained for some time breathless and motionless, with my eyes riveted upon her person. Alas! its emaciation was excessive, and not one vestige of the former being lurked in any single line of the contour. My burning glances at length fell upon the face.

[1] For as Jove, during the winter season, gives twice seven days of warmth, men have called this clement and temperate time the nurse of the beautiful Halcyon.—SIMONIDES.

The forehead was high and very pale, and singularly placid. The once jet hair fell partially over it, and over-shadowed the hollow temples with innumerable ringlets now of a vivid yellow, that jarred discordantly in their fantastic character with the reigning melancholy of the countenance. The eyes were lifeless and lusterless, and seemingly pupil-less, and I shrank involuntarily from their glassy stare to the contemplation of the thin and shrunken lips. They parted; in a smile of peculiar meaning, *the teeth* of the changed Berenice disclosed themselves slowly to my view. Would to God that I had never beheld them, or that, having done so, I had died!

✲

The shutting of a door disturbed me. Looking up, I found that my cousin had departed from the chamber. But from the disordered chamber of my brain, had not alas, departed, and would not be driven away, the white and ghastly *spectrum* of the teeth. Not a speck on their surface, not a shade on their enamel, not an indenture in their edges, but what the sight of her smile had suf-ficed to brand in upon my memory. I saw them *now* even more unequivocally than I beheld them *then*. The teeth! The teeth! They were here, and there, and everywhere, visibly and palpably before me—long, narrow, and exces-sively white, with the pale lips writhing about them, as though I still beheld their terrible development.

Then came the full fury of my *monomania*, and I strug-gled in vain against its strange and irresistible influence.

In the multiplied objects of the external world I had no thoughts but for the teeth. For these I longed with a frenzied desire. All other matters and all other interests became absorbed in their single contemplation. They—they alone were present to my mental eye, and they, in their sole individuality, became the essence of my mental life. I held them in every light. I turned them in every attitude. I surveyed their characteristics. I dwelt upon their peculiarities. I pondered upon their conformation. I mused upon the alteration in their nature. I shuddered as I assigned to them in imagination a sensitive and sentient power, and even when unassisted by the lips, a capability of moral expresson. Of the Mlle. Sallé it has been well said, "*que tous ses pas étaient des sentiments,*" and of Berenice I more seriously believed *que toutes ses dents étaient des idées. Des idées!* Ah here was the idiotic thought that destroyed me! Ideas! Ah therefore it was that I coveted them so madly! I felt that only their possession could ever restore me to peace, and give me back to reason.

The evening closed in upon me thus, and then the darkness came, tarried and went, and the day again dawned. The mists of a second night were now gathering around, and still I sat motionless in that solitary room. Still I sat buried in meditation, and still the *phantasma* of the teeth maintained its terrible ascendency as, with the most vivid and hideous distinctness, it floated about amid the changing lights and shadows of the chamber. At length there broke in upon my dreams a cry of horror and dismay; and thereunto, after a pause, succeeded the sound of troubled voices, intermingled with many low moanings of sorrow, or of pain. I arose from my seat and, throwing open one of the doors of the library, saw standing out in the ante-chamber a servant maid, all in tears, who told me that Berenice was—no more. She had been seized with epilepsy in the early morning, and now, at the closing of the night, the grave was ready for its tenant, and all the preparations for the burial were completed.

❋

I found myself sitting in the library, and again sitting there alone. It seemed that I had newly awakened from a confused and exciting dream. I knew that it was now midnight, and I was well aware that since the setting of the sun Berenice had been interred. But of that dreary period which intervened I had no positive, at least no definite, comprehension. Yet its memory was replete with horror—horror more horrible from being vague, and terror more terrible from ambiguity. It was a fearful page in the record of my existence, written all over with dim, hideous and unintelligible recollections. I strived to decipher them in vain, while ever and anon, like the spirit of a departed sound, the shrill and piercing shriek of a female voice seemed to be ringing in my ears. I had done a deed. What was it? I asked myself the question aloud, and the whispering echoes of the chamber answered me. "What was it?"

On the table beside me burned a lamp, and near it lay a little box. It was of no remarkable character, and I had seen it frequently before, for it was the property of the family physician; but how came it *there*, upon my table, and why did I shudder in regarding it? These things were in no manner to be accounted for, and my eyes at length dropped to the open pages of a book, and to a sentence underscored therein. The words were the singular but simple ones of the poet Ebn Zaiat, *"Dicebant mihi sodales si sepulchrum amicae visitarem, curas meas aliquantulum fore levatas."* Why then, as I perused them, did the hairs of my head erect themselves on end, and the blood of my body congeal within my veins?

There came a light tap at the library door, and pale as the tenant of a tomb, a menial entered upon tiptoe. His looks were wild with terror, and he spoke to me in a voice tremulous, husky and low. What said he? Some broken sentences I heard. He told of a wild cry disturbing the silence of the night, of the gathering together of the household, of a search in the direction of the sound. And then his tones grew thrillingly distinct as he whispered me of a violated grave—of a disfigured body, enshrouded yet still breathing, still palpitating, still *alive!*

He pointed to my garments; they were muddy and clotted with gore. I spoke not, and he took me gently by the hand. It was indented with the impress of human nails. He directed my attention to some object against the wall. I looked at it for some minutes—it was a spade.

With a shriek I bounded to the table, and grasped the box that lay upon it. But I could not force it open. In my tremor it slipped from my hands and fell heavily, and burst open. From it, with a rattling sound, there rolled out some instruments of dental surgery, intermingled with thirty-two small, ivory-white substances that were scattered to and fro about the floor.

THE MASQUE OF THE RED DEATH

THE Red Death had long devastated the country. No pestilence had ever been so fatal or so hideous. Blood was its avatar and its seal, the redness and horror of blood. There were sharp pains, and sudden dizziness, and then profuse bleeding at the pores, with dissolution. The scarlet stains upon the body and especially upon the face of the victim were the pest ban which shut him out from the aid and from the sympathy of his fellow men. And the whole seizure, progress, and termination of the disease were the incidents of but half an hour's duration.

But the Prince Prospero was happy and dauntless and sagacious. When his dominions were half-depopulated, he summoned to his presence a thousand hale and light-hearted friends from among the knights and dames of his court, and with these retired to the deep seclusion of one of his castellated abbeys. This was an extensive and magnificent structure, the creation of the prince's own eccentric yet august taste. A strong and lofty wall girdled it in.

This wall had gates of iron. The courtiers, having entered, brought furnaces and massive hammers and welded the bolts. They resolved to leave means neither of ingress nor egress to the sudden impulses of despair or of frenzy from within or without. The abbey was amply provisioned. With such precautions the courtiers might bid defiance to contagion. The external world could take care of itself. In the meantime it was folly to grieve or to think. The prince had provided all the appliances of pleasure. There were buffoons, there were improvisatori, there were ballet dancers, there were musicians, there was beauty, there was wine. All these and security were within. Without was the Red Death.

It was toward the close of the fifth or sixth month of his seclusion, and while the pestilence raged most furiously abroad, that the Prince Prospero entertained his thousand friends at a masked ball of the most unusual magnificence.

It was a voluptuous scene, that masquerade. But first let me tell of the rooms in which it was held. These were seven, an imperial suite. In many palaces, however, such suites form a long and straight vista, while the folding doors slide back nearly to the walls on either hand so that the view of the whole extent is scarcely impeded. Here the case was very different, as might have been expected from the duke's love of the bizarre. The apartments were so irregularly disposed that the vision embraced but little more than one at a time. There was a sharp turn at every twenty or thirty yards, and at each turn a novel effect. To the right and left, in the middle of each wall, a tall and narrow Gothic window looked out upon a closed corridor which pursued the windings of the suite. These windows were of stained glass whose color varied in accordance with the prevailing hue of the decorations of the chamber into which it opened. That at the eastern extremity was hung, for example, in blue, and vividly blue were its windows. The second chamber was purple in its ornaments and tapestries, and here the panes were purple. The third was green throughout, and so were the casements. The fourth was furnished and lighted with orange, the fifth with white, the sixth with violet. The seventh apartment was closely shrouded in black velvet tapestries that hung all over the ceiling and down the walls, falling in heavy folds upon a carpet of the same material and hue. But in this chamber only the color of the windows failed to correspond with the decorations. The panes here were scarlet, a deep blood color. Now in no one of the seven apartments was there any lamp or candelabrum amid the profusion of golden ornaments that lay scattered to and fro or hung down from the roof. There was no light of any kind emanating from lamp or candle within the suite of chambers. But in the corridors that followed the suite there stood, opposite to each window, a heavy tripod, bearing a brazier of fire that projected its rays through the tinted glass, and so glaringly illumined the room. And thus were produced a multitude of gaudy and fantastic appearances. But in the western or black chamber the effect of the firelight that streamed upon the dark hangings through the blood-tinted panes was ghastly in the extreme, and produced so wild a look upon the countenances of those who entered that there were few of the company bold enough to set foot within its precincts at all.

It was in this apartment also that there stood against the western wall a gigantic clock of ebony. Its pendulum swung to and fro with a dull, heavy, monotonous clang; and when the minute hand made the circuit of the face and the hour was to be struck, there came from the brazen lungs of the clock a sound which was clear and loud and deep and exceedingly musical, but of so peculiar a note and emphasis that at each lapse of an hour the musicians of the orchestra were constrained to pause momentarily in their performance to harken to the sound. And thus the waltzers perforce ceased their evolutions, and there was a brief disconcert of the whole gay company. And while the chimes of the clock yet rang, it was observed that the giddiest grew pale, and the more aged and sedate passed their hands over their brows as if in confused reverie or meditation. But when the echoes had fully ceased, a light laughter at once pervaded the assembly; the musicians looked at each other and smiled, as if at their own nervousness and folly, and made whispering vows each to the other that the next chiming of the clock should produce in them no similar emotion. Then, after the lapse of sixty minutes (which embrace three thousand and six hundred seconds of the time that flies), there came yet another chiming of the clock, and then were the same disconcert and tremulousness and meditation as before.

In spite of these things it was a gay and magnificent revel. The tastes of the duke were peculiar. He had a fine eye for colors and effects. He disregarded the decorum of mere fashion. His plans were bold and fiery, and his conceptions glowed with barbaric luster. There are some who would have thought him mad. His followers felt that he was not. It was necessary to hear and see and touch him to be sure that he was not.

He had directed in great part the movable embellishments of the seven chambers upon the occasion of this great fête; and it was his own guiding taste which had also given character to the *masqueraders*. Be sure, they were grotesque. There was much glare and glitter and piquancy and phantasm—much of what has been since seen in *Hernani*. There were arabesque figures with unsuited limbs and appointments. There were delirious fancies such as the madman fashions. There was much of the beautiful, much of the wanton, much of the bizarre, something of the terrible, and not a little of that which might have excited disgust. To and fro in the seven chambers there stalked, in fact, a multitude of dreams. And these, the dreams, writhed in and about, taking hue from the rooms, and causing the wild music of the orchestra to seem as the echo of their steps. And anon there strikes the ebony clock which stands in the hall of the velvet. And then for a moment all is still, and all is silent save the voice of the clock. The dreams are stiff-frozen as they stand. But the echoes of the chime die away; they have endured but an instant, and a light, half-subdued laughter floats after them as they depart. And now again the music swells, and the dreams live, and writhe to and fro more merrily than ever, taking hue from the many-tinted windows through which stream the rays from the tripods. But to the chamber which lies most westward of the seven none of the maskers now venture; for the night is waning away, and there flows a ruddier light through the blood-colored panes. The blackness of the sable drapery appals; and to him whose foot falls upon the sable carpet, there comes from the near clock of ebony a muffled peal more solemnly emphatic than any which reaches the ears of those who indulged in the more remote gaieties of the other apartments.

But these other apartments were densely crowded, and in them beat feverishly the heart of life. And the revel went whirlingly on, until at length there commenced the sounding of midnight upon the clock. Then the music ceased, as I have told, and the evolutions of the waltzers were quieted, and there was an uneasy cessation of all things as before. But now there were twelve strokes to be sounded by the bell of the clock; and thus it happened, perhaps, that more of thought crept, with more of time, into the meditations of the thoughtful among those who reveled. And thus too it happened, that before the last echoes of the last chime had utterly sunk into silence, there were many individuals in the crowd who had become aware of the presence of a masked figure which had arrested the attention of no single individual before. And the rumor of this new presence having spread itself whisperingly around, there arose at length from the whole company a buzz, or murmur expressive of disapprobation and surprise—then finally, of terror, of horror, and of disgust.

In an assembly of phantasms such as I have painted, it may well be supposed that no ordinary appearance could have excited such sensation. In truth the masquerade license of the night was nearly unlimited; but the figure in question had out Heroded Herod and gone beyond the bounds of even the prince's indefinite decorum. There are chords in the hearts of the most reckless which cannot be touched without emotion. Even with the utterly lost, to whom life and death are equally jests, there are matters of which no jest can be made. The whole company, indeed, seemed now deeply to feel that in the costume and bearing of the stranger neither wit nor propriety existed. The figure was tall and gaunt and shrouded from head to foot in the habiliments of the grave. The mask which concealed the visage was made so nearly to resemble the countenance of a stiffened corpse that the closest scrutiny must have had difficulty in detecting the cheat. And yet all this might have been endured, if not approved, by the mad revelers around. But the mummer had gone so far as to assume the type of the Red Death. His vesture was dabbled in *blood,* and his broad brow, with all the features of the face, was sprinkled with the scarlet horror.

When the eyes of Prince Prospero fell upon this spectral image (which, with a slow and solemn movement, as if more fully to sustain its rôle, stalked to and fro among the waltzers), he was seen to be convulsed in the first moment with a strong shudder either of terror or distaste; but in the next his brow reddened with rage.

"Who dares," he demanded hoarsely of the courtiers who stood near him, "insult us with this blasphemous mockery? Seize him and unmask him, that we may know whom we have to hang at sunrise from the battlements!"

It was in the eastern or blue chamber in which stood the Prince Prospero as he uttered these words. They rang throughout the seven rooms loudly and clearly, for the prince was a bold and robust man, and the music had ceased at the waving of his hand.

It was in the blue room where stood the prince, with a group of pale courtiers by his side. At first, as he spoke, there was a slight rushing movement of this group in the direction of the intruder, who at the moment was also near at hand, and now, with deliberate and stately step, made closer approach to the speaker. But from a certain nameless awe with which the mad assumptions of the mummer had inspired the whole party, there were found none who put forth hand to seize him. Unimpeded, he passed within a yard of the prince's person. And while the vast assembly, as if with one impulse, shrank from the center of the room to the walls, he made his way uninterruptedly, but with the same solemn and measured step which had distinguished him from the first, through the blue chamber to the purple, through the purple to the green, through the green to the orange, through this again to the white, and even thence to the violet, ere a decided movement had been made to arrest him. It was then, however, that the Prince Prospero, maddened with rage and shame at his own momentary cowardice, rushed hurriedly through the six chambers. None followed him; a deadly terror had seized them all. The prince bore aloft a drawn dagger, and had approached in rapid impetuosity to within three or four feet of the retreating figure when the latter, having attained the extremity of the velvet apartment, turned suddenly and confronted his pursuer. There was a sharp cry—and the dagger dropped gleaming upon the sable carpet, upon which, instantly afterward, fell prostrate in death the Prince Prospero. Then summoning the wild courage of despair, a throng of the revelers at once threw themselves into the black apartment, and seizing the mummer, whose tall figure stood erect and motionless within the shadow of the ebony clock, gasped in unutterable horror at finding the grave cerements and corpselike mask, which they handled with so violent a rudeness, untenanted by any tangible form.

And now was acknowledged the presence of the Red

Death. He had come like a thief in the night. And one by one dropped the revelers in the blood-bedewed halls of their revel, and died each in the despairing posture of his fall. And the life of the ebony clock went out with that of the last of the gay. And the flames of the tripods expired. And darkness and decay and the Red Death held illimitable dominion over all.

THE FALL OF THE HOUSE OF USHER

DURING the whole of a dull, dark and soundless day in the autumn of the year, when the clouds hung oppressively low in the heavens, I had been passing alone on horseback through a singularly dreary tract of country. At length I found myself, as the shades of the evening drew on, within view of the melancholy House of Usher. I know not how it was, but with the first glimpse of the building a sense of insufferable gloom pervaded my spirit. I say insufferable, for the feeling was unrelieved by any of that half-pleasurable, because poetic, sentiment with which the mind usually receives even the sternest images of the desolate or terrible.

I looked upon the scene before me—upon the mere house and the simple landscape features of the domain, upon the bleak walls and the vacant eyelike windows, upon a few rank sedges and white trunks of decayed trees—with an utter depression of soul. I can compare it to no earthly sensation more properly than to the after-dream of the reveler of opium—the bitter lapse into everyday life, the hideous dropping off of the veil. There was an iciness, a sinking, a sickening of the heart—an unredeemed dreariness of thought which no goading of the imagination could torture into aught of the sublime.

What was it, I paused to think, that so unnerved me in the contemplation of the House of Usher? It was a mystery all insoluble; nor could I grapple with the shadowy fancies that crowded upon me as I pondered. I was forced to fall back upon the unsatisfactory conclusion that while, beyond doubt, there *are* combinations of very simple natural objects which have the power of thus affecting us, still the analysis of this power lies among considerations beyond our depth. It was possible, I reflected, that a mere different arrangement of the *particulars* of the scene, of the details of the picture, would be sufficient to modify, or perhaps to annihilate its capacity for sorrowful impression.

Acting upon this idea, I reined my horse to the precipitous brink of a black and lurid tarn that lay in unruffled luster by the dwelling, and gazed down—but with a shudder even more thrilling than before—upon the remodeled and inverted images of the gray sedge, the ghastly tree stems, and the vacant and eyelike windows.

Nevertheless, in this mansion of gloom I proposed now to myself a sojourn of some weeks. Its proprietor, Roderick Usher, had been one of my boon companions in boyhood; but many years had elapsed since our last meeting. A letter, however, had lately reached me in a distant part of the country, a letter from him which, in its wildly importunate nature, had admitted of no other than a reply in person. The letter gave evidence of nervous agitation. The writer spoke of acute bodily illness, or a mental disorder which oppressed him, and of an earnest desire to see me, his best and indeed his only, personal friend with a view of attempting, by the cheerfulness of my society, some alleviation of his malady. It was the manner in which all this, and much more, was said—it was the apparent *heart* that went with his request—which allowed me no room for hesitation. I accordingly obeyed forthwith what I still considered a very singular summons.

Although as boys we had been even intimate associates, yet I really knew little of my friend. His reserve had always been excessive and habitual. I was aware, however, that his very ancient family had been noted, time out of mind, for a peculiar sensibility of temperament, displayed through long ages in many works of exalted art, and manifested of late in repeated deeds of munificent yet unobtrusive charity—as well as in a passionate devotion to the intricacies, perhaps even more than to the orthodox and easily recognizable beauties, of musical science.

I had learned, too, the very remarkable fact that the stem of the Usher race, all time-honored as it was, had put forth at no period any enduring branch. In other words, the entire family lay in the direct line of descent, and had always, with very trifling and very temporary variation, so lain. I considered this deficiency, while running over in thought the perfect keeping of the character of the premises with the accredited character of the people, and while speculating upon the possible influence which the one, in the long lapse of centuries, might have exercised upon the other. It was perhaps this deficiency of collateral issue, and the consequent undeviating transmission from sire to son of the patrimony with the name, which had at length so identified the two, as to merge the original title of the estate in the quaint and equivocal appellation of the House of Usher—an appellation which seemed to include, in the minds of the peasantry who used it, both the family and the family mansion.

I have said that the sole effect of my somewhat childish experiment—that of looking down within the tarn—had been to deepen the first singular impression. There can be no doubt that the consciousness of the rapid increase of my superstition—for why should I not so term it?— served mainly to accelerate the increase itself. Such, I have long known, is the paradoxical law of all sentiments having terror as a basis. And it might have been for this reason only that, when I again lifted my eyes, from the image in the pool to the house itself, there grew in my mind a strange fancy—a fancy so ridiculous, indeed, that I but mention it to show the vivid force of the sensations which oppressed me. I had so worked upon my imagination as really to believe that about the whole mansion and domain there hung an atmosphere peculiar to themselves and their immediate vicinity. It was an atmosphere which had no affinity with the air of heaven, but which had reeked up from the decayed trees, and the gray walls, and the silent tarn—a pestilent and mystic vapor, dull, sluggish, faintly discernible, and leaden-hued.

Shaking off from my spirit what *must* have been a dream, I scanned more narrowly the real aspect of the building. Its principal feature seemed to be that of an excessive antiquity. The discoloration of ages had been great. Minute fungi overspread the whole exterior, hanging in a fine tangled webwork from the eaves. Yet all this was apart from any extraordinary dilapidation. No portion of the masonry had fallen; and there appeared to be a wild inconsistency between its still perfect adaptation of parts, and the crumbling condition of the individual stones.

In this there was much that reminded me of the specious totality of old woodwork, which has rotted for long years in some neglected vault with no disturbance from the breath of the external air. Beyond this indication of extensive decay, however, the fabric gave little token of instability. A scrutinizing observer's eye might perhaps have discovered there a barely perceptible fissure, which, extending from the roof of the building in front, made its way down the wall in a zigzag direction, until it became lost in the sullen waters of the tarn.

Noticing these things, I rode over a short causeway to the house. A servant in waiting took my horse, and I entered the Gothic archway of the hall. A valet of stealthy step thence conducted me in silence through many dark and intricate passages in my progress to the studio of his master. Much that I encountered on the way contributed, I know not how, to heighten the vague sentiments of which I have already spoken. The objects around me—the carvings of the ceilings, the somber tapestries of the walls, the ebon blackness of the floors, and the phantasmagoric armorial trophies which rattled as I strode—were matters to which I had been accustomed from my infancy, and I hesitated not to acknowledge how familiar was all this. Still I wondered at the unfamiliar fancies which ordinary images were stirring up. On one of the staircases I met the physician of the family. His countenance, I thought, wore a mingled expression of low cunning and perplexity. He accosted me with trepidation and passed on. The valet now ushered me into the presence of his master.

The room in which I found myself was very large and lofty. The windows were long, narrow and pointed, and at so vast a distance from the black oaken floor as to be altogether inaccessible from within. Feeble gleams of encrimsoned light made their way through the trellised panes, and served to render sufficiently distinct the more prominent objects around. The eye, however, struggled in vain to reach the remoter angles of the chamber, or the recesses of the vaulted and fretted ceiling. Dark draperies hung upon the walls. The general furniture was profuse, comfortless, antique and tattered. Many books and musical instruments lay scattered about, but failed to give any vitality to the scene. I felt that I breathed an atmosphere of sorrow. An air of stern, deep and irredeemable gloom hung over and pervaded all.

Upon my entrance, Usher arose from a sofa on which he had been lying at full length, and greeted me with a vivacious warmth which had much in it, I at first thought, of an overdone cordiality, of the constrained effort of the *ennuyé* man of the world. A glance at his countenance, however, convinced me of his perfect sincerity. We sat down; and for some moments, while he spoke not, I gazed upon him with a feeling half of pity, half of awe. Surely man had never before so terribly altered in so brief a period as had Roderick Usher! It was with difficulty that I could identify the wan being before me with the companion of my early boyhood.

Yet the character of his face had been at all times remarkable. A cadaverousness of complexion, an eye large, liquid and luminous beyond comparison, lips somewhat thin and very pallid but of a surpassingly beautiful curve, a nose of a delicate Hebrew model but with an unusual breadth of nostril, a finely moulded chin speaking, in its want of prominence, of a want of moral energy, hair of a more than weblike softness and tenuity—these features, with an inordinate expansion above the regions of the temple, made up altogether a countenance not easily forgotten.

And now in the mere exaggeration of the prevailing character of these features, and of the expression they were wont to convey, lay such change that I doubted to whom I spoke. The now ghastly pallor of the skin and the now miraculous luster of the eye, above all things, startled and even awed me. The silken hair, too, had been suffered to grow all unheeded; and as in its wild gossamer texture it floated rather than fell about the face, I could not even with effort, connect its arabesque array with any idea of simple humanity.

In the manner of my friend I was at once struck with an incoherence—an inconsistency; and I soon found this to arise from a series of feeble and futile struggles to overcome an habitual trepidation, an excessive nervous agitation. For something of this nature I had indeed been prepared, no less by his letter than by reminiscences of certain boyish traits, and by conclusions deduced from his peculiar physical conformation and temperament. His action was alternately vivacious and sullen. His voice varied rapidly from a tremulous indecision, when the animal spirits seemed utterly in abeyance, to that species of energetic concision—that abruptly, weighty, unhurried and hollow-sounding enunciation, that leaden, self-balanced and perfectly modulated guttural utterance which may be observed in the lost drunkard, or the irreclaimable eater of opium, during periods of intense excitement.

It was thus that Usher spoke of the object of my visit, of his earnest desire to see me, and of the solace he expected me to afford him. He entered at some length into what he conceived to be the nature of his malady. It was, he said, a constitutional and a family evil, and one for which he despaired to find a remedy—a mere nervous affection, he immediately added, which would undoubtedly soon pass off. It displayed itself in a host of unnatural sensations. Some of these, as he detailed them, interested and bewildered me, although perhaps the terms and the general manner of the narration had their weight. He suffered much from a morbid acuteness of the senses. The most insipid food was alone endurable. He could wear only garments of certain texture. The odors of all flowers were oppressive. His eyes were tortured by even a faint light. And there were but a few peculiar sounds, and these from stringed instruments, which did not inspire him with horror.

To an anomalous species of terror I found him a bounden slave. "I shall perish," said he, "I *must* perish in this deplorable folly. Thus, thus, and not otherwise, shall I be lost. I dread the events of the future, not in themselves, but in their results. I shudder at the thought of even the most trivial incident which may operate upon this intolerable agitation of soul. I have indeed no abhorrence of danger, except in its absolute effect—terror. In this unnerved, this pitiable condition, I feel that the period will sooner or later arrive when I must abandon life and reason together, in some struggle with the grim phantasm, *fear*."

I learned, moreover, at intervals, and through broken and equivocal hints, another singular feature of his mental condition. He was enchained by certain superstitious

145

impressions in regard to the house, whence for many years he had never ventured forth. An influence whose supposed force was conveyed in terms too shadowy to be restated here—an influence which some peculiarities in the mere form and substance of his family mansion *had*, by dint of long sufferance obtained over his spirit. It was an effect which the physique of the gray walls and turrets, and of the dim tarn into which they all looked down, had at length wrought upon the morale of his existence.

He admitted, although with hesitation, that much of the peculiar gloom which thus afflicted him could be traced to a more natural and far more palpable origin. It was the severe and long-continued illness, indeed the evidently approaching dissolution, of a tenderly beloved sister—his sole companion for long years, and his last and only relative on earth. Her decease, he said, with a bitterness which I can never forget, would leave him (him the hopeless and the frail) the last of the ancient race of the Ushers.

While he spoke, the Lady Madeline (for so was she called) passed slowly through a remote portion of the apartment, and without having noticed my presence, disappeared. I regarded her with an utter astonishment not unmingled with dread, and yet I found it impossible to account for such feelings. A sensation of stupor oppressed me as my eyes followed her retreating steps. When a door, at length, closed upon her, my glance sought instinctively and eagerly the countenance of the brother. But he had buried his face in his hands, and I could only perceive that a far more than ordinary wanness had overspread the emaciated fingers through which trickled many passionate tears.

The disease of the Lady Madeline had long baffled the skill of her physicians. A settled apathy, a gradual wasting away of the person, and frequent but usually transient afflictions of a peculiar cataleptic character, were the unusual diagnosis. Hitherto she had steadily borne up against the pressure of her malady and had not betaken herself finally to bed. But on the closing in of the evening of my arrival at the house, she succumbed, as her brother told me at night with the inexpressible agitation, to the prostrating power of the destroyer. I learned that the glimpse I had obtained of her would thus probably be the last I should obtain—that the lady, at least while living, would be seen by me no more.

For several days ensuing, her name was not mentioned by either Usher or myself: and during this period I was busied in earnest endeavors to alleviate the melancholy of my friend. We painted and read together; or I listened, as if in a dream, to the wild improvisations of his guitar. And thus, as a closer and still closer intimacy admitted me more unreservedly into the recesses of his spirit, the more bitterly did I perceive the futility of all attempt at cheering a mind from which darkness, as if it were his inherent quality, poured forth upon all objects of the moral and physical universe, in one unceasing radiation of gloom.

I shall ever bear about me a memory of the many solemn hours I thus spent alone with the master of the House of Usher. Yet I should fail in any attempt to convey an idea of the exact character of the studies or of the occupations in which he involved me, or led me the way. An excited and highly distempered ideality threw a sulphureous luster over all. His long, improvised dirges will ring forever in my ears. Among other things, I hold painfully in mind a certain singular perversion and amplification of the wild air of the last waltz of von Weber. From the paintings over which his elaborate fancy brooded, and which grew, under his touch, into a vagueness at which I shuddered, knowing not why—from these paintings (vivid as their images now are before me, I would, in vain, endeavor to educe more than a small portion which should lie within the compass of written words. By the utter simplicity, by the nakedness of his designs, he arrested and overawed attention. If ever mortal painted an idea, that mortal was Roderick Usher. For me, in the circumstances then surrounding me, there arose out of the pure abstractions which the hypochondriac contrived to throw upon his canvas, an intensity of intolerable awe, no shadow of which I have ever yet felt in the contemplation of the certainly glowing yet too concrete reveries of Fuseli.

One of the phantasmagoric conceptions of my friend, partaking not so rigidly of the spirit of abstraction, may be shadowed forth, although feebly, in words. A small picture presented the interior of an immensely long and rectangular vault or tunnel, with low walls, smooth, white, and without interruption or device. Certain accessory points of the design served well to convey the idea that this excavation lay at an exceeding depth below the surface of the earth. No outlet was observed in any portion of its vast extent, and no torch, or other artificial source of light was discernible. Yet a flood of intense rays rolled throughout, and bathed the whole in a ghastly and inappropriate splendor.

I have just spoken of that morbid condition of the auditory nerve which rendered all music intolerable to the sufferer, with the exception of certain effects of stringed instruments. It was, perhaps, the narrow limits to which he thus confined himself upon the guitar which gave birth, in great measure, to the fantastic character of his performances.

But the fervid facility of his impromptus could not be so accounted for. They must have been, and were, in the notes as well as in the words of his wild fantasias (for he not infrequently accompanied himself with rhymed verbal improvisations), the result of that intense mental collectedness and concentration to which I have previously alluded as observable only in particular moments of the highest artificial excitement.

The words of one of these rhapsodies I have easily remembered. I was perhaps the more forcibly impressed with it as he gave it, because in the undercurrent of its mystic meaning I fancied that I perceived, for the first time, a full consciousness on the part of Usher of the tottering of his lofty reason upon her throne. The verses, which were entitled *The Haunted Palace,* ran very nearly, if not accurately, thus:

I

In the greenest of our valleys,
    By good angels tenanted,
Once a fair and stately palace—
    Radiant palace—reared its head.
In the monarch thought's dominion
    It stood there!
Never seraph spread a pinion
    Over fabric half so fair.

II

Banners yellow, glorious, golden,
    On its roof did float and flow;
(This—all this—was in the olden
    time long ago.)
And every gentle air that dallied,
    In that sweet day,
Along the ramparts plumed and pallid,
    A winged odor went away.

III

Wanderers in that happy valley
    Through two luminous windows saw
Spirits moving musically
    To a lute's well-tuned law,
Round about a throne, where sitting
    (Porphyrogene!)
In state his glory well-befitting,
    The ruler of the realm was seen.

IV

And all with pearl and ruby glowing
　　was the fair palace door,
Through which came flowing, flowing, flowing
　　And sparkling evermore,
A troop of echoes, whose sweet duty
　　Was but to sing,
In voices of surpassing beauty,
　　The wit and wisdom of their king.

V

But evil things, in robes of sorrow,
　　Assailed the monarch's high estate;
(Ah, let us mourn, for never morrow
　　Shall dawn upon him, desolate!)
And, round about his home, the glory
　　That blushed and bloomed
Is but a dim-remembered story
　　Of the old time entombed.

VI

And travelers now within that valley,
　　Through the red-lighted windows, see
Vast forms that move fantastically
　　To a discordant melody;
While, like a rapid ghastly river,
　　Through the pale door,
A hideous throng rush out forever,
　　And laugh—but smile no more.

I well remember that suggestions arising from this bal-
lad led us into a train of thought wherein there became
manifest an opinion of Usher's which I mention not so
much on account of its novelty (for men have thought
thus), as on account of the pertinacity with which
he maintained it. This opinion, in its general form, was

that of the sentience of all vegetable things. But in his disordered fancy the idea had assumed a more daring character, and trespassed, under certain conditions, upon the kingdom of inorganization. I lack words to express the full extent, or the earnest *abandon* of his persuasion.

The belief, however, was connected (as I have previously hinted) with the gray stones of the home of his forefathers. The conditions of the sentience had been here, he imagined, fulfilled in the method of collocation of these stones—in the order of their arrangement as well as in that of the many fungi which overspread them, in the decayed trees which stood around, and above all, in the long undisturbed endurance of this arrangement, and its reduplication in the still waters of the tarn. Its evidence —the evidence of the sentience—was to be seen, he said (and here I started as he spoke) in the gradual yet certain condensation of an atmosphere of their own about the waters and the walls. The result was discoverable, he added, in that silent yet importunate and terrible influence which for centuries had moulded the destinies of his family, and which made him what I now saw him, what he was. Such opinions need no comment, and I will make none.

Our books—the books which for years had formed no small portion of the mental existence of the invalid—were, as might be supposed, in strict keeping with this character of phantasm. We pored together over such works as the *Ververt et Chartreuse* of Gresset, the *Belphegor* of Machiavelli, the *Heaven and Hell* of Swedenborg, the *Subterranean Voyage of Nicholas Klimm* by Holberg, the *Chiromancy* of Robert Flud, of Jean D'Indaginé and of De la Chambre, the *Journey into the Blue Distance* of Tieck, and the *City of the Sun* of Campanella. One favorite volume was a small octavo edition of the *Directorium Inquisitorum*, by the Dominican Eymeric de Gironne. And there were passages in *Pomponius Mela*, about the old African satyrs and aegipans, over which Usher would sit dreaming for hours. His chief delight, however, was in the perusal of an exceedingly rare and curious book in quarto Gothic, the manual of a forgotten church, the *Vigiliae Mortuorum Chorum Ecclesiae Maguntinae*.

I could not help thinking of the wild ritual of this work, and of its probable influence upon the hypochondriac, when, one evening, having informed me abruptly that the Lady Madeline was no more, he stated his intention of preserving her corpse for a fortnight previous to its final interment, in one of the numerous vaults within the main walls of the building.

The worldly reason, however, assigned for this singular proceeding was one which I did not feel at liberty to dispute. The brother had been led to his resolution (so he told me) by consideration of the unusual character of the malady of the deceased, of certain obtrusive and eager inquiries on the part of her medical men, and of the remote and exposed situation of the burial ground of the family. I will not deny that when I called to mind the sinister countenance of the person whom I met upon the staircase, on the day of my arrival at the house, I had no desire to oppose what I regarded as at best but a harmless, and by no means an unnatural, precaution.

At the request of Usher, I personally aided him in the arrangements for the temporary entombment. The body having been encoffined, we two alone bore it to its rest. The vault in which we placed it, and which had been so long unopened that our torches, half-smothered in its oppressive atmosphere, gave us little opportunity for investigation, was small, damp, and entirely without means of admission for light. It lay at great depth, immediately beneath that portion of the building in which was my own sleeping apartment. It had been used, apparently, in remote feudal times for the worst purpose of a dungeon, and in later days as a place of deposit for powder or some other highly combustible substance, as a portion of its floor and the whole interior of a long archway through which we reached it, were carefully sheathed with copper. The door, of massive iron, had been similarly protected. Its immense weight caused an unusually sharp grating sound as it moved upon its hinges.

Having deposited our mournful burden upon trestles within this region of horror, we partially turned aside the yet unscrewed lid of the coffin, and looked upon the face of the tenant. A striking similitude between the brother and sister now first arrested my attention. And Usher, divining, perhaps, my thoughts, murmured out some few words from which I learned that the deceased and himself had been twins, and that sympathies of a scarcely intelligible nature had always existed between them. Our glances, however, rested not long upon the dead, for we could not regard her unawed. The disease which had thus entombed the lady in youthful maturity had left, as is usual in all maladies of a strictly cataleptic character, the mockery of a faint blush upon the bosom and the face, and that suspiciously lingering smile upon the lip which is so terrible in death. We replaced and screwed down the lid, and, having secured the door of iron, made our way into the scarcely less gloomy apartments of the upper portion of the house.

And now, some days of bitter grief having elapsed, an observable change came over the features of the mental disorder of my friend. His ordinary manner had vanished. His ordinary occupations were neglected or forgotten. He roamed from chamber to chamber with hurried, unequal and objectless step. The pallor of his countenance had assumed, if possible, a more ghastly hue, but the luminousness of his eye had utterly gone out. The once occasional huskiness of his tone was heard no more, and a tremulous quaver, as if of extreme terror, habitually characterized his utterance. There were times, indeed, when I thought his unceasingly agitated mind was laboring with some oppressive secret, to divulge which he struggled for the necessary courage. At times, again, I was obliged to resolve all into the mere inexplicable vagaries of madness, for I beheld him gazing upon vacancy for long hours, in an attitude of the profoundest attention, as if listening to some imaginary sound. It was no wonder that his condition terrified, that it infected me. I felt creeping upon me, by slow yet certain degrees, the wild influences of his own fantastic yet impressive superstitions.

It was especially upon retiring to bed late in the night of the seventh or eighth day after the placing of the Lady Madeline within the dungeon that I experienced the full power of such feelings. Sleep came not near my couch, while the hours waned and waned away. I struggled to reason off the nervousness which had dominion over me. I endeavored to believe that much, if not all, of what I felt was due to the bewildering influence of the gloomy furniture of the room—of the dark and tattered draperies, which, tortured into motion by the breath of a rising tempest, swayed fitfully to and fro upon the walls and rustled uneasily about the decorations of the bed. But my efforts were fruitless. An irrepressible tremor gradually pervaded my frame. At length there sat upon my very heart an incubus of utterly causeless alarm. Shaking this off with a gasp and a struggle, I uplifted myself upon the pillows, and peering earnestly within the intense darkness of the chamber, hearkened—I know not why, except that an instinctive spirit prompted me—to certain low and indefinite sounds which came, through the pauses of the storm, at long intervals, I knew not whence. Overpowered by an intense sentiment of horror, unaccountable yet unendurable, I threw on my clothes with haste, for I felt that I should sleep no more during the night, and endeavored to arouse myself from the pitiable condition into which I had fallen, by pacing rapidly to and fro through the apartment.

I had taken but few turns in this manner, when a light step on an adjoining staircase arrested my attention. I presently recognized it as that of Usher. In an instant afterward he rapped with a gentle touch at my door, and entered, bearing a lamp. His countenance was as usual cadaverously wan—but there was a species of mad hilarity in his eyes, an evidently restrained *hysteria* in his whole demeanor. His air appalled me, but anything was preferable to the solitude which I had so long endured, and I even welcomed his presence as a relief.

"And you have not seen it?" he said abruptly, after having stared about him for some moments in silence. "You have not then seen it? But, stay! You shall." Thus speaking, and having carefully shaded his lamp, he hurried to one of the casements and threw it freely open to the storm.

The impetuous fury of the entering gust nearly lifted us from our feet. It was indeed a tempestuous yet sternly beautiful night, and one wildly singular in its terror and its beauty. A whirlwind had apparently collected its force in our vicinity, for there were frequent and violent alterations in the direction of the wind. And the exceeding density of the clouds (which hung so low as to press upon the turrets of the house) did not prevent our perceiving the lifelike velocity with which they flew careering from all points against each other without passing away into the distance. I say that even their exceeding density did not prevent our perceiving this, yet we had no glimpse of the moon or stars, nor was there any flashing forth of the lightning. But the undersurfaces of the huge masses of agitated vapor, as well as all terrestrial objects immediately around us, were glowing in the unnatural light of a faintly luminous and distinctly visible gaseous exhalation which hung about and enshrouded the mansion.

"You must not, you shall not behold this!" said I, shudderingly to Usher as I led him, with a gentle violence, from the window to a seat. "These appearances which bewilder you are merely electrical phenomena not uncommon, or it may be that they have their ghastly origin in the rank miasma of the tarn. Let us close this casement. The air is chilling and dangerous to your frame. Here is one of your favorite romances. I will read and you shall listen—and so we will pass away this terrible night together."

The antique volume which I had taken up was the *Mad Trist* of Sir Launcelot Canning; but I had called it a favorite of Usher's more in sad jest than in earnest. In truth, there is little in its uncouth and unimaginative prolixity which could have had interest for the lofty and spiritual ideality of my friend. It was, however, the only book immediately at hand; and I indulged a vague hope that the excitement which now agitated the hypochondriac, might find relief (for the history of mental disorder is full of similar anomalies) even in the extremity of the folly which I should read. Could I have judged, indeed, by the wild overstrained air of vivacity with which he hearkened, or apparently hearkened, to the words of the tale, I might well have congratulated myself upon the success of my design.

I had arrived at that well-known portion of the story where Ethelred, the hero of the *Trist,* having sought in vain for peaceable admission into the dwelling of the hermit, proceeds to make good an entrance by force. The words of the narrative run thus:

And Ethelred, who was by nature of a doughty heart, and who was now mighty withal, on account of the powerfulness of the wine which he had drunken, waited no longer to hold parley with the hermit, who, in sooth, was of an obstinate and maliceful turn, but feeling the rain upon his shoulders, and fearing the rising of the tempest, uplifted his mace outright, and with blows, made quickly room in the plankings of the door for his gauntleted hand; and now pulling therewith sturdily, he so cracked and ripped and tore all asunder, that the noise of the dry and hollow-sounding wood alarmed and reverberated throughout the forest.

At the termination of this sentence I started, and for

a moment, paused; for it appeared to me (although I at once concluded that my excited fancy had deceived me) that, from some very remote portion of the mansion there came indistinctly to my ears what might have been, in its exact similarity of character, the echo (but a stifled and dull one certainly) of the very cracking and ripping sound which Sir Launcelot had so particularly described. It was, beyond doubt, the coincidence alone which had arrested my attention; for, amid the rattling of the sashes of the casements, and the ordinary commingled noises of the still increasing storm, the sound in itself was nothing, surely, which should have interested or disturbed me. I continued the story:

But the good champion Ethelred, now entering within the door, was sore enraged and amazed to perceive no signal of the maliceful hermit; but, in the stead thereof, a dragon of a scaly and prodigious demeanor and of a fiery tongue, which sate in guard before a palace of gold, with a floor of silver; and upon the wall there hung a shield of shining brass with this legend engraved upon it:
Who entereth herein, a conqueror hath bin;
Who slayeth the dragon, the shield he shall win.
Ethelred uplifted his mace and struck upon the head of the dragon, which fell before him, and gave up his pestilent breath with a shriek so horrid and harsh and withal so piercing, that Ethelred had fain to close his ears with his hands against the dreadful noise of it, the like whereof was never before heard.

Here again I paused abruptly, and now with a feeling of wild amazement—for there could be no doubt whatever that in this instance I did actually hear, although from what direction it proceeded I found it impossible to say, a low and apparently distant, but harsh, protracted and most unusual screaming or grating sound—the exact counterpart of what my fancy had already conjured up for the dragon's unnatural shriek as described by the romancer.

Oppressed as I certainly was upon the occurrence of the second and most extraordinary coincidence, by a thousand conflicting sensations in which wonder and extreme terror were predominant, I still retained sufficient presence of mind to avoid exciting, by any observation, the sensitive nervousness of my companion. I was by no means certain that he had noticed the sounds in question, although assuredly a strange alteration had, during the last few minutes, taken place in his demeanor. From a position facing me, he had gradually brought round his chair so as to sit with his face to the door of the chamber; and thus I could but partially perceive his features, although I saw that his lips trembled as if he were murmuring inaudibly. His head had dropped upon his breast, yet I knew that he was not asleep, for I caught a glimpse of the wide and rigid opening of his eye, in profile. The motion of his body, too, was at variance with this idea, for he rocked from side to side with a gentle yet constant and uniform sway. Having rapidly taken notice of all this, I resumed the narrative of Sir Launcelot, which thus proceeded:

And now the champion, having escaped from the terrible fury of the dragon and bethinking himself of the brazen shield, and of the breaking up of the enchantment which was upon it, removed the carcass from out of the way before him, and approached valorously over the silver pavement of the castle to where the shield was upon the wall; which in sooth tarried not for his full comnig, but fell down at his feet upon the silver floor, with a mighty great and terrible ringing sound.

No sooner had these syllables passed my lips, than—as if a shield of brass had indeed, at the moment, fallen heavily upon a floor of silver—I became aware of a distinct, hollow, metallic and clangorous yet apparently muffled reverberation. Completely unnerved, I leaped to my feet, but the measured rocking movement of Usher was undisturbed. I rushed to the chair in which he sat. His eyes were bent fixedly before him, and throughout his whole countenance there reigned a stony rigidity. But, as I placed my hand upon his shoulder, there came a strong shudder over his whole person. A sickly smile quivered about his lips, and I saw that he spoke in a low, hurried and gibbering murmur, as if unconscious of my presence. Bending closely over him, I at length drank in the hideous import of his words.

"Not hear it? Yes, I hear it, and *have* heard it. Long—long—long—many minutes, many hours, many days, have I heard it, yet I dared not—oh, pity me, miserable wretch that I am! I dared not, I *dared* not speak! *We have put her living in the tomb!* Said I not that my senses were acute?

I *now* tell you that I heard her first feeble movements in the hollow coffin. I heard them many, many days ago— yet I dared not, *I dared not speak!* And now, tonight— Ethelred—ha! ha! The dragon of the hermit's door, and the death cry of the dragon, and the clangor of the shield! Say rather the rending of her coffin, and the grating of the iron hinges of her prison, and her struggles within the coppered archway of the vault! Oh whither shall I fly? Will she not be here anon? Is she not hurrying to upbraid me for my haste? Have I not heard her footstep on the stair? Do I not distinguish that heavy and horrible beating of her heart? *Madman!*" Here he sprang furiously to his feet, and shrieked out his syllables, as if in the effort he were giving up his soul. "*Madman! I tell you that she stands without the door!*"

As if in the superhuman energy of his utterance there has been found the potency of a spell, the huge antique panels to which the speaker pointed moved slowly back, upon the instant, their ponderous and ebony jaws. It was the work of the rushing gust, but then without those doors there *did* stand the lofty and enshrouded figure of the Lady Madeline of Usher. There was blood upon her white robes, and the evidence of some bitter struggle upon every portion of her emaciated frame. For a moment she remained trembling and reeling to and fro upon the threshold, then with a low moaning cry, fell heavily inward upon the person of her brother, and in her violent and now final death agonies, bore him to the floor a corpse, and a victim to the terrors he had anticipated.

From that chamber and from that mansion, I fled aghast. The storm was still abroad in all its wrath as I found myself crossing the old causeway. Suddenly there shot along the path a wild light, and I turned to see whence a gleam so unusual could have issued, for the vast house and its shadows were alone behind me. The radiance was that of the full, setting, and blood-red moon which now shone vividly through that once barely discernible fissure of which I have before spoken as extending from the roof of the building, in a zigzag direction, to the base. While I gazed, this fissure rapidly widened—there came a fierce breath of the whirlwind—the entire orb of the satellite burst at once upon my sight—my brain reeled as I saw the mighty walls rushing asunder—there was a long tumultuous shouting sound like the voice of a thousand waters—and the deep and dark tarn at my feet closed sullenly and silently over the fragments of the *House of Usher.*

THE BLACK CAT

FOR the most wild yet most homely narrative which I am about to pen, I neither expect nor solicit belief. Mad indeed would I be to expect it in a case where my very senses reject their own evidence. Yet mad am I not, and very surely do I not dream. But tomorrow I die, and today I would unburden my soul. My immediate purpose is to place before the world, plainly, succinctly, and without comment, a series of mere household events. In their consequences, these events have terrified, have tortured, have destroyed me. Yet I will not attempt to expound them. To me, they have presented little but horror—to many they will seem less terrible than *baroque*. Hereafter, perhaps, some intellect may be found which will reduce my phantasm to the commonplace. Some calmer intellect, more logical, less excitable than mine will perceive in the circumstances I detail with awe, nothing more than an ordinary succession of very natural causes and effects.

From my infancy I was noted for the docility and humanity of my disposition. My tenderness of heart was even so conspicuous as to make me the jest of my companions. I was especially fond of animals, and was indulged by my parents with a great variety of pets. With these I spent most of my time, and never was so happy as when feeding and caressing them. This peculiarity of character grew with my growth, and in my manhood I derived from it one of my principal sources of pleasure. To those who have cherished an affection for a faithful and sagacious dog, I need hardly be at the trouble of explaining the nature or the intensity of the gratification thus derived. There is something in the unselfish and self-sacrificing love of a brute which goes directly to the heart of him who has had frequent occasion to test the paltry friendship and gossamer fidelity of mere man.

I married early and was happy to find in my wife a disposition not uncongenial with my own. Observing my partiality for domestic pets, she lost no opportunity of procuring those of the most agreeable kind. We had birds, goldfish, a fine dog, rabbits, a small monkey, and a cat.

This latter was a remarkably large and beautiful animal, entirely black, and sagacious to an astonishing degree. In speaking of his intelligence, my wife, who at heart was not a little tinctured with superstition, made frequent allusion to the ancient popular notion which regarded all black cats as witches in disguise. Not that she was ever *serious* upon this point. That I mention the matter at all is for no better reason than that it happens, just now, to be remembered.

Pluto—this was the cat's name—was my favorite pet and playmate. I alone fed him, and he attended me wherever I went about the house. It was even with difficulty that I could prevent him from following me through the streets.

Our friendship lasted in this manner for several years, during which my general temperament and character—through the instrumentality of the fiend intemperance—had experienced a radical alteration for the worse. I grew day by day more moody, more irritable, more regardless of the feelings of others. I suffered myself to use intemperate language to my wife and at length I even offered her personal violence. My pets, of course, were made to feel the change in my disposition. I not only neglected, but ill-used them. For Pluto, however, I still retained sufficient regard to restrain me from maltreating him, as I made no scruple of maltreating the rabbits, the monkey, or even the dog, when by accident or through affection they got in my way. But my disease grew upon me—for what disease is like alcohol? And at length even Pluto, who was now becoming old and consequently somewhat peevish, began to experience the effects of my ill temper.

One night, returning home much intoxicated from one of my haunts about town, I fancied that the cat avoided my presence. I seized him; and in his fright at my violence he inflicted a slight wound upon my hand with his teeth. The fury of a demon instantly possessed me. I knew myself no longer. My original soul seemed at once to take flight from my body, and a more than fiendish malevolence, gin-nurtured, thrilled every fiber of my frame. I took from my waistcoat pocket a penknife, opened it, grasped the poor beast by the throat, and deliberately cut one of its eyes from the socket! I blush, I burn, I shudder, while I pen the damnable atrocity.

When reason returned with the morning—when I had slept off the fumes of the night's debauch—I experienced a sentiment half of horror, half of remorse for the crime of which I had been guilty; but it was at best a feeble and equivocal feeling, and the soul remained untouched. I again plunged into excess and soon drowned in wine all memory of the deed.

In the meantime the cat slowly recovered. The socket of the lost eye presented, it is true, a frightful appearance, but he no longer appeared to suffer any pain. He went about the house as usual, but as might be expected, fled in extreme terror at my approach. I had so much of my old heart left as to be at first grieved by this evident dislike on the part of a creature which had once so loved me. But this feeling soon gave place to irritation. And then came, as if to my final and irrevocable overthrow, the spirit of *perverseness*. Of this spirit philosophy takes no account. Yet I am not more sure that my soul lives than that perverseness is one of the primitive impulses of the human heart—one of the indivisible primary faculties, or sentiments, which give direction to the character of man. Who has not, a hundred times, found himself committing a vile or a silly action for no other reason than because he knows he should *not*? Have we not a perpetual inclination, in the teeth of our best judgment, to violate that which is law, merely because we understand it to be such? This spirit of perverseness, I say, came to my final overthrow. It was this unfathomable longing of the soul to vex itself—to offer violence to its own nature—to do wrong for wrong's sake only—that urged me to continue and finally to consummate the injury I had inflicted upon the unoffending brute. One morning, in cold blood, I slipped a noose about its neck and hung it to the limb of a tree, hung it with the tears streaming from my eyes and with the bitterest remorse at my heart, hung it *because* I knew that it had loved me and had given me no reason of offense—hung it because I knew that in so doing I was committing a sin, a deadly sin that would so jeopardize my immortal soul as to place it (if such a thing were possible) even beyond the reach of the infinite mercy of the most merciful and most terrible God.

On the night of the day on which this cruel deed was done I was aroused from sleep by the cry of "Fire!" The curtains of my bed were in flames. The whole house was blazing. It was with great difficulty that my wife, a servant and myself made our escape from the conflagration. The destruction was complete. My entire worldly wealth was swallowed up, and I resigned myself thenceforward to despair.

I am above the weakness of seeking to establish a sequence of cause and effect between the disaster and the atrocity. But I am detailing a chain of facts and wish not to leave even a possible link imperfect. On the day succeeding the fire, I visited the ruins. The walls, with one exception, had fallen in. This exception was found in a compartment wall, not very thick, which stood about the middle of the house and against which had rested the head of my bed. The plastering had here in great measure resisted the action of the fire, a fact which I attributed to its having been recently spread. About this wall a dense crowd had collected, and many persons seemed to be examining a particular portion of it with very minute and eager attention. Their words strange, singular, and other similar expressions excited my curiosity. I approached and saw, as if graven in bas-relief upon the white surface, the figure of a gigantic *cat*. The impression was given with an accuracy truly marvelous. There was a rope about the animal's neck.

When I first beheld this apparition—for I could scarcely regard it as less—my wonder and my terror were extreme. But at length reflection came to my aid. The cat, I remembered, had been hung in a garden adjacent to the house. Upon the alarm of fire this garden had been immediately filled by the crowd. Someone must have cut down the animal from the tree and thrown it through an open window into my chamber. This had probably been done with the view of arousing me from sleep. The falling of other walls had compressed the victim of my cruelty into the substance of the freshly spread plaster, the lime of which, with the flames and the ammonia from the carcass, had then accomplished the portraiture as I saw it.

Although I thus readily accounted to my reason, if not altogether to my conscience, for the startling fact just detailed, it did not fail to make a deep impression upon my fancy. For months I could not rid myself of the phantasm of the cat; and during this period there came back into my spirit a half-sentiment that seemed, but was not, remorse. I went so far as to regret the loss of the animal, and to look about me among the vile haunts which I now habitually frequented for another pet of the same species, and of somewhat similar appearance, to take its place.

One night as I sat, half-stupefied, in some den of infamy, my attention was suddenly drawn to a black object reposing on the head of one of the immense casks of gin, or of rum, which constituted the chief furniture of the apartment. I had been looking steadily at the top of this cask for some minutes, and what now caused me surprise was the fact that I had not sooner perceived the object thereupon. I approached it and touched it with my hand. It was a black cat and a very large one, fully as large as Pluto, and closely resembling him in every respect but one. Pluto had not a white hair upon any portion of his body, but this cat had a large, although indefinite, splotch of white, covering nearly the whole region of the breast.

Upon my touching him he immediately arose, purred loudly, rubbed against my hand, and appeared delighted with my notice. This, then, was the very creature of which I was in search. I at once offered to purchase it of the landlord; but this person made no claim to it, knew nothing of it, and had never seen it before.

I continued my caresses, and when I prepared to go home, the animal evinced a disposition to accompany me. I permitted it to do so, occasionally stooping and patting it as I proceeded. When it reached the house, it domesticated itself at once, and became immediately a great favorite with my wife.

For my own part, I soon found a dislike to it arising within me. This was just the reverse of what I had anticipated. I know not how or why it was, but its evident fondness for myself rather disgusted and annoyed me. By slow degrees these feelings of disgust and annoyance rose into the bitterness of hatred. I avoided the creature; yet a certain sense of shame and the remembrance of my former deed of cruelty prevented me from physically abusing it. I did not for some weeks strike or otherwise violently ill-use it; but gradually, very gradually, I came to look upon it with unutterable loathing, and to flee silently from its odious presence, as from the breath of a pestilence.

What added, no doubt, to my hatred of the beast was the discovery, on the morning after I brought it home,

THE BLACK CAT

that, like Pluto, *it also had been deprived of one of its eyes.* This circumstance, however, only endeared it to my wife, who, as I have already said, possessed in a high degree that humanity of feeling which had once been my distinguishing trait and the source of many of my simplest and purest pleasures.

With my aversion to this cat, however, its partiality for myself seemed to increase. It followed my footsteps with a pertinacity which it would be difficult to make the reader comprehend. Whenever I sat, it would crouch beneath my chair, or spring upon my knees, covering me with its loathsome caresses. If I arose to walk, it would get between my feet and thus nearly throw me down, or, fastening its long and sharp claws in my clothes, clamber in this manner to my breast. At such times, although I longed to destroy it with a blow, I was yet withheld from doing so, partly by a memory of my former crime, but chiefly—let me confess it at once—by absolute *dread* of the beast.

This dread was not exactly a dread of physical evil, and yet I should be at a loss how otherwise to define it. I am almost ashamed to own—yes, even in this felon's cell I am almost ashamed to own—that the terror and horror with which the animal inspired me had been heightened by one of the merest chimeras it would be possible to conceive. My wife had called my attention more than once to the character of the mark of white hair, of which I have spoken and which constituted the sole visible difference

173

between the strange beast and the one I had destroyed. The reader will remember that this mark, although large, had been originally very indefinite; but by slow degrees— degrees nearly imperceptible and which for a long time my reason struggled to reject as fanciful—it had at length assumed a rigorous distinctness of outline. It was now the representation of an object that I shudder to name—and for this above all I loathed, and dreaded, and would have rid myself of the monster had I dared. It was now, I say, the image of a hideous, of a ghastly thing—the *gallows!* Oh mournful and terrible engine of horror and of crime, of agony and of death!

And now I was indeed wretched beyond the wretched- ness of mere humanity. A brute beast, whose fellow I had contemptuously destroyed, a brute beast to work out for me, a man fashioned in the image of the high God, so much insufferable woe! Alas! Neither by day nor by night knew I the blessing of rest any more! During the day the creature left me no moment alone, and in the night I started hourly from dreams of unutterable fear to find the hot breath of the *thing* upon my face, and its vast weight —an incarnate nightmare that I had no power to shake off —incumbent eternally upon my heart!

Beneath the pressure of torments such as these, the feeble remnant of the good within me succumbed. Evil thoughts became my sole intimates, the darkest and most evil of thoughts. The moodiness of my usual temper in- creased to hatred of all things and of all mankind; while from the sudden, frequent, and ungovernable outbursts of a fury to which I now blindly abandoned myself, my uncomplaining wife, alas, was the most usual and the most patient of sufferers.

One day she accompanied me upon some household errand into the cellar of the old building which our poverty compelled us to inhabit. The cat followed me down the steep stairs, and, nearly throwing me headlong, exasperated me to madness. Uplifting an axe, and forgetting in my wrath the childish dread which had hitherto stayed my hand, I aimed a blow at the animal which, of course, would have proved instantly fatal had the axe descended as I wished. But this blow was arrested by the hand of my wife. Goaded by the interference into a rage more than demoniacal, I withdrew my arm from her grasp and buried the axe in her brain. She fell dead upon the spot, without a groan.

This hideous murder accomplished, I set myself forthwith, and with entire deliberation, to the task of concealing the body. I knew that I could not remove it from the house, either by day or by night, without running the risk of being observed by the neighbors. Many projects entered my mind. At one period I thought of cutting the corpse into minute fragments and destroying them by fire. At another, I resolved to dig a grave for it in the floor of the cellar. Again, I deliberated about casting it into the well in the yard, or packing it in a box, like merchandise, and getting a porter to take it from the house. Finally I hit upon what I considered a far better expedient than either of these. I determined to wall it up in the cellar, as the monks of the Middle Ages are recorded to have walled up their victims.

For a purpose such as this the cellar was well adapted. Its walls were loosely constructed, and had lately been plastered throughout with a rough plaster which the dampness of the atmosphere had prevented from hardening. Moreover, in one of the walls was a projection, caused by a false chimney or fireplace, that had been filled up and made to resemble the rest of the cellar. I had no doubt that I could readily displace the bricks at this point, insert the corpse, and wall the whole up as before, so that no eye could detect anything suspicious.

And in this calculation I was not deceived. By means of a crowbar I easily dislodged the bricks, and having carefully deposited the body against the inner wall, I propped it in that position, while with little trouble I relaid the whole structure as it had originally stood. Having procured mortar, sand and hair with every possible precaution, I prepared a plaster which could not be distinguished from the old. With this I very carefully went over the new brickwork. When I had finished, I felt satisfied that all was right. The wall did not present the slightest appearance of having been disturbed. The rubble on the floor, the only evidence of my work, I picked up with the minutest care. I looked around triumphantly and said to myself, "Here at least, then, my labor has not been in vain."

My next step was to look for the beast which had been the cause of so much wretchedness, for I had at length firmly resolved to put it to death. Had I been able to meet with it at the moment, there could have been no doubt of its fate, but it appeared that the crafty animal had been alarmed at the violence of my previous anger and forbore to present itself in my present mood. It is impossible to describe or to imagine the deep, the blissful sense of relief which the absence of the detested creature occasioned in my bosom. It did not make its appearance during the night, and thus for the first night since its introduction into the house I soundly and tranquilly slept— aye, slept even with the burden of murder upon my soul.

The second and the third day passed, and still my tormentor came not. Once again I breathed as a free man. The monster, in terror, had fled the premises forever! I should behold it no more! My happiness was supreme! The guilt of my dark deed disturbed me but little. Some few inquiries had been made, but these had been readily answered. A search had even been instituted, but of course nothing was to be discovered. I looked upon my future felicity as finally secure.

Upon the fourth day of the assassination, a party of the police came unexpectedly into the house, and proceeded again to make rigorous investigation of the premises. Secure in the inscrutability of my place of concealment, I felt no embarrassment whatever. The officers bade me accompany them in their search. They left no nook or corner unexplored. At length, for the third or fourth time, they descended into the cellar. I quivered not in a muscle. My heart beat as calmly as that of one who slumbers in innocence. I walked the cellar from end to end. I folded my arms upon my bosom and roamed easily to and fro. The police were thoroughly satisfied, and prepared to depart. The glee in my heart was too strong to be restrained. I burned to say a word, by way of triumph, and to render doubly sure their assurance of my guiltlessness.

"Gentlemen," I said at last, as the party ascended the steps, "I am delighted to have allayed your suspicions. I wish you all health and a little more courtesy. By the way, gentlemen, this—this is a very well-constructed house." (In the rabid desire to say something easily, I scarcely knew what I uttered.) "I may say an *excellently* well-constructed house. These walls—are you going, gentlemen? These walls are solidly put together."

Here, through the mere frenzy of bravado, I rapped heavily upon that very portion of the brickwork behind which stood the corpse of my wife.

But may God shield and deliver me from the fangs of the archfiend! No sooner had the reverberation of my blows sunk into silence than I was answered by a voice from within the tomb—by a cry at first muffled and broken, like the sobbing of a child, and then quickly swelling into one long, loud and continuous scream, utterly anomalous and inhuman—a howl, a wailing shriek, half of horror and half of triumph, such as might have arisen only out of hell conjointly from the throats of the damned in their agony and of the demons that exult in the damnation.

Of my own thoughts it is folly to speak. Swooning, I staggered to the opposite wall. For one instant, the party on the stairs remained motionless through extremity of terror and of awe. In the next, a dozen stout arms were toiling at the wall. It fell bodily. The corpse, already greatly decayed and clotted with gore, stood erect before the eyes of the spectators. Upon its head, with red extended mouth and solitary eye of fire, sat the hideous beast whose craft had seduced me into murder, and whose informing voice had consigned me to the hangman. I had walled the monster up within the tomb!

A TALE OF THE RAGGED MOUNTAINS

DURING the fall of the year 1827, while residing near Charlottesville, Virginia, I casually made the acquaintance of Mr. Augustus Bedloe. This young gentleman was remarkable in every respect, and excited in me a profound interest and curiosity. I found it impossible to comprehend him either in his moral or his physical relations. Of his family I could obtain no satisfactory account. Whence he came, I never ascertained. Even about his age, although I call him a young gentleman, there was something which perplexed me in no little degree. He certainly *seemed* young, and he made a point of speaking about his youth, yet there were moments when I should have had little trouble in imagining him a hundred years of age. But in no regard was he more peculiar than in his personal appearance. He was singularly tall and thin. He stooped greatly. His limbs were exceedingly long and emaciated. His forehead was broad and low. His complexion was absolutely bloodless. His mouth was large and inflexible, and his teeth were more wildly uneven, although sound, than I had ever before seen teeth in a human head. The expression of his smile, however, was by no means unpleasing, as might be supposed, but it had no variation whatever. It was one of profound melancholy, of a phaseless and unceasing gloom. His eyes were abnormally large, and round like those of a cat. The pupils, too, upon any accession or diminution of light, underwent contraction or dilation, just such as is observed in the feline tribe. In moments of excitement the orbs grew bright to a degree almost inconceivable, seeming to emit luminous rays, not of a reflected but of an intrinsic luster, as does a candle; yet their ordinary condition was so totally vapid, filmy and dull, as to convey the idea of the eyes of a long-interred corpse.

These peculiarities of person appeared to cause him much annoyance, and he was continually alluding to them in a sort of half-explanatory, half-apologetic strain, which, when I first heard it, impressed me very painfully. I soon, however, grew accustomed to it and my uneasiness wore off. It seemed to be his design rather to insinuate than directly to assert that, physically, he had not always been what he was—that a long series of neuralgic attacks had reduced him from a condition of more than usual personal beauty to that which I saw. For many years past he had been attended by a physician, named

Templeton, an old gentleman, perhaps seventy years of age whom he had first encountered at Saratoga, and from whose attention while there, he either received, or fancied that he received, great benefit. The result was that Bedloe, who was wealthy, had made an arrangement with Dr. Templeton, by which the latter, in consideration of a liberal annual allowance, had consented to devote his time and medical experience exclusively to the care of the invalid.

Doctor Templeton had been a traveler in his younger days, and at Paris had become a convert, in great measure, to the doctrine of Mesmer. It was altogether by means of magnetic[1] remedies that he had succeeded in alleviating the acute pains of his patient; and this success had very naturally inspired the latter with a certain degree of confidence in the opinions from which the remedies had been educed. The doctor, however, like all enthusiasts, had struggled hard to make a thorough convert of his pupil, and finally so far gained his point as to induce the sufferer to submit to numerous experiments. By a frequent repetition of these, a result had arisen, which of late days has become so common as to attract little or no attention, but which, at the period of which I write, had very rarely been known in America. I mean to say, that between Dr. Templeton and Bedloe there had grown up, little by little, a very distinct and strongly marked rapport, or magnetic relation. I am not prepared to assert, however, that this rapport extended beyond the limits of the simple sleep-producing power; but this power itself had attained great intensity. At the first attempt to induce the magnetic somnolency, the mesmerist entirely failed. In the fifth or sixth he succeeded very partially, and after long-continued effort. Only at the twelfth was the triumph complete. After this, the will of the patient succumbed rapidly to that of the physician, so that, when I first became acquainted with the two, sleep was brought about almost instantaneously by the mere volition of the operator, even when the invalid was unaware of his presence. It is only now, in the year 1845, when similar miracles are witnessed daily by thousands, that I dare venture to record this apparent impossibility as a matter of serious fact.

The temperament of Bedloe was in the highest degree sensitive, excitable, enthusiastic. His imagination was singularly vigorous and creative; and no doubt it derived additional force from the habitual use of morphine, which he swallowed in great quantity, and without which he would have found it impossible to exist. It was his practice to take a very large dose of it immediately after breakfast each morning, or rather immediately after a cup of strong coffee, for he ate nothing in the forenoon, and then set forth alone, or attended only by a dog, upon a long ramble among the chain of wild and dreary hills that lie westward and southward of Charlottesville, and are there dignified by the title of the Ragged Mountains.

Upon a dim, warm, misty day, toward the close of November, and during the strange *interregnum* of the seasons which in America is termed the Indian summer, Mr. Bedloe departed as usual for the hills. The day passed, and still he did not return.

About eight o'clock at night, having become seriously alarmed at his protracted absence, we were about to set out in search of him, when he unexpectedly made his appearance, in health no worse than usual, and in rather more than ordinary spirits. The account which he gave of his expedition, and of the events which had detained him, was a singular one indeed.

"You will remember," said he, "that it was about nine in the morning when I left Charlottesville. I bent my steps immediately to the mountains, and about ten, entered a gorge which was entirely new to me. I followed the windings of this pass with much interest. The scenery which presented itself on all sides, although scarcely entitled to be called grand, had about it an indescribable and to me a delicious aspect of dreary desolation. The solitude seemed absolutely virgin. I could not help believing that the green sods and the gray rocks upon which I trod had been trodden never before by the foot of a human being. So entirely secluded, and inaccessible, in fact, except through a series of accidents, is the entrance of the ravine, that it is by no means impossible that I was the first adventurer—the very first and sole adventurer who had ever penetrated its recesses.

"The thick and peculiar mist, or smoke, which distinguishes the Indian summer, and which now hung heavily over all objects, served, no doubt, to deepen the vague impressions which these objects created. So dense was this pleasant fog that I could at no time see more than a dozen yards of the path before me. This path was excessively sinuous, and as the sun could not be seen, I soon lost all idea of the direction in which I journeyed. In the meantime the morphine had its customary effect, that of enduing all the external world with an intensity of interest. In the quivering of a leaf, in the hue of a blade of grass, in the shape of a trefoil, in the humming of a bee, in the gleaming of a dewdrop, in the breathing of the wind, in the faint odors that came from the forest, there came a whole universe of suggestion—a gay and motley train of rhapsodical and immethodical thought.

"Busied in this, I walked on for several hours, during which the mist deepened around me to so great an extent that at length I was reduced to an absolute groping of the way. And now an indescribable uneasiness possessed me, a species of nervous hesitation and tremor. I feared to tread, lest I should be precipitated into some abyss. I remembered, too, strange stories told about these Ragged Hills, and of the uncouth and fierce races of men who tenanted their groves and caverns. A thousand vague fancies oppressed and disconcerted me, fancies the more distressing because vague. Very suddenly my attention was arrested by the loud beating of a drum.

"My amazement was, of course, extreme. A drum in

these hills was a thing unknown. I could not have been more surprised at the sound of the trump of the archangel. But a new and still more astounding source of interest and perplexity arose. There came a wild rattling or jingling sound, as if of a bunch of large keys, and upon the instant a dusky-visaged and half-naked man rushed past me with a shriek. He came so close to my person that I felt his hot breath upon my face. He bore in one hand an instrument composed of an assemblage of steel rings, and shook them vigorously as he ran. Scarcely had he disappeared in the mist before, panting after him with open mouth and glaring eyes, there darted a huge beast. I could not be mistaken in its character. It was a hyena.

"The sight of this monster rather relieved than heightened my terrors, for I now made sure that I dreamed, and endeavored to arouse myself to waking consciousness. I stepped boldly and briskly forward. I rubbed my eyes. I called aloud. I pinched my limbs. A small spring of water presented itself to my view, and here, stooping, I bathed my hands and my head and neck. This seemed to dissipate the equivocal sensations which had hitherto annoyed me. I arose, as I thought, a new man, and proceeded steadily and complacently on my unknown way.

"At length, quite overcome by exertion, and by a certain oppressive closeness of the atmosphere, I seated myself beneath a tree. Presently there came a feeble gleam of sunshine, and the shadow of the leaves of the tree fell faintly but definitely upon the grass. At this shadow I

gazed wonderingly for many minutes. Its character stupefied me with astonishment. I looked upward. The tree
was a palm.

"I now rose hurriedly, and in a state of fearful agitation, for the fancy that I dreamed would serve me no
longer. I felt that I had perfect command of my senses,
and these senses now brought to my soul a world of
novel and singular sensation. The heat became all at
once intolerable. A strange odor loaded the breeze. A low,
continuous murmur, like that arising from a full, but
gently flowing river, came to my ears, intermingled with
the peculiar hum of multitudinous human voices.

"While I listened in an extremity of astonishment which
I need not attempt to describe, a strong and brief gust
of wind bore off the incumbent fog as if by the wand of an
enchanter.

"I found myself at the foot of a high mountain, and
looking down into a vast plain, through which wound a
majestic river. On the margin of this river stood an East-
ern-looking city, such as we read of in Arabian tales, but
of a character even more singular than any there described. From my position, which was far above the level
of the town, I could perceive its every nook and corner, as
if delineated on a map. The streets seemed innumerable,
and crossed each other irregularly in all directions, but
were rather long winding alleys than streets, and absolutely swarmed with inhabitants. The houses were wildly
picturesque. On every hand was a wilderness of balconies,

of verandas, of minarets, of shrines, and fantastically carved oriels. Bazaars abounded, and there were displayed rich wares in infinite variety and profusion—silks, muslins, the most dazzling cutlery, the most magnificent jewels and gems.

"Besides these things, were to be seen on all sides, banners and palanquins, litters with stately dames close-veiled, elephants gorgeously caparisoned, idols grotesquely hewn, drums, banners, and gongs, spears, silver and gilded maces. And amid the crowd, and clamor, and general intricacy and confusion, amid the million black and yellow men, turbaned and robed and of flowing beard, there roamed a countless multitude of holy filleted bulls, while vast legions of the filthy but sacred apes clambered, chattering and shrieking, on the cornices of the mosques, or climbed up to the minarets and oriels. From the swarming streets to the banks of the river, there descended innumerable flights of steps leading to bathing places, while the river itself seemed to force a passage with difficulty through the vast fleets of deeply burdened ships that far and wide encountered its surface. Beyond the limits of the city arose the palm and the cocoa, with other gigantic and weird trees of vast age; and here and there might be seen a field of rice, the thatched hut of a peasant, a tank, a stray temple, a gipsy camp, or a solitary graceful maiden taking her way, with a pitcher upon her head, to the banks of the magnificent river.

"You will say now, of course, that I dreamed, but not

so. What I saw, what I heard, what I felt, what I thought, had about it nothing of the unmistakable idiosyncrasy of the dream. All was rigorously self-consistent. At first, doubting that I was really awake, I entered into a series of tests which soon convinced me that I really was. Now when one dreams, and in the dream suspects that he dreams, the suspicion never fails to confirm itself, and the sleeper is almost immediately aroused. Thus Novalis errs not in saying that 'we are near waking when we dream that we dream.' Had the vision occurred to me as I describe it, without my suspecting it as a dream, then a dream it might absolutely have been, but, occurring as it did, and suspected and tested as it was, I am forced to class it among other phenomena."

"In this I am not sure that you are wrong," observed Dr. Templeton. "But proceed. You arose and descended into the city."

"I arose," continued Bedloe, regarding the Doctor with an air of profound astonishment, "I arose as you say, and descended into the city. On my way I fell in with an immense populace, crowding through every avenue, all in the same direction, and exhibiting in every action the wildest excitement. Very suddenly, and by an impulse I could not fathom, I became intensely imbued with personal interest in what was going on. I seemed to feel that I had an important part to play, without exactly understanding what it was. Against the crowd which environed me, however, I experienced a deep sentiment of animosity. I shrank from amid them, and, swiftly, by a circuitous path, reached and entered the city. Here all was the wildest tumult and contention. A small party of men, clad in garments half-Indian, half-European, and officered by gentlemen in a uniform partly British, were engaged, at great odds, with the swarming rabble of the allies. I joined the weaker party, arming myself with the weapons of a fallen officer, and fighting I knew not whom with the nervous ferocity of despair. We were soon overpowered by numbers, and driven to seek refuge in a species of kiosk. Here we barricaded ourselves, and, for the present, were secure. From a loophole near the summit of the kiosk, I perceived a vast crowd, in furious agitation, surrounding and assaulting a gay palace that overhung the river. Presently, from an upper window of this palace, there descended an effeminate-looking person, by means of a string made of the turbans of his attendants. A boat was at hand in which he escaped to the opposite bank of the river.

"And now a new object took possession of my soul. I spoke a few hurried but energetic words to my companions, and, having succeeded in gaining over a few of them to my purpose, made a frantic sally from the kiosk. We rushed amid the crowd that surrounded it. They retreated, at first, before us. They rallied, fought madly, and retreated again. In the meantime we were borne far from the kiosk, and became bewildered and entangled among the narrow streets of tall, overhanging houses, into the recesses of which the sun had never shone. The rabble pressed impetuously upon us, harassing us with their spears and overwhelming us with flights of arrows. These latter were very remarkable, and resembled in some respects the writhing creese of the Malay. They were made to imitate the body of a creeping serpent, and were long and black, with a poisoned barb. One of them struck me upon the right temple. I reeled and fell. An instantaneous and dreadful sickness seized me. I struggled, I gasped, I died."

"You will hardly persist *now*," said I, smiling, "in believing that the whole of your adventure was not a dream. You are not prepared to maintain that you are dead?"

When I said these words, I of course expected some lively sally from Bedloe in reply; but to my astonishment, he hesitated, trembled, became fearfully pallid, and remained silent. I looked toward Templeton. He sat erect and rigid in his chair. His teeth chattered, and his eyes were starting from their sockets. "Proceed!" he at length said hoarsely to Bedloe.

"For many minutes," continued the latter, "my sole sentiment, my sole feeling, was that of darkness and nonentity, with the consciousness of death. At length there seemed to pass a violent and sudden shock through my soul, as if of electricity. With it came the sense of elasticity and of light. This latter I felt, not saw. In an instant I seemed to rise from the ground. But I had no bodily—no visible, audible or palpable presence. The crowd had departed. The tumult had ceased. The city was in comparative repose. Beneath me lay my corpse, with the arrow in my temple, the whole head greatly swollen and disfigured. But all these things I felt, not saw. I took interest in nothing. Even the corpse seemed a matter in which I had no concern. Volition I had none, but appeared to be impelled into motion, and flitted buoyantly out of the city, retracing the circuitous path by which I had entered it. When I had attained that point of the ravine in the mountains at which I had encountered the hyena, I again experienced a violent shock; the sense of weight, of volition, of substance, returned. I became my original self, and bent my steps eagerly homeward. But the past had not lost the vividness of the real, and not now, even for an instant, can I compel my understanding to regard it as a dream."

"Nor was it," said Templeton, with an air of deep solemnity. "Yet it would be difficult to say how otherwise it should be termed. Let us suppose only that the soul of the man of today is upon the verge of some stupendous psychic discoveries. Let us content ourselves with this supposition. For the rest I have some explanation to make. Here is a watercolor drawing, which I should have shown you before, but which an accountable sentiment of horror has hitherto prevented me from showing."

We looked at the picture which he presented. I saw nothing in it of an extraordinary character; but its effect upon Bedloe was prodigious. He nearly fainted as he gazed. And yet it was but a miniature portrait—a miraculously accurate one, to be sure—of his own very remarkable features. At least this was my thought as I regarded it.

"You will perceive," said Templeton, "the date of this picture—it is here, scarcely visible, in this corner—1780. In this year was the portrait taken. It is the likeness of a dead friend, a Mr. Oldeb, to whom I became much attached at Calcutta, during the administration of Warren Hastings. I was then only twenty years old. When I first saw you, Mr. Bedloe, at Saratoga, it was the miraculous similarity which existed between yourself and the painting which induced me to accost you, to seek your friendship, and to bring about those arrangements which resulted in my becoming your constant companion. In accomplishing this point, I was urged partly, and perhaps principally, by a regretful memory of the deceased, but also, in part, by an uneasy and not altogether horrorless curiosity respecting yourself.

"In your detail of the vision which presented itself to you amid the hills, you have described, with the minutest accuracy, the Indian city of Benares, upon the holy Ganges River. The riots, the combat and massacre were the actual events of the insurrection of Cheyte Sing, which took place in 1780, when Hastings was put in imminent peril of his life. The man escaping by the string of turbans was Cheyte Sing himself. The party in the kiosk were sepoys and British officers, headed by Hastings. Of this party I was one, and did all I could to prevent the rash and fatal sally of the officer who fell, in the crowded alleys, by the poisoned arrow of a Bengali. That officer was my dearest friend. It was Oldeb. You will perceive by these manuscripts"—here the speaker produced a note-book in which several pages appeared to have been freshly written—"that at the very period in which you fancied these things amid the hills I was engaged in de-tailing them upon paper here at home."

In about a week after this conversation, the following paragraphs appeared in a Charlottesville paper:

"We have the painful duty of announcing the death of Mr. Augustus Bedlo, a gentleman whose amiable man-ners and many virtues have long endeared him to the citi-zens of Charlottesville.

"Mr. B., for some years past, has been subject to neural-gia, which has often threatened to terminate fatally, but this can be regarded only as the indirect cause of his de-cease. The proximate cause was one of special singularity. In an excursion to the Ragged Mountains a few days since, a slight cold and fever were contracted, attended with great determination of blood to the head. To relieve this, Dr. Templeton resorted to topical bleeding. Leeches were applied to the temples. In a fearfully brief period the patient died, when it appeared that in the jar contain-ing the leeches, had been introduced, by accident, one of the venomous vermicular sangsues which are now and then found in the neighboring ponds. This creature fastened itself upon a small artery in the right temple. Its close resemblance to the medicinal leech caused the mistake to be overlooked until too late.

"N. B. The poisonous sangsue of Charlottesville may always be distinguished from the medicinal leech by its blackness, and especially by its writhing or vermicular motions, which very nearly resemble those of a snake."

I was speaking with the editor of the paper in question, upon the topic of this remarkable accident, when it occurred to me to ask how it happened that the name of the deceased had been given as Bedlo.

"I presume," said I, "you have authority for this spelling, but I have always supposed the name to be written with an *e* at the end."

"Authority? No," he replied. "It is a mere typographical error. The name is Bedloe, with an *e* all the world over; I never knew it to be spelt otherwise in my life."

"Then," said I mutteringly, as I turned upon my heel, "then indeed has it come to pass that one truth is stranger than any fiction, for Bedlo without the *e*—what is it but Oldeb reversed? And this man tells me it is a mere typographical error!"

THE OBLONG BOX

SOME years ago, I engaged passage from Charleston, S. C., to the city of New York, in the fine packet ship *Independence*, Captain Hardy. We were to sail on the fifteenth of June, weather permitting. On the fourteenth I went on board to arrange some matters in my stateroom.

I found that we were to have a great many passengers, including a more than usual number of ladies. On the list were several of my acquaintances; and among other names, I was rejoiced to see that of Mr. Cornelius Wyatt, a young artist for whom I entertained feelings of warm friendship. He had been with me a fellow student at C—— University, where we were very much together. He had the usual temperament of genius, and was a compound of misanthropy, sensibility and enthusiasm. To these qualities he united the warmest and truest heart which ever beat in a human bosom.

I observed that his name was carded upon three staterooms; and, upon again referring to the list of passengers,

I found that he had engaged a passage for himself, wife, and his two sisters. The staterooms were sufficiently roomy, and each had two berths, one above the other. These berths, to be sure, were so exceedingly narrow as to be insufficient for more than one person; still, I could not comprehend why there were three staterooms for these four persons. I was at that time, in that moody frame of mind which makes a man abnormally inquisitive about trifles. And I confess, with shame, that I busied myself in a variety of ill-bred and preposterous conjectures about this matter of the supernumerary stateroom. It was no business of mine, to be sure; but with none the less pertinacity did I occupy myself in attempts to solve the enigma.

At last I reached a conclusion which wrought in me great wonder why I had not arrived at it before. "It is a servant, of course," I said. "What a fool I am, not to have thought of so obvious a solution sooner!" And then I again repaired to the list. But here I saw distinctly that no servant was to come with the party, although in fact it had been the original design to bring one—for the words "and servant" had been overscored.

"Oh, extra baggage, to be sure," I now said to myself. "Something he does not wish to be put in the hold—something to be kept under his own eye. Ah, I have it! A painting or so! And this is what he has been bargaining about with Nicolino, the art dealer." This idea satisfied me and I dismissed my curiosity for the nonce.

Wyatt's two sisters I knew very well, and most amiable and clever girls they were. He had newly married, and I had never yet seen his wife. He had often talked about her in my presence, however, and in his usual style of enthusiasm. He described her as of surpassing beauty, wit and accomplishment. I was therefore quite anxious to make her acquaintance.

On the day in which I visited the ship, on the fourteenth, Wyatt and party were also to visit it, or so the captain informed me. I waited on board an hour longer than I had designed in hope of being presented to the bride, but then an apology came. Mrs. Wyatt was a little indisposed, and would decline coming on board until to-morrow, at the hour of sailing.

The morrow having arrived, I was going from my hotel to the wharf, when Captain Hardy met me and said that, owing to circumstances (a stupid but convenient phrase), he rather thought the *Independence* would not sail for a day or two, and that when all was ready, he would send up and let me know. This I thought strange, for there was a stiff southerly breeze; but as "the circumstances" were not forthcoming, even though I pumped for them with much perseverance, I had nothing to do but to return home and digest my impatience at leisure.

I did not receive the expected message from the captain for nearly a week. It came at length, however, and I immediately went on board. The ship was crowded with passengers, and everything was in the bustle attendant upon making sail. Wyatt's party arrived about ten minutes after me. There were the two sisters, the bride and the artist—the latter in one of his customary fits of moody misanthropy. I was too well used to these, however, to pay them any special attention. He did not even introduce me to his wife; this courtesy devolved, perforce, upon his sister Marian, a very sweet and intelligent girl, who, in a few hurried words, made us acquainted.

Mrs. Wyatt had been closely veiled. When she raised her veil in acknowledging my bow, I confess that I was profoundly astonished. I should have been much more so, however, had not long experience advised me not to trust with too implicit a reliance the enthusiastic descriptions of my friend, the artist, when he was indulging in comments upon the loveliness of woman. When beauty was the theme I well knew with what facility he soared into the regions of the purely ideal.

The truth is, I could not help regarding Mrs. Wyatt as a decidedly plain-looking woman. If not positively ugly, she was not, I think, very far from it. She was dressed, however, in exquisite taste—and then I had no doubt that she had captivated my friend's heart by the more enduring graces of the intellect and soul. She said very few words, and passed at once into her stateroom with Wyatt.

My old inquisitiveness now returned. There was no servant; that was a settled point. I looked therefore for the extra baggage. After some delay a cart arrived at the wharf with an oblong pine box, which seemed to be everything that had been expected. Immediately upon its arrival we made sail, and in a short time were safely over the bar and standing out to sea.

The box in question was, as I say, oblong. It was about six feet in length by two and a half in breadth. I observed it attentively and like to be precise. Now this shape was *peculiar,* and no sooner had I seen it than I took credit to myself for the accuracy of my guessing. I had reached the conclusion, it will be remembered, that the extra baggage of my friend the artist would prove to be pictures, or at least a picture, for I knew he had been for several weeks in conference with Nicolino. And now here was a box which, from its shape, could possibly contain nothing in the world but a copy of Leonardo's *The Last Supper.* I had known that a copy of *The Last Supper,* done by Rubini the younger, at Florence, had for some time been in the possession of Nicolino. This point therefore I considered as sufficiently settled. I chuckled excessively when I thought of my acumen. It was the first time I had ever known Wyatt to keep from me any of his artistic secrets, but here he evidently intended to steal a march upon me and smuggle a fine picture to New York under my very nose, expecting me to know nothing of the matter. I resolved to quiz him well, now and hereafter.

One thing, however, annoyed me not a little. The box did not go into the extra stateroom. It was deposited in Wyatt's own, and there, too, it remained, occupying very nearly the whole of the floor, no doubt to the exceeding discomfort of the artist and his wife—this the more especially as the tar or paint with which it was lettered in sprawling capitals emitted a strong, disagreeable, and to my fancy, a peculiarly disgusting odor. On the lid were painted the words,

> *Mrs. Adelaide Curtis,*
> *Albany, New York,*
> *Charge of Cornelius Wyatt, Esq.*
> *This side up. To be handled with care.*

Now, I was aware that Mrs. Adelaide Curtis, of Albany, was the artist's wife's mother—but then I looked upon the whole address as a mystification, intended especially for myself. I made up my mind, of course, that the box and contents would never get further north than the Chambers Street, New York, studio of my misanthropic friend.

For the first three or four days we had fine weather although the wind was dead ahead, having chopped round to the northward immediately upon our losing sight of the coast. The passengers were, consequently, in high spirits and disposed to be social. I must except, however, Wyatt and his sisters, who behaved stiffly, and, I could not help thinking, uncourteously to the rest of the party. Wyatt's conduct I did not so much regard. He was gloomy, even beyond his usual habit—in fact he was morose—but in him I was prepared for eccentricity. For the sisters, however, I could make no excuse. They secluded themselves in their staterooms during the greater part of the passage, and absolutely refused, although I repeatedly urged them, to hold communication with any person on board.

Mrs. Wyatt herself was far more agreeable. That is to say, she was chatty, and to be chatty is no slight recommendation at sea. She became excessively intimate with most of the ladies, and to my profound astonishment, evinced no equivocal disposition to coquet with the men. She amused us all very much. I say "amused"—and scarcely know how to explain myself. The truth is, I soon found Mrs. Wyatt was far oftener laughed *at* than *with.* The gentlemen said little about her, but the ladies, in a little while, pronounced her "a good-hearted thing, rather indifferent-looking, totally uneducated, and decidedly vulgar." The great wonder was, how Wyatt had been entrapped into such a match. Wealth was the general solution. But this I knew to be no solution at all, for Wyatt had told me that she neither brought him a dollar nor had any expectations from any source whatever. He had married, he said, for love, and for love only, and his bride was far more than worthy of his love.

When I thought of these expressions on the part of my friend I confess that I felt indescribably puzzled. Could it be possible that he was taking leave of his senses? What else could I think? He, so refined, so intellectual, so fastidious, with so exquisite a perception of the faulty, and so keen an appreciation of the beautiful! To be sure the lady seemed especially fond of him, particularly so in his absence, when she made herself ridiculous by frequent quotations of what had been said by her "beloved husband, Mr. Wyatt." The word husband seemed forever— to use one of her own delicate expressions—on the tip of her tongue.

In the meantime, it was observed by all on board that he avoided her in the most pointed manner, and for the most part, shut himself up alone in his stateroom, where in fact he might have been said to live altogether, leaving his wife at full liberty to amuse herself as she thought best, in the public society of the main cabin.

My conclusion from what I saw and heard was that the artist, by some unaccountable freak of fate, or perhaps in some fit of enthusiastic and fanciful passion, had been induced to unite himself with a person altogether beneath him, and that the natural result, a deep disgust, had speedily ensued. I pitied him from the bottom of my heart—but could not, for that reason, quite forgive his incommunicativeness in the matter of *The Last Supper*. For this I resolved to have my revenge.

One day he came upon deck, and taking his arm as had been my wont I sauntered with him backward and forward. His gloom, however (which I considered quite natural under the circumstances), seemed entirely unabated. He said little, and that moodily, and with evident effort. I ventured a jest or two, and he made a sickening attempt at a smile. Poor fellow! As I thought of his wife, I wondered that he could have the heart to put on even a semblance of mirth. At last I ventured a home thrust. I determined to commence a series of covert insinuations, or innuendoes, about the oblong box—just to let him perceive, gradually, that I was not altogether the butt or victim of his little bit of pleasant mystification. My first observation was by way of opening a masked battery. I said something about the "peculiar shape of that box" and, as I spoke the words, I smiled knowingly, winked, and touched him gently with my forefinger in the ribs.

The manner in which Wyatt received this harmless pleasantry convinced me at once that he was mad. At first he stared at me as if he found it impossible to comprehend the witticism of my remark; but as its point made its way slowly into his brain, his eyes in the same proportion protruded from their sockets. Then he grew very red, then hideously pale. Then, as if highly amused with what I had insinuated, he began a loud and boisterous laugh which, to my astonishment, he kept up with gradually increasing vigor for ten minutes or more. In conclusion, he fell flat and heavily upon the deck. When I ran to lift him up to all appearance he was *dead*.

I called assistance, and with much difficulty we brought him to himself. Upon reviving he spoke incoherently for some time. At length we bled him and put him to bed. The next morning he was quite recovered, at least as far as his bodily health was concerned. Of his mind I say nothing. I avoided him during the rest of the passage by advice of the captain, who seemed to coincide with me altogether in my views of his insanity, but cautioned me to say nothing about this to any person on board.

Several circumstances occurred immediately after this fit of Wyatt's, which contributed to heighten the curiosity with which I was already possessed. Among other things, this: I had been nervous, drank too much strong green tea, and slept ill at night. In fact, for two nights I could not properly say I slept at all. Now my stateroom opened into the main cabin, or dining room, as did those of all the single men on board. Wyatt's three rooms were in the after-cabin, which was separated from the main one by a slight sliding door, and never locked, even at night. As we were almost constantly on a wind and the breeze was not a little stiff, the ship heeled to leeward very considerably. Whenever her starboard side was to leeward, the sliding door between the cabins slid open and so remained. No one took the trouble to get up and shut it. But my berth was in such a position that when my own stateroom door was open, as well as the sliding door in question (and my own door was *always* open on account of the heat), I could see into the after-cabin quite distinctly, and just at that portion of it, too, where were situated the staterooms of Mr. Wyatt. Well, during two nights (not consecutive) while I lay awake, I clearly saw Mrs. Wyatt, about eleven o'clock each night, steal cautiously from Wyatt's stateroom and enter the extra room, where she remained until daybreak, when she was called by her husband and went back. That they were virtually separated was clear. They had separate apartments—no doubt in contemplation of a more permanent divorce; here after all, I thought, was the mystery of the extra stateroom.

There was another circumstance, too, which interested me very much. During the two wakeful nights in question, and immediately after the disappearance of Mrs. Wyatt into the extra stateroom, I was attracted by certain singular, subdued noises coming from her husband's room. After listening to them for some time, with thoughtful attention, I at length succeeded perfectly in translating their import. They were sounds occasioned by the artist in prying open the oblong box, by means of a chisel and mallet—the latter being apparently muffled or deadened by some soft woolen or cotton substance in which its head was enveloped.

In this manner I fancied I could distinguish the precise moments when he disengaged the lid, when he removed it altogether, and when he deposited it upon the lower berth in his room. This latter point I knew by certain slight taps which the lid made in striking against the wooden edges of the berth as he endeavored to lay it down very gently; there was no room for it on the floor. After this there was a dead stillness, and I heard nothing more upon either occasion until nearly daybreak—unless, perhaps, I may mention a low sobbing or murmuring sound, so suppressed as to be nearly inaudible, if indeed this latter noise was not rather produced by my own imagination. I say it seemed to *resemble* sobbing or sighing, but of course it could not have been either. I rather think it was ringing in my own ears. Mr. Wyatt no doubt, according to custom, was merely giving the rein to one of his hobbies—indulging in one of his fits of artistic enthusiasm. He had opened his oblong box in order to feast his eyes on the pictorial treasure within. There was nothing in this, however, to make him *sob*. I repeat, therefore, that it must have been simply a freak of my own fancy, distempered by good Captain Hardy's green tea. Just before dawn on each of the two nights of which I speak, I distinctly heard Mr. Wyatt replace the lid upon the oblong box and force the nails into their old places by means of the muffled mallet. Having done this, he issued from his stateroom, fully dressed, and proceeded to call Mrs. Wyatt from hers.

We had been at sea seven days, and were now off Cape Hatteras, when there came a tremendously heavy blow from the southwest. We were in a measure prepared for it, however, as the weather had been threatening for some time. Everything was made snug, alow and aloft. As the wind steadily freshened, we lay to at length under spanker and fore-topsail, both double-reefed.

In this trim we rode safely enough for forty-eight hours —the ship proving herself an excellent sea boat in many respects, and shipping no water of any consequence. At the end of this period, however, the gale had freshened into a hurricane, and our aftersail split into ribbons, bringing us so much in the trough of the water that we shipped several prodigious seas, one immediately after the other. By this accident we lost three men overboard with the caboose, and nearly the whole of the larboard bulwarks. Scarcely had we recovered our senses before the fore-topsail went into shreds. Then we got up a storm staysail, and with this did pretty well for some hours, the ship heading the sea much more steadily than before.

The gale still held on, however, and we saw no signs of its abating. The rigging was found to be ill-fitted and greatly strained; and on the third day of the blow, about five in the afternoon, our mizzenmast, in a heavy lurch to windward, went by the board. For an hour or more we tried in vain to get rid of it, on account of the prodigious rolling of the ship. Before we had succeeded, the carpenter came aft and announced four feet of water in the hold. To add to our dilemma, we found that the pumps were choked, and very nearly useless.

All was now confusion and despair—but an effort was made to lighten the ship by throwing overboard as much of her cargo as could be reached, and by cutting away the two masts that remained. This we at last accomplished —but we were still unable to do anything at the pumps, and in the meantime the leak gained on us fast.

At sundown the gale had sensibly diminished in violence, and as the sea went down with it, we still entertained faint hopes of saving ourselves in the boats. At eight p.m., the clouds broke away to windward, and we had the advantage of a full moon—a piece of good fortune which served wonderfully to cheer our drooping spirits.

After incredible labor, we succeeded at length in getting the longboat over the side without material accident, and into this we crowded the whole of the crew and most of the passengers. This party made off immediately, and after undergoing much suffering, finally arrived in safety, at Ocracoke Inlet, on the third day after the wreck.

Fourteen passengers, with the captain, remained on board, resolving to trust their fortunes to the jolly boat at the stern. We lowered it without difficulty, although it was only by a miracle that we prevented it from swamping as it touched the water. It contained, when afloat, the captain and his wife, Mr. Wyatt and party, a Mexican officer, his wife and four children, myself and a valet.

We had no room, of course, for anything except a few necessary instruments, some provisions, and the clothes upon our backs. No one had even thought of attempting to save anything more. What might have been the astonishment of all, then, when having proceeded a few fathoms from the ship, Mr. Wyatt stood up in the stern sheets, and coolly demanded of Captain Hardy that the boat should be put back for the purpose of taking in his oblong box!

"Sit down, Mr. Wyatt," replied the captain, somewhat

sternly. "You will capsize us if you do not sit quite still. Our gunwale is almost in the water now."

"The box!" vociferated Mr. Wyatt, still standing. "The box, I say! Captain Hardy, you cannot, you *will* not refuse me. Its weight will be but a trifle—it is nothing, mere nothing. By the mother who bore you! For the love of Heaven! By your hope of salvation, I *implore* you to put back for the box!"

The captain, for a moment seemed touched by the earnest appeal of the artist, but he regained his stern composure and merely said:

"Mr. Wyatt, you are mad. I cannot listen to you. Sit down, I say, or you will swamp the boat. Stay—hold him! Seize him! He is about to spring overboard! There—I knew it—he is over!"

As the captain said this Mr. Wyatt, in fact, sprang from the boat, and as we were yet in the lee of the wreck, succeeded by almost superhuman exertion, in getting hold of a rope which hung from the forechains. In another moment he was on board, and rushing frantically down into the cabin.

In the meantime, we had been swept astern of the ship, and being quite out of her lee, were at the mercy of the tremendous sea which was still running. We made a determined effort to put back, but our little boat was like a feather in the breath of the tempest. We saw at a glance that the doom of the unfortunate artist was sealed.

As our distance from the wreck rapidly increased, the

madman (for as such only could we regard him) was seen to emerge from the companionway, up which, by dint of strength that appeared gigantic, he dragged the oblong box. While we gazed in the extremity of astonishment, he passed rapidly several turns of a three-inch rope, first around the box, and then around his body. In another instant both body and box were in the sea—disappearing suddenly, at once and forever.

We lingered awhile sadly upon our oars, with our eyes riveted upon the spot. At length we pulled away. The silence remained unbroken for an hour. Finally I hazarded a remark.

"Did you observe, captain, how suddenly they sank? Was not that an exceedingly singular thing? I confess that I entertained some feeble hope of his final deliverance when I saw him lash himself to the box and commit himself to the sea."

"They sank as a matter of course," replied the captain, "and that like a shot. They will soon rise again, however, but not till the salt melts."

"The salt!" I ejaculated.

"Hush!" said the captain, pointing to the wife and sisters of the deceased. "We must talk of these things at some more appropriate time."

We suffered much, and made a narrow escape; but fortune befriended us, as well as our mates in the longboat. We landed more dead than alive after four days of intense distress, upon the beach opposite Roanoke Island. We remained here a week, and at length obtained a passage to New York.

About a month after the loss of the *Independence*, I happened to meet Captain Hardy on Broadway. Our conversation turned, naturally, upon the disaster, and especially upon the sad fate of poor Wyatt. I thus learned the following particulars.

The artist had engaged passage for himself, wife, two sisters, and a servant. His wife was indeed as she had been represented, a most lovely and most accomplished woman. On the morning of the fourteenth of June (the day in which I first visited the ship), the lady suddenly sickened and died. The young husband was frantic with grief—but circumstances imperatively forbade his deferring the voyage to New York. It was necessary to take to her mother the corpse of his adored wife; on the other hand, the universal prejudice which would prevent his doing so openly was well known. Nine-tenths of all the passengers would have abandoned the ship rather than take passage with a dead body.

In this dilemma, Captain Hardy arranged that the corpse, being first partially embalmed, and packed with a large quantity of salt in a box of suitable dimensions, should be conveyed on board as merchandise. Nothing was to be said of the lady's decease; and as it was well understood that Mr. Wyatt had engaged passage for his wife, it became necessary that some person should personate her during the voyage. This the deceased lady's maid was easily prevailed on to do. The extra stateroom, originally engaged for this girl during her mistress's life, was now merely retained. In this stateroom the pseudo-wife slept, of course, every night. In the daytime she performed, to the best of her ability, the part of her mistress —whose person, it had been carefully ascertained, was unknown to any of the passengers on board.

My own mistake arose, naturally enough, through too careless, too inquisitive, and too impulsive a temperament. But of late, it is a rare thing that I sleep soundly at night. There is a countenance which haunts me, turn as I will. There is a hysterical laugh which will forever ring within my ears.

THE CASK OF AMONTILLADO

THE thousand injuries of Fortunato I had borne as I best could; but when he ventured upon insult, I vowed revenge. You, who so well know the nature of my soul, will not suppose, however, that I gave utterance to a threat. At length I would be avenged. This was a point definitely settled, but the very definitiveness with which it was resolved precluded the idea of risk. I must not only punish but punish with impunity. A wrong is unredressed when retribution overtakes its redresser. It is equally unredressed when the avenger fails to make himself felt as such to him who has done the wrong.

It must be understood that neither by word nor deed had I given Fortunato cause to doubt my good will. I continued as was my wont, to smile in his face, and he did not perceive that my smile now was at the thought of his immolation.

He had a weak point, this Fortunato, although in other regards he was a man to be respected and even feared. He prided himself on his connoisseurship in wine. Few Italians now have the true virtuoso spirit. For the most part their enthusiasm has been adapted to suit the time and opportunity. In painting and gemmary Fortunato, like certain of his countrymen, was a quack, but in the matter of old wines he was sincere. In this respect I did not differ from him materially. I was skillful in the vintages myself, and bought largely whenever I could.

It was about dusk one evening during the supreme madness of the carnival season that I encountered my friend. He accosted me with excessive warmth, for he had been drinking heavily. The man wore motley. He had on a tight-fitting parti-striped costume and his head was surmounted by the conical cap and bells. I was so pleased to see him that I thought I should never have done wringing his hand.

I said to him, "My dear Fortunato, you are luckily met. How remarkably well you are looking today. I have just received a pipe of what passes for amontillado, but I have my doubts."

"How's that?" said he. "Amontillado? A pipe? Impossible! And in the middle of the carnival!"

"I have my doubts," I replied. "And I was silly enough to pay the full amontillado price without consulting you in the matter. You were not to be found, and I was fearful of losing a bargain."

"Amontillado!"

"I have my doubts."

"Amontillado!"

"And I must satisfy them."

"Amontillado!"

"As you are engaged, I am on my way to Luchesi. If anyone has a critical turn, it is he. He will tell me——"

"Luchesi cannot tell amontillado from any other sherry."

"And yet some fools will have it that his taste is a match for your own."

"Come, let us go."

"Whither?"

"To your vaults."

"My friend, no. I will not impose upon your good nature. I perceive you have an engagement. Luchesi——"

"I have no engagement. Come."

"My friend, no. It is not the engagement, but the severe cold with which I perceive you are afflicted. The vaults are insufferably damp. They are encrusted with niter."

"Let us go, nevertheless. The cold is merely nothing. Amontillado! You have been imposed upon. And as for Luchesi, he cannot distinguish ordinary sherry from amontillado."

Thus speaking, Fortunato possessed himself of my arm. And putting on a mask of black silk and drawing a *roquelaure* closely about my person, I suffered him to hurry me to my palazzo.

There were no attendants at home; they had absconded to make merry in honor of the time. I had told them that I should not return until the morning, and had given them explicit orders not to stir from the house. These orders were sufficient, I well knew, to insure their immediate disappearance, one and all, as soon as my back was turned.

I took from their sconces two flambeaux, and giving one to Fortunato, bowed him through several suites of rooms to the archway that led into the vaults. I passed down a long and winding staircase, requesting him to be cautious as he followed. We came at length to the foot of the descent, and stood together upon the damp ground of the catacombs of the Montresors.

The gait of my friend was unsteady, and the bells upon his cap jingled as he strode.

"The pipe," he said.

"It is farther on," said I, "but observe the white web-work which gleams from these cavern walls."

He turned towards me, and looked into my eyes with two filmy orbs that distilled the rheum of intoxication.

"Niter?" he asked, at length.

"Niter," I replied. "How long have you had that cough?"

"Ugh! ugh! ugh!—ugh! ugh! ugh!—ugh! ugh! ugh!— ugh! ugh! ugh!—ugh! ugh! ugh!"

My poor friend found it impossible to reply for many minutes.

"It is nothing," he said at last.

"Come," I said with decision. "We will go back. Your health is precious. You are rich, respected, admired, beloved. You are happy, as once I was. You are a man to be missed. For me it is no matter. We will go back. You will be ill and I cannot be responsible. Besides, there is Luchesi——"

"Enough," he said. "The cough is a mere nothing; it will not kill me. I shall not die of a cough."

"True—true," I replied. "And indeed, I had no intention of alarming you unnecessarily. But you should use all proper caution. A draught of this Médoc will defend us from the damps."

Here I knocked off the neck of a bottle which I drew from a long row of its fellows that lay upon the mould.

"Drink," I said, presenting him the wine.

He raised it to his lips with a leer. He paused and nodded to me familiarly, while his bells jingled.

"I drink to the buried that repose around us," he said.

"And I to your long life."

He again took my arm, and we proceeded.

"These vaults," he said, "are extensive."

"The Montresors," I replied, "were a great and numerous family."

"I forget your arms."

"A huge human foot d'or, in a field azure; the foot crushes a serpent rampant whose fangs are imbedded in the heel."

"And the motto?"

"*Nemo me impune lacessit.*"

"Good" he said.

The wine sparkled in his eyes, and the bells jingled. My own fancy grew warm with the Médoc. We had passed along walls of piled skeletons, with casks and puncheons intermingling, into the inmost recesses of the catacombs. I paused again, and this time I made bold to seize Fortunato by an arm above the elbow.

"The niter!" I said. "See, it increases. It hangs like moss upon the vaults. We are below the river's bed. The drops of moisture trickle among the bones. Come, we will go back ere it is too late. Your cough——"

"It is nothing," he said. "Let us go on. But first, another draught of the Médoc."

I broke and handed him a flagon of Graves. He emptied it at a breath. His eyes flashed with a fierce light. He laughed and threw the bottle upwards with a gesticulation I did not understand.

I looked at him in surprise. He repeated the movement, a grotesque one.

"You do not comprehend?" he said.

"Not I," I replied.

"Then you are not of the brotherhood."

"How?"

"You are not of the Masons."

"Yes, yes," I said. "Yes, yes."

"You? Impossible! A Mason?"

"A Mason," I replied.

"A sign," he said, "a sign."

"It is this," I answered, producing from beneath the

folds of my *roquelaure* a trowel.

"You jest," he exclaimed, recoiling a few paces. "But let us proceed to the amontillado."

"Be it so," I said, replacing the tool beneath the cloak and again offering my arm. He leaned upon it heavily. We continued our route in search of the amontillado. We passed through a range of low arches, descended, passed on, and descending again, arrived at a deep crypt, in which the foulness of the air caused our flambeaux rather to glow than flame.

At the most remote end of the crypt there appeared another less spacious crypt. Its walls had been lined with human remains, piled to the vault overhead, in the fashion of the great catacombs of Paris. Three sides of this interior crypt were still ornamented in this manner. From the fourth side the bones had been thrown down, and lay promiscuously upon the earth, forming at one point a mound of some size. Within the wall thus exposed by the displacing of the bones, we perceived a still more interior crypt or recess, in depth about four feet, in width three, in height six or seven. It seemed to have been constructed for no special use, but was merely the interval between two of the colossal supports for the roof of the catacombs. It was backed by one of their circumscribing walls of solid granite.

It was in vain that Fortunato, uplifting his dull torch, endeavored to pry into the depth of the recess. Its termination the feeble light did not enable us to see.

"Proceed," I said. "Herein is the amontillado. As for Luchesi——"

"He is an ignoramus," interrupted my friend, as he stepped unsteadily forward. I followed immediately at his heels. In an instant he had reached the extremity of the niche, and finding his progress arrested by the rock, stood stupidly bewildered. A moment more and I had fettered him to the granite. In its surface were two horizontal iron staples, distant from each other about two feet. From one of these hung a short chain, from the other a padlock. Throwing the links about his waist, it was but the work of a few seconds to secure it. He was too much astounded to resist. Withdrawing the key I stepped back from the recess.

"Pass your hand," I said, "over the wall; you cannot help feeling the niter. Indeed, it is very damp. Once more let me *implore* you to return. No? Then I must positively leave you. But I must first render you all the little attentions in my power."

"The amontillado!" ejaculated my friend, not yet recovered from his astonishment.

"True," I replied. "The amontillado."

As I said these words I busied myself among the pile of bones of which I have before spoken. Throwing them aside, I soon uncovered a quantity of building stone and mortar. With these materials and with the aid of my trowel, I began vigorously to wall up the entrance of the niche.

I had scarcely laid the first tier of the masonry when I discovered that the intoxication of Fortunato had in a great measure worn off. The earliest indication I had of this was a low moaning cry from the depth of the recess. It was not the cry of a drunken man. There was then a long and obstinate silence. I laid the second tier, and the third, and the fourth; and then I heard the furious vibrations of the chain. The noise lasted for several minutes, during which, that I might hearken to it with the more satisfaction, I ceased my labors and sat down upon the bones. When at last the clanking subsided I resumed troweling, and finished without interruption the fifth, the sixth, and the seventh tier. The wall was now nearly upon a level with my breast. I again paused, and holding the flambeaux over the masonwork, threw a few feeble rays upon the figure within.

A succession of loud and shrill screams, bursting suddenly from the throat of the chained form, seemed to thrust me violently back. For a brief moment I hesitated, I trembled. Unsheathing my rapier, I began to grope with it about the recess, but the thought of an instant reassured me. I placed my hand upon the solid fabric of the catacombs, and felt satisfied. I reapproached the wall; I replied to the yells of him who clamored. I re-echoed, I aided, I surpassed them in volume and in strength. I did this, and the clamorer grew still.

It was now midnight, and my task was drawing to a close. I had completed the eighth, the ninth, and the tenth tier. I had finished a portion of the last, the eleventh. There remained but a single stone to be fitted and plastered in. I struggled with its weight. I placed it partially in its destined position. But now there came from out the niche a low laugh that erected the hairs upon my head. It was succeeded by a sad voice, which I had difficulty in recognizing as that of the noble Fortunato. The voice said:

"Ha! ha! ha! He! he! a very good joke, indeed. An excellent jest. We shall have many a rich laugh about it at the palazzo—he! he! he!—over our wine—he! he! he!"

"The amontillado!" I said.

"He! he! he!—he! he! Yes, the amontillado. But is it not getting late? Will not they be awaiting us at the palazzo, the Lady Fortunato and the rest? Let us be gone."

"Yes," I said, "let us be gone."

"For the love of God, Montresor!"

"Yes," I said, "for the love of God!"

But to these words I hearkened in vain for a reply. I grew impatient. I called aloud, "Fortunato!"

No answer.

I called again, "Fortunato!"

No answer still. I thrust a torch through the remaining aperture and let it fall within. There came forth in return only a jingling of the bells. My heart grew sick; it was the dampness of the catacombs that made it so. I hastened to make an end of my labor. I forced the last stone into its position; I plastered it up. Against the new masonry I re-erected the old rampart of bones. For half century no mortal has disturbed them. *In pace requiescat!*

METZENGERSTEIN

INTRODUCTION

Horror and fatality have been stalking abroad in all ages. Why then give a date to the story I have to tell? Let it suffice to say that at the period of which I speak there existed, in the interior of Hungary, a settled although hidden belief in the doctrines of the metempsychosis.[1] Of the doctrines themselves—that is of their falsity or of their probability—I say nothing. I assert, however, that much of our incredulity (as La Bruyère says of all our unhappiness) *"vient de ne pouvoir être seuls."* [2]

But there were some points in the Hungarian superstition which were fast verging to absurdity. They, the Hungarians, differed very essentially from their Eastern authorities. For an example of the former I give the words of an acute and intelligent Parisian: *"L'âme [the soul] ne demeure qu'une seule fois dans un corps sensible; au reste, une cheval, un chien, un homme même, n'est que la ressemblance peu tangible de ces animaux."*

[1] Transmigration of souls.

[2] Mercier, in *"L'An deux mille quatre cents quarante,"* seriously maintains the doctrines of the metempsychosis, and J. D'Israeli says that "no system is so simple and so little repugnant to the understanding." Colonel Ethan Allen, the Green Mountain Boy, is also said to have been a serious metempsychosist.

METZENGERSTEIN

THE families of Berlifitzing and Metzengerstein had been
at variance for centuries. Never before were two houses,
so illustrious, so mutually embittered by hostility so
deadly. The origin of this enmity seems to be found in
the words of an ancient prophecy: "A lofty name shall
have a fearful fall when, as the rider over his horse, the
mortality of Metzengerstein shall triumph over the immortality of Berlifitzing."

To be sure, the words themselves had little or no meaning. But more trivial causes have given rise, and that no
long while ago, to consequences equally eventful. Besides
the estates, which were contiguous, had long exercised a
rival influence in the affairs of a busy government. Moreover, near neighbors are seldom friends; and the inhabitants of the Castle Berlifitzing might look from their lofty
buttresses, into the very windows of the Palace Metzengerstein. Least of all had the more than feudal magnificence, thus discovered, a tendency to allay the irritable
feelings of the less ancient and less wealthy Berlifitzing.
What wonder then, that the words, however silly, of that
prediction should have succeeded in setting and keeping
at variance two families already predisposed to quarrel
by every instigation of hereditary jealousy? The prophecy
seemed to imply, if it implied anything, a final triumph on
the part of the already more powerful house; and was of
course remembered with the more bitter animosity by

the weaker and less influential.

Wilhelm, Count Berlifitzing, although loftily descended, was at the epoch of this narrative an infirm and doting old man, remarkable for nothing but an inordinate and inveterate personal antipathy to the family of his rival, and so passionate a love of horses and of hunting, that neither bodily infirmity, great age, nor mental incapacity prevented his daily participation in the dangers of the chase.

Frederick, Baron Metzengerstein, was on the other hand not yet of age. His father, the Minister G——, died young. His mother, the Lady Mary, followed him quickly. Frederick was at that time in his eighteenth year. In a city eighteen years is no long period; but in a wilderness, in so magnificent a wilderness as that old principality, the pendulum vibrates with deeper meaning.

From some peculiar circumstances attending the administration of his father, the Baron Metzengerstein, after his father's decease, entered immediately upon his vast possessions. Such estates were seldom before held by a nobleman of Hungary. His castles were without number. The chief in point of splendor and extent was the Palace Metzengerstein. The boundary line of his dominions was never clearly defined, but his principal park embraced a circuit of fifty miles.

Upon the succession of a proprietor so young and with a character so well known, to a fortune so unparalleled, little speculation was afloat in regard to his probable course of conduct. And indeed for the space of three days, the behavior of the heir out-Heroded Herod, and fairly surpassed the expectations of his most enthusiastic admirers. Shameful debaucheries, flagrant treacheries, unheard-of atrocities, gave his trembling vassals quickly to understand that no servile submission on their part, no punctilios of conscience on his own, were thenceforward to prove any security against the remorseless fangs of a petty Caligula. On the night of the fourth day, the stables of the Castle Berlifitzing were discovered to be on fire; and the unanimous opinion of the neighborhood added the crime of the incendiary to the already hideous list of the Baron's misdemeanors and enormities.

But during the tumult occasioned by this occurrence, the young nobleman himself sat apparently buried in meditation, in a vast and desolate upper apartment of the family palace of Metzengerstein. The rich although faded tapestry hangings which swung gloomily upon the walls represented the shadowy and majestic forms of a thousand illustrious ancestors. Here, rich ermined priests and pontifical dignitaries, familiarly seated with the autocrat and the sovereign, put a veto on the wishes of a temporal king, or restrained with the fiat of papal supremacy the rebellious scepter of the archenemy. There, the dark, tall statures of the Princes Metzengerstein, their muscular war coursers plunging over the carcasses of fallen foes, startled the steadiest nerves with their vigorous expression; while here, again, the voluptuous and swanlike figures of the dames of days gone by floated away in the mazes of an unreal dance, to the strains of imaginary melody.

But as the Baron listened, or affected to listen, to the gradually increasing uproar in the stables of Berlifitzing— or perhaps pondered upon some more novel, some more decided act of audacity—his eyes were turned unwittingly to the figure of an enormous, and unnaturally colored horse, represented in the tapestry as belonging to a Saracen ancestor of the family of his rival. The horse itself, in the foreground of the design, stood motionless and statue-like—while, farther back, its discomfited rider perished by the dagger of a Metzengerstein.

On Frederick's lip arose a fiendish expression, as he became aware of the direction which his glance had, without his consciousness, assumed. Yet he did not remove it. On the contrary, he could by no means account for the overwhelming anxiety which appeared falling like a pall upon his senses. It was with difficulty that he reconciled his dreamy and incoherent feelings with the certainty of being awake. The longer he gazed the more absorbing became the spell—the more impossible did it appear that he could ever withdraw his glance from the fascination of that tapestry. But the tumult without becoming suddenly more violent, with a compulsory exertion he diverted his attention to the glare of ruddy light thrown full by the flaming stables upon the windows of the apartment.

The action, however, was but momentary; his gaze returned mechanically to the wall. To his extreme horror and astonishment, the head of the gigantic steed had in the meantime altered its position. The neck of the animal before arched, as if in compassion, over the prostrate body of its lord, was now extended at full length, in the direction of the Baron. The eyes, before invisible, now wore an energetic and human expression, while they gleamed with a fiery and unusual red; and the distended lips of the apparently enraged horse left in full view his sepulchral and disgusting teeth.

Stupefied with terror, the young nobleman tottered to the door. As he threw it open, a flash of red light streaming far into the chamber flung his shadow with a clear outline against the quivering tapestry; and he shuddered to perceive that shadow—as he staggered awhile upon the threshold—assuming the exact position, and precisely filling up the contour of the relentless and triumphant murderer of the Saracen Berlifitzing.

To lighten the depression of his spirits, the Baron hurried into the open air. At the principal gate of the palace he encountered three equerries. With much difficulty, and at the imminent peril of their lives, they were restraining the conclusive plunges of a gigantic and fiery-colored horse.

"Whose horse? Where did you get him?" demanded the youth, in a querulous and husky tone, as he became instantly aware that the mysterious steed in the tapestried chamber was the very counterpart of the furious animal before his eyes.

"He is your own property, sire," replied one of the equerries, "at least he is claimed by no other owner. We caught him flying, all smoking and foaming with rage, from the burning stables of the Castle Berlifitzing. Supposing him to have belonged to the old Count's stud of foreign horses, we led him back as an estray. But the grooms there disclaim any title to the creature; which is strange, since he bears evident marks of having made a narrow escape from the flames."

"The letters W. V. B. are also branded very distinctly on his forehead," interrupted a second equerry. "I supposed them of course to be the initials of William Von Berlifitzing—but all at the castle are positive in denying any knowledge of the horse."

"Extremely singular!" said the young Baron, with a musing air, and apparently unconscious of the meaning of his words. "He is as you say, a remarkable horse, a prodigious horse, although as you very justly observe, of a suspicious and untractable character. Let him be mine, however," he added, after a pause. "Perhaps a rider like Frederick of Metzengerstein may tame even the devil from the stables of Berlifitzing."

"You are mistaken, my lord. The horse, as I think we mentioned, is *not* from the stables of the Count. If such had been the case, we know our duty better than to bring him into the presence of a noble of your family."

"True!" observed the Baron, drily. At that instant a page of the bedchamber came from the palace with a heightened color and a precipitate step. He whispered into his master's ear a strange account—of the sudden disappearance of a small portion of the tapestry in an apartment which he designated, entering at the same time, into particulars of a minute and circumstantial character; but from the low tone of voice in which these details communicated, nothing escaped to gratify the excited curiosity of the equerries.

During the conference, the young Frederick seemed agitated by a variety of emotions. He soon, however, recovered his composure, and an expression of determined malignancy settled upon his countenance as he gave peremptory orders that the apartment in question should be immediately locked up, and the key placed in his own possession.

"Have you heard of the unhappy death of the old hunter, Berlifitzing?" said one of his vassals to the Baron as, after the departure of the page, the huge steed which that nobleman had adopted as his own, plunged and curveted, with redoubled fury, down the long avenue which extended from the palace to the stables of Metzengerstein.

"No!" said the Baron, turning abruptly toward the speaker. "Dead, say you?"

"It is indeed true, my lord; and to the noble of your name it is, I imagine, no unwelcome intelligence."

A rapid smile shot over the countenance of the listener. "How died he?"

"In his rash exertions to rescue a favorite portion of the hunting stud, he has himself perished miserably in the flames."

"I-n-d-e-e-d!" ejaculated the Baron, as if slowly and deliberately impressed with the truth of some exciting idea.

"Indeed!" repeated the vassal.

"Shocking!" said the youth calmly, and turned quietly into the palace.

From this date a marked alteration took place in the outward demeanor of the dissolute young Baron Frederick von Metzengerstein. Indeed, his behavior disappointed every expectation, and proved little in accordance with the views of many a maneuvering mamma, while his habits and manner, were if anything even less congenial than formerly with those of the neighboring aristocracy. He was never to be seen beyond the limits of his own domain, and in his wide and socially limitless world, was utterly companionless—unless indeed that unnatural, impetuous and fiery-colored horse which he henceforward continually bestrode, had any mysterious right to the title of his friend.

Numerous invitations on the part of the neighborhood for a long time, however, periodically came in. "Will the Baron honor our festivals with his presence?" "Will the Baron join us in a hunting of the boar?"—"Metzengerstein does not hunt," "Metzengerstein will not attend," were the haughty and laconic answers.

These repeated insults were not to be endured by an

imperious nobility. Such invitations became less cordial, less frequent; in time they ceased altogether. The widow of the unfortunate Count Berlifitzing was even heard to express a hope that the Baron might be at home when he did not wish to be at home, since he disdained the company of his equals; and ride when he did not wish to ride, since he preferred the society of a horse. This, to be sure, was a very silly explosion of hereditary pique; and merely proved how singularly unmeaning our sayings are apt to become, when we desire to be unusually energetic.

The charitable, nevertheless, attributed the alteration in the conduct of the young nobleman to the natural sorrow of a son for the untimely loss of his parents—forgetting, however, his atrocious and reckless behavior during the short period immediately succeeding that bereavement. Some there were, indeed, who suggested a too haughty idea of self-consequence and dignity. Others again (among whom may be mentioned the family physician) did not hesitate in speaking of morbid melancholy, and hereditary ill-health; while dark hints of a more equivocal nature, were current among the multitude.

Indeed, the Baron's perverse attachment to his lately acquired charger—an attachment which seemed to attain new strength from every fresh example of the animal's ferocious and demonlike propensities—at length became, in the eyes of all reasonable men, a hideous and unnatural fervor. In the glare of noon, at the dead hour of night, in sickness or in health, in calm or in tempest, the young

Metzengerstein seemed riveted to the saddle of that colossal horse, whose intractable audacities so well accorded with his own spirit.

There were circumstances, moreover, which, coupled with late events, gave an unearthly and portentous character to the mania of the rider, and to the capabilities of the steed. The space passed over in a single leap had been accurately measured, and was found to exceed, by an astounding difference, the wildest expectations of the most imaginative. The Baron, besides, had no particular name for the animal, although all the rest in his collection were distinguished by characteristic appellations. This horse's stable, too, was appointed at a distance from the rest; and, with regard to grooming and other necessary offices, none but the owner in person had ventured to officiate, or even to enter the enclosure of that horse's particular stall. It was also to be observed that although the three grooms who had caught the steed as he fled from the conflagration at Berlifitzing had succeeded in arresting his course by means of a chain-bridle and noose, yet not one of the three could with any certainty affirm that he had, during that dangerous struggle, or at any period thereafter, actually placed his hand upon the body of the beast. Instances of peculiar intelligence in the demeanor of a noble and high-spirited horse are not to be supposed capable of exciting unreasonable attention, but there were certain circumstances which intruded themselves perforce upon the most skeptical and phlegmatic; and it is said there were times when the animal caused the gaping crowd who stood around to recoil in horror from the deep and impressive meaning of his terrible stamp—times when the young Metzengerstein turned pale and shrunk away from the rapid and searching expression of his human-looking eye.

Among all the retinue of the Baron, however, none were found to doubt the ardor of that extraordinary affection which existed on the part of the young nobleman for the fiery qualities of his horse; at least, none but an insignificant and misshapen little page, whose deformities were in everybody's way, and whose opinions were of the least possible importance. He (if his ideas are worth mentioning at all) had the effrontery to assert that his master never vaulted into the saddle without an unaccountable and almost imperceptible shudder; and that, upon his return from every long-continued and habitual ride, an expression of triumphant malignity distorted every muscle in his countenance.

One tempestuous night, Metzengerstein, awaking from a heavy slumber, descended like a maniac from his chamber, and, mounting in hot haste, bounded away into the mazes of the forest. An occurrence so common attracted no particular attention, but his return was looked for with intense anxiety on the part of his domestics, when, after some hours' absence, the stupendous and magnificent battlements of the Palace Metzengerstein were discovered crackling and rocking to their very foundation, under the influence of a dense and livid mass of ungovernable fire.

As the flames, when first seen, had already made so terrible a progress that all efforts to save any portion of the building were evidently futile, the astonished neighborhood stood idly around in silent if not pathetic wonder. But a new and fearful object soon riveted the attention of the multitude, and proved how much more intense is the excitement wrought in the feelings of a crowd by the contemplation of human agony, than that brought about by the most appalling spectacles of inanimate matter.

Up the long avenue of aged oaks which led from the forest to the main entrance of the Palace Metzengerstein, a steed, bearing an unbonneted and disordered rider, was seen leaping with an impetuosity which outstripped the very demon of the tempest.

The career of the horseman was indisputably, on his own part, uncontrollable. The agony of his countenance, the convulsive struggle of his frame gave evidence of superhuman exertion; but no sound, save a solitary shriek, escaped from his lacerated lips, which were bitten through and through in the intensity of terror. One instant, and the clattering of hoofs resounded sharply and shrilly above the roaring of the flames and the shrieking of the winds—another and, clearing at a single plunge the gateway and the moat, the steed bounded far up the tottering staircases of the palace, and, with its rider, disappeared amid the whirlwind of chaotic fire.

The fury of the tempest immediately died away, and a dead calm sullenly succeeded. A white flame still enveloped the building like a shroud, and, streaming far away into the quiet atmosphere, shot forth a glare of preternatural light; while a cloud of smoke settled heavily over the battlements in the distinct colossal figure of— *a horse.*

THE PIT AND THE PENDULUM

I WAS sick—sick unto death with that long agony; and when they at length unbound me, and I was permitted to sit, I felt that my senses were leaving me. The sentence— the dread sentence of death—was the last distinct accentuation which reached my ears. After that the sound of the inquisitorial voices seemed merged in one dreamy indeterminate hum. It conveyed to my soul the idea of a revolving wheel—perhaps from its association in fancy with the burr of a mill wheel. This only for a brief period, for presently I heard no more. Yet, for a while, I saw— but with how terrible an exaggeration I saw the lips of the black-robed judges. They appeared to me white, whiter than the sheet upon which I trace these words, and thin even to grotesqueness—thin with the intensity of their expression of firmness, of immovable resolution, of stern contempt for human suffering. I saw the decrees of what to me was fate were still issuing from those lips. I saw them writhe with a deadly locution. I saw them fashion the syllables of my name, and I shuddered because no sound succeeded. I saw, too, for a few moments of delirious horror, the soft and nearly imperceptible waving of the sable draperies which enwrapped the walls of the apartment. And then my vision fell upon the seven tall candles upon the table. At first they wore the aspect of charity, and seemed white slender angels who would save me; but then, all at once, there came a most deadly nausea over my spirit, and I felt every fiber in my frame thrill with shock, while the angel forms became meaningless specters, with heads of flame, and I saw that from them there would be no help. And then there stole into my fancy, like a rich musical note, the thought of what sweet rest there must be in the grave. The thought came gently and stealthily, and it seemed long before it attained full appreciation; but just as my spirit came at length properly to feel and entertain it, the figures of the judges vanished, as if magically, from before me; the tall candles sank into nothingness; their flames went out utterly; the blackness of darkness supervened; all sensations appeared swallowed up in a mad rushing descent as of the soul into Hades. Then all was silence, and stillness, and night.

I had swooned; but I will not say that all consciousness was lost. What remained I will not attempt to define, or even to describe; yet all was not lost. In the deepest slumber—no! In delirium—no! In a swoon—no! In death—no! Even in the grave all *is not* lost. Else there is no immortality for man. Arousing from the most profound of slum-

bers, we break the gossamer web of *some* dream. Yet in
a second afterward (so frail may that web have been) we
remember not that we have dreamed. In the return to life
from the swoon there are two stages: first, the returning
mental or spiritual sense, and then the sense of physical
existence. It seems probable that if on reaching the second stage we could recall the impressions of the *first,* we
should find these impressions eloquent in memories of the
gulf beyond. And that gulf is—what? How shall we distinguish its shadows from those of the tomb? But if the
impressions of what I have termed the first stage, are not
recalled at will, yet do they not come unbidden after a
long interval while we marvel whence they come?

He who has never swooned is not he who finds strange
palaces and familiar faces in the glowing embers. It is not
he who beholds floating in mid-air sad visions that the
many may not view. *He* ponders not over the perfume of
some novel flower, nor does he grow bewildered with the
meaning of some musical cadence which has never before arrested his attention.

Amid frequent and thoughtful endeavors to remember,
amid earnest struggles to regather some token of the state
of seeming nothingness into which my soul then lapsed,
there have been brief, very brief periods when I conjured
up remembrances which my lucid reason assures me
could refer only to that condition of seeming unconsciousness. These shadows of memory tell, indistinctly, of tall
figures that lifted and bore me in silence down—down—

still down—till a hideous dizziness oppressed me at the mere idea of the interminableness of the descent. They tell also of a vague horror at my heart, on account of that heart's unnatural stillness. Then comes a sense of sudden motionlessness throughout all things; as if those who bore me (a ghastly train!) had outrun, in their descent, the limits of the limitless, and paused from the wearisomeness of their toil. After this I call to mind flatness and dampness; and then all is *madness*—the madness of a memory which busies itself among forbidden things.

Very suddenly there came back to my soul motion and sound—the tumultuous motion of my heart, and in my ears the sound of its beating. Then a pause in which all is blank. Then again sound, and motion, and touch—a tingling sensation pervaded my frame. Then the mere consciousness of existence, without thought, a condition which lasted a long time. Then very suddenly, *thought* and shuddering terror, and an earnest endeavor to comprehend my true state. Then a strong desire to lapse into insensibility. Then a rushing revival of soul and a successful effort to move. And now a full memory of the trial, of the judges, of the sable draperies, of the sentence, of the sickness of the swoon. Then entire forgetfulness of all that followed; of all that a later day and much earnestness of endeavor have enabled me vaguely to recall.

So far, I had not opened my eyes. I felt that I lay upon my back, unbound. I reached out my hand; it fell heavily upon something damp and hard. There I let it remain for many minutes, while I strove to imagine where and *what* I could be. I longed, yet dared not, to employ my vision. I dreaded the first glance at objects around me. It was not that I feared to look upon things horrible, but that I grew aghast lest there should be *nothing* to see.

At length, with a wild desperation at heart, I unclosed my eyes. My worst thoughts, then, were confirmed. The blackness of eternal night encompassed me. I struggled for breath. The intensity of the darkness seemed to oppress and stifle me. The atmosphere was intolerably close. I still lay quietly, and made effort to exercise my reason. I brought to mind the Inquisitorial proceedings, and attempted from that point to deduce my real condition. The sentence had been passed; and it appeared to me that a very long interval of time had since elapsed. Yet I did not really suppose myself actually dead. Such a supposition, notwithstanding what we read in fiction, is inconsistent with real existence—but where and in what state was I? The condemned to death, I knew, usually perished at the *auto-da-fè,* and one had been held on the very night of the day of my trial. Had I been remanded to my dungeon, to await the next sacrifice, which would not take place for many months? This I at once saw could not be. Victims had been in immediate demand. Moreover, my dungeon as well as all the condemned cells at Toledo had stone floors, and light was not altogether excluded.

A fearful idea now suddenly drove the blood in torrents upon my heart, and for a brief period I once more relapsed into insensibility. Upon recovering, I at once started to my feet, trembling convulsively in every fiber. I thrust my arms wildly above and around me in all directions. I felt nothing; yet dreaded to move a step, lest I should be impeded by the walls of a *tomb*. Perspiration burst from every pore, and stood in cold big beads upon my forehead. The agony of suspense grew at length intolerable, and I cautiously moved forward, with my arms extended, and my eyes straining from their sockets in the hope of catching some faint ray of light. I proceeded for many paces; but still all was blackness and vacancy. I breathed more freely. It seemed evident that mine was not, at least, the most hideous of fates.

And now, as I still continued to step cautiously onward, there came thronging upon my recollection a thousand vague rumors of the horrors of Toledo. Of the dungeons there had been strange things narrated—fables I had always deeemed them—but yet strange and too ghastly to repeat, save in a whisper. Was I left to perish of starvation in this subterranean world of darkness; or what fate, perhaps even more fearful, awaited me? That the result would be death, and a death of more than customary bitterness, I knew too well from the character of my judges, to doubt. The mode and the hour were all that occupied or distracted me.

My outstretched hands at length encountered some solid obstruction. It was a wall, seemingly of stone masonry—very smooth, slimy and cold. I followed it along, stepping with all the careful distrust with which certain antique narratives had inspired me. This process, however, afforded me no means of determining the dimensions of my dungeon; I might make its circuit and return to the point whence I set out without being aware of the fact, so perfectly uniform seemed the wall. I therefore sought the knife which had been in my pocket when led into the Inquisitorial chamber, but it was gone; my clothes had been exchanged for a wrapper of coarse serge. I had thought of forcing the blade into some minute crevice of the masonry, to identify my point of departure. The difficulty, nevertheless, was trivial, although it seemed, to my disordered fancy, at first insuperable. I tore a part of the hem from the robe and placed the fragment at full length, at right angles to the wall. In groping my way around the prison, I could not fail to encounter this rag upon completing the circuit. So, at least, I thought; but I had not counted upon the extent of the dungeon, or upon my own weakness. The ground was moist and slippery. I staggered onward for some time, when I stumbled and fell. I remained prostrate with fatigue, and sleep soon overtook me as I lay.

Upon awaking, and stretching forth an arm, I found beside me a loaf and a pitcher with water. I was too much exhausted to reflect upon this circumstance, but ate and drank with avidity. Shortly afterward, I resumed my tour around the prison, and with much toil came at last upon the fragment of the serge. Up to the period when I fell, I had counted fifty-two paces. Resuming my walk, I counted forty-eight more when I came again to the rag. There were in all, then, a hundred paces; and, allowing two paces to a yard, I estimated the dungeon to be fifty yards in circuit. I had met, however, with many angles in the wall, and thus I could form no guess at the *shape* of the vault, for vault I could not help supposing it to be.

I had little object—certainly no hope—in these researches, but a vague curiosity prompted me to continue them. Quitting the wall, I resolved to cross the area of the enclosure. At first I proceeded with extreme caution, for the floor, although seemingly of solid material, was treacherous with slime. At length, however, I took courage, and did not hesitate to step firmly—endeavoring to cross in as direct a line as possible. I had advanced some ten or twelve paces in this manner, when the remnant of the torn hem of my robe became entangled between my legs. I stepped on it, and fell violently on my face.

In the confusion attending my fall, I did not immediately apprehend a startling circumstance, which a few seconds afterward arrested my attention, while I still lay prostrate. It was this: my chin rested upon the floor of the prison, but my lips, and the upper portion of my head, although seemingly at a less elevation than the chin, touched nothing. At the same time, my forehead seemed bathed in a clammy vapor, and the peculiar smell of decayed fungus arose to my nostrils. I put forward my arm, and shuddered to find that I had fallen at the very brink of a circular pit, whose extent, of course, I had no means of ascertaining at the moment. Groping about the masonry just below the margin, I succeeded in dislodging a small fragment, and let it fall into the abyss. For many seconds I harkened to its reverberations as it dashed against the sides of the chasm in its descent; at length, there was a sullen plunge into water, succeeded by loud echoes. At the same moment, there came a sound resembling the quick opening and as rapid closing of a door overhead, while a faint gleam of light flashed suddenly through the gloom, and as suddenly faded away.

I saw clearly the doom which had been prepared for me, and congratulated myself upon the timely accident by which I had escaped. Another step before my fall, and the world had seen me no more. And the death just avoided was of that very character which I had regarded as fabulous and frivolous in the tales respecting the Inquisition. To the victims of its tyranny, there was the choice of death with its direct physical agonies, or death with its most hideous moral horrors. I had been reserved for the latter. By long suffering, my nerves had been unstrung until I trembled at the sound of my own voice. I had become in every respect a fitting subject for the species of torture which awaited me.

Shaking in every limb, I groped my way back to the wall—resolving there to perish rather than risk the terrors of the wells, which my imagination now pictured in various positions about the dungeon. In other conditions of mind, I might have had courage to end my misery at once, by a plunge into one of these abysses, but now I was the veriest of cowards. Neither could I forget what I had read of these pits—that the *sudden* extinction of life formed no part of their most horrible plan.

Agitation of spirit kept me awake for many long hours, but at length I again slumbered. Upon arousing, I found by my side, as before, a loaf and a pitcher of water. A burning thirst consumed me, and I emptied the vessel at a draught. It must have been drugged, for scarcely had I drunk before I became irresistibly drowsy. A deep sleep fell upon me—a sleep like that of death. How long it lasted, of course I know not; but when, once again, I unclosed my eyes, the objects around me were visible. By a wild, sulphurous luster, the origin of which I could not at first determine, I was enabled to see the extent and aspect of the prison.

In its size I had been greatly mistaken. The whole circuit of its walls did not exceed twenty-five yards. For some minutes this fact occasioned me a world of vain trouble; vain indeed—for what could be of less importance, under the terrible circumstances which environed me, than the mere dimensions of my dungeon? But my soul took a wild interest in trifles, and I busied myself in endeavors to account for the error I had committed in my measurement. The truth at length flashed upon me. In my first attempt at exploration I had counted fifty-two paces up to the time when I fell. I must then have been within a pace or two of the fragment of serge, had, in fact, nearly performed the circuit of the vault. I then slept; upon awaking I must have turned upon my steps, thus supposing the circuit nearly double what it actually was. My confusion of mind prevented me from observing that I had begun my tour with the wall to the left, and ended with the wall to the right.

I had been deceived, too, in respect to the shape of the enclosure. In feeling my way I had found many angles, and thus deduced an idea of great irregularity, so potent is the effect of total darkness upon one arousing from lethargy or sleep! The angles were simply those of a few slight depressions, or niches at odd intervals. The general shape of the prison was square. What I had taken for masonry seemed now to be iron, or some other metal, in huge plates, whose sutures or joints occasioned the depression. The entire surface of this metallic enclosure was rudely daubed in all the hideous and repulsive devices to which the charnel superstition of the monks has given rise. The figures of fiends in aspects of menace, with skeleton forms, and other more really fearful images, overspread and disfigured the walls. I observed that the outlines of these monstrosities were sufficiently distinct, but that the colors seemed faded and blurred, as if from the effects of a damp atmosphere. I now noticed the floor, too, which was of stone. In the center yawned the circular pit from whose jaws I had escaped, but it was the only one in the dungeon.

All this I saw indistinctly and by much effort, for my personal condition had been greatly changed during slumber. I now lay upon my back, and at full length, on a species of low framework of wood. To this I was securely bound by a long strap resembling a surcingle. It passed in many convolutions about my limbs and body, leaving at liberty only my head and my left arm to such extent that, by dint of much exertion, I could supply myself with food from an earthen dish which lay by my side on the floor. I saw, to my horror, that the pitcher had been removed. I say to my horror—for I was consumed with intolerable thirst. This thirst it appeared to be the design of my persecutors to stimulate—for the food in the dish was meat pungently seasoned.

Looking upward, I surveyed the ceiling of my prison. It was some thirty or forty feet overhead, and constructed much as the side walls. In one of its panels a very singular figure riveted my whole attention. It was the painted figure of Time as he is commonly represented, save that in lieu of a scythe he held what, at a casual glance, I had taken to be the pictured image of a huge *pendulum*, such as we see on antique clocks. There was something, however, in the appearance of this machine which caused me to regard it more attentively. While I gazed directly upward at it—its position was immediately over my own— I fancied that I saw it in motion. In an instant afterward the fancy was confirmed. Its sweep was brief, and of course slow. I watched it for some minutes somewhat in fear, but more in wonder. Wearied at length with observing its dull movement, I turned my eyes upon the other objects in the cell.

A slight noise attracted my notice, and, looking to the floor, I saw several enormous rats traversing it. They had issued from the well which lay just within view to my right. Even then, while I gazed, they came up in troops, hurriedly, with ravenous eyes, allured by the scent of the meat. From this it required much effort and attention to scare them away.

It might have been half an hour, perhaps even an hour (for I could take but imperfect note of time), before I again cast my eyes upward. What I then saw confounded and amazed me. The sweep of the pendulum had increased in extent by nearly a yard. As a natural consequence its velocity was also much greater. But what mainly disturbed me was the idea that it had perceptibly *descended*. I now observed—with what horror it is needless to say—that its neither extremity was formed of a crescent of glittering steel, about a foot in length from horn to horn; the horns upward, and the under edge evidently as keen as that of a razor. Like a razor, also, it seemed massive and heavy, tapering from the edge into a solid and broad structure above. It was appended to a weighty rod of brass, and the whole *hissed* as it swung through the air.

I could no longer doubt the doom prepared for me by monkish ingenuity in torture. My cognizance of the pit had become known to the Inquisitorial agents—the pit, whose horrors had been destined for so bold a recusant as myself—the pit, typical of hell and regarded by rumor as the Ultima Thule of all their punishments. The plunge into this pit I had avoided by the merest of accidents, and I knew that surprise, or entrapment into torment, formed an important portion of all the grotestquerie of these dungeon deaths. Having failed to fall, it was no part of the demon plan to hurl me into the abyss; thus, there being no alternative, a different and a milder destruction awaited me. Milder! I half-smiled in my agony as I thought of such application of such a term.

What boots it to tell of the long, long hours of horror more than mortal, during which I counted the rushing oscillations of the steel! Inch by inch—line by line—with a descent only appreciable at intervals that seemed ages —down and still down it came! Days passed—it might have been that many days passed—ere it swept so closely over me as to fan me with its acrid breath. The odor of the sharp steel forced itself into my nostrils. I prayed—I wearied heaven with my prayer for its more speedy descent. I grew frantically mad, and struggled to force myself upward against the sweep of the fearful scimitar. And then I fell suddenly calm, and lay smiling at the glittering death, as a child at some rare bauble.

There was another interval of utter insensibility. It was brief, for upon again lapsing into life, I saw that there had been no perceptible descent in the pendulum. But it might have been long—for I knew there were demons who took note of my swoon, and who could have arrested the vibration at pleasure. I felt very—oh inexpressibly, sick and weak, as if through long inanition. Even amid the agonies of that period my human nature craved food. With painful effort I outstretched my left arm as far as my bonds permitted, and took possession of the small remnant which had been spared me by the rats. As I put a portion of it within my lips, there rushed to my mind a half-formed thought of joy—of hope. Yet what business had *I* with hope? It was, as I say, a half-formed thought —man has many such, which are never completed. I felt that it was of joy, of hope; but I felt also that it had perished in its formation. In vain I struggled to regain it. Long suffering had nearly annihilated all my ordinary powers of mind. I was an imbecile, an idiot.

The vibration of the pendulum was at right angles to my length. I saw that the crescent was designed to cross the region of the heart. It would fray the serge of my robe; it would return and repeat its operations, again and again. Notwithstanding its terrifically wide sweep (some thirty feet or more), and the hissing vigor of its descent, still, the fraying of my robe would be all that, for several minutes, it would accomplish. And at this thought I paused. I dared not go further than this reflection. I dwelt upon it with a pertinacity of attention—as if, in so dwelling, I could arrest *here* the descent of the steel. I forced myself to ponder upon the sound of the crescent as it should pass across the garment, upon the peculiar thrilling sensation which the friction of cloth produces on the nerves. I pondered over all this frivolity until my teeth were on edge.

Down—steadily down it crept. I took a frenzied pleasure in contrasting its downward with its lateral velocity. To the right, to the left, far and wide—with the shriek of a damned spirit! Toward my heart, it crept, with the stealthy pace of the tiger! I alternately laughed and howled, as the one or the other idea grew predominant.

Down, certainly, relentlessly down! It vibrated within three inches of my bosom! I struggled violently, furiously, to free my left arm, which was free only from the elbow to the hand. With great effort, I could reach with this hand from the platter beside me to my mouth, but no further. Could I have broken the fastenings *above* the elbow, I would have seized and attempted to arrest the pendulum. I might as well have attempted to arrest an avalanche!

Down—still unceasingly, still inevitably down! I gasped and struggled at each vibration. I shrunk convulsively at its every sweep. My eyes followed its outward or upward whirls with the eagerness of unmeaning despair, then I closed them spasmodically at the descent; yet death would have been a relief, oh, how unspeakable! Still I quivered in every nerve to think how slight a sinking of the machinery would precipitate that keen, listening axe upon my bosom. It was *hope* that prompted the nerve to quiver, the frame to shrink. It was hope, the hope that triumphs on the rack—that whispers to the death-condemned even in a dungeon of the Inquisition.

I saw that some ten or twelve vibrations would bring the steel in actual contact with my robe, and with this observation there suddenly came over my spirit all the keen, collected calmness of despair. For the first time during many hours, or perhaps days, I *thought*. It now occurred to me, that the bandage, or surcingle which enveloped me was *unique*. I was tied by no other cord. The first stroke of the razorlike crescent athwart any portion of the band would so detach it that it might be unwound from my person by means of my left hand. But how fearful, in that case, the proximity of the steel! The result of the slightest struggle, how deadly! Was it likely, moreover, that the minions of the tortured had not foreseen and provided for this possibility? Was it probable that the bandage crossed my bosom in the track of the pendulum? Dreading to find my faint and, as it seemed, my last hope frustrated, I so far elevated my head as to obtain a distinct view of my breast. The surcingle enveloped my limbs and body close in all directions—*save in the path of the destroying crescent.*

Scarcely had I dropped my head back into its original position, when there flashed upon my mind what I cannot better describe than as the unformed half of that idea of deliverance to which I have previously alluded, and of which a moiety had floated indeterminately through my brain when I raised food to my burning lips. The whole thought was now present—feeble, scarcely sane, scarcely definite—but still entire. I proceeded at once, with the nervous energy of despair, to attempt its execution.

For many hours the immediate vicinity of the low framework upon which I lay had been literally swarming with rats. They were wild, bold, ravenous—their red eyes glaring upon me as if they waited but for motionlessness on my part to make me their prey. "To what food," I thought, "have they been accustomed in the well?"

They had devoured, in spite of all my efforts to prevent them, all but a small remnant of the contents of the dish. I had fallen into an habitual seesaw or wave of the hand about the platter; and at length the unconscious uniformity of the movement deprived it of effect. In their voracity, the vermin frequently fastened their sharp fangs in my fingers. With the particles of the oily and spicy viand which now remained, I thoroughly rubbed the bandage wherever I could reach it then, slowly raising my hand from the floor, I lay breathlessly still.

At first, the ravenous animals were startled and terrified at the change—at the cessation of movement. They shrank alarmedly back; many sought the well. But this was only for a moment. I had not counted in vain upon their voracity. Observing that I remained without motion, one or two of the boldest leaped upon the framework, and smelt of the surcingle. This seemed the signal for a general rush. Forth from the well they hurried in fresh troops. They clung to the wood—they overran it, and leaped in hundreds upon my person. The measured movement of the pendulum disturbed them not at all. Avoiding its strokes, they busied themselves with the anointed bandage. They pressed—they swarmed upon me in ever accumulating heaps. They writhed upon my throat; their cold lips sought my own; I was half-stifled by their thronging pressure. Disgust for which the world has no name swelled my bosom and chilled, with a heavy clamminess, my heart. Yet one minute, and I felt that the struggle would be over. Plainly I perceived the loosening of the bandage. I knew that in more than one place it must be already severed. With a more than human resolution I lay still.

Nor had I erred in my calculations—nor had I endured in vain. I at length felt that I was free. The surcingle hung in ribands from my body. But the stroke of the pendulum already pressed upon my bosom. It had divided the serge of the robe. It had cut through the linen beneath. Twice again it swung, and a sharp sense of pain shot through every nerve. But the moment of escape had arrived. At a wave of my hand my deliverers hurried tumultuously away. With a steady movement—cautious, sidelong, shrinking and slow—I slid from the embrace of the bandage and beyond the reach of the scimitar. For the moment, at least, I was free.

Free—and in the grasp of the Inquisition! I had scarcely stepped from my wooden bed of horror upon the stone floor of the prison, when the motion of the hellish machine ceased, and I beheld it drawn up, by some invisible force, through the ceiling. This was a lesson which I took desperately to heart. My every motion was undoubtedly watched. Free! I had but escaped death in one form of agony, to be delivered unto worse than death in some other. With that thought I looked nervously around at the barriers of iron that hemmed me in. Something unusual, some change which at first I could not appreciate distinctly had obviously taken place in the apartment. For many minutes of a dreamy and trembling abstraction, I busied myself in vain, unconnected conjecture. During this period, I became aware, for the first time, of the origin of the sulphurous light which illumined the cell. It proceeded from a fissure about half an inch in width, extending entirely around the prison at the base of the walls, which it thus appeared, were completely separated from the floor. I endeavored, but of course in vain, to look through the aperture.

As I arose from the attempt, the mystery of the alteration in the chamber broke at once upon my understanding. I have observed that, although the outlines of the figures upon the walls were sufficiently distinct, yet the colors seemed blurred and indefinite. These colors had now assumed, and were momentarily assuming, a startling and most intense brilliancy, that gave to the spectral and fiendish portraitures an aspect that might have thrilled even firmer nerves than my own. Demon eyes, of a wild and ghastly vivacity, glared upon me in a thousand directions, where none had been visible before, and gleamed with the lurid luster of a fire that I could not force my imagination to regard as unreal.

Unreal! Even while I breathed there came to my nostrils the breath of the vapor of heated iron! A suffocating odor pervaded the prison. A deeper glow settled each moment in the eyes that glared at my agonies. A richer tint of crimson diffused itself over the pictured horrors of blood. I panted, I gasped for breath! There could be no doubt of the design of my tormentors—oh most unrelenting, most demoniac of men! I shrank from the glowing metal to the center of the cell. Amid the thought of the fiery destruction that impended, the idea of the coolness of the well came over my soul like balm. I rushed to its deadly brink. I threw my straining vision below. The glare from the enkindled roof illumined its inmost recesses. Yet for a wild moment did my spirit refuse to comprehend the meaning of what I saw. At length it forced, it wrestled its way into my soul; it burned itself in upon my shuddering reason. Oh, for a voice to speak!—oh, horror! Oh! Any horror but this! With a shriek I rushed from the margin, and buried my face in my hands, weeping bitterly.

The heat rapidly increased, and once again I looked up, shuddering as with a fit of the ague. There had been a second change in the cell—and now the change was obviously in the *form*. As before, it was in vain that I at first endeavored to appreciate or understand what was taking place. But not long was I left in doubt. The Inquisitorial vengeance had been hurried by my twofold escape, and there was to be no more dallying with the king of terrors. The room had been square. I saw that two of its iron angles were now acute—two, consequently, obtuse. The fearful difference quickly increased with a low rumbling or moaning sound. In an instant the apartment had shifted its form into that of a lozenge. But the alteration stopped not here; I neither hoped nor desired it to stop. I could have clasped the red walls to my bosom as a garment of eternal peace. "Death," I said, "any death but that of the pit!" Fool! might I not have known that *into the pit* it was the object of the burning iron to urge me? Could I resist its glow? or if even that, could I withstand its pressure? And now, flatter and flatter grew the lozenge, with a rapidity that left me no time for contemplation. Its center, and of course its greatest width, came just over the yawning gulf. I shrank back—but the walls, closing, pressed me resistlessly onward. At length for my seared and writhing body there was no longer an inch of foothold on the firm floor of the prison. I struggled no more, but the agony of my soul found vent in one loud, long and final scream of despair. I felt that I tottered upon the brink—I averted my eyes—

There was a discordant hum of human voices! There was a loud blast as of many trumpets! There was a harsh grating as of a thousand thunders! The fiery walls rushed back! An outstretched arm caught my own as I fell, fainting, into the abyss. It was that of General Lasalle. The French army had entered Toledo. The Inquisition was in the hands of its enemies.

A DESCENT INTO THE MAELSTRÖM

We had now reached the summit of the loftiest crag. For some minutes the old man seemed too much exhausted to speak.

"Not long ago," he said at length, "I could have guided you on this route as well as the youngest of my sons. But about three years past something happened to me that has never before happened to mortal man—or, at least, that no man ever survived to tell of—and the six hours of deadly terror which I then endured have broken me body and soul. You suppose me a very old man—but I am not. It took less than a single day to change these hairs from jet-black to white, to weaken my limbs, and to unstring my nerves so that I tremble at the least exertion and am frightened at a shadow. Do you know I can scarcely look over this little cliff without getting giddy?"

The "little cliff," upon whose edge he had so carelessly thrown himself down to rest that the weightier portion of his body hung over it, while he was kept from falling only by the tenure of his elbow on its extreme and slippery edge—this "little cliff" arose, a sheer unobstructed precipice of black shining rock, some fifteen or sixteen hundred feet from the world of crags beneath us. Nothing would have tempted me to be within half a dozen yards of its brink. In truth so deeply was I excited by the perilous position of my companion, that I fell at full length upon the ground, clung to the shrubs around me, and dared not even glance upward at the sky—while I struggled in vain to divest myself of the idea that the very foundations of the mountain were in danger from the fury of the winds. It was long before I could reason myself into sufficient courage to sit up and look out into the distance.

"You must get over these fancies," said the guide. "For I have brought you here that you might have the best possible view of the scene of that event I mentioned—and to tell you the whole story with the spot just under your eye.

"We are now," he continued, in that particularizing manner which distinguished him, "close upon the Norwegian coast, in the sixty-eight degree of latitude in the great province of Nordland, and in the dreary district of Lofoten. The mountain upon whose top we sit is Helseggen the Cloudy. Now raise yourself up a little higher—hold on to the grass if you feel giddy, so— and look out beyond the belt of vapor beneath us into the sea."

I looked dizzily, and beheld a wide expanse of ocean, whose waters wore so inky a hue as to bring at once to my mind the Nubian geographer's account of the *Mare Tenebrarum*. A panorama more deplorably desolate no human imagination can conceive. To the right and left, as far as the eye could reach, there lay outstretched, like ramparts of the world, lines of horridly black and beetling cliff, whose character of gloom was but the more forcibly illustrated by the surf which reared high up against it its white and ghastly crest, howling and shrieking forever. Just opposite the promontory upon whose apex we were placed, and at a distance of some five or six miles out at sea, there was visible a small, bleak-looking island, or, more properly, its *position* was *discernible* through the wilderness of surge in which it was enveloped. About two miles nearer the land rose another island of smaller size, hideously craggy and barren, and encompassed at various intervals by a cluster of dark rocks.

The appearance of the ocean, in the space between the more distant island and the shore, had something very unusual about it. Although at the time so strong a gale was blowing landward that a brig in the remote distance lay to under a double-reefed trysail, and constantly plunged her whole hull out of sight, still there was here nothing like a regular swell, but only a short, quick, angry cross-dashing of water in every direction—in the teeth of the wind as well. Except in the immediate vicinity of the rocks, there was little foam.

"The island in the distance," resumed the old man, "is called by the Norwegians Vagoy. The one midway is Moskenaes. Do you hear anything? Do you see any change in the water?"

We had now been about ten minutes upon the top of Helseggen, to which we had ascended from the interior of Lofoten, so that we had caught no glimpse of the sea until it had burst upon us from the summit. As the old man spoke, I became aware of a loud and gradually increasing sound, like the moaning of a vast herd of buffaloes upon an American prairie. At the same moment I perceived that what seamen term the *chopping* character of the ocean beneath us was rapidly changing into a current which set to the eastward. Even while I gazed, this current acquired a monstrous velocity. Each moment added to its speed, to its headlong impetuosity. In five minutes the whole sea as far as Vagoy was lashed into ungovernable fury. But it was between Moskenaes and the coast that the main uproar held its sway. Here the vast bed of the waters, seamed and scarred into a thousand conflicting channels, burst suddenly into frenzied convulsion—heaving, boiling, hissing, gyrating in gigantic and innumerable vortices, and all whirling and plunging on to the eastward with a rapidity which water never elsewhere assumes, except in precipitous descents.

In a few minutes there came over the scene another

radical alteration. The general surface grew somewhat more smooth, and the whirlpools one by one disappeared, while prodigious streaks of foam became apparent where none had been seen before. These streaks, at length, spreading out to a great distance and entering into combination, took unto themselves the gyratory motion of the subsided vortices, and seemed to form the germ of another, more vast vortex. Suddenly, very suddenly, this assumed a distinct and definite existence, in a circle of more than a mile in diameter. The edge of the whirl was represented by a broad belt of gleaming spray. But no particle of this slipped into the mouth of the terrific funnel whose interior, as far as the eye could fathom it, was a smooth, shining and jet-black wall of water, inclined to the horizon at an angle of some forty-five degrees, speeding dizzily round and round with a swaying and sweltering motion, and sending forth to the winds an apalling voice, half shriek, half roar, such as not even the mighty cataract of Niagara ever lifts up in its agony to heaven.

The mountain trembled to its very base, and the cliff rocked. I threw myself upon my face, and clung to the scant herbage in an excess of nervous agitation.

"This," said I at length to the old man—"*can* be nothing else than the great whirlpool of the Maelström."

"So it is sometimes termed," said he. "We Norwegians call it the Moskenström, from the island of Moskenaes in the midway."

The ordinary account of this vortex had by no means prepared me for what I saw. That of Jonas Ramus, which is perhaps the most circumstantial of any, cannot impart the faintest conception either of the magnificence, or of the horror of the scene—or of the wild bewildering sense of the *novel* which confounds the beholder. I am not sure from what point of view the writer in question surveyed it, nor at what time, but it could neither have been from the summit of Helseggen nor during a storm. There are some passages of his description, nevertheless, which may be quoted for their details, although their effect is exceedingly feeble in conveying an impression of the spectacle.

"Between the other Lofoten islands and Moskenaes," he says, "the depth of the water is between thirty-six and forty fathoms; but on the other side, toward Vagoy, this depth decreases so that a vessel runs the risk of splitting on the rocks. And this sometimes happens even in the calmest weather. When it is flood, the stream runs up the country between the other Lofoten islands and Moskenaes with a boisterous rapidity; but the roar of its impetuous ebb to the sea is scarcely equaled by the loudest and most dreadful cataract, the noise being heard several leagues off. And its vortices or pits are of such an extent and depth that, if a ship comes within its attraction, it is inevitably absorbed and carried down to the bottom and there beat to pieces against the rocks; when the water relaxes, the fragments thereof are thrown up again. But these intervals of tranquility are only at the turn of the ebb and flood, and in calm weather, and last but a quarter of an hour; its violence gradually returns. When the stream is most boisterous, and its fury heightened by a storm, it is dangerous to come within a Norway mile of it. Boats, yachts, and ships have been carried away by not guarding against it before they were carried within its reach. It likewise happens frequently that whales come too near the stream and are overpowered by its violence; and then it is impossible to describe their howling and bellowings in their fruitless struggles to disengage themselves. Once a bear, attempting to swim from the other Lofoten islands to Moskenaes was caught by the stream and borne down, while he roared so as to be heard on shore. Large stocks of firs and pine trees, after being absorbed by the current, rise again broken and torn to such a degree they look as if bristles grew upon them. This plainly shows the bottom to consist of craggy rocks, among which they are whirled to and fro. This stream is regulated by the flux of the sea, it being constantly high and low water every six hours. In the year 1645, early in the morning of Sexagesima Sunday, it raged with such noise and impetuosity that the stones fell from the houses along the coast."

In regard to the depth of the water, I could not see how this could have been ascertained at all in the immediate vicinity of the vortex. The "forty fathoms" must have reference only to portions of the channel close upon the shore either of Moskenaes or the other Lofoten islands. The depth in the center of the Moskenström must be unmeasurably greater; and no better proof of this fact is necessary than can be obtained from even the sidelong glance into the abyss of the whirl which may be had from the highest crag of Helseggen. Looking down from this pinnacle upon the howling Phlegethon below, I could not help smiling at the simplicity with which the honest Jonas Ramus recorded, as a matter difficult of belief, the anecdotes of the whales and the bears, for it appeared to me a self-evident thing that the largest ships in existence, coming within the influence of that deadly attraction, could resist it as little as a feather in a hurricane, and must disappear at once.

The attempts to account for the phenomenon—some of which, I remember, seemed to me sufficiently plausible in perusal—now wore a very different and unsatisfactory aspect. The idea generally received is that this, as well as three smaller vortices among the Ferroe Islands, "have no other cause than the collision of waves rising and falling at high and low tide against a ridge of rocks and shelves, which confines the water so that it precipitates itself like a cataract; and thus the higher the flood rises, the deeper must the fall be, and the natural result of all is a whirlpool or vortex, the prodigious suction of which is sufficiently known by lesser experiments."—These are the words of the *Encyclopædia Britannica*.

Kircher and others imagine that in the center of the channel of the Maelström is an abyss penetrating the globe, and issuing in some very remote part—the Gulf of Bothnia being somewhat decidedly named in one instance. This opinion, idle in itself, was the one to which, as I gazed, my imagination most readily assented; upon mentioning it to the guide, I was rather surprised to hear him say that although it was the view almost universally entertained of the subject by the Norwegians, it nevertheless was not his own. As to the "confinement of water" theory, he confessed his inability to comprehend it; and here I agreed with him—for, however, conclusive on paper, it becomes altogether unintelligible, and even absurd, amid the thunder of the abyss.

"You have had a good look at the whirl now," said the old man, "and if you creep round this crag, so as to get in its lee and deaden the roar of the water, I will tell you a story that will convince you I ought to know something of the Moskenström."

I placed myself as desired, and he proceeded.

"Myself and my two brothers once owned a schooner-rigged smack of about seventy tons with which we were in the habit of fishing among the islands beyond Moskenaes, nearly to Vagoy. In all violent eddies at sea there is good fishing at proper opportunities, if one has only the courage to attempt it. But among the whole of the Lofoten coastmen, we three were the only ones who made a regular business of going out to the islands, as I tell you. The usual grounds are a great way lower down to the southward. There, fish can be got at all hours without much risk, and therefore these places are preferred. The choice spots over here among the rocks, however, not only yield the finest variety, but in far greater abundance; so that we often got in a single day what the more timid of the craft could not scrape together in a week. In fact, we made it a matter of desperate speculation—the risk of life standing instead of labor, and courage answering for capital.

"We kept the smack in a cove about five miles higher up the coast than this; and it was our practice, in fine weather, to take advantage of the fifteen minutes' slack to push across the main channel of the Moskenström, far above the pool, and then drop anchor somewhere near the smaller islands, where the eddies are not so violent as elsewhere. Here we used to remain until nearly time for slack water again, when we weighed and made for home. We never set out upon this expedition without a steady side wind for going and coming, one that we felt sure would not fail us before our return, and we seldom made a miscalculation upon this point. Twice during six years we were forced to stay all night at anchor on account of a dead calm, which is a rare thing indeed just about here; and once we had to remain on the grounds nearly a week, starving to death, owing to a gale which blew up shortly after our arrival and made the channel too boisterous to be thought of. Upon this occasion we should have been driven out to sea in spite of everything (for the whirlpools threw us round and round so violently, that at length we fouled our anchor and dragged it) if it had not been that we drifted into one of the innumerable cross currents—here today and gone tomorrow—which drove us under the lee of Flimen where, by good luck, we brought up.

"I could not tell you the twentieth part of the difficulties we encountered 'on the ground'—it is a bad spot to be in, even in good weather—but we made shift always to run the gauntlet of the Moskenström itself without accident, although at times my heart has been in my mouth when we happened to be a minute or so behind or before the slack. The wind sometimes was not as strong as we thought it at starting, and then we made rather less headway than we could wish, while the current rendered the smack unmanageable. My eldest brother had a son eighteen years old, and I had two stout boys of my own. These would have been of great assistance at such times, in using the sweeps as well as afterward in fishing, but somehow although we ran the risk ourselves, we had not the heart to let the young ones get into the danger—for, after all is said and done, it *was* a horrible danger, and that is the truth.

"It is now within a few days of three years since what I am going to tell you occurred. It was on the tenth of July, 18—,a day which the people of this part of the world will never forget, for it was one in which blew the most terrible hurricane that ever came out of the heavens. And yet all the morning and indeed until late in the afternoon there was a gentle and steady breeze from the southwest, while the sun shone so brightly that the oldest seaman among us could not have foreseen what was to follow.

"The three of us, my two brothers and myself, had crossed over to the islands about two p.m., and soon nearly loaded the smack with fine fish which, we all remarked, were more plentiful that day than we had ever known them. It was just seven, by my watch, when we weighed and started for home, in order to make the worst of the Ström at slack water, which we knew would be at eight.

"We set out with a fresh wind on our starboard quarter, and for some time spanked along at a great rate, never dreaming of danger for indeed we saw not the slightest reason to apprehend it. All at once we were taken aback by a breeze from over Helseggen. This was most unusual—something that had never happened to us before—and I began to feel a little uneasy without exactly knowing why. We put the boat on the wind, but could make no headway at all for the eddies, and I was upon the point of proposing to return to our point of anchorage when, looking astern, we saw the whole horizon covered with a singular copper-colored cloud that rose with the most amazing velocity.

"In the meantime the breeze that had headed us off

fell away and we were dead becalmed, drifting about in every direction. This state of things, however, did not last long enough to give us time to think about it. In less than a minute the storm was upon us. In less than two the sky was entirely overcast, and what with this and the driving spray, it became suddenly so dark that we could not see each other in the smack.

"Such a hurricane as then blew would be folly to attempt to describe. The oldest seaman in Norway never experienced anything like it. We had let our sails go by the run before it took us. But at the first puff both our masts went by the board as if they had been sawed off, the mainmast taking with it my youngest brother, who had lashed himself to it for safety.

"Our boat was the lightest feather of a thing that ever sat upon water. It had a complete flush deck with only a small hatch near the bow, and this hatch it had always been our custom to batten down when about to cross the Ström, by way of precaution against the chopping seas. But for this circumstance we should have foundered at once, for we lay entirely buried for some moments. How my elder brother escaped destruction I cannot say, for I never had an opportunity of ascertaining. For my part, as soon as I had left the foresail run I threw myself flat on deck with my feet against the narrow gunwale of the bow, and with my hands grasping a ringbolt near the foot of the foremost. It was mere instinct that prompted me to do this, and it was undoubtedly the best thing I could have done, for I was too much flurried to think.

"For some moments we were completely deluged, as I say, and all this time I held my breath and clung to the bolt. When I could stand it no longer I raised myself upon my knees, still keeping hold with my hands, and thus got my head clear. Presently our little boat gave herself a shake, just as a dog does in coming out of the water, and thus rid herself in some measure of the seas. I was now trying to get the better of the stupor that had come over me and to collect my senses so as to see what was to be done when I felt somebody grasp my arm. It was my elder brother, and my heart leaped for joy, for I had been sure that he was overboard. But the next moment all this joy was turned into horror, for he put his mouth close to my ear and screamed out the word '*Moskenström!*'

"No one ever will know what my feelings were at that moment. I shook from head to foot as if I had had the most violent fit of the ague. I knew what he meant by that one word well enough—I knew what he wished to make me understand. With the wind that now drove us on, we were bound for the whirl of the Ström and nothing could save us!

"You perceive that in crossing the Ström channel we always went a long way up above the whirl even in the calmest weather, and then had to wait and watch carefully for the slack. But now we were driving right upon the pool itself, and in such a hurricane as this! To be sure, I thought, we shall get there just about the slack. There is some little hope in that. But in the next moment I cursed myself for being so great a fool as to dream of hope at all. I knew very well that we were doomed had we been ten times a ninety-gun ship.

"By this time the first fury of the tempest had spent itself, or perhaps we did not feel it so much as we scudded before it. But at all events the seas which at first had been kept down by the wind and lay flat and frothing, now got up into absolute mountains. A singular change, too, had come over the heavens. Around in every direction it was still as black as pitch, but nearly overhead there burst out, all at once, a circular rift of clear sky—as clear as I ever saw, and of a deep bright blue—and through it there blazed forth the full moon with a luster that I never before knew her to wear. She lit up everything about us with the greatest distinctness —but oh God, what a scene it was to light up!

"I now made one or two attempts to speak to my brother. But in some manner which I could not understand, the din had so increased that I could not make him hear a single word although I screamed at the top of my voice in his ear. Presently he shook his head, looking as pale as death, and held up one of his fingers as if to say 'listen!'

"At first I could not make out what he meant, but soon a hideous thought flashed upon me. I dragged my watch from its fob. It was not going. I glanced at its face by the moonlight, and then burst into tears as I flung it far away into the ocean. *It had run down at seven o'clock!* We were behind the time of the slack, and the whirl of the Ström was in full fury!

"When a boat is well-built, properly trimmed, and not deep laden, the waves in a strong gale when she is going large, seem always to slip from beneath her—it appears strange to a landsman—and this is what is called 'riding,' in sea phrase.

"Well, so far we were riding the swells very cleverly. But presently a gigantic sea happened to take us right under the counter and bore us with it as it rose—up— up—as if into the sky. I would not have believed that any wave could rise so high. And then down we came with a sweep, a slide, and a plunge that made me feel sick and dizzy, as if I were falling from some lofty mountaintop in a dream. But while we were up I had thrown a quick glance around—and that one glance was all-sufficient. I saw our exact position in an instant. The Moskenström whirlpool was about a quarter of a mile dead ahead—but no more like the everyday Moskenström than the whirl as you now see it is like a millrace. If I had not known where we were and what we had to expect, I should not have recognized the place at all. As it was I involuntarily closed my eyes in horror. The lids clenched themselves together as if in a spasm.

"It could not have been more than two minutes afterwards until we suddenly felt the waves subside, and were enveloped in foam. The boat made a sharp half turn to larboard, and then shot off in its new direction like a thunderbolt. At the same moment the roaring noise of the water was completely drowned in a kind of shrill shriek—such a sound as you might imagine given out by the water pipes of many thousand steam vessels letting off their steam all together. We were now in the belt of surf that always surrounds the whirl; and I thought of course that another moment would plunge us into the abyss, down which we could only see indistinctly on account of the amazing velocity with which we were borne along. The boat did not seem to sink into the water at all, but to skim like an air bubble upon the surface of the surge. Her starboard side was next the whirl, and on the larboard arose the world of ocean we had left. It stood like a huge writhing wall between us and the horizon.

"It may appear strange, but now when we were in the very jaws of the gulf I felt more composed than when we were only approaching it. Having made up my mind to hope no more I got rid of a great deal of that terror which unmanned me at first. I suppose it was despair that strung my nerves.

"It may look like boasting, but what I tell you is the truth. I began to reflect how magnificent a thing it was to die in such a manner, and how foolish it was in me to think of so paltry a consideration as my own individual life, in view of so wonderful a manifestation of God's power. I do believe that I blushed with shame when this idea crossed my mind. After a little while I became possessed with the keenest curiosity about the whirl itself. I positively felt a *wish* to explore its depths, even at the sacrifice I was going to make; and my principal grief was that I should never be able to tell my old companions on shore about the mysteries I should see. These, no doubt, were singular fancies to occupy a man's mind in such extremity—and I have often thought since that the revolutions of the boat around the pool might have rendered me a little lightheaded.

"There was another circumstance which tended to restore my self-possession; and this was the cessation of the wind, which could not reach us in our present situation. For as you saw for yourself, the belt of the surf is considerably lower than the general bed of the ocean, and this latter now towered above us, a high, black, mountainous ridge. If you have never been at sea in a heavy gale you can form no idea of the confusion of mind occasioned by the wind and spray together. They blind, deafen, and strangle you, and take away all power of action or reflection. But we were now in a great measure rid of these annoyances, just as death-condemned felons in prison are allowed petty indulgences forbidden them while their doom is yet uncertain.

"How often we made the circuit of the belt it is impossible to say. We careered round and round for perhaps an hour, flying rather than floating, getting gradually more and more into the middle of the surge, and then nearer and nearer to its horrible inner edge. All this time I had never let go of the ringbolt. My brother was at the stern holding on to a small empty water cask which had been securely lashed under the coop of the counter. It was the only thing on deck that had not been swept overboard when the gale first took us. As we approached the brink of the pit he let go his hold upon this and made for the ring from which, in the agony of his terror, he endeavored to force my hands as it was not large enough to afford us both a secure grasp. I never felt deeper grief than when I saw him attempt this act, although I knew he was a madman when he did it—a raving maniac through sheer fright. I did not care however to contest the point with him. I knew it could make no difference whether either of us held on at all. So I let him have the bolt and went astern to the cask. This there was no great difficulty in doing, for the smack flew round steadily enough and upon an even keel, only swaying to and fro with the immense sweeps and swelters of the whirl. Scarcely had I secured myself in my new position, when we gave a wild lurch to starboard and rushed headlong into the abyss. I muttered a hurried prayer to God and thought all was over.

"As I felt the sickening sweep of the descent, I had instinctively tightened my hold upon the barrel, and closed my eyes. For some seconds I dared not open them. I expected instant destruction and wondered that I was not already in my death struggles with the water. But moment after moment elapsed. I still lived. The sense of falling had ceased, and the motion of the vessel seemed much as it had been before while in the belt of foam, with the exception that she now lay more along. I took courage and looked once again upon the scene.

"Never shall I forget the sensation of awe, horror and admiration with which I gazed about me. The boat appeared to be hanging, as if by magic, midway down upon the interior surface of a funnel vast in circumference, prodigious in depth, and whose perfectly smooth sides might have been mistaken for ebony but for the bewildering rapidity with which they spun around, and for the gleaming and ghastly radiance they shot forth. The rays of the full moon from that circular rift amid the clouds, which I have already described, streamed in a flood of golden glory along the black walls and far away down into the inmost recesses of the abyss.

"At first I was too much confused to observe anything accurately. The general burst of terrific grandeur was all that I beheld. When I recovered myself a little, however, my gaze fell instinctively downward. In this direction I was able to obtain an unobstructed view, from the manner in which the smack hung on the inclined surface of the pool. She was quite upon an even keel—that is to say, her deck lay in a plane parallel with that of the water. But this latter sloped at an angle of more than forty-five degrees so that we seemed to be lying upon our beam-ends. I could not help observing nevertheless that I had scarcely more difficulty in maintaining my hold and footing in this situation than if we had been upon a dead level. This, I suppose, was owing to the speed at which we revolved.

"The rays of the moon seemed to search the very bottom of the profound gulf. But still I could make out nothing distinctly on account of a thick mist in which everything there was enveloped, and over which there hung a magnificent rainbow, like that narrow and tottering bridge which Mussulmans say is the only pathway between time and eternity. This mist, or spray, was no doubt occasioned by the clashing of the great walls of the funnel as they all met together at the bottom—but the yell that went up to the heavens from out of that mist I dare not attempt to describe.

"Our first slide into the abyss itself from the belt of foam above had carried us to a great distance down the slope, but our further descent was by no means proportionate. Round and round we swept, not with any uniform movement, but in dizzying swings and jerks that sent us sometimes only a few hundred yards, sometimes nearly the complete circuit of the whirl. Our progress downward at each revolution was slow but very perceptible.

"Looking about me upon the wide waste of liquid

ebony on which we were thus borne, I perceived that
our boat was not the only object in the embrace of the
whirl. Both above and below us were visible fragments
of vessels, large masses of building timber and trunks
of trees, with many smaller articles, such as pieces of
furniture, broken boxes, barrels and staves. I have
already described the unnatural curiosity which had
taken the place of my original terrors. It appeared to
grow upon me as I drew nearer and nearer to my
dreadful doom. I now began to watch with a strange
interest the numerous things that floated in our company. I must have been delirious, for I even sought
amusement in speculating upon the relative velocities
of their several descents toward the foam below. 'This
fir tree,' I found myself at one time saying, 'will certainly be the next thing that takes the awful plunge
and disappears'—and then I was disappointed to find
that the wreck of a Dutch merchant ship overtook it
and went down before. At length after making several
guesses of this nature and being deceived in all, this
fact—the fact of my invariable miscalculation—set me
upon a train of reflection that made my limbs again
tremble and my heart beat heavily once more.

"It was not a new terror that thus affected me but
the dawn of something more exciting—*hope*. This hope
arose partly from memory and partly from present observation. I called to mind the great variety of buoyant
matter that strewed the coast of Lofoten, having been

absorbed and then thrown forth by the Moskenström. By far the greater number of the articles were shattered in the most extraordinary way, so chafed and roughened as to have the appearance of being stuck full of splinters —but then I distinctly recollected that there were some of them which were not disfigured at all.

Now I could not account for this difference except by supposing that the roughened fragments were the only ones which had been completely absorbed; that the others had entered the whirl at so late a period of the tide, or from some reason had descended so slowly after entering, that they did not reach the bottom before the turn of the flood or the ebb, as the case might be. I conceived it possible in either instance that they might thus be whirled up again to the level of the ocean without undergoing the fate of those which had been drawn in earlier, or absorbed more rapidly. I also made three important observations. The first was that as a general rule the larger the bodies were, the more rapid their descent. The second was that between two masses of equal extent, the one spherical and the other of any other shape, the superiority in speed of descent was with the sphere—and the third, that between two masses of equal size, the one cylindrical and the other of any other shape, the cylinder was absorbed the more slowly. Since my escape I have had several conversations on this subject with an old schoolmaster of the district; it was from him that I learned the use of the words 'cylinder' and 'sphere.' He explained to me, although I have forgotten the explanation, how what I observed was, in fact, the natural consequence of the forms of the floating fragments; and he showed me how it happened that a cylinder swimming in a vortex offered more resistance to its suction and was drawn in with greater difficulty than an equally bulky body, of any form whatever.[1]

"There was one startling circumstance which went a great way in enforcing these observations, and in rendering me anxious to turn them to account. This was that at every revolution we passed something like a barrel, or else the spar or the mast of a vessel, and many of these things which had been on our level when I first opened my eyes upon the wonders of the whirlpool, were now high up above us, and seemed to have moved but little from their original station.

"I no longer hesitated what to do. I resolved to lash myself securely to the water cask to which I now held, to cut it loose from the counter, and to throw myself with it into the water. I attracted my brother's attention by signs, pointed to the floating barrels that came near us, and did everything in my power to make him understand what I was about to do. I thought at length that he comprehended my design. But whether this was the case or not, he shook his head despairingly and refused to move from his station by the ringbolt. It was impos-

[1] See Archimedes, "*De Incidentibus in Fluido*," lib. 2.

sible to reach him. The emergency admitted of no delay. And so with a bitter struggle I resigned him to his fate, fastened myself to the cask by means of the lashings which secured it to the counter, and precipitated myself with it into the sea without another moment's hesitation.

"The result was precisely what I hoped it might be. As it is myself who now tell you this tale, you can see that I *did* escape. And as you are already in possession of the mode in which this escape was effected and must therefore anticipate all that I have to say further, I will bring my story quickly to conclusion. It might have been an hour or thereabouts after my quitting the smack when, having descended to a vast distance beneath me, the boat made three or four wild gyrations in rapid succession and bearing my loved brother with it plunged headlong, at once and forever, into the chaos of foam below. The barrel to which I was attached sunk very little further than half the distance between the bottom of the gulf and the spot at which I leaped overboard, before a great change took place in the character of the whirlpool. The slope of the sides of the vast funnel became moment by moment less and less steep. The gyrations of the whirl grew gradually less and less violent. By degrees the froth and the rainbow disappeared, and the bottom of the gulf seemed slowly to uprise. The sky was clear, the winds had gone down, and the full moon was setting radiantly in the west when I found myself on the surface of the ocean in full view of the shores of

Lofoten, and above the spot where the pool of the Moskenström had been. It was the hour of the slack, but the sea still heaved in mountainous waves from the effects of the hurricane. I was borne violently into the channel of the Ström, and in a few minutes was hurried down the coast into the 'grounds' of the fishermen. A boat picked me up, exhausted from fatigue, and now that the danger was removed, speechless from the memory of its horror. Those who drew me on board were my old mates and daily companions, but they knew me no more than they would have known a traveler from the spirit land. My hair, which had been raven black the day before, was as white as you see it now. They say too that the whole expression of my countenance had changed. I told them my story; they did not believe it. I now tell it to *you*, and I can scarcely expect you to put more faith in it than did the merry fishermen of Lofoten."

THE PREMATURE BURIAL

THERE are certain themes of which the interest is all-absorbing, but which are too entirely horrible for the purposes of legitimate fiction. These the mere romanticist must eschew, if he does not wish to offend or to disgust. They are with propriety handled only when the severity and majesty of truth sanctify and sustain them. We thrill, for example, with the most intense of "pleasurable pain" over the accounts of Napoleon's crossing of the Berezina, of the earthquake at Lisbon, of the plague at London, of the Massacre of St. Bartholomew, or of the stifling of one hundred and twenty-three prisoners in the Black Hole of Calcutta. But in these accounts it is the fact, it is the reality, it is the history which excites. As inventions we should regard them with simple abhorrence.

I have mentioned some few of the more prominent and august calamities on record; but in these it is extent no less than the character of the calamity, which so vividly impresses the fancy. I need not remind the reader that, from the long and weird catalogue of human miseries, I might have selected many individual instances more replete with essential suffering than any of these vast generalities of disaster. The true wretchedness, indeed the ultimate woe, is particular, not diffuse. That the ghastly extremes of agony are endured by man the unit and never by man the mass—for this let us thank a merciful God!

To be buried while alive is beyond question the most terrific of these extremes which has ever fallen to the lot of mere mortality. That it has frequently, very frequently, so fallen will scarcely be denied by those who think. The boundaries which divide life from death are at best shadowy and vague. Who will say where the one ends and where the other begins? We know that there are diseases in which occur total cessations of all the apparent functions of vitality, and yet these cessations are merely suspensions, properly so called. They are only temporary pauses in the incomprehensible mechanism. A certain period elapses, and some unseen mysterious principle again sets in motion the magic pinions and the wizard wheels. The silver cord was not forever loosed, nor the golden bowl irreparably broken. But where, meantime, was the soul?

Apart, however, from the inevitable conclusion, a priori that such causes must produce such effects (the well-known occurrence of such cases of suspended animation must naturally give rise now and then to premature interments)—apart from this consideration, we have the direct testimony of medical and ordinary experience to prove that a vast number of such interments have actually taken place. I might refer at once, if necessary, to a hundred well-authenticated instances. One of very remarkable character, and of which the circumstances may be fresh in the memory of some of my readers, occurred not very long ago in the neighboring city of Baltimore, where it occasioned a painful, intense and widely extended excitement. It concerned the wife of one of its most respectable citizens, a lawyer of eminence and a member of Congress. She was seized with a sudden and unaccountable illness which completely baffled the skill of her physicians. After much suffering she died, or was supposed to die. No one suspected, or indeed, had reason to suspect, that she was not actually dead. She presented all the ordinary appearances of death. The face assumed the usual pinched and sunken outline. The lips were of the usual marble pallor. The eyes were lusterless. There was no warmth. Pulsation had ceased. For three days the body was preserved unburied, during which it had acquired a stony rigidity. The funeral was hastened on account of the rapid advance of, supposedly, decomposition.

The lady was deposited in her family vault, which for three subsequent years was undisturbed. At the expiration of this term it was opened for the reception of a sarcophagus. But alas! how fearful a shock awaited the husband, who, personally, threw open the door! As its portals swung outwardly back, some white-appareled object fell rattling within his arms. It was the skeleton of his wife in her yet unmoulded shroud.

A careful investigation rendered it evident that she had revived within two days after her entombment; that her struggles within the coffin had caused it to fall from a ledge, or shelf, to the floor, where it was so broken as to permit her escape. A lamp, which had been accidentally left full of oil within the tomb, was found empty; it might have been exhausted, however, by evaporation. On the uppermost of the steps which led down into the dread chamber was a large fragment of the coffin, with which it seemed that she had endeavored to arrest attention by striking the iron door. While thus occupied, she probably swooned or possibly died, through sheer terror; and in falling her shroud became entangled in some ironwork which projected interiorly. Thus she remained, and thus she rotted, erect.

In the year 1810, a case of living inhumation happened in France, attended with circumstances which go far to warrant the assertion that truth is indeed stranger than fiction. The heroine of the story was a Mademoiselle Victorine Lafourcade, a young girl of illustrious family, of wealth, and of great personal beauty. Among her numerous suitors was Julien Bossuet, a poor *littérateur*, or journalist, of Paris. His talents and general amiability had recommended him to the notice of the heiress, by whom he seems to have been truly beloved; but her pride of birth decided her finally to reject him and to wed a Monsieur Renelle, a banker and a diplomatist of some eminence. After marriage, however, this gentleman neglected and perhaps even more positively ill-treated her. Having passed with him some wretched years she died, or at least her condition so closely resembled death as to deceive everyone who saw her. She was buried, not in a vault but in an ordinary grave in the village of her nativity.

Filled with despair and still inflamed by the memory of a profound attachment, the lover journeys from the capital to the remote province in which the village lies, with the romantic purpose of disinterring the corpse, and possessing himself of its luxuriant tresses. He reaches the grave. At midnight he unearths the coffin, opens it, and is in the act of detaching the hair when he is arrested by the unclosing of the beloved eyes.

In fact the lady had been buried alive. Vitality had not altogether departed, and she was aroused by the caresses of her lover from the lethargy which had been mistaken for death. He bore her frantically to his lodgings in the village. He employed certain powerful restoratives suggested by no little medical learning. In fine, she revived. She recognized her preserver. She remained with him until, by slow degrees, she fully recovered her original health. Her woman's heart was not adamant, and this last lesson of love sufficed to soften it. She bestowed it upon Bossuet. She returned no more to her husband, but concealing from him her resurrection, fled with her lover to America.

Twenty years afterward, the two returned to France, in the persuasion that time had so greatly altered the lady's appearance that her friends would be unable to recognize her. They were mistaken however; for at the first meeting, Monsieur Renelle did actually recognize and make claim to his wife. This claim she resisted, and a judicial tribunal sustained her in her resistance, deciding that the peculiar circumstances, with the long lapse of years, had extinguished not only equitably, but legally, the authority of the husband.

The *Chirurgical Journal* of Leipsic, a periodical of high authority and merit, which some American booksellers would do well to translate and republish, records in a late number a very distressing event of the character in question.

An officer of artillery, a man of gigantic stature and of robust health, being thrown from an unmanageable horse, received a very severe contusion upon the head which rendered him insensible at once; the skull was slightly fractured, but no immediate danger was apprehended. Trepanning was accomplished successfully. He was bled, and many other of the ordinary means of relief were adopted. Gradually, however, he fell into a more and more hopeless state of stupor, and finally it was thought that he died.

The weather was warm, and he was buried with indecent haste in one of the public cemeteries. His funeral took place on Thursday. On the Sunday following, the grounds of the cemetery were, as usual, much thronged with visitors. About noon an intense excitement was created by the declaration of a peasant that, while sitting upon the grave of the officer, he had distinctly felt a commotion of the earth, as if occasioned by someone struggling beneath. At first little attention was paid to the man's asseveration; but his evident terror, and the dogged obstinacy with which he persisted in his story, had at length their natural effect upon the crowd. Spades were hurriedly procured, and the grave, which was shamefully shallow, was in a few minutes so far thrown open that the head of its occupant appeared. He was then seemingly dead; but he sat nearly erect within his coffin, the lid of which, in his furious struggles, he had partially uplifted.

He was forthwith conveyed to the nearest hospital, and there pronounced to be still living, although in an asphyctic condition. After some hours he revived, recognized individuals of his acquaintance, and in broken sentences spoke of his agonies in the grave.

From what he related, it was clear that he must have been conscious of life for more than an hour, while inhumed, before lapsing into insensibility. The grave was carelessly and loosely filled with an exceedingly porous soil, and thus some air was necessarily admitted. He heard the footsteps of the crowd overhead, and endeavored to make himself heard in turn. It was the tumult within the grounds of the cemetery, he said, which appeared to awaken him from a deep sleep, but no sooner was he awake than he became fully aware of the awful horrors of his position.

This patient, it is recorded, was doing well and seemed to be in a fair way of ultimate recovery, but fell a victim to the quackeries of medical experiment. The galvanic battery was applied, and he suddenly expired in one of those ecstatic paroxysms which it occasionally superinduces.

Nevertheless, the mention of the galvanic battery recalls to my memory a well-known and very extraordinary case in point, where its action proved the means of restoring to animation a young attorney of London, who had been interred for two days. This occurred in 1831, and created at the time a very profound sensation wherever it was made the subject of converse.

The patient, Mr. Edward Stapleton, had died, apparently, of typhus fever, accompanied with some anomalous symptoms which had excited the curiosity of his medical attendants. Upon his seeming decease, his friends were requested to sanction a post-mortem examination, but declined to permit it. As often happens when such refusals are made, the practitioners resolve to disinter the body and dissect it at leisure, in private. Arrangements were easily effected with some of the numerous corps of body snatchers with which London abounds; upon the third night after the funeral, the supposed corpse was unearthed from a grave eight feet deep, and deposited in the operating chamber of one of the private hospitals.

An incision of some extent had been actually made in the abdomen, when the fresh and undecayed appearance of the subject suggested an application of the battery. One experiment succeeded another, and the customary effects supervened, with nothing to characterize them in any respect, except upon one or two occasions a more than ordinary degree of lifelikeness in the convulsive action.

It grew late. The day was about to dawn; and it was thought expedient to proceed at once to the dissection. However, a student who was especially desirous of testing a theory of his own, insisted upon applying the battery to one of the pectoral muscles. A rough gash was made and a wire hastily brought in contact. The patient, with a hurried but quite unconvulsive movement, arose from the table, stepped into the middle of the floor, gazed about him uneasily for a few seconds, and then—spoke. What he said was unintelligible, but words were uttered; the syllabification was distinct. Having spoken, he fell heavily to the floor.

For some moments all were paralyzed with awe—but the urgency of the case soon restored them their presence of mind. It was seen that Mr. Stapleton was alive, although in a swoon. Upon a light application of ether, he revived, and was rapidly restored to health and to the society of his friends—from whom, however, all knowledge of his resuscitation was withheld until a relapse was no longer to be apprehended. Their wonder, their rapturous astonishment, may be conceived.

The most thrilling peculiarity of this incident, nevertheless, is involved in what Mr. S. himself asserts. He declares that at no period was he altogether insensible. Dully and confusedly he was aware of everything which happened to him, from the moment in which he was pronounced dead by his physicians, to that in which he fell swooning to the floor of the hospital. "I am alive," were the uncomprehended words which, upon recognizing the locality of the dissecting room, he had endeavored, in his extremity, to utter.

It would be an easy matter to multiply such histories as these. But I forbear, for indeed we have no need of such to establish the fact that premature interments occur. When we reflect how very rarely, from their very nature, we have it in our power to detect them, we must admit that they may *frequently* occur without our cognizance. Scarcely, in truth, is a graveyard ever encroached upon that skeletons are not found in postures which suggest the most fearful of suspicions.

Fearful indeed the suspicion, but more fearful the doom! It may be asserted without hesitation that no event is so terribly well adapted to inspire the extremity of bodily and of mental distress as is burial before death. There is the unendurable oppression of the lungs, the stifling fumes of the damp earth, the clinging to the death garments, the rigid embrace of the narrow house, the blackness of the absolute night, the silence like a sea that overwhelms, and the unseen but palpable presence of the conqueror worm. These things, with the thoughts of the air and grass above, with memory of dear friends who would fly to save us if but informed of our fate, and with consciousness that of this fate they can never be informed—for our hopeless portion is that of the really dead—these considerations, I say, carry into the heart which still palpitates a degree of appalling and intolerable horror from which the most daring imagination must recoil. We know of nothing so agonizing upon Earth; we can dream of nothing half so hideous in the realms of the nethermost hell. And thus all narratives upon this topic have a profound interest; an interest, nevertheless which, through the sacred awe of the topic itself, very properly and very peculiarly depends upon our conviction of the *truth* of the matter narrated. What I have now to tell is of my own actual knowledge, of my own positive and personal experience.

For several years I had been subject to attacks of the singular disorder which physicians have agreed to term catalepsy in default of a more definitive title. Although both the immediate and the predisposing causes, and even the actual diagnosis, of this disease are still mysterious, its obvious and apparent character is sufficiently well understood. Its variations seem to be chiefly of degree. Sometimes the patient lies for a day, or for an even shorter period, in a species of exaggerated lethargy. He is senseless and externally motionless, but the pulsation of the heart is still faintly perceptible; some traces of warmth remain. A slight color lingers within the center of the cheek, and upon application of a mirror to the lips, we can detect a torpid, unequal and vacillating action of the lungs. Then again the duration of the trance may be for weeks, even for months, while the closest scrutiny and the most rigorous medical tests fail to establish any material distinction between the state of the sufferer and what we conceive of as absolute death. Very usually he is saved from premature interment by the knowledge of his friends that he has been previously subject to catalepsy, by the consequent suspicion excited and, above all, by the nonappearance of decay. The advances of the malady are luckily gradual. The first manifestations, although marked, are unequivocal. The fits grow successively more and more distinctive, and endure each for a longer term than the preceding. In this lies the principal security from inhumation. The unfortunate whose first attack should be of the extreme character which is occasionally seen, would almost inevitably be consigned alive to the tomb.

My own case differed in no important particular from those mentioned in medical books. Sometimes, without any apparent cause, I sank little by little into a condition of semisyncope, or half-swoon; and in this condition, without pain, without ability to stir, or strictly speaking, to think, but with a dull lethargic consciousness of life and of the presence of those who surrounded my bed, I remained until the crisis of the disease restored me, suddenly, to perfect sensation.

At other times I was quickly and impetuously smitten. I grew sick, and numb, and chilly, and dizzy, and so fell prostrate at once. Then, for weeks, all was void and black and silent, and nothing became the universe. Total annihilation could be no more. From these latter attacks I awoke, however, with a gradation slow in proportion to the suddenness of the seizure. Just as the day dawns to the friendless and houseless beggar who roams the streets throughout the long desolate winter night, just so tardily, just so wearily, just so cheerily came back the light of the soul to me.

Apart from the tendency to trance, however, my general health appeared to be good, nor could I perceive that it was at all affected by the one prevalent malady—unless, indeed, an idiosyncrasy in my ordinary sleep may be looked upon as superinduced. Upon awakening from slumber, I could never gain thorough possession of my senses at once, and always remained for many minutes in much bewilderment and perplexity—the mental faculties in general, but the memory in particular, being in a condition of absolute abeyance.

In all that I endured there was no physical suffering, but of moral distress an infinitude. My fancy grew charnel. I talked of worms, of tombs, of epitaphs. I was lost in reveries of death, and the idea of premature burial held continual possession of my brain. The ghastly danger to which I was subjected haunted me day and night. In the former, the torture of meditation was excessive; in the latter, supreme. When the grim darkness overspread the earth, then with every horror of thought, I shook—shook as the quivering plumes upon the hearse. When nature could endure wakefulness no longer, it was with a struggle that I consented to sleep, for I shuddered to reflect that upon awaking, I might find myself the tenant of a grave. And when, finally, I sank into slumber, it was only to rush at once into a world of phantasms above which, with vast, sable, overshadowing wings, hovered predominant the one sepulchral idea.

From the innumerable images of gloom which thus oppressed me in dreams, I select for record but a solitary vision. Methought I was immersed in a cataleptic trance of more than usual duration and profundity. Suddenly there came an icy hand upon my forehead, and an impatient gibbering voice whispered "Arise!"

I sat erect. The darkness was total. I could not see the figure of him who had aroused me. I could call to mind neither the period at which I had fallen into the trance nor the locality in which I then lay. While I remained motionless, and busied in endeavors to collect my thoughts, the cold hand grasped me fiercely by the wrist, shaking it petulantly, while the gibbering voice said again:

"Arise! did I not bid thee arise?"

"And who," I demanded, "art thou?"

"I have no name in the regions which I inhabit," replied the voice, mournfully. "I was mortal, but am fiend. I am merciless, but am pitiful. Thou dost feel that I shudder. My teeth chatter as I speak, yet it is not with the chilliness of the night, of the night without end. But this hideousness is insufferable. How canst *thou* tranquilly sleep? I cannot rest for the cry of these great agonies. These sights are more than I can bear. Get thee up! Come with me unto the outer night, and let me unfold to thee the graves. Is not this a spectacle of woe? Behold!"

I looked. The unseen figure, which still grasped me by the wrist, had caused to be thrown open the graves of all mankind. From each issued the faint phosphoric radiance of decay, so that I could see into the innermost recesses, and there view the shrouded bodies in their sad and solemn slumbers with the worm. But alas! the real sleepers were fewer by many millions than those who slumbered not at all. And there was a feeble struggling, and there was a general and sad unrest; and from out the depths of the countless pits there came a melancholy rustling from the garments of the buried. And of those who seemed tranquilly to repose, I saw that a vast number had changed, in a greater or less degree, the rigid and uneasy position in which they had originally been entombed. And the voice again said to me as I gazed:

"Is it not—oh! is it *not* a pitiful sight?"

But, before I could find words to reply, the figure had

ceased to grasp my wrist. The phosphoric lights expired, and the graves were closed with a sudden violence, while from out them arose a tumult of despairing cries, saying again, "Is it not—O God! is it *not* a very pitiful sight?"

Phantasies such as these, presenting themselves at night, extended their terrific influence far into my waking hours. My nerves became thoroughly unstrung, and I fell a prey to perpetual horror. I hesitated to ride, or to walk, or to indulge in any exercise that would carry me from home. In fact, I no longer dared trust myself out of the immediate presence of those who were aware of my proneness to catalepsy lest, falling into one of my usual fits, I should be buried before my real condition could be ascertained. I doubted the care, the fidelity of my dearest friends. I dreaded that in some trance of more than customary duration they might be prevailed upon to regard me as irrecoverable. I even went so far as to fear that, as I occasioned much trouble, they might be glad to consider any very protracted attack as sufficient excuse for getting rid of me altogether. It was in vain they endeavored to reassure me by the most solemn promises. I exacted the most sacred oaths, that under no circumstances they would bury me until decomposition had so materially advanced as to render further preservation impossible. And even then my mortal terrors would listen to no reason, would accept no consolation.

I entered into a series of elaborate precautions. Among other things, I had the family vault so remodeled as to admit of being readily opened from within. The slightest pressure upon a long lever that extended far into the tomb would cause the iron portals to fly back. There were arrangements also for the free admission of air and light, and convenient receptacles for food and water within immediate reach of the coffin intended for my reception. This coffin was warmly and softly padded, and was provided with a lid, fashioned upon the principle of the vault door, with the addition of springs so contrived that the feeblest movement of the body would be sufficient to set it at liberty. Besides all this, there was suspended from the roof of the tomb, a large bell, the rope of which, it was designed, should extend through a hole in the coffin, and so be fastened to one of the hands of the corpse. But, alas, what avails the vigilance against the destiny of man? Not even these well-contrived securities sufficed to save, from the uttermost agonies of living inhumation, a wretch to these agonies foredoomed!

There arrived an epoch, as often before there had arrived, in which I found myself emerging from total unconsciousness into the first feeble and indefinite sense of existence. Slowly, with a tortoise gradation, approached the faint gray dawn of the psychal day. A torpid uneasiness. An apathetic endurance of dull pain. No care, no hope, no effort. Then after a long interval, a ringing in the ears. Then after a lapse still longer, a prickling or tingling sensation in the extremities; then a seemingly eternal period of pleasurable quiescence, during which the awakening feelings are struggling into thought. Then a brief re-sinking into nonentity; then a sudden recovery. At length the slight quivering of an eyelid, and immediately thereupon, an electric shock of a terror, deadly and indefinite, which sends the blood in torrents from the temples to the heart. And now the first positive effort to think. And now the first endeavor to remember. And now a partial and evanescent success. And now the memory has so far regained its dominion, that in some measure, I am cognizant of my state. I feel that I am not awaking from ordinary sleep. I recollect that I have been subject to catalepsy. And now, at last, as if by the rush of an ocean, my shuddering spirit is overwhelmed by the one grim danger, by the one spectral and ever-prevalent idea.

For some minutes after this fancy possessed me, I remained without motion. And why? I could not summon courage to move. I dared not make the effort which was to satisfy me of my fate—and yet there was something at my heart which whispered to me *it was sure*. Despair—such as no other species of wretchedness ever calls into being—despair alone urged me, after long irresolution, to uplift the heavy lids of my eyes. I uplifted them. It was dark, all dark. I knew that the fit was over. I knew that the crisis of my disorder had long passed. I knew that I had now fully recovered the use of my visual faculties, and yet it was dark, all dark—the intense and utter raylessness of the night that endureth forevermore.

I endeavored to shriek; and my lips and my parched

tongue moved convulsively together in the attempt—but no voice issued from the cavernous lungs which, oppressed as if by the weight of some incumbent mountain, gasped and palpitated with the heart at every elaborate and struggling inspiration.

The movement of the jaws, in this effort to cry aloud, showed me that they were bound up, as is usual with the dead. I felt, too, that I lay upon some hard substance; and by something similar my sides were, also, closely compressed. So far, I had not ventured to stir any of my limbs, but now I violently threw up my arms, which had been lying at length, with the wrists crossed. They struck a solid wooden substance, which extended above my person at an elevation of not more than six inches from my face. I could no longer doubt that I reposed within a coffin at last.

And now, amid all my infinite miseries, came sweetly the cherub hope, for I thought of my precautions. I writhed, and made spasmodic exertions to force open the lid; it would not move. I felt my wrists for the bell rope; it was not to be found. And now the comforter fled forever, and a still sterner despair reigned triumphant, for I could not help perceiving the absence of the paddings which I had so carefully prepared. And then, too, there came suddenly to my nostrils the strong peculiar odor of moist earth. The conclusion was irresistible, I was not within the vault. I had fallen into a trance while absent from home, while among strangers—when or how, I could not remember. And it was they who had buried me as a dog, nailed up in some common coffin—and thrust, deep, deep, and forever into some ordinary and nameless *grave*.

As this awful conviction forced itself, thus, into the innermost chambers of my soul, I once again struggled to cry aloud. And in this second endeavor I succeeded. A long, wild and continuous shriek, or yell of agony, resounded through the realms of the subterranean night.

"Hillo! hillo, there!" said a gruff voice in reply.

"What the devil's the matter now!" said a second.

"Get out o' that!" said a third.

"What do you mean by yowling in that 'ere kind of style, like a cattymount?" said a fourth; and hereupon I was seized and shaken without ceremony, for several minutes, by a junto of very rough-looking individuals. They did not arouse me from my slumber, for I was wide awake when I screamed, but they restored me to the full possession of my memory.

This adventure occurred near Richmond, Virginia. Accompanied by a friend, I had proceeded, upon a gunning expedition, some miles down the banks of the James River. Night approached, and we were overtaken by a storm. The cabin of a small sloop lying at anchor in the stream, and laden with garden mould, afforded us the only available shelter. We made the best of it, and passed the night on board. I slept in one of the only two berths in the vessel; the berths of a sloop of sixty or seventy tons need scarcely be described. That which I occupied had no bedding of any kind. Its extreme width was eighteen inches. The distance of its bottom from the deck overhead was precisely the same. I found it a matter of exceeding difficulty to squeeze myself in. Nevertheless I slept soundly; and the whole of my vision, for it was no dream, and no nightmare, arose naturally from the circumstances of my position, from my ordinary bias of thought, and from the difficulty to which I have alluded, of collecting my senses, and especially of regaining my memory, for a long time after awaking from slumber. The men who shook me were the crew of the sloop, and some laborers engaged to unload it. From the load itself came the earthy smell. The bandage about the jaws was a silk handkerchief in which I had bound up my head, in default of my customary nightcap.

The tortures endured, however, were indubitably quite equal, for the time, to those of actual sepulture. They were fearfully, they were inconceivably, hideous; but out of evil proceeded good, for their very excess wrought in my spirit an inevitable revulsion. My soul acquired tone, acquired temper. I went abroad. I took vigorous exercise. I breathed the free air of heaven. I thought upon other subjects than death. I discarded my medical books. *Buchan* I burned. I read no *Night Thoughts,* no fustian about churchyards, no bugaboo tales—such as this. In short I became a new man, and lived a man's life. From that memorable night, I dismissed forever my charnel apprehensions, and with them vanished the cataleptic disorder, of which, perhaps, they had been less the consequence than the cause.

There are moments when, even to the sober eye of reason, the world of our sad humanity may assume the semblance of a hell—but the imagination of man is no Carathis, to explore with impunity its every cavern. Alas! the grim legion of sepulchral terrors cannot be regarded as altogether fanciful. But, like the demons in whose company Afrasiab made his voyage down the Oxus, they must sleep, or they will devour us; they must be suffered to slumber or we perish.

THE SPHINX

DURING the dread reign of the cholera in New York, I had accepted the invitation of a relative to spend a fortnight with him in the retirement of his cottage on the banks of the Hudson. He had here all the ordinary means of summer amusement. And with rambling in the woods, sketching, boating, fishing, bathing, music and books we should have passed the time pleasantly enough, but for the fearful intelligence which reached us every morning from the populous city. Not a day elapsed which did not bring us news of the decease of some acquaintance. Then, as the fatality increased, we learned to expect daily the loss of some friend. At length we trembled at the approach of every messenger. The very air from the south seemed to us redolent with death. That palsying thought, indeed, took entire possession of my soul. I could neither speak, think, nor dream of anything else. My host was of a less excitable temperament, and, although greatly depressed in spirits, exerted himself to sustain my own. His richly philosophical intellect was not at any time affected by unrealities. To the substances of terror he was sufficiently alive, but of its shadows he had no apprehension.

His endeavors to arouse me from the condition of abnormal gloom into which I had fallen were frustrated in great measure by certain volumes which I had found in his library. These were of a character to force into germination whatever seeds of hereditary superstition lay latent in my bosom. I had been reading these books without his knowledge, and thus he was often at a loss to account for the forcible impressions which had been made upon my fancy.

A favorite topic with me was the popular belief in omens—a belief which at this one epoch of my life I was almost seriously disposed to defend. On this subject we had long and animated discussions. He maintained the utter groundlessness of faith in such matters; I contended that a popular sentiment, arising with absolute spontaneity—that is to say, without apparent traces of suggestion —had in it unmistakable elements of truth.

The fact is that soon after my arrival at the cottage, there had occurred to me an incident so entirely inexplicable, and which had in it so much of the portentous character, that I might well have been excused for regarding it as an omen. It appalled, and at the same time so confounded and bewildered me, that many days elapsed before I could make up my mind to communicate the circumstance to my friend.

Near the close of an exceedingly warm day I was sitting, book in hand, at an open window commanding, through a long vista of the riverbanks, a view of a distant hill. Its nearer face had been denuded by a landslide of the principal portion of its trees. My thoughts had long been wandering from the volume before me to the gloom and desolation of the neighboring city. Lifting my eyes from the page, I glanced at the naked face of the hill. There my eyes perceived an object—it was a living monster of hideous conformation, which very rapidly made its way from the summit to the bottom of the hill, disappearing finally in the dense forest below. When I first saw this creature I doubted my own sanity—or at least the evidence of my own eyes, and many minutes passed before I succeeded in convincing myself that I was neither mad nor in a dream. Yet when I describe the monster (which I distinctly saw, and calmly surveyed through the whole period of its progress) my readers, I fear, will feel even more difficulty in being convinced of these points than I did.

Estimating the size of the creature by comparison with the diameter of the large trees near which it passed—the few giants of the forest which had escaped the fury of the landslide—I concluded it to be far larger than any ship in existence. I say ship, because the shape of the monster suggested the idea.

The mouth of the animal was situated at the extremity of a proboscis some sixty or seventy feet in length, and about as thick as the body of an ordinary elephant. Near the root of this trunk was an immense quantity of black shaggy hair—more than could have been supplied by the coats of a score of buffaloes; and projecting from this hair downwardly and laterally, sprang two gleaming tusks not unlike those of the wild boar, but of infinitely greater dimension. Extending forward, parallel with the proboscis and on each side of it was a gigantic staff, thirty or forty feet in length, formed seemingly of pure crystal, and in shape a perfect prism. It reflected in the most gorgeous manner the rays of the declining sun. The trunk was fashioned like a wedge, with the apex to the earth.

From it there were outspread two pairs of wings—each wing nearly one hundred yards in length—one pair being placed above the other, and all thickly covered with metal scales; each scale was apparently some ten or twelve feet in diameter. I observed that the upper and lower tiers of wings were connected by a strong chain. But the chief peculiarity of this horrible thing, was the representation of a *death's-head,* which covered nearly the whole surface of its breast, and which was as accurately traced in glaring white upon the dark ground of the body, as if it had been carefully designed by an artist.

I regarded this terrific animal, and especially the device on its breast, with a feeling of horror and awe, with a sentiment of forthcoming evil, which I found it impossible to quell by any effort of the reason. Then I perceived the huge jaws at the extremity of the proboscis suddenly

313

expand themselves, and from them there proceeded a sound so loud and so expressive of woe, that it struck upon my nerves like a knell, and as the monster disappeared at the foot of the hill, I fell fainting to the floor.

Upon recovering, my first impulse of course was to inform my friend of what I had seen and heard—and I can scarcely explain what feeling of repugnance operated, in the end, to prevent me.

At length, one evening, some three or four days after the occurrence, we were sitting together in the room in which I had seen the apparition. I occupied the same seat at the same window; he lounged on a sofa near at hand. The association of the place and time impelled me to give him an account of the phenomenon. He heard me to the end, at first laughing heartily, then lapsing into an excessively grave demeanor, as if my insanity was a thing beyond suspicion. At this instant I again had a distinct view of the monster, to which, with a shout of absolute terror, I now directed his attention. He looked eagerly, but maintained that he saw nothing although I designated minutely the course of the creature, as it made its way down the naked face of the hill.

I was now immeasurably alarmed, for I considered the vision either as an omen of my death, or worse, as the forerunner of an attack of mania. I threw myself passionately back in my chair, and for some moments buried my face in my hands. When I uncovered my eyes, the apparition was no longer visible.

My host, however, had in some degree resumed the calmness of his demeanor, and questioned me very rigorously in respect to the conformation of the visionary creature. When I had fully satisfied him on the matter, he sighed deeply, as if relieved of some intolerable burden, and went on to talk with what I thought a cruel calmness of various points of speculative philosophy, which had heretofore been a subject of discussion between us. I remember his insisting very particularly upon the idea that the principal source of error in all human investigations lay in the liability of the understanding to underrate or to overvalue the importance of an object, through improper measurement of its propinquity.

"For example," he said, "to estimate properly the influence of democratic ideas on mankind, one must take into account the time required for the thorough dissemination of those ideas—or, in other words, the *distance* from the present to the point at which such thorough dissemination may be accomplished. Yet can you tell me one writer on the subject of government who has ever thought this particular branch of the subject worthy of discussion at all?"

He here paused for a moment, stepped to a bookcase, and brought forth one of the ordinary synopses of natural history. Requesting me then to exchange seats with him that he might better distinguish the fine print of the volume, he took my armchair at the window, and opening the book, resumed his discourse very much in the same tone as before.

"But for your exceeding minuteness," he said, "in describing the monster, I might never have had it in my power to demonstrate to you what it was. In the first place, let me read to you a schoolboy account of the genus *sphinx,* of the family *crepuscularia,* of the order *lepidoptera,* of the class *insecta.* The account runs thus:

> Four membraneous wings covered with little coloured scales of a metallic appearance; mouth forming a rolled proboscis, produced by an elongation of the jaws, upon the sides of which are found the rudiments of mandibles and downy palpi; the inferior wings retained to the superior by a stiff hair; antennae in the form of an elongated club, prismatic; abdomen pointed. The death's-head, or sphinx moth has occasioned much terror among the vulgar, at times, by the melancholy kind of cry which it utters, and the insignia of death on its corselet.

Here he closed the book and leaned forward in the chair, placing himself accurately in the position which I had occupied at the moment of beholding the monster.

"Ah, here it is!" he presently exclaimed. "It is reascending the face of the hill, and a very remarkable looking creature I admit it to be. Still it is by no means so large or so distant as you imagined it. For the fact is that, as it wiggles its way up a thread which some spider has spun across the window, I find it to be about a sixteenth of an inch in its entire length, and also about a sixteenth of an inch distant from the pupil of my eye."

THE IMP OF THE PERVERSE

INTRODUCTION

In the consideration of the faculties and impulses, of the *prima mobilia* or prime movers of the human soul, the phrenologists have failed to make room for a propensity which, although obviously existing as a radical, primitive, irreducible sentiment, has been equally overlooked by all the moralists who have preceded them. In the pure arrogance of reason, we have all overlooked it. We have suffered its existence to escape our senses solely through want of belief, of faith—whether it be faith in revelation, or faith in the cabala. The idea of it has never occurred to us, simply because of its supererogation. We saw no need of the impulse, the propensity. We could not perceive its necessity. We could not have understood, had the notion of this particular *primum mobile* ever obtruded itself. We could not have understood in what manner it might be made to further the objects of humanity, either temporal or eternal. It cannot be denied that phrenology and in great measure all metaphysics have been concocted a priori. The intellectual or logical man, rather than the understanding or observant man, set himself to imagine designs, to dictate purposes to God. Having thus fathomed, to his satisfaction, the intentions of Jehovah, out of these intentions he built his innumerable systems of mind. In the matter of phrenology, for example, we first determined, naturally enough, that it was the design of the deity that man should eat. We then assigned to man the faculty of alimentation, and this faculty is the scourge with which the deity compels man, will I nill I, into eating. Secondly, having settled it to be God's will that man should continue his species, we discovered the faculty of amativeness, forthwith. And so with combativeness, with ideality, with causality, with constructiveness—so, in short, with every faculty, whether representing a propensity, a moral sentiment, or a faculty of the pure intellect. And in these arrangements of the *principia* of human action, the Spurzheimites, whether right or wrong, in part or in whole, have but followed the footsteps of their predecessors, deducing and establishing everything from the preconceived destiny of man, and on the ground of the objects of his creator.

It would have been wiser, it would have been safer, to classify upon the basis of what man usually or occasionally did, and was always occasionally doing, rather than upon the basis of what we took it for granted the deity intended him to do. If we cannot comprehend God in his visible works, how then in his inconceivable thoughts, that call the works into being? If we cannot understand him in his objective creatures, how then in his substantive moods and phases of creation?

Induction, a posteriori, would have brought phrenology to admit, as an innate and primitive principle of human action, a paradoxical something which we may call *perverseness*, for want of a more characteristic term. In the sense I intend, it is in fact a *mobile* or mover without motive. Through its promptings we act without a comprehensible object; or if this shall be understood as a contradiction in terms, we may so far modify the proposition as to say that through its promptings we act for the reason that we should *not*. In theory, no reason can be more unreasonable; but in fact there is none more strong. With certain minds, under certain conditions, it becomes absolutely irresistible. I am not more certain that I breathe, than that the assurance of the wrong or error of any action is often the one unconquerable *force* which impels us, and alone impels us to its prosecution. Nor will this overwhelming tendency to do wrong for the wrong's sake admit of analysis or resolution into ulterior elements. It is a radical, a primitive impulse—elementary.

It will be said, I am aware, that when we persist in acts because we feel we should *not* persist in them, our conduct is but a modification of that which ordinarily springs from the *combativeness* of phrenology. But a glance will show the fallacy of this idea. The phrenological combativeness has, for its essence, the necessity of

319

self-defense. It is our safeguard against injury. Its principle regards our well-being, and thus the desire to be well is excited simultaneously with its development. It follows that the desire to be well must be excited simultaneously with any principle which is a modification of combativeness, but in the case of that something which I term *perverseness*, the desire to be well is not only *not* aroused, but a strongly antagonistic sentiment exists.

An appeal to one's own heart is, after all, the best confirmation of this seeming sophistry. No one who trustingly consults and thoroughly questions his own soul will wholly deny the radical propensity in question. It is not more incomprehensible than distinctive.

There lives no man who at some period has not been tormented, for example, by an earnest desire to tantalize a listener by circumlocution. The speaker is aware that he displeases. He has every intention to please. He is usually curt, precise and clear. The most laconic and luminous language is struggling for utterance upon his tongue, and it is only with difficulty that he restrains himself from giving it flow. He dreads and deprecates the anger of him whom he addresses, yet the thought strikes him that by certain involutions and parentheses this anger may be engendered. And that single thought is enough. The impulse increases to a wish, the wish to a desire, the desire to an uncontrollable longing, and the longing, to the deep regret and mortification of the speaker is, in defiance of all consequences, indulged.

Or, we have a task before us which must be speedily performed. We know that it will be ruinous to make delay. The most important crisis of our life calls, trumpet-tongued, for immediate energy and action. We glow. We are consumed with eagerness to commence the work. With the anticipation of the glorious result our whole souls are on fire. It must, it shall be, undertaken today, and yet we put it off until tomorrow. Why? There is no answer, except that we feel *perverse*, using the word with no comprehension of a principle. Tomorrow arrives, and with it a more impatient anxiety to do our duty, but with this very increase of anxiety there arrives also a nameless, positively fearful because unfathomable, craving for delay. This craving gathers strength as the moments fly. The last hour for action is at hand. We tremble with the violence of the conflict within us, of the definite with the indefinite, of the substance with the shadow. But if the contest has proceeded thus far, it is the shadow which prevails, and we struggle in vain. The clock strikes; it is the knell of our welfare. At the same time, it is the chanti-cleer-note to the ghost that has so long overawed us. It flies, it disappears, and we are free. The old energy returns. We will labor now. But alas, it is *too late!*

Or, we stand upon the brink of a precipice. We peer into the abyss; we grow sick and dizzy. Our first impulse is to shrink from the danger. Unaccountably we remain. By slow degrees our sickness and dizziness and horror become merged in a cloud of unnamable feeling. By gradations still more imperceptible this cloud assumes shape, as did the vapor from the bottle out of which arose the genie in the *Arabian Nights*. But out of *our* cloud upon the precipice's edge there grows into palpability a shape far more terrible than any genie or any demon of a tale, and yet it is but a thought, although a fearful one, and one which chills the very marrow of our bones with the fierceness of delight in its horror. It is merely the idea of what would be our sensations during the sweeping precipitancy of a fall from such a height. And this fall, this rushing annihilation, for the very reason that it involves one of the most ghastly and loathsome images of death and suffering which have ever presented themselves to our imagination—for this very cause we now most vividly desire it. And because our reason violently deters us from the brink, *therefore* do we the most impetuously approach it. There is no passion in nature so demoniacally impatient as that of him who, shuddering upon the edge of a precipice, thus meditates a plunge. To indulge, for a moment, in any attempt at *thought*, is to be inevitably lost; for reflection but urges us to forbear, and *therefore* it is, I say, that we *cannot*. If there be no friendly arm to check us, or if we fail in a sudden effort to prostrate ourselves backward from the abyss, we plunge and are destroyed.

Examine these and similar actions as we will, we shall find them resulting solely from the spirit of the *perverse*. We perpetrate them merely because we feel that we should *not*. Beyond or behind this there is no intelligible principle; and we might, indeed, deem this perverseness a direct instigation of the archfiend, were it not occasion- . ally known to operate in furtherance of good as well as evil.

I have said thus much, that in some measure I may answer your question, that I may explain to you why I am here, that I may assign to you something that shall have at least the faint aspect of a cause for my wearing these fetters, and for my tenanting this cell of the condemned. Had I not been thus prolix, you might either have misunderstood me altogether or, with the rabble, have fancied me mad. As it is, you will easily perceive that I am one of the many uncounted victims of the imp of the perverse.

THE IMP OF THE PERVERSE

It is impossible that any deed could have been wrought with a more thorough deliberation. For weeks, for months, I pondered upon the means of the murder. I rejected a thousand schemes, because their accomplishment involved a *chance* of detection. At length, in reading some French memoirs, I found an account of a nearly fatal illness that occurred to Madame Pilau, through the agency of a candle accidentally poisoned. The idea struck my fancy at once. I knew my victim's habit of reading in bed. I knew, too, that his apartment was narrow and ill-ventilated. But I need not vex you with impertinent details. I need not describe the easy artifices by which I substituted, in his bedroom candlestand, a waxlight of my own making for the one which I there found. The next morning he was discovered dead in his bed, and the coroner's verdict was—"death by the visitation of God."

Having inherited his estate, all went well with me for years. The idea of detection never once entered my brain. Of the remains of the fatal taper I had myself carefully disposed. I had left no shadow of a clue by which it would be possible to convict, or even suspect, me of the crime. It is inconceivable how rich a sentiment of satisfaction arose in my bosom as I reflected upon my absolute security. For a very long period of time I was accustomed to revel in this sentiment. It afforded me more real delight than all the mere worldly advantages accruing from my sin. But there arrived at length an epoch, from which the pleasurable feeling grew, by scarcely perceptible gradations, into a haunting and harassing thought. It harassed me because it haunted. I could scarcely get rid of it for an instant. It is quite a common thing to be thus annoyed with the ringing in our ears, or rather in our memories, of the burden of some ordinary song, or some unimpressive snatches from an opera. Nor will we be the less tormented if the song in itself be good, or the opera air meritorious. In this manner, at last, I would perpetually catch myself pondering upon my security, and repeating, in a low undertone, the phrase, "I am safe."

One day, while sauntering along the streets, I arrested myself in the act of murmuring half-aloud these customary syllables. In a fit of petulance I remodeled them thus: "I am safe—I am safe. Yes, if I be not fool enough to make open confession."

No sooner had I spoken these words, then I felt an icy chill creep to my heart. I had had some experience in these fits of perversity (whose nature I have been at some trouble to explain), and I remembered well that in no instance had I successfully resisted their attacks. And now my own casual self-suggestion, that I might possibly be fool enough to confess the murder of which I had been guilty, confronted me, as if the very ghost of him whom I had murdered beckoned me on to death.

At first, I made an effort to shake off this nightmare of the soul. I walked vigorously, faster, still faster—at length I ran. I felt a maddening desire to shriek aloud. Every succeeding wave of thought overwhelmed me with new terror, for, alas! I well, too well, understood that to *think*, in my situation, was to be lost. I still quickened my pace. I bounded like a madman through the crowded thoroughfares. At length, the populace took the alarm and pursued me. I felt then the consummation of my fate. Could I have torn out my tongue I would have done it, but a rough voice resounded in my ears—a rougher grasp seized me by the shoulder. I turned, I gasped for breath. For a moment I experienced all the pangs of suffocation; I became blind, and deaf, and giddy. And then some invisible fiend, I thought, struck me with his broad palm upon the back. The long-imprisoned secret burst forth from my soul.

They say that I spoke with a distinct enunciation, but with marked emphasis and passionate hurry, as if in dread of interruption before concluding the brief but pregnant sentences that consigned me to the hangman and to hell.

Having related all that was necessary for the fullest judicial conviction, I fell prostrate in a swoon.

But why shall I say more? Today I wear these chains, and am *here!* Tomorrow I shall be fetterless—*but where?*

THE CONVERSATION OF EIROS AND CHARMION

EIROS. Why do you call me Eiros?

CHARMION. So henceforward will you always be called. You must forget, too, my earthly name, and speak to me as Charmion.

EIROS. This is indeed no dream!

CHARMION. Dreams are with us no more, but of these mysteries anon. I rejoice to see you looking lifelike and rational. The film of the shadow has already passed from off your eyes. Be of good heart, and fear nothing. Your allotted days of stupor have expired; and, tomorrow, I will myself induct you into the full joys and wonders of your novel existence.

EIROS. True, I feel no stupor, none at all. The wild sickness and the terrible darkness have left me, and I hear no longer that mad, rushing, horrible sound, like "the voice of many waters." Yet my senses are bewildered, Charmion, with the keenness of their perception of *the new.*

CHARMION. A few days will remove all this; but I fully understand you and feel for you. It is now ten earthly years since I underwent what you undergo, yet the remembrance of it hangs by me still. You have now suffered all of pain, however, which you will suffer in Aidenn.

EIROS. In Aidenn?

CHARMION. In Aidenn.

EIROS. Oh, God! Pity me, Charmion! I am overburdened with the majesty of all things—of the unknown now known, of the speculative Future merged in the august and certain Present.

CHARMION. Grapple not now with such thoughts. Tomorrow we will speak of this. Your mind wavers, and its agitation will find relief in the exercise of simple memories. Look not around, nor forward—but back. I am burning with anxiety to hear the details of that stupendous event which threw you among us. Tell me of it. Let us converse of familiar things, in the old familiar language of the world which has so fearfully perished.

EIROS. Most fearfully, fearfully! This is indeed no dream.

CHARMION. Dreams are no more. Was I much mourned, my Eiros?

EIROS. Mourned, Charmion? Oh, deeply. To that last hour of all, there hung a cloud of intense gloom and devout sorrow over your household.

CHARMION. And that last hour—speak of it. Remember, that beyond the naked fact of the catastrophe itself,

I know nothing. When, coming out from among mankind, I passed into night through the grave—at that period, if I remember aright, the calamity which overwhelmed you was utterly unanticipated. But, indeed, I knew little of the speculative philosophy of the day.

EIROS. The individual calamity was, as you say, entirely unanticipated, but analogous misfortunes had been long a subject of discussion with astronomers. I need scarce tell you, my friend, that even when you left us, men had agreed to understand those passages in the most holy writings which speak of the final destruction of all things by fire, as having reference to the orb of the earth alone.

But in regard to the immediate agency of the ruin, speculation in astronomical knowledge had been at fault, during that period, by which the comets were divested of the terrors of flame. The very moderate density of these bodies had been well established. They had been observed to pass among the satellites of Jupiter, without bringing about any sensible alteration either in the masses or in the orbits of these secondary planets. We had long regarded the wanderers as vapory creations of inconceivable tenuity, and as altogether incapable of doing injury to our substantial globe, even in the event of contact. But contact was not in any degree dreaded, for the elements of all the comets were accurately known. That among *them* we should look for the agency of the threatened fiery destruction had been for many years considered an inadmissible idea. But wonders and wild fancies had been, of late days, strangely rife among mankind; and although it was only with a few of the ignorant that actual apprehension prevailed, at the announcement by astronomers of a *new* comet, yet this announcement was generally received with I know not what of agitation and mistrust.

The elements of the strange orb were immediately calculated, and it was at once conceded by all observers that its path, at perihelion, would bring it into very close proximity with the earth. There were two or three astronomers of secondary note who resolutely maintained that a contact was inevitable. I cannot very well express to you the effect of this intelligence upon the people. For a few short days they would not believe an assertion which their intellect, so long employed among worldly considerations, could not in any manner grasp. But the truth of a vitally important fact soon makes its way into the understanding of even the most stolid. Finally, all men saw that astronomical knowledge lied not, and they awaited the comet.

Its approach was not, at first, seemingly rapid, nor was its appearance of very unusual character. It was of a dull red, and had little perceptible train. For seven or eight days we saw no material increase in its apparent diameter, and but a partial alteration in its color. Meanwhile the ordinary affairs of men were discarded, and all interests absorbed in a growing discussion, instituted by the philosophic, in respect to the cometary nature. Even the grossly ignorant aroused their sluggish capacities to such considerations. The learned now gave their intellect, their soul, to no such points as the allaying of fear, or to the sustenance of loved theory. They sought, they panted for right views. They groaned for perfected knowledge. Truth arose in the purity of her strength and exceeding majesty, and the wise bowed down and adored.

That material injury to our globe or to its inhabitants would result from the apprehended contact, was an opinion which hourly lost ground among the wise; and the wise were now freely permitted to rule the reason and the fancy of the crowd. It was demonstrated, that the density of the comet's nucleus was far less than that of our rarest gas; and the harmless passage of a similar visitor among the satellites of Jupiter was a point strongly insisted upon, and which served greatly to allay terror.

Theologists, with an earnestness fear-enkindled, dwelt upon the biblical prophecies, and expounded them to the people with a directness and simplicity of which no previous instance had been known. That the final destruction of the earth must be brought about by the agency of fire, was urged with a spirit that enforced everywhere conviction; and that the comets were of no fiery nature (as all men now knew), was a truth which relieved all, in a great measure, from the apprehension of the great calamity foretold. It is noticeable that the popular prejudices and vulgar errors in regard to pestilences and wars—errors which were wont to prevail upon every appearance of a comet—were now altogether unknown. As if by some sudden convulsive exertion, Reason had at once hurled Superstition from her throne. The feeblest intellect had derived vigor from excessive interest.

What minor evils might arise from the contact were points of elaborate question. The learned spoke of slight geological disturbances, of probable alterations in climate and consequently in vegetation, of possible magnetic and electric influences. Many held that no visible or perceptible effect would in any manner be produced. While such discussions were going on, their subject gradually approached, growing larger in apparent diameter, and of a more brilliant luster. Mankind grew paler as it came. All human operations were suspended.

There was an epoch in the course of the general sentiment when the comet had attained, at length, a size surpassing that of any previously recorded visitation. The people now, dismissing any lingering hope that the astronomers were wrong, experienced all the certainty of evil. The chimerical aspect of their terror was gone. The hearts of the stoutest of our race beat violently within their bosoms.

A very few days sufficed, however, to merge even such feelings in sentiments more unendurable. We could no longer apply to the strange orb any accustomed thoughts. Its historical attributes had disappeared. It oppressed us with a hideous novelty of emotion. We saw it not as an astronomical phenomenon in the heavens, but as an incubus upon our hearts, and a shadow upon our brains. It had taken, with inconceivable rapidity, the character of a gigantic mantle of rare flames, extending from horizon to horizon.

Yet a day, and men breathed with greater freedom. It was clear that we were already within the influence of the comet, yet we lived. We even felt an unusual elasticity of frame and vivacity of mind. The exceeding tenuity of the object of our dread was apparent, for all heavenly objects were plainly visible through it. Meantime, our vegetation had perceptibly altered; and we gained faith, from this predicted circumstance, in the foresight of the wise. A wild luxuriance of foliage, utterly unknown before, burst out upon every vegetable thing.

Yet another day, and the evil was not altogether upon us. It was now evident that its nucleus would first reach us. A wild change had come over all men, and the first sense of *pain* was the wild signal for general lamentation and horror. This first sense of pain lay in a rigorous constriction of the breast and lungs, and an insufferable dryness of the skin. It could not be denied that our atmosphere was radically affected. The conformation of this atmosphere, and the possible modifications to which it might be subjected, were now the topics of discussion. The result of investigation sent an electric thrill of the intensest horror through the universal heart of man.

It had been long known that the air which encircled us was a compound of oxygen and nitrogen gases, in the proportion of twenty-one measures of oxygen and seventy-nine of nitrogen in every one hundred of the atmosphere. Oxygen, which was the principle of combustion and the vehicle of heat, was absolutely necessary to the support of animal life, and was the most powerful and energetic agent in nature. Nitrogen, on the contrary, was incapable of supporting either animal life or flame. An unnatural excess of oxygen would result, it had been ascertained, in just such an elevation of the animal spirits as we had latterly experienced.

It was the pursuit, the extension of the idea, which had engendered awe. What would be the result of a *total extraction of the nitrogen?* A combustion irresistible, all-devouring, omniprevalent, immediate—the entire fulfillment, in all their minute and terrible details, of the fiery and horror-inspiring denunciations of the prophecies of the Holy Book.

Why need I paint, Charmion, the now disenchained frenzy of mankind? That tenuity in the comet which had previously inspired us with hope, was now the source of the bitterness of despair. In its impalpable gaseous character we clearly perceived the consummation of fate.

Meantime a day again passed, bearing away with it the last shadow of hope. We gasped in the rapid modification of the air. The red blood bounded tumultuously through its strict channels. A furious delirium possessed all men. With arms rigidly outstretched toward the threatening heavens, they trembled and shrieked aloud. But the nucleus of the destroyer was now upon us; even here in Aidenn, I shudder while I speak. Let me be brief—brief as the ruin that overwhelmed. For a moment there was a wild lurid light alone, visiting and penetrating all things. Then—let us bow down, Charmion, before the excessive majesty of the great God—there came a shouting and pervading sound, as if from the mouth itself of Him; while the whole incumbent mass of ether in which we existed burst at once into a species of intense flame, for whose surpassing brilliancy and all-fervid heat even the angels in the high heaven of pure knowledge have no name. Thus ended all.

WILLIAM WILSON

INTRODUCTION

LET me call myself, for the present, William Wilson. The fair page now lying before me need not be sullied with my real appellation. This has been already too much an object for the scorn, for the horror, for the detestation of my race. To the uttermost regions of the globe have not the indignant winds bruited its unparalleled infamy? Oh, outcast of all outcasts most abandoned! To the earth thou art forever dead—to its honors, to its flowers, to its golden aspirations. And a cloud, dense, dismal and limitless hangs eternally between thy hopes and heaven.

I would not here embody, if indeed I could, the record of my later years of unspeakable misery and unpardonable crime. This epoch, these later years, took unto themselves a sudden elevation in turpitude, whose origin alone it is my present purpose to assign. Men usually grow base by degrees. From me in an instant all virtue dropped bodily as a mantle. From comparatively trivial wickedness I passed, with the stride of a giant, into more than the enormities of an Elagabalus. Bear with me while I relate the chance, the single event, which brought this evil thing to pass. Death approaches, and the shadow which foreruns him has thrown a softening influence over my spirit. I long, in passing through the dim valley, for the sympathy—I had nearly said for the pity—of my fellow men. I would have them believe that I have been, in some measure, the slave of circumstances beyond human control. I would wish them to seek out for me in the details I am about to give, some little oasis of *fatality* amid a wilderness of error. I would have them allow that, although temptation as great may have existed ere this, man was never *thus*, at least, tempted before—certainly, never thus fell. And is it therefore that he has never thus suffered? Have I not indeed been living in a dream? And am I not now dying a victim to the horror and the mystery of the wildest of all sublunary visions?

WILLIAM WILSON

I AM the descendant of a race whose imaginative and easily excitable temperament has at all times rendered it remarkable; and in my earliest infancy I gave evidence of having fully inherited the family character. As I advanced in years it was more strongly developed, becoming, for many reasons, a cause of serious disquietude to my friends and of positive injury to myself. I grew self-willed, addicted to the wildest caprices, and a prey to the most ungovernable passions. Weak-minded and beset with constitutional infirmities akin to my own, my parents could do but little to check the evil propensities which distinguished me. Some feeble and ill-directed efforts resulted in complete failure on their part, and, of course, in total triumph on mine. Thenceforward my voice was a household law. And at an age when few children have abandoned their leading strings, I was left to the guidance of my own will, and became in all but name the master of my own actions.

My earliest recollections of school life are connected with a large, rambling, Elizabethan house, in a misty-looking village of England, where were a vast number of gigantic and gnarled trees and where all the houses were excessively ancient. In truth it was a dreamlike and spirit-soothing place, that venerable old town. At this moment, in fancy, I feel the refreshing chilliness of its deeply shadowed avenues, inhale the fragrance of its thousand shrubberies, and thrill anew with undefinable delight at the deep hollow note of the church bell, breaking each hour with sullen and sudden roar upon the stillness of the dusky atmosphere in which the fretted Gothic steeple lay imbedded and asleep.

It gives me, perhaps, as much pleasure as I can now in any manner experience to dwell upon minute recollections of the school and its concerns. Steeped in misery as I am—misery, alas, only too real—I shall be pardoned for seeking relief, however slight and temporary, in the weakness of a few rambling details. These details, utterly trivial and even ridiculous in themselves, assume adventitious importance in my fancy, for they were connected with a period and a locality wherein I recognize the first ambiguous monitions of the destiny which afterwards so fully overshadowed me. Let me then remember.

The house, I have said, was old and irregular. The grounds were extensive, and a high and solid brick wall, topped with a bed of mortar and broken glass, encompassed the whole. This prisonlike rampart formed the limit of our domain. Beyond it we went but thrice a week —once every Saturday afternoon when, attended by two ushers, we were permitted to take brief walks in a body through some of the neighboring fields; and twice during Sunday, when we were paraded in the same formal manner to the morning and evening service in the one church of the village.

The principal of our school was pastor of this church. With how deep a spirit of wonder and perplexity was I wont to regard him from our remote pew in the gallery as with solemn step and slow he ascended the pulpit! This reverend man—with countenance so demurely benign, with robes so glossy and so clerically flowing, with wig so minutely powdered, so rigid and so vast—could this be he who, of late, with sour visage and in snuffy habiliments, administered, ferule in hand, the Draconian laws of the academy? Oh gigantic paradox, too utterly monstrous for solution!

At an angle of the ponderous wall frowned a more ponderous gate. It was riveted and studded with iron bolts and surmounted with jagged iron spikes. What impressions of deep awe did it inspire! It was never opened save for the three periodical egressions and ingressions already mentioned. Then, in every creak of its mighty hinges we found a plenitude of mystery—a world of matter for solemn remark or for more solemn meditation.

The extensive enclosure was irregular in form, having many capacious recesses. Of these, three or four of the largest constituted the playground. It was level and covered with fine hard gravel. I well remember it had no trees nor benches, nor anything similar within it. Of course it was in the rear of the house. In front lay a small parterre, planted with box and other shrubs; but through this sacred division we passed only upon rare occasions indeed—such as a first advent to school or final departure thence, or perhaps, when a parent or friend having called for us, we joyfully took our way home for the Christmas or midsummer holidays.

But the house! How quaint an old building was this! To me how veritably a palace of enchantment! There was really no end to its windings, to its incomprehensible sub-divisions. It was difficult, at any given time, to say with certainty upon which of its two stories one happened to be. From each room to every other there were three or four steps either in ascent or descent. Then the wings were innumerable, inconceivable, and so turned in upon themselves that our ideas of the entire mansion were not far different from those with which we regarded infinity. During the five years of my residence here I was never able to ascertain with precision in what remote locality lay the little sleeping apartment assigned to myself and some eighteen or twenty other scholars.

The schoolroom was the largest in the house, and I could not help thinking, in the world. It was very long, narrow, and dismally low, with pointed Gothic windows and a ceiling of oak. In a remote and terror-inspiring angle was a square enclosure of eight or ten feet, com-prising the sanctum, during school hours, of our princi-pal, the Reverend Dr. Bransby. It was a solid structure with a massive door, which, sooner than open in the absense of the Dominie, we would all have willingly perished by the *peine forte et dure*. In other angles were two other similar boxes, far less reverenced, indeed, but still matters of awe. One of these was the pulpit of the classics usher, one of the English and mathematics usher. Interspersed about the room, crossing and recrossing in endless irregularity, were innumerable benches and desks, black, ancient and time worn. They were piled desperately with much-bethumbed books, and so beseamed with initial letters, names at full length, grotesque figures and other multiplied efforts of the knife, as to have entirely lost what little of original form might have been their portion in days long departed. A huge bucket with water stood at one extremity of the room, and a clock of stupendous dimensions at the other.

Encompassed by the massive walls of this venerable academy I passed, yet not in tedium or disgust, my tenth to my fifteenth year. The teeming brain of childhood requires no external world of incident to occupy or amuse it; and the apparently dismal monotony of the school was replete with more intense excitement than my riper youth has derived from luxury, or my full manhood from crime. Yet I must believe that my first mental development had in it much of the uncommon, even of the *outré*. Upon mankind at large the events of very early existence rarely leave in mature age any definite impression. All is gray shadow, a weak and irregular remembrance, an in-

distinct regathering of feeble pleasures and phantasmagoric pains. With me this is not so. In childhood I must
have felt with the energy of a man what I now find
stamped upon memory in lines as vivid, as deep, and as
durable as the *exergues* of the Carthaginian medals.

Yet actually, from an outsider's view, how little there
was to remember! The morning's awakening and nightly
summons to bed, the connings and recitations, the peri-
odic half-holidays and perambulations, the playground
with its broils, its pastimes, its intrigues—these, by a mental sorcery long forgotten, were made to involve a wilderness of sensation, a world of rich incident, a universe of
varied emotion, of excitement most passionate and spirit-
stirring.

The ardor, the enthusiasm and the imperiousness of
my disposition soon rendered me a marked character
among my schoolmates, and by slow but natural gradations, gave me an ascendency over all not greatly older
than myself—over all with a single exception. This exception was a scholar who, although no relation, bore the
same Christian and surname as myself, a circumstance in
fact little remarkable; for notwithstanding a noble descent, mine was one of those everyday appellations which
seem by prescriptive right to have been time out of mind
the common property of the mob. In this narrative I have
therefore designated myself as William Wilson, a fictitious
title not very dissimilar to the real. My namesake alone,
of those who in school phraseology constituted "our set,"

presumed to compete with me in classroom studies and in the sports and broils of the playground, and to refuse implicit belief in my assertions or to submit to my will. Indeed, he was the only one to interfere with my arbitrary dictation in any respect whatsoever. If there is on earth a supreme and unqualified despotism, it is the despotism of a master mind in boyhood over the less energetic spirit of his companions.

Wilson's rebellion was to me a source of the greatest embarrassment—the more so as, in spite of the bravado with which in public I made a point of treating him and his pretensions, I secretly felt that I feared him. I could not help thinking that the equality which he maintained so easily with me was a proof of his true superiority, since not to be overcome cost me a perpetual struggle.

Yet this superiority, even this equality, was in truth acknowledged by no one but me. Our associates, by some unaccountable blindness, seemed not even to suspect it. For his competition, his resistance, and especially his impertinent and dogged interference with my purposes were not more pointed than private. He appeared to be destitute alike of the ambition which urged me, and of the passionate energy of mind which enabled me, to excel. In his rivalry he might have been actuated solely by a whimsical desire to thwart, astonish or mortify me; although there were times when I could not help observing, with a feeling made up of wonder, abasement and pique, that he mingled with his injuries, insults or contradictions an inappropriate, and assuredly most unwelcome, *affectionateness* of manner. I could only think that this singular manner arose from a consummate self-conceit, disguised as patronage.

Perhaps it was this manner, conjoined with our identity of name and the mere accident of our having entered the school on the same day, which set afloat the notion among the senior classes in the academy that we were brothers. Seniors do not usually inquire with much strictness into the affairs of their juniors. I have said or should have said before, that Wilson was not in the remotest degree connected with my family. But assuredly if we *had* been brothers we must have been twins; for after leaving Dr. Bransby's, I casually learned that my namesake was born on the nineteenth of January, 1813—the day is precisely that of my own nativity.

It may seem strange that in spite of my continual anxiety, occasioned by the rivalry of Wilson and his intolerable spirit of contradiction, I could not bring myself to hate him altogether. To be sure we had, nearly every day, a quarrel in which he yielded me publicly the palm of victory, yet in some manner contrived to make me feel that it was *he* who had deserved it. Yet a sense of pride on my part and a real dignity on his, kept us always on speaking terms. And there were many points of strong congeniality in our tempers, operating to awaken in me a sentiment which our position alone, perhaps, prevented from ripening into friendship.

Indeed it is difficult to define or even to describe my real feelings towards him. They were so mixed—some petulant animosity which was not yet hatred, some esteem, more respect, much fear, and a world of uneasy curiosity. To the moralist it will be unnecessary to say, in addition, that Wilson and myself were the most inseparable of companions.

It was no doubt the anomalous state of affairs existing between us which turned all my attacks, either open or covert, upon him into the channel of banter or practical joke (giving pain while assuming the aspect of mere fun), rather than into a more serious and determined hostility. But my endeavors were by no means uniformly successful, even when my plans were the most wittily concocted, for my namesake had much about him of that unassuming and quiet austerity; while enjoying the poignancy of his own jokes, he himself had no heel of Achilles. I could find, indeed, but one vulnerable point. That lay in a personal peculiarity arising, perhaps, from a constitutional disease, and would have been spared by any antagonist less at his wit's end than myself. My rival had a weakness in the faucial or guttural organs, which prevented him from raising his voice at any time above a very low whisper. Of this defect I did not fail to take what poor advantage lay in my power.

Wilson's retaliations in kind were many, and there was one form of his practical wit that disturbed me beyond measure. How he first discovered that so petty a thing would vex me is a question I could never solve, but having done so, he habitually practiced the annoyance. I had always felt aversion to my uncourtly surname, and my very common, if not plebeian given name. The words were venom in my ears; when on the day of my arrival a second William Wilson came to the academy, I felt angry with him for bearing the name. I was doubly disgusted because another William Wilson would be the cause of its twofold repetition. He would be constantly in my presence, and his concerns in the ordinary routine of the school business must inevitably, on account of the detestable coincidence, be confused with those of mine.

The feeling of vexation grew stronger with every circumstance that showed a resemblance, moral or physical, between my rival and myself. I had not then discovered the remarkable fact that we were of the same age; but I saw that we were of the same height, and I perceived that we were singularly alike in general contour of person and outline of feature. I was galled, too, by the rumor current in the upper forms, based on our identical names, that we were related. Nothing could more seriously disturb me (although I scrupulously concealed it) than an allusion to a similarity existing between us of mind, person or condition.

But in truth I had no reason to believe that this similarity had ever been made a subject of comment, or even observed at all by our schoolfellows. That *he* observed it in all its bearings, and as fixedly as I, was apparent; but that he could discover in such circumstances so fruitful a field of annoyance can only be attributed, as I said before, to his more than ordinary penetration.

His method was to imitate me to perfection in both words and actions, and most admirably did he play the part. My dress was an easy matter to copy; my gait and general manner were without difficulty appropriated; in spite of his constitutional defect, even my voice did not escape him. My louder tones were, of course, impossible for him, but the *quality* was identical, and in his singular whisper grew the very echo of my voice.

How greatly this exquisite portraiture (for it could not justly be termed a caricature) harassed me I will not venture to describe. I had but one consolation—in the fact that the imitation was apparently noticed by me alone, and that I had to endure only the knowing and strangely sarcastic smiles of my namesake himself. Satisfied with having produced in my bosom the intended effect, he seemed to chuckle in secret over the sting he had inflicted, and characteristically disregarded the public applause which the success of his witty endeavors might so easily have elicited. That the school indeed did not feel his design, perceive its accomplishment, and participate in his sneer was for many anxious months a riddle I could not resolve. Perhaps the *gradation* of his copy rendered it not readily perceptible; or more possibly, I owed my security to the masterly air of the copyist who, disdaining the letter, gave the full spirit of his original for my individual contemplation and chagrin.

I have already spoken more than once of the disgusting air of patronage which he assumed toward me, and of his frequent officious interference with my will. This interference often took the ungracious form of advice, advice not openly given but hinted or insinuated. I received it with a repugnance which gained strength as I grew in years. Yet, at this distant day let me acknowledge that I can recall no occasion when his suggestions were on the side of errors and follies so usual to our immature age and inexperience. His moral sense, if not his general talents and worldly wisdom, was far keener than mine. I might today have been a better and thus a happier man, had I less frequently rejected the counsels of those meaning whispers which I then cordially hated and bitterly despised.

As it was, I grew restive in the extreme under his distasteful supervision, and daily resented more openly what I considered his intolerable arrogance. I have said that in the first years of our connection as schoolmates, my feelings toward him might easily have ripened into friendship. But in the latter months of my residence at the academy, although the intrusion of his ordinary manner had beyond doubt abated in some measure, my sentiments, in similar proportion, partook of positive hatred. Upon one occasion he saw this, I think, and afterwards avoided me, or at least made a show of avoiding me.

It was about the same period, if I remember aright, that in an altercation of violence with him when he was more than usually thrown off his guard, he spoke and acted with an openness of demeanor rather foreign to his nature. I discovered, or fancied I discovered in his accent, his air and general appearance, something which first startled and then deeply interested me. It brought to mind dim visions of my earliest infancy—wild, confused and thronging memories of a time when memory herself was yet unborn. I cannot better describe the sensation which oppressed me than by saying that I could only with difficulty shake off the belief that I had been acquainted with him long ago—at some infinitely remote point of the past. The delusion however faded as rapidly as it came; and I mention it in order to define the day of the last conversation I held with him at school.

The huge old house, with its countless subdivisions, had several large chambers communicating with each other, where slept the greater number of the students. There were, however (as must necessarily happen in a building so awkwardly planned), many little nooks or recesses, the odds and ends of the structure; these the economic ingenuity of Dr. Bransby had also fitted up as dormitories, although being the merest closets, they were capable of accommodating but a single individual. One of these small apartments was occupied by Wilson.

It was late at night, about the close of my fith year at the school and immediately after the altercation just mentioned, when I arose from bed and, lamp in hand, stole through a wilderness of narrow passages from my bedroom to that of my rival. I had long been plotting one of those ill-natured pieces of practical wit in which I had hitherto been so unsuccessful. It was now my intention to put my scheme in operation, and to make him feel the whole extent of my malice. I noiselessly entered his closet, leaving the lamp on the outside. I advanced a step, and listened to the sound of his tranquil breathing. Assured that he was asleep, I took the light, and with it again approached the bed. Close curtains were around it, which I slowly and quietly withdrew. The bright rays fell vividly upon the sleeper. I looked, and a numbness, an iciness of feeling instantly pervaded my frame. My breast heaved, my knees tottered, my whole spirit was possessed with an objectless yet intolerable horror. Gasping for breath, I lowered the lamp still nearer to the face. Were these the lineaments of William Wilson? I saw, indeed, that they were his, but I shook with fear in fancying they were not. What *was* there about them to confound me in this manner? I gazed, while my brain reeled with a multitude of incoherent thoughts. Not thus he appeared, assuredly not *thus*, in his waking hours. The same name! the same contour of person! The same day of arrival at the academy! And then his dogged and meaningless imitation of my gait, my voice, my habits and my manner! Was it in truth within the bounds of human possibility, that what I now saw was merely the result of the habitual practice of this sarcastic imitation? Awe-stricken, and with a creeping shudder, I extinguished the lamp, passed silently from the chamber, and left the halls of that old academy at once, never to enter them again.

After a lapse of some months, spent at home in idleness, I found myself at Eton. The brief interval had been sufficient to dim my memory of the events at Dr. Bransby's, or at least to change the nature of the feelings with which I remembered them. The truth, the tragedy, of the drama was gone. I could now find room to doubt. If I called up the subject at all it was to wonder at the extent of my credulity, and smile at the vivid imagination which I hereditarily possessed. Nor was this skepticism likely to be diminished by the life I led at Eton. The vortex of thoughtless folly into which I so immediately and so recklessly plunged there washed away all but the froth of my past hours, engulfed every serious impression, and left to memory only the levities of my former existence.

I do not wish to detail my miserable profligacy here— a profligacy which defied the laws, while it eluded the vigilance of the institution. Three years of folly, passed without profit, had given me rooted habits of vice when, after a week of dissipation, I invited a small party of the most dissolute students to a secret carousal in my chambers. We met at a late hour of the night, for our debaucheries were to be faithfully protracted until morning. The wine flowed freely, and other more dangerous seductions were not wanting. The gray dawn had already appeared in the east, while our delirious extravagance was at its height. Madly flushed with cards and intoxication, I was in the act of insisting upon a toast of more than usual profanity when my attention was suddenly drawn to the violent opening of the door of the apartment, and by the eager voice of a servant. He said that some person, apparently in great haste, demanded to speak with me in the hall.

Wildly excited with wine, the unexpected interruption rather delighted than surprised me. I staggered forward at once, and a few steps brought me to the vestibule of the building. In this small low room there was no light save that of the feeble dawn which made its way through the semicircular window. As I stepped over the threshold I saw a youth about my own height. He wore a white kerseymere morning frock coat in the novel fashion of the one I myself was wearing. This the faint light enabled me to perceive, but I could not distinguish the features of his face. He strode hurriedly up to me, and seizing me by the arm with a gesture of petulant impatience, whispered the words "William Wilson!" in my ear.

I grew perfectly sober in an instant.

In the manner of the stranger, and in the tremulous shake of his uplifted finger as he held it between my eyes and the light, there was that which filled me with amazement and dread; but it was not this which so violently moved me. It was the solemn admonition in the singular, low, hissing utterance, and above all it was the character, the tone, the *quality,* of those simple and familiar yet *whispered* syllables, which brought back a thousand thronging memories of bygone days, and shocked my soul. Ere I could recover my senses he was gone.

Although this event failed not in its vivid effect upon my disordered imagination, yet it was as evanescent as vivid. For some weeks I busied myself in earnest inquiry, or brooded in morbid speculation. I did not pretend to hide from myself the identity of the individual who thus interfered with my affairs, and harassed me with his insinuated counsel.

Who and what was this Wilson? Whence came he? What were his purposes? Upon none of these points could I be satisfied, merely ascertaining that a sudden accident in his family had caused him to leave Dr. Bransby's academy on the afternoon of the day in which I myself had eloped.

But in a brief period I ceased to think upon the subject. My attention was all absorbed in a contemplated departure for Oxford. Thither I soon went. My parents had furnished me with an outfit and annual stipend which would permit me to indulge at will in the luxury already so dear to my heart, and to vie in expenditure with the haughtiest heirs of the wealthiest earldoms in Great Britain.

Excited by such provision for vice, my constitutional temperament broke forth with redoubled ardor, and I spurned even the common restraints of decency in my mad revels. But it would be absurd to detail my extravagance. Let it suffice, that among spendthrifts I outdid them all. To give name to the multitude of my novel follies, I would have added no brief appendix to the long catalogue of vices then usual in the most dissolute university of Europe.

It is incredible that I had, even at this point, so utterly fallen from the gentlemanly estate as to seek acquaintance with the vilest arts of the professional gambler. Having become an adept in his despicable science, I practiced it habitually, as a means of increasing my already enormous income, at the expense of the weak-minded among my fellow collegians. Such, nevertheless, was the fact. And the enormity of this offense against all manly and honorable sentiment was beyond doubt the main reason for the fact that I committed it. Who indeed among my most abandoned associates would not rather have disputed the clearest evidence of his senses than have suspected of such vile tricks the gay, the frank, the generous William Wilson, noblest and most liberal commoner at Oxford, whose follies (said his parasites) were but the follies of youth and unbridled fancy, whose errors but inimitable whim, and whose darkest vice but a careless and dashing extravagance?

I had now been successfully busied in this way for two years, when there came to the university a young *parvenu* nobleman, Glendinning—rich, said report, as Croesus, and his riches had been easily acquired. I soon found him of weak intellect, and of course marked him as a fitting subject for my skill. I frequently engaged him in play, and contrived with the gambler's usual art to let him win considerable sums, the more effectually to entangle him in my snares. At length, my schemes being ripe, I met him (with the full intention that this meeting should be final and decisive) at the chambers of a fellow commoner, Mr. Preston. My fellow commoner was equally intimate with both of us, but to do him justice, entertained not even a remote suspicion of my design. To give it a better coloring, I had contrived to assemble a party of some eight or ten, and was solicitously careful that the introduction of cards should appear accidental, and originate in the proposal of my contemplate dupe himself. To be brief upon a vile topic, I omitted none of the low finesse, so customary upon similar occasions that it is cause for wonder how any can still be found so besotted as to fall victim.

We had protracted our sitting far into the night, and I had at length effected the maneuver of getting Glendinning as my sole antagonist. The game, too, was my favorite *écarté*. The rest of the company, interested in the extent of our play, had abandoned their own cards and were standing around us as spectators. The *parvenu*, who had been induced by my artifices early in the evening to drink deeply, now shuffled, dealt or played with a wild nervousness of manner, for which his intoxication I thought might partially, but could not altogether, account. In a very short period he had become my debtor to a large amount, when having taken a long draught of port he did precisely what I had been coolly anticipating —he proposed to double our already extravagant stakes. With a well-feigned show of reluctance, and not until after my repeated refusal had seduced him into some angry words which gave a color of *pique* to my compliance, did I finally comply.

The result of course proved how entirely he was in my hands; in less than an hour he had quadrupled his debt. For some time his countenance had been losing the florid tinge lent it by the wine; but now, to my astonishment, I perceived that it had grown to a pallor truly fearful. I say to my astonishment. Glendinning had been represented to my eager inquiries as immeasurably wealthy, and the sums which he had as yet lost, although vast, could not I supposed seriously annoy, much less so violently affect him. That he was overcome by the wine just swallowed was the idea which most readily presented itself; and, rather with a view to the preservation of my own character in the eyes of my associates, than from any less interested motive, I was about to insist, peremptorily, upon a discontinuance of the play, when some expressions at my elbow from among the company, and an ejaculation evincing utter despair on the part of Glendinning, gave me to understand that I had effected his total ruin under circumstances which, rendering him an object for the pity of all, should have protected him from the ill offices even of a fiend.

What now might have been my conduct it is difficult to say. The pitiable condition of my dupe had thrown an air of embarrassed gloom over all; and for some moments there was a profound silence, during which I felt my cheeks tingle with the burning glances of scorn and reproach cast on me by the less abandoned of the party.

I will own that an intolerable weight of anxiety was for an instant lifted from my bosom by the sudden and extraordinary interruption which ensued. The heavy folding doors of the apartment were all at once thrown open to their full extent with a vigorous and rushing impetuosity that extinguished, as if by magic, every candle in the room. Their light, in dying, enabled us to perceive that a stranger, about my own height and closely muffled in a cloak, had entered. The darkness, however, was now total, and we could only *feel* that he was standing in our midst. Before any one of us could recover from the extreme astonishment into which this rudeness had thrown all, we heard the voice of the intruder.

"Gentlemen," he said, in the low, distinct, never-to-be-forgotten *whisper* which thrilled me to the marrow of my bones. "I make no apology for this behavior, because in thus behaving I am fulfilling a duty. You are beyond doubt uninformed of the true character of the person who has tonight won at *écarté* a large sum of money from Lord Glendinning. I will therefore put you upon an expeditious and decisive plan of obtaining this very necessary information. Please to examine, at your leisure, the inner linings of the cuff of his left sleeve, and the several little packages which may be found in the somewhat capacious pockets of his embroidered morning wrapper."

While he spoke, so profound was the stillness that one might have heard a pin drop upon the floor. He departed at once, and as abruptly as he had entered. Can I, shall I, describe my sensations? Must I say that I felt all the horrors of the damned? Most assuredly I had little time for reflection. Many hands roughly seized me upon the spot, and lights were immediately reprocured. A search ensued. In the lining of my sleeve were found all the court cards essential in *écarté*, and in the pockets of my wrapper, a number of packs, facsimiles of those used at our sittings, with the single exception that mine were of the species called, technically, *arrondées;* the honors were slightly convex at the ends, the lower cards slightly convex at the sides. In this disposition, the dupe who cuts at the length of the pack, will invariably find that he cuts his antagonist an honor; while the gambler, cutting at the breadth, will as certainly cut nothing for his victim which may count in the records of the game.

Any burst of indignation upon this discovery would have affected me less than the silent contempt and sarcastic composure of the company.

"Mr. Wilson," said our host, stooping to remove from beneath his feet an exceedingly luxurious cloak of rare furs, "Mr. Wilson, this is your property."

The weather was cold; and, upon quitting my own

room, I had thrown a cloak over my dressing-wrapper, putting it off upon reaching the scene of play.

"I presume it is supererogatory to seek here"—he eyed the folds of the garment with a bitter smile—"for any further evidence of your skill. Indeed, we have had enough. You will see the necessity, I hope, of quitting Oxford—at all events, of quitting my chambers instantly."

Abased, humbled to the dust as I then was, it is probable that I should have answered this galling language by personal violence had not my whole attention been arrested by the cloak. My cloak was of a rare fur, how rare, how extravagantly costly I shall not venture to say. Its fashion too was of my own fantastic invention, for I was fastidious to an absurd degree in matters of this nature. When, therefore, Mr. Preston handed me the cloak which he had picked up from the floor near the folding doors of the apartment, it was with astonishment nearly bordering upon terror that I perceived my own already hanging on my arm, where I had no doubt unwittingly placed it. Yet the one presented me was its exact counterpart in every particular. The singular being who had so disastrously exposed me had been muffled, I remembered, in a cloak; and none had been worn by any of the other members of our party. Retaining some presence of mind, I took the one offered me by Preston, placed it unnoticed over my own, left the apartment with a resolute scowl of defiance, and next morning before dawn, commenced a hurried journey from Oxford to the continent, in a perfect agony of horror and of shame.

I fled in vain. My evil destiny pursued me as if in exultation, and proved indeed that the exercise of its mysterious dominion had as yet only begun. Scarcely had I set foot in Paris ere I had fresh evidence of the detestable interest taken in my concerns by this Wilson. Years flew, yet I experienced no relief. Villain! At Rome with how untimely, yet with how spectral an officiousness, he stepped between me and my ambition! At Vienna, too, at Berlin, and at Moscow! Where, in truth, had I *not* bitter cause to curse him within my heart? From his inscrutable tyranny did I at length flee, panic-stricken, as from a pestilence; and to the very ends of the earth I fled in vain.

Again and again, in secret communion with my own spirit, would I ask, "Who is he—whence came he—what are his objects?" But I found no answer. Then I scrutinized, with a minute scrutiny, the forms, the methods and the leading traits of his impertinent supervision. But even here there was little matter for conjecture. It was noticeable, indeed, that in no instance in which he had of late appeared had he crossed my path except to frustrate my schemes, or to disturb my actions, which might have resulted in bitter mischief.

I had also been forced to notice that my tormentor for a very long period of time (while scrupulously and with miraculous dexterity maintaining his whim of an identity of apparel with myself), had so contrived it, in his varied interference with my will, that I never saw his face. Be

Wilson what he might, *this,* at least, was affectation, and folly. Could he for an instant have supposed that in my admonisher at Eton, in the destroyer of my honor at Oxford, in him who thwarted my ambition at Rome, my revenge at Paris, my passionate love at Naples, or what he falsely termed my avarice in Egypt, that in my archenemy and evil genius I could fail to recognize the William Wilson of my schoolboy days—the namesake, companion and rival, the hated and dreaded rival, at Dr. Bransby's? Impossible! But let me hasten to the last eventful scene of the drama.

Thus far I had succumbed supinely to this imperious domination. I habitually regarded, with sentiments of deep awe, the elevated character, the majestic wisdom, the apparent omnipresence and omnipotence of Wilson. These, added to the feeling of terror with which certain other traits in his nature and assumptions inspired me, had operated hitherto, to impress me with an idea of my own utter weakness and helplessness, and to suggest an implicit although bitterly reluctant submission to his will. But of late days I had given myself up entirely to wine; its maddening influence upon my hereditary temper rendered me more and more impatient of control. I began to murmur, to hesitate, to resist. And was it only fancy which induced me to believe that, with the increase of my own firmness, that of my tormentor underwent a proportional diminution? Be this as it may, I now began to feel the inspiration of a burning hope, and at length nurtured in my secret thoughts a stern and desperate resolution that I would no longer be enslaved.

It was at Rome, during the Carnival of 18—, that I attended a masquerade in the palazzo of the Neapolitan Duke di Broglio. I had indulged more freely than usual in the excesses of the wine table; and now the suffocating atmosphere of the crowded rooms irritated me beyond endurance. The difficulty, too, of forcing my way through the maze of company contributed to the ruffling of my temper, for I was anxiously seeking the young, gay, and beautiful wife of the aged and doting di Broglio. With a too unscrupulous confidence, she had previously communicated to me the costume she would be wearing. Now, having caught a glimpse of her, I was hurrying to her. At this moment I felt a light hand placed upon my shoulder, and that ever-remembered, low damnable *whisper* within my ear.

In an absolute frenzy of wrath I turned at once upon him who had thus interrupted me, and seized him violently by the collar. He was attired, as I had expected, in a costume altogether similar to mine, a Spanish cloak of blue velvet, belted about the waist with a crimson sash and wearing a rapier. A mask of black silk entirely covered his face.

"Scoundrel!" I said in a voice husky with rage, while every syllable I uttered added fuel to my fury. "Scoundrel! Impostor! Accursed villain! You shall not—you *shall not* dog me unto death! Follow me, or I stab you where you stand!" I pushed my way from the ballroom into a small antechamber adjoining, dragging him unresistingly with me as I went.

Upon entering, I thrust him furiously from me. He staggered against the wall, while I closed the door with an oath and commanded him to draw. He hesitated an instant; then with a slight sigh he drew, in silence, and put himself upon his defense.

The contest was brief indeed. I was frantic with wild excitement, and felt superhuman energy and power within my single arm. In a few seconds I forced him by sheer strength against the wainscoting, and thus had him at my mercy. I plunged my sword with brute ferocity repeatedly through and through his bosom.

At that instant some person tried the latch of the door. I hastened to prevent an intrusion, and then immediately returned to my dying antagonist. But what human language can adequately portray that astonishment, that horror which possessed me at the spectacle then presented to view? The brief moment in which I averted my eyes had been sufficient to produce, apparently, a material change in the arrangements at the upper or further end of the room. A large mirror—so at first it seemed to me in my confusion—now stood where none had been perceptible before; and as I stepped up to it in extremity of terror, my own image, but with features all pale and dabbled in blood, advanced to meet me with a feeble and tottering gait.

Thus it appeared, I say, but was not. It was my antag-onist—it was Wilson who stood before me in the agonies of death. His mask and cloak lay where he had thrown them, upon the floor. Not a thread in all his clothing, not a line in all the marked and singular lineaments of his face, which was not—my own!

It was Wilson, but he spoke no longer in a whisper. And I fancied that I was speaking when he said:

"*You have conquered, and I yield. Yet, henceforward you are also dead—dead to the world, to heaven, and to hope! In me did you exist—and in my death, see by this image which is your own, how utterly you have mur-dered yourself.*"

LIGEIA

I CANNOT, for my soul, remember how, when, or even precisely where I first became acquainted with the Lady Ligeia. Long years have since elapsed, and my memory is feeble through much suffering. Or, perhaps, I cannot *now* bring these points to mind, because, in truth, the character of my beloved, her rare learning, her singular yet placid cast of beauty, and the thrilling and enthralling eloquence of her low musical language made their way into my heart by paces so steadily and stealthily progressive that they have been unnoticed and unknown. Yet I believe that I met her first and most frequently in some large, old, decaying city near the Rhine. Of her family I have surely heard her speak. That it is of a remotely ancient date cannot be doubted! Ligeia! Ligeia! I am buried in studies of a nature more than all else adapted to deaden impressions of the outward world; it is by that sweet word alone—by Ligeia—that I bring before mine eyes in fancy the image of her who is no more. And now, while I write, a recollection flashes upon me that I have never known the

paternal name of her who was my friend and my be-
trothed, and who became the partner of my studies, and finally the wife of my bosom. Was it a playful charge on the
part of my Ligeia? Or was it a test of my strength of affection that I should institute no inquiries upon this point? Or
was it rather a caprice of my own, a wildly romantic offering on the shrine of the most passionate devotion? I but
indistinctly recall the fact itself. What wonder that I have
utterly forgotten the circumstances which originated or
attended it? And, indeed, if ever that spirit which is entitled Romance presided over a marriage ill-omened, then
most surely she presided over mine.

There is one dear topic, however, on which my memory fails me not. It is the person of Ligeia. In stature
she was tall, somewhat slender, and, in her latter days,
even emaciated. I would in vain attempt to portray the
majesty, the quiet ease of her demeanor, or the incomprehensible lightness and elasticity of her footfall. She
came and departed as a shadow. I was never made aware
of her entrance into my closed study save by the dear
music of her low sweet voice as she placed her marble
hand upon my shoulder. In beauty of face no maiden ever
equaled her. It was the radiance of an opium dream, an
airy and spirit-lifting vision more wildly divine than the
phantasies which hovered about the slumbering souls of
the daughters of Delos. Yet her features were not of that
regular mould which we have been falsely taught to wor-
ship in the classical labors of the heathen. "There is no

exquisite beauty," says Bacon, Lord Verulam, speaking truly of all the forms and genera of beauty, "without some strangeness in the proportion." Yet, although I saw that the features of Ligeia were not of a classic regularity, although I perceived that her loveliness was indeed "exquisite," and felt that there was much of "strangeness" pervading it, yet I have tried in vain to detect the irregularity and to trace home my own perception of "the strange." I examined the contour of the pale and lofty forehead. It was faultless. How cold indeed that word when applied to a majesty so divine—the skin rivaling the purest ivory, the commanding extent and repose, the gentle prominence of the regions above the temples; and then the raven-black, the glossy, the luxuriant and naturally-curling tresses, setting forth the full force of the Homeric epithet, "hyacinthine"! I looked at the delicate outlines of the nose, and nowhere but in the graceful medallions of the Hebrews had I beheld a similar perfection. There were the same luxurious smoothness of surface, the same scarcely perceptible tendency to the aquiline, the same harmoniously curved nostrils speaking the free spirit. I regarded the sweet mouth. Here was indeed the triumph of all things heavenly—the magnificent turn of the short upper lip, the soft, voluptuous slumber of the under, the dimples which sported, the color which spoke, and the teeth glancing back, with a brilliancy almost startling, every ray of the holy light which fell upon them in her serene and placid, yet most exultingly radiant of all smiles. I scrutinized the formation of the chin. And here, too, I found the gentleness of breadth, the softness and the majesty, the fullness and the spirituality of the Greek.

And then I peered into the large eyes of Ligeia. It might have been that in these very eyes of my beloved lay the secret to which Lord Verulam alludes. They were, I must believe, far larger than the ordinary eyes of our own race. They were even fuller than the fullest of the gazelle eyes of the tribe of the valley of Nourjahad. Yet it was only at intervals, in moments of intense excitement, that this peculiarity became more than slightly noticeable in Ligeia. And at such moments was her beauty—in my heated fancy thus it appeared perhaps—the beauty of beings either above or apart from the earth, the beauty of the fabulous houri of the Turk. The hue of the orbs was the most brilliant of black, and far over them hung jet lashes of great length. The brows, slightly irregular in outline, had the same tint. The "strangeness," however, which I found in the eyes was of a nature distinct from the formation or the color or the brilliancy of the features, and must, after all, be referred to as the expression. Ah, word of no meaning behind whose vast latitude of mere sound we intrench our ignorance of so much of the spiritual. The expression of the eyes of Ligeia! How for long hours have I pondered upon it! How have I, through the whole of a midsummer night, struggled to fathom it! What was it—that something more profound than the well of

Democritus—which lay far within the pupils of my beloved? What *was* it? I was possessed with a passion to discover. Those eyes! Those large, those shining, those divine orbs! They became to me twin stars of Leda, and I to them the most devout of astrologers.

There is no point among the many incomprehensible anomalies of the science of mind more thrillingly exciting than the fact—never, I believe, noticed in the schools—that, in our endeavors to recall to memory something long forgotten, we often find ourselves upon the very verge of remembrance without being able, in the end, to remember. And thus how frequently in my intense scrutiny of Ligeia's eyes have I felt approaching the full knowledge of their expression—felt it approaching, yet not quite mine, and so at length entirely gone from me! And strange, oh strangest mystery of all, I found in the commonest objects of the universe a circle of analogies to that expression. I mean to say that subsequent to the period when Ligeia's beauty passed into my spirit, there dwelling as in a shrine, I derived from many existences in the material world a sentiment such as I felt always aroused within me by her large and luminous orbs. Yet I could not define that sentiment, or analyze, or even steadily view it. I recognized it, let me repeat, sometimes in the survey of a rapidly-growing vine, in the contemplation of a moth, a butterfly, a chrysalis, a stream of running water. I have felt it in the ocean, in the falling of a meteor. I have felt it in the glances of unusually aged people. And there are one or two stars in heaven (one especially, a star of the sixth magnitude, double and changeable, to be found near the large star in Lyra) in a telescopic scrutiny of which I have been made aware of the feeling. I have been filled with it by certain sounds from stringed instruments, and not infrequently by passages from books. Among innumerable other instances, I well remember something in a volume of Joseph Glanvill, which (perhaps merely from its quaintness—who shall say?) never failed to inspire me with the sentiment:

"And the will therein lieth which dieth not. Who knoweth the mysteries of the will, with its vigor? For God is but a great will pervading all things by nature of its intentness. Man doth not yield himself to the angels, nor unto death utterly, save only through the weakness of his feeble will."

Length of years and subsequent reflection have enabled me to trace, indeed, some remote connection between this passage in the English moralist and a portion of the character of Ligeia. An intensity in thought, action or speech was possibly, in her, a result or at least an index of that gigantic volition which, during our long intercourse, failed to give other and more immediate evidence of its existence. Of all the women whom I have ever known, she, the outwardly calm, the ever-placid Ligeia, was the most violently a prey to the tumultuous vultures of stern passion. And of such passion I could form no estimate, save by the miraculous expansion of those eyes which at once so delighted and appalled me, by the almost magical melody, modulation, distinctness and placidity of her very low voice, and by the fierce energy (rendered doubly effective by contrast with her manner of utterance) of the wild words which she habitually uttered.

I have spoken of the learning of Ligeia; it was immense, such as I have never known in woman. In the classical tongues she was deeply proficient, and as far as my own acquaintance extended in regard to the modern dialects of Europe, I have never known her at fault. Indeed upon any theme of the most admired, because simply the most abstruse of the boasted erudition of the academy, have I ever found Ligeia at fault? How singularly, how thrillingly, this one point in the nature of my wife has forced itself, at this late period only, upon my attention! I said her knowledge was such as I have never known in woman. But where breathes the man who has traversed, and successfully, *all* the wide areas of moral, physical, and mathematical science? I saw not then what I now clearly perceive, that the acquisitions of Ligeia were gigantic, were astounding; yet I was sufficiently aware of her infinite supremacy to resign myself, with a childlike confidence, to her guidance through the chaotic world of metaphysical investigation at which I was most busily occupied during the earlier years of our marriage. With how vast a triumph, with how vivid a delight, with how much of all that is ethereal in hope did I feel, as she bent over me in

studies but little sought and even less known, that delicious vista by slow degrees expanding before me, down
whose long, gorgeous, and all untrodden path I might at
length pass onward to the goal of a wisdom too divinely
precious not to be forbidden!

How poignant, then, must have been the grief with
which after some years I beheld my well-grounded expectations take wings to themselves and fly away! Without Ligeia I was but as a child groping benighted. Her
presence, her readings alone, rendered vividly luminous
the many mysteries of the transcendentalism in which we
were immersed. Wanting the radiant luster of her eyes,
letters lambent and golden grew duller than Saturnian
lead. And now those eyes shone less and less frequently
upon the pages over which I pored. Ligeia grew ill. The
wild eyes blazed with a too, too glorious effulgence; the
pale fingers became of the transparent waxen hue of the
grave; and the blue veins upon the lofty forehead swelled
and sank impetuously with the tides of the most gentle
emotion.

I saw that she must die, and I struggled desperately in
spirit with the grim Azrael. And the struggles of the passionate wife were, to my astonishment, even more energetic than my own. There had been much in her stern
nature to impress me with the belief that, to her, death
would have come without its terrors; but not so. Words
are impotent to convey any just idea of the fierceness of
resistance with which she wrestled with the Shadow. I

groaned in anguish at the pitiable spectacle. I would have soothed, I would have reasoned; but in the intensity of her wild desire for life—for life—*but* for life—solace and reason were alike the uttermost of folly. Yet not until the last instance, amid the most convulsive writhings of her fierce spirit, was the external placidity of her demeanor shaken. Her voice grew more gentle, grew more low; yet I would not wish to dwell upon the wild meaning of the quietly uttered words. My brain reeled as I hearkened, entranced, to a melody more than mortal, to assumptions and aspirations which mortality had never before known.

That she loved me I should not have doubted; and I might have been easily aware that, in a bosom such as hers, love would have reigned no ordinary passion. But in death only was I fully impressed with the strength of her affection. For long hours, detaining my hand, would she pour out before me the overflowing of a heart whose more than passionate devotion amounted to idolatry. How had I deserved to be so blessed by such confessions? How had I deserved to be so cursed with the removal of my beloved in the hour of her making them? But upon this subject I cannot bear to dilate. Let me say only that in Ligeia's more than womanly abandonment to a love—alas, all unmerited, all unworthily bestowed—I at length recognized the principle of her longing, with so wildly earnest a desire, for the life which was now fleeing so rapidly away. It is this wild longing, it is this eager vehemence of desire for life—for life itself—that I have no power to portray, no utterance capable of expressing.

At high noon before the night in which she departed, beckoning me peremptorily to her side, she bade me repeat certain verses composed by herself not many days before. I obeyed her. They were these:

> Lo! 'tis a gala night
>   Within the lonesome latter years!
> An angel throng, bewinged, bedight
>   In veils, and drowned in tears,
> Sit in a theater, to see
>   A play of hopes and fears,
> While the orchestra breathes fitfully
>   The music of the spheres.
>
> Mimes, in the form of God on high,
>   Mutter and mumble low,
> And hither and thither fly—
>   Mere puppets they, who come and go
> At bidding of vast formless things
>   That shift the scenery to and fro,
> Flapping from out their condor wings
>   Invisible woe!
>
> That motley drama!—oh, be sure
>   It shall not be forgot!
> With its phantom chased forevermore,
>   By a crowd that seize it not
> Through a circle that ever returneth in
>   To the selfsame spot;
> And much of madness, and more of sin
>   And horror, the soul of the plot.

But see, amid the mimic rout,
   A crawling shape intrude!
A blood-red thing that writhes from out
   The scenic solitude!
It writhes! It writhes! With mortal pangs
   The mimes become its food,
And the seraphs sob at vermin fangs
   In human gore imbued.

Out, out are the lights—out all!
   And over each quivering form,
The curtain, a funeral pall,
   Comes down with the rush of a storm—
And the angels, all pallid and wan,
   Uprising, unveiling, affirm
That the play is the tragedy, *Man*.
   And its hero, the Conqueror Worm.

"O God!" half-shrieked Ligeia, leaping to her feet and extending her arms aloft with a spasmodic movement, as I made an end of these lines. "O God! O Divine Father! Shall these things be undeviatingly so? Shall this conqueror be not once conquered? Are we not part and parcel in Thee? Who—who knoweth the mysteries of the will, with its vigor? Man doth not yield himself to the angels, nor unto death utterly, save only through the weakness of his feeble will."

And now, as if exhausted with emotion, she suffered her white arms to fall, and returned solemnly to her bed of death. And as she breathed her last sighs, there came mingled with them a low murmur from her lips. I bent to them my ear and distinguished, again, the concluding words of the passage in Glanvill:

Man doth not yield himself to the angels, nor unto death utterly, save only through the weakness of his feeble will.

She died. And I, crushed into the very dust with sorrow, could not longer endure the lonely desolation of my dwelling in the dim and decaying city by the Rhine. I had no lack of what the world calls wealth. Ligeia had brought me far more, far, far more, than ordinarily falls to the lot of mortals.

After a few months of weary and aimless wandering, I purchased and put in some repair an abbey, which I shall not name, in one of the wildest and least frequented portions of fair England. The gloomy and dreary grandeur of the building, the almost savage aspect of the domain, the many melancholy and time-honored memories connected with both had much in unison with the feelings of utter abandonment which had driven me into that remote and unsocial region of the country.

Yet although the external abbey with its verdant decay hanging about it suffered but little alteration, I gave way, with a childlike perversity, and perchance with a faint hope of alleviating my sorrows, to a display of more than regal magnificence within. For such follies, even in childhood, I had imbibed a taste, and now they came back to me as if in the dotage of grief. Alas, I feel how much even of incipient madness might have been discovered in the gorgeous and fantastic draperies, in the solemn carvings of Egypt, in the wild cornices and furniture, in the bedlam patterns of the carpets of tufted gold! I had become a slave to opium, and my labors and my orders had taken a coloring from my dreams. But these absurdities I must not pause to detail. Let me speak only of that one chamber, ever accursed, whither in a moment of mental alienation I led from the altar as my bride—as the successor of the unforgotten Ligeia—the fair-haired and blue-eyed Lady Rowena Trevanion of Tremaine.

There is no individual portion of the architecture and decoration of that bridal chamber which is not now visibly before me. Where were the souls of the haughty family of the bride when, through thirst of gold they permitted to pass over the threshold of an apartment so bedecked, a maiden and a daughter so beloved? I have said that I minutely remember the details of the chamber— yet I am sadly forgetful on topics of deep moment; and here there was no system, no keeping, in the fantastic display to take hold upon the memory. The room lay in a high turret of the castellated abbey, was pentagonal in shape, and of capacious size. Occupying the whole southern face of the pentagon was the sole window—an immense sheet of unbroken glass from Venice—a single pane tinted of a leaden hue, so that the rays of either the sun or moon, passing through it fell with a ghastly luster on the objects within. Over the upper portion of this huge window extended the trelliswork of an aged vine, which clambered up the massive walls of the turret. The ceiling, of gloomy-looking oak, was excessively lofty, vaulted, and elaborately fretted with the wildest and most grotesque specimens of a semi-Gothic, semi-druidical device. From out the most central recess of this melancholy vaulting, hung, by a single chain of gold with long links, a huge censer of the same metal, Saracenic in pattern, and with many perforations so contrived that there writhed in and out of them, as if endued with a serpent vitality, a continual succession of varicolored fires.

Some few ottomans and golden candelabra of Eastern figure were in various stations about, and there was the couch, too—the bridal bed—of an Indian model, low and sculptured of solid ebony, with a pall-like canopy above. In each of the angles of the chamber stood on end a gigantic sarcophagus of black granite, from the tombs of the Egyptian kings at Luxor, with their aged lids full of immemorial sculpture. But in the draping of the apartment lay, alas, the chief phantasy of all. The lofty walls, gigantic in height, even unproportionably so, were hung from summit to foot in vast folds of a heavy, massive-looking tapestry—tapestry of a material which was found alike as a carpet on the floor, as a covering for the ottomans and the ebony bed, as a canopy for the bed, and as the gorgeous volutes of the curtains which partially shaded the window. The material was the richest cloth of gold. It was spotted all over, at irregular intervals, with arabesque figures, about a foot in diameter, and wrought upon the

cloth in patterns of jet-black. But these figures partook of
the true character of the arabesque only when regarded
from a single point of view. By a contrivance now common, and indeed traceable to a very remote period of antiquity, they were made changeable in aspect. To one
entering the room, they bore the appearance of simple
monstrosities; but upon a farther advance, this appearance gradually departed; and step by step, as the visitor
moved his station in the chamber, he saw himself surrounded by an endless succession of the ghastly forms
which belong to the superstition of the Norman, or arise
in the guilty slumbers of the monk. The phantasmagoric
effect was vastly heightened by the artificial introduction
of a strong continual current of wind behind the draperies,
giving a hideous and uneasy animation to the whole.

In halls such as these, in a bridal chamber such as
this, I passed with the Lady of Tremaine the unhallowed
hours of the first month of our marriage—passed them
with but little disquietude. That my wife dreaded the
fierce moodiness of my temper, that she shunned me and
loved me but little, I could not help perceiving; but it
gave me rather pleasure than otherwise. I loathed her
with a hatred belonging more to demon than to man.
My memory flew back (oh, with what intensity of regret!) to Ligeia, the beloved, the august, the beautiful,
the entombed. I reveled in recollections of her purity, of
her wisdom, of her lofty ethereal nature, of her passionate
idolatrous love. Now did my spirit fully and freely burn

with more than all the fires of her own. In the excitement of my opium dreams (for I was habitually fettered in the shackles of the drug), I would call aloud upon her name during the silence of the night, or among the sheltered recesses of the glens by day, as if, through the wild eagerness, the solemn passion, the consuming ardor of my longing for the departed, I could restore her to the pathway she had abandoned—*could* it be forever?—on the earth.

At the beginning of the second month of the marriage, the Lady Rowena was attacked with sudden illness, from which her recovery was slow. The fever which consumed her rendered her nights uneasy; and in her perturbed state of half-slumber she spoke of sounds and of motions in and about the chamber of the turret, which I concluded had no origin save in the distemper of her fancy, or perhaps in the phantasmagoric influences of the chamber itself. She became at length convalescent—finally well. Yet but a brief period elapsed ere a second more violent disorder again threw her upon a bed of suffering; and from this attack her frame, at all times feeble, never altogether recovered. Her illnesses were, after this epoch, of alarming character and of more alarming recurrence, defying alike the knowledge and the great exertions of her physicians.

With the increase of the chronic disease which had apparently taken too sure hold upon her constitution to be eradicated by human means, I could not fail to observe a similar increase in the nervous irritation of her temperament, and in her excitability to trivial causes of fear. She spoke again, and now more frequently, of the sounds —of the slight sounds—and of the unusual motions among the tapestries.

One night, near the closing in of September, she pressed this distressing subject with more than usual emphasis upon my attention. She had just awakened from an unquiet slumber, and I had been watching with feelings half of anxiety, half of vague terror the workings of her emaciated countenance. I sat by the side of her ebony bed upon one of the ottomans. She partly arose, and spoke in an earnest low whisper of sounds which she heard but which I could not hear, of motions which she saw but which I could not perceive. The wind was rushing hurriedly behind the tapestries, and I wished to show her (though let me confess, I could not believe it) that those almost inarticulate breathings and those very gently variations of the figures upon the wall were but the natural effects of that customary rushing of the wind. But a deadly pallor, overspreading her face, had proved to me that my exertions to reassure her would be fruitless. She appeared to be fainting, and no attendants were within call.

I remembered a decanter of light wine which had been ordered by her physicians, and hastened across the chamber to procure it. But, as I stepped beneath the light of the censer, two circumstances of a startling nature attracted my attention. I had felt that some palpable although invisible object had passed lightly by my person; and I saw that there lay upon the golden carpet, in the very middle of the rich luster thrown from the censer, a shadow—a faint, indefinite shadow of angelic aspect—such as might be fancied for the shadow of a shade. But I was wild with the excitement of opium, and heeded these things but little.

Having found the wine I recrossed the chamber, and poured out a gobletful which I held to the lips of the fainting lady. She had now partially recovered and took the vessel herself, while I sank upon an ottoman near me, with my eyes fastened upon her. It was then that I became distinctly aware of a gentle footfall upon the carpet, near the couch. In a second thereafter, as Rowena was in the act of raising the wine to her lips, I saw, or may have dreamed that I saw, fall within the goblet, as if from some invisible spring in the atmosphere of the room, three or four large drops of a brilliant and ruby-colored fluid. If this I saw, not so Rowena. She swallowed the wine unhesitatingly, and I forbore to speak to her of a circumstance which must after all, I considered, have been but the suggestion of a vivid imagination rendered morbidly active by the terror of the lady, by the opium, and by the hour.

Yet I cannot conceal it from my own perception that, immediately subsequent to the fall of the ruby drops, a rapid change for the worse took place in the disorder of my wife; so that on the third subsequent night the hands of her menials prepared her for the tomb, and on the fourth I sat alone with her shrouded body in that fantastic chamber which had received her as my bride. Wild visions, opium-engendered, flitted shadow-like before me. I gazed with an unquiet eye upon the sarcophagi in the angles of the room, upon the varying figures of the drapery, and upon the writhing of the varicolored fires in the censer overhead. My eyes then fell to the spot beneath the glare of the censer where I had seen the faint traces of the shadow. It was there, however, no longer; and breathing with greater freedom, I turned my glances to the pallid and rigid figure upon the bed. Then rushed upon me a thousand memories of Ligeia, and then came back upon my heart, with the turbulent violence of a flood, the whole of that unutterable woe with which I had regarded *her* thus enshrouded. The night deepened; and still, with a bosom full of bitter thoughts of the one only and supremely beloved, I remained gazing upon the body of Rowena.

It might have been midnight, or perhaps earlier or later, for I had taken no note of time, when a sob, low, gentle, but very distinct, startled me from my reverie. I *felt* that it came from the bed of ebony, the bed of death. I listened in an agony of superstitious terror, but there was no repetition of the sound. I strained my vision to detect any motion in the corpse, but there was not the slightest perceptible. Yet I could not have been deceived. I *had* heard the noise, however faint, and my soul was awakened within me. I resolutely and perseveringly kept my attention riveted upon the body. Many minutes elapsed before any circumstance occurred tending to throw light upon the mystery. At length it became evident that a very feeble and barely noticeable tinge of color had flushed up within the cheeks and along the sunken small veins of the eyelids. Through a species of unutterable horror and awe, for which the language of mortality has no sufficiently energetic expression, I felt my heart cease to beat, my limbs grow rigid where I sat. Yet a sense of duty finally operated to restore my self-possession. I could no longer doubt that we had been precipitate in our preparations, that Rowena still lived. It was necessary that some immediate exertion be made, yet the turret was altogether apart from the portion of the abbey tenanted by the servants. There were none within call. I had no means of summoning them to my aid without leaving the room for many minutes, and this I could not venture to do. I therefore struggled alone in my endeavors to call back the spirit still hovering. In a short period it was certain, however, that a relapse had taken place: the color disappeared from both eyelid and cheek, leaving a wanness even more than that of marble; the lips became doubly shriveled and pinched up in the ghastly expression of death; a repulsive clamminess and coldness overspread rapidly the surface of the body; and all the usual rigorous stiffness immediately supervened. I fell back with a shudder upon the couch from which I had been so startlingly aroused, and again gave myself up to passionate waking visions of Ligeia.

An hour thus elapsed when (could it be possible?) I was a second time aware of some vague sound issuing from the region of the bed. I listened in extremity of horror. The sound came again—it was a sigh. Rushing to the corpse. I saw, distinctly saw, a tremor upon the lips. In a minute afterwards they relaxed, disclosing a bright line of the pearly teeth. Amazement now struggled in my bosom with the profound awe which had hitherto reigned there alone. I felt that my vision grew dim, that my reason wandered, and it was only by a violent effort that I at length succeeded in nerving myself to the task which duty thus once more had pointed out. There was now a partial glow upon the forehead and upon the cheek and throat; a perceptible warmth pervaded the whole frame; there was even a slight pulsation at the heart. The lady *lived;* and with redoubled ardor I betook myself to the task of restoration. I chafed and bathed the temples and the hands, and used every exertion which experience, and no little medical reading, could suggest. But in vain. Suddenly the color fled, the pulsation ceased, the lips resumed the expression of the dead, and an instant afterwards the whole body took upon itself the icy chilliness, the livid hue, the intense rigidity, the sunken outline, and all the loathsome peculiarities of that which has been for many days a tenant of the tomb.

And again I sunk into visions of Ligeia. And again

(what marvel that I shudder while I write?), *again* there reached my ears a low sob from the region of the ebony bed. But why shall I minutely detail the unspeakable horrors of that night? Why shall I pause to relate how, time after time until near the period of the gray dawn, this hideous drama of revivification was repeated—how each terrific relapse was only into a sterner and apparently more irredeemable death—how each agony wore the aspect of a struggle with some invisible foe—and how each struggle was succeeded by I know not what wild change in the personal appearance of the corpse? Let me hurry to the conclusion.

The greater part of the fearful night had worn away, and she who had been dead once again stirred—and now more vigorously than hitherto, although arousing from a dissolution more appalling in its utter hopelessness than any. I had long ceased to struggle or to move, and remained sitting rigidly upon the ottoman, a helpless prey to a whirl of violent emotions, of which extreme awe was perhaps the least terrible, the least consuming. The corpse, I repeat, stirred, and now more vigorously than before. The hues of life flushed up with unwonted energy into the countenance, the limbs relaxed, and, save that the eyelids were yet pressed heavily together and that the bandages and draperies of the grave still imparted their charnel character to the figure, I might have dreamed that Rowena had indeed shaken off, utterly, the fetters of death. But if this idea was not, even then, altogether adopted, I could at least doubt no longer when, arising from the bed, tottering with feeble steps, with closed eyes, and in the manner of one bewildered in a dream, the thing that was enshrouded advanced boldly and palpably into the middle of the apartment.

I trembled not, I stirred not; for a crowd of unutterable fancies connected with the air, the stature, the demeanor of the figure, rushing hurriedly through my brain, had paralyzed, had chilled me into stone. I stirred not, but gazed upon the apparition. There was a mad disorder in my thoughts, a tumult unappeasable. Could it indeed be the living Rowena who confronted me? Could it indeed be Rowena *at all*—the fair-haired, the blue-eyed Lady Rowena Trevanion of Tremaine? Why, *why* should I doubt it? The bandage lay heavily about the mouth, but then might it not be the mouth of the breathing Lady of Tremaine? And the cheeks—there were the roses as in her noon of life—yes, these might indeed be the fair cheeks of the living Lady of Tremaine. And the chin, with its dimples, as in health, might it not be hers?—but *had she then grown taller since her malady?*

What inexpressible madness seized me with that thought? One bound, and I had reached her feet! Shrinking from my touch, she let fall from her head, unloosened, the ghastly cerements which had confined it, and there streamed forth, into the rushing atmosphere of the chamber, huge masses of long and disheveled hair. It was blacker than the raven wings of the midnight! And now slowly opened the *eyes* of the figure which stood before me.

"Here then, at least," I shrieked aloud, "can I never be mistaken! These are the full, the black, the wild eyes of my lost love—of the *Lady Ligeia.*"

MORELLA

WITH a feeling of deep yet most singular affection I regarded my friend Morella. Thrown by accident into her society many years ago, my soul from our first meeting burned with fires it had never before known. But the fires were not of Eros, and bitter and tormenting to my spirit was the gradual conviction that I could not define their unusual meaning, or regulate their vague intensity. We met; fate bound us together at the altar, yet I never spoke of passion nor thought of love. She, however, shunned society, and attaching herself to me alone, rendered me happy. For it is a happiness to wonder and to dream.

Morella's erudition was profound. Her talents were of no common order; her powers of mind were gigantic. I felt this, and in many matters became her pupil. Soon, and perhaps on account of her Presburg education, she placed before me a number of those mystical writings which are usually considered the mere dross of the early German literature. These, for what reason I could not imagine, were her favorite and constant study. That in the process of time they became my own, should be attributed to the simple but effectual influence of habit and example.

My reason had little to do with all this. My convictions, or I forget myself, were in no manner acted upon by the ideal, nor was any tincture of the mysticism which I read to be discovered, unless I am greatly mistaken, either in my deeds or in my thoughts. Persuaded of this, I abandoned myself implicitly to the guidance of my wife, and entered with an unflinching heart into the intricacies of her studies. And then—then, when poring over forbidden pages I felt a forbidden spirit enkindling within me— Morella would place her cold hand upon my own, and rake up from the ashes of a dead philosophy some low singular words whose strange meaning burned themselves in upon my memory.

Hour after hour I would linger by her side and dwell upon the music of her voice, until at length its melody was tainted with terror. And there fell a shadow upon my soul—I grew pale and shuddered inwardly at those too unearthly tones. Thus joy suddenly faded into horror and the most beautiful became the most hideous, as Hinnom became Gehenna.

It is unnecessary to state the exact character of those inquiries which, growing out of the volumes I have mentioned, formed for so long a time almost my sole conversation with Morella. By those learned in what might be termed theological morality these inquiries will be readily conceived, and by the unlearned they would, at all events, be little understood. The wild pantheism of Fichte; the modified mysticism of the Pythagoreans, and above all the doctrines of *identity* urged by Schelling, were the philosophies presenting the most beauty to the imaginative Morella.

Mr. Locke, I think, truly defines that identity which is termed *personal* to mean the *sanity* of a rational being. Since by *person* we mean an intelligent essence having reason, and since there is a consciousness which always accompanies our individual thinking, we arrive at that which we call self, or personal identity. But the notion of identity, *which at death is or is not lost forever,* was to me at all times a consideration of intense interest—not more from the perplexing and exciting nature of its consequences than from the marked and agitated manner in which Morella mentioned them.

But, indeed, the time had now arrived when the mystery of my wife's manner oppressed me as a spell. I could no longer bear the touch of her wan fingers, nor the low tone of her musical language, nor the luster of her melancholy eyes. And she knew all this but did not upbraid; she seemed conscious of my weakness or folly, and, smiling, called it fate. She seemed also conscious of a cause, to me unknown, for the gradual alienation of my regard, but she gave no hint or token of its nature. Yet was she woman, and pined away daily. In time, the crimson spot settled steadily upon the cheek, and the blue veins upon the pale forehead became prominent; one instant my nature melted into pity, but in the next I met the glance of her meaning eyes, and then my soul sickened and became giddy with the giddiness of one who gazes downward into some dreary and unfathomable abyss.

Shall I then say that I longed with an earnest and consuming desire for the moment of Morella's decease? I did; but the fragile spirit clung to its tenement of clay for many days, for many weeks and irksome months, until my tortured nerves obtained the mastery over my mind. I grew furious through delay and with the heart of a fiend cursed the days, and the hours, and the bitter moments which seemed to lengthen and lengthen as her gentle life declined—like shadows in the dying of the day.

But one autumnal evening, when the winds lay still in heaven, Morella called me to her bedside. There was a dim mist over all the earth, and a warm glow upon the waters, and amid the rich October leaves of the forest, a rainbow from the firmament had surely fallen.

"It is a day of days," she said as I approached, "a day of all days either to live or die. It is a fair day for the sons of earth and life—ah, more fair for the daughters of heaven and death!"

I kissed her forehead, and she continued,

"I am dying, yet shall I live."

"Morella!"

"The days have never been when you could love me, but her whom in life you did abhor, in death you shall adore."

"Morella!"

"I repeat that I am dying. But within me is a pledge of

that affection—ah, how little!—which you did feel for me, Morella. And when my spirit departs the child shall live—your child and mine, Morella's. But your days shall be days of sorrow, that sorrow which is the most lasting of impressions, as the cypress is the most enduring of trees. For the hours of your happiness are over; and joy is not gathered twice in a life, as the roses of Paestum twice in a year. You shall no longer, then, play the Teian with time, but being ignorant of the myrtle and the vine, you shall bear about with you your shroud on earth as do the Moslems at Mecca."

"Morella!" I cried, "Morella! How know you this?" But she turned away her face upon the pillow, and a slight tremor came over her limbs. She died thus, and I heard her voice no more.

Yet, as she had foretold, her child, a daughter—to which in dying she had given birth and which breathed not until the mother breathed no more—lived. The child grew strangely in stature and intellect, and was the perfect resemblance of her who had departed, and I loved her with a love more fervent than I had believed it possible to feel for any denizen of earth.

But ere long the heaven of this pure affection became darkened, and gloom, horror, and grief swept over it in clouds. I said the child grew strangely in stature and intelligence. Strange indeed was her rapid increase in bodily size—but terrible, oh terrible were the tumultuous thoughts which crowded upon me while watching the development of her mental being! Could it be otherwise, when I daily discovered in the conceptions of the child the adult powers and faculties of a woman? When lessons of experience fell from the lips of infancy? And when I found the wisdom or the passions of maturity hourly gleaming from her full and speculative eye? When, I say, all this became evident to my appalled senses—when I could no longer hide it from my soul, nor throw it off from those perceptions which trembled to receive it—is it to be wondered at that suspicions of a nature fearful and exciting crept in upon my spirit, or that my thoughts fell back aghast upon the wild tales and thrilling theories of the entombed Morella? I snatched from the scrutiny of the world a being whom destiny compelled me to adore, and in the rigorous seclusion of my home watched with an agonizing anxiety over all which concerned the beloved.

As years rolled away and I gazed, day after day, upon her holy, mild and eloquent face, and pored over her maturing form, I discovered, day after day, new points of resemblance in the child to her mother, the melancholy, dead Morella. And hourly these shadows of similitude grew darker, and fuller and more definite, more perplexing, and more hideously terrible in their aspect. That her smile was like her mother's I could bear, but I shuddered at its too perfect *identity*. That her eyes were like Morella's I could endure, but then they too often looked into the depths of my soul with Morella's own intense and bewildering meaning. And in the contour of the high forehead, in the ringlets of the silken hair, in the wan fingers which buried themselves therein, in the sad musical tones of her speech, and, above all, in the phrases and expressions of the dead on the lips of the loved and the living, I found food for consuming thought and horror—for a worm that *would* not die.

Thus passed away ten years of her life, and as yet my daughter remained nameless upon the earth. "My child," and "my love," were the designations usually prompted by my affection, and the rigid seclusion of her days precluded all other intercourse. Morella's name had died with her at her death. Of the mother I had never spoken to the daughter—it was impossible to speak. Indeed, during the brief period of her existence, the latter had received no impressions from the outer world, save those afforded by the narrow limits of her privacy. But at length the ceremony of baptism presented to my mind, in its unnerved and agitated condition, a present deliverance from the terrors of my destiny.

At the baptismal font I hesitated for a name. Many titles of the wise and beautiful from old and modern times, and of my own and foreign lands came thronging to my lips, many of them fair titles of the gentle, the happy and the good. What prompted me then to disturb the memory of the buried dead? What demon urged me to breathe that sound, which in its very recollection was wont to cause my blood to rush in torrents from my temples to my heart? What fiend spoke from the recesses of my soul, when amid those dim aisles and in the silence of the night, I whispered within the ears of the holy man the name *Morella?* What more than fiend convulsed the features of my child and overspread them with hues of death, as starting at that scarcely audible sound, she turned her glassy eyes from earth to heaven, and falling prostrate on the black slabs of our ancestral vault, responded, "I am here!"

Distinct, coldly, calmly distinct, fell those few simple sounds within my ear, and thence like molten lead, rolled hissingly into my brain. Years may pass away, but the memory of that moment—never! Nor was I indeed ignorant of the flowers and the vine, but the hemlock and the cypress overshadowed me night and day. I kept no reckoning of time or place. The stars of my fate faded from heaven and the earth grew dark. Its figures passed by me like flitting shadows, and among them all I beheld only—Morella. The winds of the firmament breathed but one sound within my ears, and the ripples upon the sea murmured evermore—Morella.

My child died. With my own hands I bore her to the tomb, and I laughed with a long and bitter laugh when I found no traces of the first, in the charnel where I laid the second, Morella.

THOU ART THE MAN

I WILL now play the Oedipus to the Rattleborough enigma. I will expound to you, as I alone can, the secret of the mechanics that effected the Rattleborough miracle —the one, the true, the admitted, the undisputed, the indisputable miracle, which put a definite end to infidelity among the Rattleburghers, and converted to the orthodoxy of the grandames all the carnal-minded who had ventured to be skeptical before.

This event, which I should be very sorry to discuss in a tone of unsuitable levity, occurred in the summer of 18—. Mr. Barnabas Shuttleworthy, one of the wealthiest and most respected citizens of the borough, had been missing for several days under circumstances which gave rise to suspicion of foul play. Mr. Shuttleworthy had set out from Rattleborough very early one Saturday morning, on horseback, with the avowed intention of proceeding to the city of ——, about fifteen miles distant, and of returning the night of the same day. Two hours after his departure, however, his horse returned without him, and without the saddlebags which had been strapped on his back at starting. The animal was wounded, too, and covered with mud. These circumstances naturally gave rise to much alarm among the friends of the missing man; and when it was found, on Sunday morning, that he had not yet made his appearance, the whole borough arose en masse to go and look for his body.

The foremost and most energetic in instituting this search was the bosom friend of Mr. Shuttleworthy—a Mr. Charles Goodfellow, or as he was universally called, "Charley Goodfellow," or "Old Charley Goodfellow." Now whether it is a marvelous coincidence, or whether a name has an imperceptible effect upon character, I have never yet been able to ascertain. But the fact is unquestionable that there never yet was any person named Charles who was not an open, manly, honest, good-natured, and frank-hearted fellow, with a rich, clear voice, that did you good to hear it, and an eye that looked you always straight in the face, as much as to say: "I have a clear conscience myself, am afraid of no man, and am altogether above doing a mean action." And thus all the hearty, careless, "walking gentlemen" of the stage are very certain to be called Charles.

Now, "Old Charley Goodfellow," although he had been in Rattleborough not longer than six months or thereabouts, and although nobody knew anything about him before he came to settle in the neighborhood, had experienced no difficulty in the world in making the acquaintance of all the respectable people in the borough. Not a man of them but would have taken his bare word for a thousand at any moment. As for the women, there is no saying what they would not have done to oblige him. And all this came of his having been christened Charles, and of his possessing, in consequence, that ingenuous face which is proverbially the very "best letter of recommendation."

I have already said that Mr. Shuttleworthy was one of the most respectable and undoubtedly the most wealthy man in Rattleborough, and "Old Charley Goodfellow" was upon as intimate terms with him as if he had been his own brother. The two old gentlemen were next door neighbors, and although Mr. Shuttleworthy seldom, if ever, visited "Old Charley," and never was known to take a meal in his house, still this did not prevent the two friends from being exceedingly intimate, as I have just observed. For "Old Charley" never let a day pass without stepping in three or four times to see how his neighbor was. Very often he would stay to breakfast or tea, and almost always to dinner; then the amount of wine that was made away with by the two cronies at a sitting would really be difficult to ascertain. "Old Charley's" favorite beverage was Château Margaux, and it appeared to do Mr. Shuttleworthy's heart good to see the old fellow swallow it, as he did, quart after quart.

One day when the wine was *in* and the wit, as a natural consequence, somewhat *out*, he said to his crony, as he slapped him upon the back: "I tell you what it is, 'Old Charley.' You are by all odds the heartiest old fellow I ever came across in all my born days. And since you love to guzzle the wine in that fashion, I'll be darned if I don't make thee a present of a big box of the Château Margaux. Od rot me." (Mr. Shuttleworthy had a sad habit of swearing, although he seldom went beyond "od rot me" or "by gosh" or "by the jolly golly"). "Od rot me," says he, "if I don't send an order to town this very afternoon for a double box of the best that can be got, and I'll make ye a present of it, I will! Ye needn't say a word now. I *will*, I tell ye, and there's an end of it. So look out for it. It will come to hand some of these fine days precisely when ye are looking for it the least!"

I mention this little bit of liberality on the part of Mr. Shuttleworthy, just by way of showing you how very intimate an understanding existed between the two friends.

Well, on the Sunday morning in question, when it came to be fairly understood that Mr. Shuttleworthy had met with foul play, I never saw anyone so profoundly affected as "Old Charley Goodfellow." When he first heard that the horse had come home without his master, and without his master's saddlebags, and all bloody from a pistol shot that had gone clean through and through the poor animal's chest without quite killing him—when he heard all this, he turned as pale as if the missing man had been his own dear brother or father, and shivered and shook all over as if he had had a fit of the ague.

At first he was too much overpowered with grief to be able to do anything at all, or to decide upon any plan of action; so that for a long time he endeavored to dissuade Mr. Shuttleworthy's other friends from making a stir about the matter, thinking it best to wait awhile—say for a week or two, or a month or two—to see if something wouldn't turn up, or if Mr. Shuttleworthy wouldn't come in the natural way and explain his reasons for sending his horse on before. I dare say you have often observed this disposition to temporize or procrastinate in people who are laboring under any very poignant sorrow. Their powers of mind seem to be rendered torpid, so that they have a horror of anything like action, and like nothing in the world so well as to lie quietly in bed and "nurse their grief," as the old ladies express it—to ruminate over their trouble.

The people of Rattleborough had so high an opinion of the wisdom and discretion of "Old Charley" that the greater part of them felt disposed to agree with him, and not make a stir in the business "until something should turn up," as the honest old gentleman worded it. I believe that, after all, this would have been the general determination, but for the very suspicious interference of Mr. Shuttleworthy's nephew, a young man of very dissipated habits, and otherwise of rather bad character. This nephew, whose name was Pennifeather, would listen to nothing like reason in the matter of lying quiet, but insisted upon making an immediate search for the corpse of the murdered man. This was the expression he employed; and Mr. Goodfellow acutely remarked at the time, that it was "a *singular* expression, to say no more." This remark of "Old Charley's" had great effect upon the crowd. And one of the party was heard to ask very impressively how it happened that young Mr. Pennifeather was so intimately cognizant of all the circumstances connected with his wealthy uncle's disappearance as to feel authorized to assert, distinctly and unequivocally, that his uncle *was* 'a murdered man.'

Hereupon some little squibbling and bickering occurred among various members of the crowd, and especially between "Old Charley" and Mr. Pennifeather, although this latter occurrence was by no means a novelty. Little good will had subsisted between the parties for the last three or four months. Matters had even gone so far that Mr. Pennifeather had actually knocked down his uncle's friend for some alleged excess of liberty that the latter had taken in the uncle's house, of which the nephew was an inmate. Upon this occasion "Old Charley" is said to have behaved with exemplary moderation and Christian charity. He arose from the blow, adjusted his clothes, and made no attempt at retaliation at all. He merely muttered a few words about "taking summary vengeance at the first convenient opportunity," a natural and very justifiable ebullition of anger, which meant nothing, however, and was beyond doubt no sooner given vent to than forgotten.

However these matters may be (which have no reference to the point now at issue), it is quite certain that the people of Rattleborough, principally through the persuasion of Mr. Pennifeather, came at length to the determination of dispersing over the adjacent country in search of the missing Mr. Shuttleworthy. I say they came to this determination in the first instance. After it had been fully resolved that a search should be made, it was considered almost a matter of course that the seekers should disperse—that is to say, distribute themselves in parties—for the more thorough examination of the region round about. I forget, however, by what ingenious train of reasoning "Old Charley" finally convinced the assembly that this was the most injudicious plan they could pursue. Convince them, however, he did—all except Mr. Pennifeather. In the end it was arranged that a search should be instituted, carefully and very thoroughly, by the burghers *en masse*, "Old Charley" himself leading the way.

For that matter, there could have been no better pioneer than "Old Charley," whom everybody knew to have the eyes of a lynx; but, although he led them into all manner of out-of-the-way holes and corners, by routes that nobody had ever suspected of existing in the neighborhood, and although the search was incessantly kept up day and night for nearly a week, still no trace of Mr. Shuttleworthy could be discovered.

When I say no trace, however, I must not be taken literally, for trace, to some extent, there certainly was. The poor gentleman had been tracked by his horse's shoes, which were peculiar, to a spot about three miles to the east of the borough on the main road leading to the city. Here the track made off into a by-path through a piece of woodland, the path coming out again into the main road and cutting off about half a mile of the regular distance.

Following the shoe marks down this lane, the party came at length to a pool of stagnant water, half-hidden by the brambles, to the right of the lane. Opposite this pool all vestige of the track was lost sight of. It appeared however that a struggle of some nature had here taken place, and it seemed as if some large and heavy body, much larger and heavier than a man, had been drawn from the by-path to the pool. This latter was carefully dragged twice, but nothing was found; and the party were upon the point of going away, in despair of coming to any result, when Providence suggested to Mr. Goodfellow the expediency of draining the water off altogether.

This project was received with cheers and many high compliments to "Old Charley," upon his sagacity and consideration. As many of the burghers had brought spades with them in the possibility that they might be called upon to disinter a corpse, the drain was easily and speedily effected. No sooner was the bottom visible than right in the middle of the mud that remained was discovered a black silk velvet waistcoat, which nearly everyone present immediately recognized as the property of

Mr. Pennifeather.

This waistcoat was much torn and stained with blood. There were several persons among the party who had a distinct remembrance of its having been worn by its owner on the very morning of Mr. Shuttleworthy's departure for the city. Others, again, were ready to testify upon oath, if required, that Mr. P. did *not* wear the garment in question at any period during the *remainder* of that memorable day, nor could anyone be found to say that he had seen it upon Mr. P.'s person at any period at all subsequent to Mr. Shuttleworthy's disappearance.

Matters now wore a very serious aspect for Mr. Pennifeather. It was observed as an indubitable confirmation of the suspicions which were excited against him that he grew exceedingly pale, and when asked what he had to say for himself, was utterly incapable of saying a word. Hereupon, the few friends his riotous mode of living had left him deserted him at once to a man, and were even more clamorous than his ancient and avowed enemies for his instantaneous arrest.

But on the other hand, the magnanimity of Mr. Goodfellow shone forth with only the more brilliant luster through contrast. He made a warm and intensely eloquent defense of Mr. Pennifeather, in which he alluded more than once to his own sincere forgiveness of that wild young gentleman—"the heir of the worthy Mr. Shuttleworthy"—for the insult which he (the young gentleman) had, no doubt in the heat of passion, thought proper to put upon him (Mr. Goodfellow). He forgave him for it, he said, from the very bottom of his heart. For himself, so far from pushing the suspicious circumstances to extremity, which, he was sorry to say, really *had* arisen against Mr. Pennifeather, he (Mr. Goodfellow) would make every exertion in his power, would employ all the little eloquence in his possession to—to—to—soften down, as much as he could conscientiously do so, the worst features of this really exceedingly perplexing piece of business.

Mr. Goodfellow went on for some half hour longer in this strain, very much to the credit both of his head and of his heart; but your warmhearted people are seldom apposite in their observations—they run into all sorts of blunders, *contretemps* and malapropisms in the hotheadedness of their zeal to serve a friend—thus, often with the kindest intentions in the world, doing infinitely more to prejudice his cause than to advance it.

So, in the present instance, it turned out that with all the eloquence of "Old Charley"—he labored earnestly in behalf of the suspected—it so happened, somehow or other, that every syllable he uttered of which the direct but unwitting tendency was not to exalt the speaker in the good opinion of his audience, had the effect of deepening the suspicion already attached to the individual whose cause he pleaded, and of arousing against him the fury of the mob.

One of the most unaccountable errors committed by

the orator was his allusion to the suspected as "the heir of the worthy old gentleman, Mr. Shuttleworthy." The people had really never thought of this before. They had only remembered certain threats of disinheritance uttered a year or two previously by the uncle (who had no living relative except the nephew), and they had therefore always looked upon this disinheritance as a matter that was settled—so single-minded a race of beings were the Rattleburghers.

But the remark of "Old Charley" brought them at once to a consideration of this point, and thus gave them to see the possibility of the threats of disinheritance having been nothing more than a threat.

And straightway, hereupon, arose the natural question of *cui bono?* The question tended even more than the waistcoat to fasten the terrible crime upon the young man. And here, lest I be misunderstood, permit me to digress for one moment merely to observe that the exceedingly brief and simple Latin phrase which I have employed, is invariably mistranslated and misconceived. *Cui bono* in all the crack novels and elsewhere—in one by Mrs. Gore, in which for example, a lady quotes all tongues from the Chaldean to Chickasaw and is helped to her learning "as needed" upon a systematic plan by Mr. Beckford—in *all* the crack novels, I say, from those of Bulwer-Lytton and Dickens to those of Turnapenny and Ainsworth, the two little Latin words *cui bono* are rendered "to what purpose" or (as if *quo bono*) "to what good."

Their true meaning, nevertheless, is "for whose advantage." *Cui*, to whom, *bono*, is it for a benefit? It is a purely legal phrase, and applicable precisely in cases such as we have now under consideration, where the probability of the doer of a deed hinges upon the probability of the benefit accruing to the individual from the deed's accomplishment.

Now, in the present instance, the question, *cui bono?* very pointedly implicated Mr. Pennifeather. His uncle had threatened him, after making a will in his favor, with disinheritance. But the threat had not actually been kept; the original will, it appeared, had not been altered. *Had* it been altered, the only supposable motive for murder on the part of the suspected would have been the ordinary one of revenge; and even this would have been counteracted by the hope of reinstatement in the good graces of the uncle. But the will being unaltered while the threat to alter it remained suspended over the nephew's head, appeared at once the very strongest possible inducement for the atrocity; so concluded, very sagaciously, the worthy citizens of the borough of Rattle.

Mr. Pennifeather was, accordingly, arrested upon the spot, and the crowd, after some further search, proceeded homeward, with him in custody. En route, however, another circumstance tended to confirm the suspicion entertained. Mr. Goodfellow, whose zeal led him to be always a little in advance of the party, was seen suddenly to run forward a few paces, stoop, and then apparently to pick up some small object from the grass. Having quickly examined it, he was observed, too, to make a sort of half-attempt at concealing it in his coat pocket. This action was noticed, as I say, and consequently prevented; the object was found to be a Spanish knife which a dozen persons at once recognized as belonging to Mr. Pennifeather. Moreover, his initials were engraved upon the handle. The blade of this knife was open and bloody.

No doubt now remained of the guilt of the nephew, and immediately upon reaching Rattleborough he was taken before a magistrate for examination.

Here matters again took a most unfavorable turn. The prisoner, on being questioned as to his whereabouts on the morning of Mr. Shuttleworthy's disappearance, had absolutely the audacity to acknowledge that on that very morning he had been out deerstalking with his rifle in the immediate neighborhood of the pool where the blood-stained waistcoat had been discovered through the sagacity of Mr. Goodfellow.

This latter now came forward, and with tears in his eyes, asked permission to be examined. He said that a stern sense of the duty he owed his Maker, not less than his fellow men, would permit him no longer to remain silent. Hitherto, the sincerest affection for the young man (notwithstanding the latter's ill-treatment of himself, Mr. Goodfellow) had induced him to make every hypothesis which imagination could suggest, by way of endeavoring to account for what appeared suspicious in the circumstances that told so seriously against Mr. Pennifeather; but these circumstances were now altogether *too* convincing, *too* damning. He would hesitate no longer. He would tell all he knew although his heart (Mr. Goodfellow's) should absolutely burst asunder in the effort.

He then went on to state that, on the afternoon of the day previous to Mr. Shuttleworthy's departure for the city, the worthy old gentleman had mentioned to his nephew, in *his* hearing (Mr. Goodfellow's), that his object in going to town on the morrow was to make a deposit of an unusually large sum of money in the Farmers' and Mechanics' Bank, and that then and there the said Mr. Shuttleworthy had distinctly avowed to the said nephew his irrevocable determination of rescinding the will originally made, and of cutting him off with a shilling. He (the witness) now solemnly called upon the accused to state whether what he (the witness) had just stated was or was not the truth in every substantial particular. Much to the astonishment of everyone present, Mr. Pennifeather frankly admitted that it was.

The magistrate now considered it his duty to send a couple of constables to search the chamber of the accused in the house of his uncle. From this search they almost immediately returned with the well-known steel-bound, russet leather pocketbook which the old gentleman had been in the habit of carrying for years. Its valuable contents, however, had been abstracted, and the magistrate in vain endeavored to extort from the prisoner the use

411

which had been made of them, or the place of their concealment. Indeed, he obstinately denied all knowledge of the matter. The constables also discovered between the bed and sacking of the unhappy man a shirt and neckerchief, both marked with the initials of his name, and both hideously besmeared with the blood of the victim.

At this juncture, it was announced that the horse of the murdered man had just expired in the stable from the effects of the wound he had received, and it was proposed by Mr. Goodfellow that a post-mortem examination of the beast should immediately be made with the view of discovering the bullet, if possible.

This was accordingly done; and as if to demonstrate beyond a question the guilt of the accused, Mr. Goodfellow, after considerable searching in the cavity of the chest, was able to detect and to pull forth a bullet of extraordinary size, which, upon trial, was found to be exactly adapted to the bore of Mr. Pennifeather's rifle, although far too large for a rifle belonging to any other person in the borough or its vicinity. To render the matter even surer, this bullet was discovered to have a flaw or seam at right angles to the usual suture; upon examination, this seam corresponded precisely with an accidental ridge or elevation in a pair of moulds acknowledged by the accused himself to be his own property.

With the finding of this bullet, the examining magistrate refused to listen to any further testimony, and immediately committed the prisoner for trial, declining resolutely to take any bail in the case, although against this severity Mr. Goodfellow very warmly remonstrated, and offered to become surety in whatever amount might be required. This generosity on the part of "Old Charley" was only in accordance with the whole tenor of his amiable and chivalrous conduct during the entire period of his sojourn in the borough of Rattle. In the present instance, the worthy man was so entirely carried away by the excessive warmth of his sympathy, that he seemed to have quite forgotten, when he offered to go bail for his young friend, that he himself (Mr. Goodfellow) did not possess a single dollar's worth of property upon the face of the earth.

The result of the committal may be readily foreseen. Mr. Pennifeather, amid the loud execrations of all Rattleborough, was brought to trial at the next criminal sessions, when the chain of circumstantial evidence (strengthened as it was by some additional damning facts, which Mr. Goodfellow's sensitive conscientiousness forbade him to withhold from the court) was considered so unbroken and so thoroughly conclusive, that the jury, without leaving their seats, returned an immediate verdict of "Guilty of murder in the first degree." Soon afterward the unhappy wretch received sentence of death, and was remanded to the county jail to await the inexorable vengeance of the law.

In the meantime, the noble behavior of "Old Charley Goodfellow" had doubly endeared him to the honest citizens of the borough. He became ten times a greater favorite than ever; and as a natural result of the hospitality with which he was treated, he relaxed the extremely parsimonious habits which his poverty had hitherto impelled him to observe. He frequently had little *réunions* at his own house, when wit and jollity reigned supreme—dampened a little, of course, by the occasional remembrance of the untoward and melancholy fate which impended over the nephew of the late-lamented bosom friend of the generous host.

One fine day, this magnanimous old gentleman was agreeably surprised at the receipt of the following letter:

> To Charles Goodfellow, Esquire:
> Dear Sir—In conformity with an order transmitted to our firm about two months since by our esteemed correspondent, Mr. Barnabas Shuttleworthy, we have the honor of forwarding this morning to your address, a double box of Château Margaux, of the antelope brand, violet seal. Box numbered and marked as per margin.
>
>> We remain, sir,
>> Your most ob'nt ser'ts,
>> HOGGS, FROGS, BOGS, & CO.
>
> City of ——, June 21, 18—.
> P.S.—The box will reach you, by wagon, on the day after your receipt of this letter. Our respects to Mr. Shuttleworthy.
>
>> H., F., B., & Co.

CHARLES GOODFELLOW, ESQ., RATTLEBOROUGH.
FROM H., F., B., & CO.
CHAT. MAR. A—NO. I.—6 DOZ. BTS. (½ GROSS).

The fact is, that Mr. Goodfellow had, since the death of Mr. Shuttleworthy, given over all expectation of ever receiving the promised Château Margaux; and he therefore looked upon it now as a sort of special dispensation of Providence in his behalf. He was highly delighted, of course, and in the exuberance of his joy invited a large party of friends to a *petit souper* on the morrow, for the purpose of broaching Mr. Shuttleworthy's gift.

Not that he said anything about "the good old Mr. Shuttleworthy" when he issued the invitations. The fact is, he thought much and concluded to say nothing at all. He did not mention to anyone—if I remember aright— that he had received a present of Château Margaux. He merely asked his friends to come and help him drink some wine of a very fine quality and rich flavor that he had ordered up from the city a couple of months ago, and of which he would be in the receipt upon the morrow. I have often puzzled myself to imagine why it was that "Old Charley" came to the conclusion to say nothing about having received the wine from his old friend, but I could never precisely understand his reason for the silence, although he had some excellent and very magnanimous reason, no doubt.

The morrow at length arrived, and with it a very large and highly respectable company at Mr. Goodfellow's house. Indeed half the borough was there—I myself among the number—but, much to the vexation of the host, the Château Margaux did not arrive until a late hour, and when the sumptuous supper supplied by "Old Charley" had been done very ample justice by the guests. It came at length, however. A monstrously big box of it there was, too, and as the whole party was in excessively good humor, it was decided, *nemine contradicente,* that it should be lifted upon the table and its contents disemboweled forthwith.

No sooner said than done. I lent a helping hand, and in a trice we had the box upon the table, in the midst of all the bottles and glasses, not a few of which were demolished in the scuffle. "Old Charley," who was pretty much intoxicated and excessively red in the face, now took a seat, with an air of mock dignity, at the head of the board, and thumped furiously upon it with a decanter, calling the company to keep order "during the ceremony of disinterring the treasure."

After some vociferation, quiet was at length fully restored, and as often happens in such cases, a profound and remarkable silence ensued. Being then requested to force open the lid, I complied, of course, "with an infinite deal of pleasure." I inserted a chisel, and giving it a few slight taps with a hammer, the top of the box flew suddenly off.

At the same instant, there sprang up into a sitting position, directly facing the host, the bruised, bloody and nearly putrid corpse of the murdered Mr. Shuttleworthy himself. It gazed for a few moments, fixedly and sorrowfully, with its decaying and lack-luster eyes, full into the countenance of Mr. Goodfellow, uttered slowly, but clearly and impressive, the words—*"Thou art the man!"* And then, falling over the side of the chest as if thoroughly satisfied, stretched out its limbs quiveringly upon the table.

The scene that ensued is altogether beyond description. The rush for the doors and windows was terrific, and many of the most robust men in the room fainted outright through sheer horror. But after the first wild, shrieking burst of affright, all eyes were directed to Mr. Goodfellow. If I live a thousand years, I can never forget the more than mortal agony which was depicted in that ghastly face of his, so lately rubicund with triumph and wine. For several minutes he sat rigidly as a statue of marble, his eyes seeming, in the intense vacancy of their gaze, to be turned inward and absorbed in the contemplation of his own miserable murderous soul. At length their expression appeared to flash suddenly out into the external world, when, with a quick leap, he sprang from his chair, and falling heavily with his head and shoulders upon the table, and in contact with the corpse, poured out rapidly and vehemently a detailed confession of the hideous crime for which Mr. Pennifeather was then imprisoned and doomed to die.

What he recounted was in substance this: He followed his victim to the vicinity of the pool. There he shot Shuttleworthy's horse with a pistol and dispatched its rider with the butt end. He possessed himself of the pocketbook; and supposing the horse dead, dragged it with great labor to the brambles by the pond. Upon his own beast he slung the corpse of Mr. Shuttleworthy, and thus bore it to a secure place of concealment a long distance off through the woods.

The waistcoat, the knife, the pocketbook and bullet had been placed by himself where found, with the view of avenging himself upon Mr. Pennifeather. He had also contrived the discovery of the stained neckkerchief and shirt.

Toward the end of the blood-chilling recital, the words of the guilty wretch faltered and grew hollow. When the record was finally exhausted, he arose, staggered backward from the table, and fell—*dead*.

The means by which this happily-timed confession was extorted, although efficient, were simple indeed. Mr. Goodfellow's excess of frankness had disgusted me, and excited my suspicions from the first. I was present when Mr. Pennifeather had struck him, and the fiendish expression which then arose upon Goodfellow's countenance, although momentary, assured me that his threat of vengeance would, if possible, be rigidly fulfilled. I was thus prepared to view the maneuvering of "Old Charley" in a very different light from that in which it was regarded by the good citizens of Rattleborough. I saw at once that all the incriminating discoveries arose, either directly or indirectly, from him. But the fact which clearly opened my eyes to the true state of the case was the affair of the bullet, found by Mr. G. in the carcass of the horse. *I* had not forgotten, although the Rattleburghers had, that there was a hole where the bullet had entered the horse, and another where it went out. If it were found in the animal then, after having made its exit, I saw clearly that it must have been deposited by the person who found it. The bloody shirt and neckkerchief confirmed the idea suggested by the bullet, for the blood on examination proved to be capital claret, and no more. When I came to think of these things, and also of the late increase of liberality and expenditure on the part of Mr. Goodfellow, I entertained a suspicion which was none the less strong because I kept it altogether to myself.

In the meantime, I instituted a rigorous private search for the corpse of Mr. Shuttleworthy, and for good reasons searched in quarters as divergent as possible from those to which Mr. Goodfellow conducted his party. The result was that after some days I came across an old dry well, the mouth of which was nearly hidden by brambles. And here, at the bottom, I discovered what I sought.

Now it so happened that I had overheard the colloquy between the two cronies, when Mr. Goodfellow had contrived to cajole his host into the promise of a box of Château Margaux. Upon this hint I acted. I procured a stiff piece of whalebone, thrust it down the throat of the corpse, and deposited the latter in an old wine box— taking care so to double the body up as to double the whalebone with it. In this manner I had to press forcibly upon the lid to keep it down while I secured it with nails; and I anticipated, of course, that as soon as these latter were removed, the top would fly *off* and the body *up*.

Having thus arranged the box, I marked, numbered, and addressed it as already told; and then writing a letter in the name of the wine merchants with whom Mr. Shuttleworthy dealt, I gave instructions to my servant to wheel the box to Mr. Goodfellow's door in a barrow, at a given signal from myself. For the words which I intended the corpse to speak, I confidently depended upon my ventriloquial abilities; for their effect, I counted upon the conscience of the murderous wretch.

I believe there is nothing more to be explained. Mr. Pennifeather was released upon the spot, inherited the fortune of his uncle, profited by the lessons of experience, turned over a new leaf, and led happily ever afterward a new life.